C0-ATA-997

# THE STORY OF
# THE STARS AND STRIPES

# THE STORY OF

By

**BUD HUTTON**

and

**ANDY ROONEY**

GREENWOOD PRESS, PUBLISHERS
WESTPORT, CONNECTICUT

Originally published in 1946
by Holt, Rinehart & Winston, Inc., New York

Reprinted with the permission
of Holt, Rinehart & Winston

First Greenwood Reprinting 1970

Library of Congress Catalogue Card Number 70-112324

SBN 8371-4712-3

Printed in the United States of America

TO THE JOES
FOR WHOM
THE PAPER
WAS PUBLISHED

# WHY
## A Preface

IN A FOXHOLE, gouged from the slope of an enemy hillside, a doughboy peers through the dust an exploding mortar has left and sees a figure in uniform crawling up from the rear. The dough squints at a green and gold patch on the uniform sleeve as the figure halts beside him. The patch says:

Stars and Stripes
U S Army
War Correspondent

The *Stars and Stripes* man talks with the dough awhile and goes off to another place. He is getting the news of the war where the news is.

Maybe not there, but somewhere across the war, another *Stars and Stripes* man drives a jeep down a road under artillery fire so that American fighting men will have their daily newspaper even thousands of miles and three or four years of war away from home.

* * *

In a Flying Fortress, four miles above the enemy flak, the pilot checks his crew over the interphone after a battle with interceptors:

"Tail gunner, you okay?" "You all right, right waist?" "Top turret?" "Ball turret?" "How about you, Stars and Stripes? How you doing in that left waist?"

"Stars and Stripes" is doing all right; he's as scared as the rest, or maybe a little more, but he's doing his job this way so that the American kids who fly the bombers into the flak and the enemy fighters will get an honest report of what they are doing and how.

Dwight Eisenhower, supreme commander of all the Allied forces, walks onto a field behind the lines to meet with a field marshal, a handful of three- or four-starred generals, and discuss exact terms of the impending surrender of Germany. Beside the supreme commander walks a square-jawed, serious soldier on whose arm there is the green and gold patch. The serious young man is a staff sergeant. He stays with the generals as they talk, takes notes on what they have to say about the men in the line.

Before night, the man with the *Stars and Stripes* patch writes his story and it goes not only to the soldiers' newspaper but to every other paper and press service in the world; and the morning's paper which the doughs read in the lines tells them, as he said it, what the supreme commander and the generals had to say about what the soldiers are doing. . . .

The Rangers landed, the infantry crossed a river, the paratroops came down—*The Stars and Stripes* was there, a collection of possibly the least martial souls on earth trying to put out a civilian newspaper in an army. They were of the army, in the army and by the army, and the army said they'd be soldiers first and newspapermen second. The staffers didn't say anything, because you can't talk back in the army, but they worked out their own compromise.

They wore uniforms, some of them learned to fight and some learned to die; and they put out newspapers in London and Rome, Paris and Frankfurt, Casablanca and Liége. They put out papers under shellfire and they put them out from luxurious chateaux, and all the time they did as best they could the one thing the army never could order successfully: publish a good newspaper.

They were against commissions for themselves, but a managing editor once told the supreme commander, in answer to a query about the obviously effective treatment of rank in the paper:

"Sir, we figured a general has every bit as much rights in *The Stars and Stripes* as a private does."

The supreme commander took a couple of takes on it and let the doctrine stand.

That was *The Stars and Stripes,* daily newspaper of the American soldier overseas.

*The Stars and Stripes* also was a variety of other things. It was probably the last refuge of the itinerant American newspaperman whom big business has driven from his desk, because it moved with the battlefront and in moving took along its own peculiar atmosphere of laissez-faire-as-long-as-you-get-the-job-done.

It was a collection of privates and corporals and sergeants who took on the whole blasted army, at one time or another, and came close to winning.

It was a bedlam. If the city room of any edition of *The Stars and Stripes* had been a movie set, the critics, no matter what else they said, would have damned it as Hollywood's idea of a newspaper city room, too front-page to be true. The truth was, the staff figured the Hollywood directors of any newspaper pictures they'd ever seen hadn't been very imaginative.

The soldiers who set up *The Stars and Stripes* and published it and somehow, with or without the assistance of the army, got it up to the fighting men every morning, had a simple conception of their job. Bob Moora, who was co-editor of the first daily in London, said it best:

"This is a paper for Joe; after that it's a newspaper; after that it's a trade journal whose specialized readers are soldiers; and after that it isn't anything else no matter what the brass says."

The paper, along that line then, tried to bring the American soldier fighting the war overseas not only news of what he was doing, but what the units on either flank were doing and the ones overhead and to the rear; what the enemy was doing, and how. Because the war news seemed most important to the Joes, there was more war news than anything else in the paper. Because the comic strip "Terry and the Pirates" seemed second most important, "Terry and the Pirates" got into the paper nightly no matter what else had to be left out. Because the soldiers wanted to know what was happening back home, the paper set up a news bureau in New York, pulled combat correspondents out of the line periodically and sent them back to the States for two months to report on the home front. Before the job was done in Europe, *Stars and Stripes* men were on the way to the Pacific, not only to establish the paper there but to cable back to the hundreds of thousands of combat men due to fight the Japs after the Germans, what the war out there was like; and they described it in the intimate terms of easy familiarity with fighting which they had learned the hard way.

Those things and virtually everything else *The Stars and Stripes* staff did or tried to do had one end: to make it a paper for Joe. But to many people *The Stars and Stripes* was many things.

Someone was always trying to make it the soldiers' and this service's, or the soldiers' and that service's, the soldiers' and this general's, or the soldiers' and that general's. (They were always careful to put the soldiers first.) Virtually no one except the staff and a fellow named Dwight Eisenhower ever figured it ought to be just the soldiers' newspaper.

And there it is: You sit down to write about maybe the most fantastic effort any newspaper ever made, or any army, for that matter—publication within an army's doctrined, ordered, protocoled ranks of a newspaper dedicated to the American principle of a free press—and what happens? You get as involved explaining it as the existence the paper and its people led, and you go off on the same sort of tangents that made the staff and *The Stars and Stripes* whatever else they were.

It is difficult to explain, because there was a mercurial unpickableupness about the paper and its creatures, and because it was illogical, being where it was. A corporal and a sergeant set up the editorial format of *The Stars and Stripes,* a private set up its business affairs. They were helped at times by various colonels and majors. Sometimes it was a corporal or a sergeant who said what was what, and sometimes it was a colonel. There never was a time when someone wasn't saying; but there it was, every morning, come Luftwaffe, come Parisian women, come buzz-bombs, come counterattacks, come closeorder drill, come generals, congressmen or Nazi spies. And with it there came to the Champs-Elysees and Piccadilly Circus, to the Via Napoli and the Strassen of the Third Reich, an unmistakably American air compounded of Main Street, cosmoline and printer's ink.

For the local equivalent of two cents—in England it was one English penny, in France it was one franc, and so on—a soldier could buy his newspaper anywhere the army was. To combat units actually on the line, *The Stars and Stripes* was delivered free of charge. We never had enough newsprint to print a paper for every soldier, because virtually every ounce of paper was hauled across the Atlantic Ocean from the States. We tried to turn out one copy for every five or six men.

At that modest sales price, the S&S in three years turned up a bookkeeping profit of three million dollars. That was possible because we paid for our plant facilities on reverse Lend Lease, or, as in Germany, just walked in and took over without bothering about a landlord; because we had no salaries to pay, and because the army maintained our rolling stock. Inasmuch as the army was getting a good many $75-to-$150-a-week newspapermen at the prevailing wages for privates, corporals, and sergeants, we never felt any qualms about boasting of our three-million-dollar profit.

It would be presumptuous to think one does justice to *The Stars and Stripes* in writing about it. We can only tell a little of *The Stars and Stripes* as we saw it. It is worth telling because the publication of the soldiers' daily newspaper may have been an important thing in American newspaper history. It was an attempt at a free-press in a part of the world where most of the free press had ceased to exist. It also sought to carry the American tradition of a free press even into the sphere of martial law, an alien grain of sand in the oyster military—although the product wasn't necessarily always a pearl.

For a long time *The Stars and Stripes* was part of the free press. Eventually the soldiers who published it lost their fight against martial law and the paper became pretty much of a military house organ. But that happened only long after S&S had spun its pin-wheeled way into the hearts of the doughboys and had established itself as the complex, unreasonable creation about which it is so difficult to tell.

It's probably best and easiest to start with the editorial rooms, which the officer in charge, whichever colonel or major he might be, entered only rarely, and then by arrangement.

# CONTENTS

# THE STORY OF THE STARS AND STRIPES

# CITY ROOM

YOU WALKED into a room which for one arrested moment was like any other newspaper editorial office in the world. Then you began to see it.

Two men sat on opposite sides of a blocky double desk, bent over typewritten sheets, and in the glare of green-shaded lights moved pencils through written words. At a desk shoved close to them a third man hammered a typewriter as if he hated it. A bonfire of wadded newspapers burned briskly beneath his chair.

As you watched, he erupted to his feet, kicked over the chair and glared through thick-lensed glasses and a bang of stringy black hair at the other men in the office until the paper burned out. He sat down, turning to kick the charred paper away, and one of the men at the big city desk said:

"Fleming, you're fidgety."

Against a window on the far side of the room, from whose unwashed panes the bleak light of a courtyard seemed to have turned away in despair, a round-faced man sat behind a desk which bore a sign: "Combat Censor." While the fire burned, he played an invisible violin with an invisible bow, and when Fleming was bawled out for being fidgety, he smirked assent and waggled a censorious finger.

To the right of the censor, a reporter still in the flying jacket he had worn to Wilhelmshaven with the bombers that morning searched for words he couldn't find on the keyboard of his typewriter.

Beyond him, beneath the dusty shelves of a bookcase that held no books, a square-faced kid talked into a telephone, took notes when he listened. In the center of the room, between you and the city desk, a lean, young individual bent his blond head over the photograph of a Hollywood bathing girl, sneered at her curves and turned to another one. Beside him, a man in a black coat, brief case under arm in the salesman's unmistakable pose, leaned forward and said, "But, Mr. Price . . ."

The individual looking at the photographs sneered at another one and spoke from the side of his mouth: "The Associated Press' idea of cheesecake is an entry for the old ladies' home!"

To your left, on a desk in front of a pigeonholed wall, a man poked through the contents of a photographer's bag with one hand and with the other spread shaving cream on his face in ruminative strokes.

In the corner beyond the photographer, a chunky individual sprawled on the floor, belly down, and peered appraisingly down the sights of a German M-42 machine gun from whose sides a belt of cartridges gleamed evilly.

There were half a dozen other men in the room. They were prosaically using typewriters to turn out stories which the next morning would be *The Stars and Stripes.* One of them wore his jacket, and as you looked at him you realized that everyone in the room wore khaki.

Maybe that was the strangest thing about *The Stars and Stripes:* the people who published it wore uniforms, and they were soldiers. Maybe that was even stranger than that the staff was only partially affected by being soldiers, or even that the army itself didn't always remember the staffers were soldiers. (Actually, the army managed to remember whenever it really wanted to.)

There were the usual desks and chairs, and the conventional mass of desk for the copyreaders. There were typewriters, even if some of them sometimes had Germanic script characters, or Arabic, or French, and there was the typewriter noise. Most of all there was the smell of a newspaper office, which superficial people or people too lazy to search have described as the smell of printer's ink, but which is much too complex for that. It is a smell of a little ink, but also of old paper, and sweat and dust, of tobacco smoke cured into the wood and walls, of rain-wet clothes which have dried where they hung, and of an old pair of overshoes.

There were the usual things of a newspaper office, but you kept seeing that machine gun, and the khaki uniforms, and after you looked awhile you saw a coat hanger in a corner, but there were two steel helmets on it along with an old straw hat with a blue band.

You looked at the walls, and they were crazy with circus-size enlargements of shapely bathing queens, with black newspaper headlines which told of news gone by and some that never happened—and never went out of the office—with the glass-studded remains of a thrown glue pot, with last year's calendar, with a photograph of Elm Street, in Dubuque, with new and old typewritten notices from colonels that this would be printed, or would not be printed, depending on which colonel signed it.

A soldier with the green and gold patch of *The Stars and Stripes* came past you in the doorway and said to the desk, "I've got a piece on the Special Services educational program," and behind him came another man with the same patch, whose tanned face was long unshaven and in whose eyes there was a certain tiredness you never saw in the other kind of newspaper, and he said in a bitterly weary tone, "Goddam jeep shot right to hell out from under me. How much do you want on this river crossing story? Those guys rate; a lot of 'em never got over."

That was the city room, heart and core, of *The Stars and Stripes,* the daily newspaper of the American soldier overseas.

England, France, Africa, the Pacific, Italy, Belgium, Germany—it was the same. The dimensions of the room, the lights, the typewriters, the faces and names of the individuals—those things might change, but they were only superficial, they didn't matter; the atmosphere was identical. It was a newspaper editorial office, and it was army, and it was a madhouse.

*The Stars and Stripes,* from the day it began publication as an eight-page weekly in London, was mad, unreasonable, implausible of behavior in the midst of an army's orderliness, a refuge for eccentrics.

But at the same time it was a well-written, well-edited, colorful, accurate, professional newspaper with (whether or no you wanted to admit it) higher editorial and moral standards than a great many civilian papers.

It was, on the authority of the army's high command, "the most important single factor" affecting the morale of the men who smashed and conquered Axis Europe.

Reporters wrote stories while other reporters built fires under them, but the paper went to press on time and in the morning did its job of making the American soldier abroad the best informed soldier in the world.

Some of its staff didn't know an "about-face" from a "parade rest," but those same individuals jumped with the paratroops, invaded with the Rangers, were gunners with the bombers, and came back to write of what other men had done. The only compulsion that sent them to do those things was their own.

Just as the city room was the heart of the hub of the paper, so the city desk was the nerve center of the editorial rooms themselves. The man on the city desk ran *The Stars and Stripes,* and as a sergeant or corporal or whatever he happened to be at the time probably wielded more immediate influence over the welfare and morale of the four million American citizens fighting in Europe than any general except Eisenhower. A lot of generals didn't like to believe that, but the privates in their commands could have told them it was so.

It was around two city desk men that *The Stars and Stripes* first was set up in London as a daily: Bob Moora, former New York *Herald-Tribune* desk man, who handled all the wire copy which poured into the first city room in London over the wires of British and American news agencies, and Bud Hutton, one-time Scripps-Howard city editor and transferee from the Canadian Army where he had been a battle photographer.

The quiet, courteous Moora and the vitriolic, nervous Hutton set down the principles of the first daily paper which were to guide it and all subsequent editions—even when the army said otherwise—across the war. They established the format by which what happened to a soldier or a group of soldiers on any given morning was translated into a news story by a soldier-reporter in the afternoon, condensed and shaped by copyreaders in the evening, and appeared in the soldier's newspaper the next breakfast-time.

The authors of this book first met in typical *S&S* fashion and under circumstances which should serve to tell of life on *The Stars and Stripes* city desk.

Rooney, battery clerk in a field artillery outfit which boasted huge 155-millimeter howitzers, each morning filled out field reports: "On hand, 12 cannons; 1,042 bullets." The howitzer men didn't like having their big guns referred to as cannons, liked less their ammunition called bullets, so when a request for newspapermen came through channels, Andy was shipped off to *The Stars and Stripes* at his own request and with the artillery's blessing. En route, he fell in with Dick Koenig, a private answering an *S&S* call for photographers.

Koenig, a mild, unpushing sort of fellow, had worked in commercial studios but he wasn't too sure about his ability as a news photographer. Gradually he confessed this feeling to Rooney, who with no reluctance whatsoever admitted to Dick that he had worked on a college newspaper at Colgate and thereafter had put in four or five days as a copy boy on the Albany (New York) *Knickerbocker News.*

They came together to the *Times* of London building which housed *The Stars and Stripes* in England, stumbled their way through the twisting dark corridors, and arrived outside the city room door just as a pastepot splattered violently against it. A figure fled wildly from the room and from inside snarled a voice:

"And don't come back here, you illiterate baboon, until you've got it right!"

Andy peered around the corner of the door. A tall, hard-faced individual with a sneer just below a black mustache was standing at the huge city desk, tugging at his hair. Rooney turned to Koenig, fishing in his pocket for a coin.

"I'll flip you, Koenig," he said. "Heads, I'm the photographer and you're the reporter. Tails, the other way around."

They flipped and entered to find that the individual with the mustache and the sneer was the city editor, and that it was for him and Bob Moora, who sat quiet and unperturbed across the desk, that they were now working.

Koenig worried about it, but Rooney today swears he just looked around the room and saw a dozen marks on the walls which were unmistakable remains of violently hurled pastepots and figured the thing was commonplace so he might as well stay and have fun.

Koenig became one of the paper's photographers and took scores of pictures of the army preparing for the invasion of the Continent. He also took one picture of Fortresses flying ahead of their vapor trails, which was reprinted throughout the world. But his fame and his claim to a place among *The Stars and Stripes* people came from a picture he not only did not make but for which he didn't even unsling his camera.

At impressive Armistice Day ceremonies in London, British and Americans joined in a huge parade. Koenig was assigned to get pictures. Four hours later, while the desk fretted and Benny Price swore his photo department couldn't make the job at that late hour, Koenig stumbled wearily into the city room. Benny grabbed at his camera and film holders while Moora demanded angrily where the hell he had been.

"I was trying to get pictures. Awful crowd," Dick sighed.

"They better be good," snarled Price as he headed for the door. Benny stopped cold, however, when Dick replied:

"There aren't any pictures. I got caught in the crowd and there were so many people I couldn't get my camera out."

Even the patient Moora exploded.

Moora and Hutton made a team as "the Desk." Charlie White, who started *The Stars and Stripes* life—to which he inevitably referred with a sigh as "my punishment"—as a rewrite man, tried hard for a month to work directly under them and then begged for a job that would move him from that third desk shoved close against the two larger ones.

"Monday, one of those two guys chews my behind," Charlie pleaded. "Next day he shuts up and the second one starts. Next day the second one's fit to live with but the other one isn't again. And I want out, because, by God, yesterday they both hit me at once and to hell with it."

Moora was a normally quiet, solid type of newspaper deskman. He knew his business, thoroughly, from one end of the editorial office to the other and knew engraving and composition as well. In addition, as long as the two were together on the desk, Bob was a patient man, poised and deliberate, and where Hutton rasped the skin off the staff's collective back, Moora caught them licking their wounds with calm and effective suggestions for correction of the things which had brought about the skinning. Thin, 32-year-old Moora was a staff sergeant when he and Hutton, a corporal, set up *The Stars and Stripes* daily. Eventually the staff decided Moora ought to have a commission because we needed someone in the shop to compromise with the army when the army demanded that something should be signed only by an officer.

The greatest compliment ever paid him, Bob held a year or

so after he had been commissioned, came the day an exasperated colonel said:

"Moora, you're no officer. You're just a Joe with an officer's uniform."

Hutton, on the other hand, remained to the end an enlisted man, although, as with virtually every man on the staff, he was offered commissions. A nervous, tough Scotch-Irishman, who could do any job on the paper as well as anyone available and then told you how well he did it, the city editor became a master sergeant. The staff said that was perfect, in view of the traditionally malevolent character attributed to master sergeants in any army.

The staff felt Desk was a good team, although it was kind of like working for a firm composed of Simon Legree and the Great White Father, which was apt to be confusing.

It was with the support and demand of the staff that the paper got off to a policy: "No matter who was sitting there, the paper was put through 'the Desk,' and nothing went except through 'the Desk.' "

It was simply sound, professional doctrine, but it worked out well in helping to keep the paper as long as possible in the format originally laid out by General Marshall in prescribing that *The Star and Stripes* should be published by the soldiers with "a minimum of official control" beyond broad policy and security. There were a lot of people who sat in positions of authority in the United States forces overseas and swore great oaths when they ran up against the policy of "clear it with the Desk."

Harry Harchar had the toughest time. Harry was a major, and executive to Lieutenant Colonel Llewellyn, the titular publisher, but he admitted he knew little about the editorial end of the newspaper business. Nonetheless, from time to time it was felt necessary for him to exert some influence "down at the *Times,*" as the business and administrative offices referred to the editorial department. (The editorial department had seen to it from the beginning that the administrative offices were somewhere else, some four miles across London, as a matter of fact.)

Thus, Harchar came to the *Times,* sat around the office for a while whistling and reading advance proofs of the comics. Whistling, as singing, was verboten in the city room. Make any noise you want to working or getting mad, was the rule (the "getting mad" part was to cover the Desk) but no noises not connected with the business.

At Harchar's first whistle, one staffer or another would stare hard. Eventually Harchar would feel the stare—sometimes he'd try for five minutes not to—and look up, appear suprised and stop. In a few minutes he started again, and this time Moora would turn slowly, clear his throat overnoisily. That usually worked. If Harchar forgot and resumed, Hutton and Moora together cleared their throats and stared. At that, Harchar would convey the message he had for the editorial department. Usually it was, "Inspection tomorrow," or in that vein. Sometimes, however, it was that a certain story had to be published because Special Services had demanded it.

As soon as it became obvious that the request or order from on high was to deal with editorial matters, the Desk would begin to burn, visibly and audibly, snarling epithets about "brass-bound bastards trying to foul up the soldiers' newspaper." (The staff could get very pious and righteous about "the soldiers' newspaper.") Moora would begin patiently, "Now, major, I think that's all right for some camp newspaper, but not here."

"It's an order from the High Command!" Harchar would claim, but his heart wasn't in it and he knew damned well it wasn't an order from the High Command and if it had been, and was that kind of order, he knew very well the sergeants and the corporals probably would say to hell with it anyway.

The major turned, each time, and walked out of the editorial rooms, and that was that until the next one.

The weekly *Stars and Stripes* and the first daily were printed in London. From there a task force of soldier-reporters went to Africa and set up *The Stars and Stripes* at Casablanca and Algiers. What then became the North African branch of the *S&S* went on to Sicily and Italy, and eventually wound up in Rome. Meanwhile the progenerator of World War II's daily established an offspring in Belfast, Northern Ireland, for the vast pool of American manpower there awaiting the invasion of Europe. When the invasion came, the paper was published in Cherbourg, in Rennes at the base of the Brittany peninsula, in Paris, and in Liége, Belgium. When the southern portion was cleared by the Allied invasion there on August 14, 1944, editions were set up in Marseille and Nice, and from there subsequent editions worked their way northeastward with the advancing armies to Besançon, Dijon, and Strasbourg on the Rhine. After the Allied crossing of the Rhine, in March, 1945, the Liége edition was too far behind the troops to service them and so was the one at Strasbourg. The staffers moved the editions designed for front-line troops to Pungstadt, a suburb of Frankfurt which had been by-passed by the war, and to Altedorf, farther east and south, so that today's paper would reach the doughs today.

Sometimes the paper lurched its way to press through falling bombs, enemy gunfire, or robot bombs; sometimes it limped to the press on crutches hastily extemporized by the staff after a flat army order had kicked the legs from under a story; every once in a while it went to press with no interruptions, no typographical errors, no complaints from the army, and just about every one of those times it was a lousy paper.

The procedure was roughly similar in each edition. . . .

Somewhere along the firing line American doughboys moved to the attack in early-morning darkness. With them was a *Stars and Stripes* reporter and, whenever we had one, a photographer. The reporter got what he could on the line, then usually stopped back at divisional headquarters where the over-all picture was a good deal clearer and where the perspective wasn't quite so narrow from the sniped-at shelter of an old barn or maybe a stone fence.

Writing a story at the divisional headquarters, the reporter handed it to a courier in a jeep who started for the nearest *Stars and Stripes* office, anywhere from fifty to a hundred miles away depending upon the sector involved. If the distance was longer, the reporter was apt to take his story back to a corps, or army headquarters where it could be censored for security and then telephone to the editorial office, where the rewrite man recorded it with headphones and typewriter.

Simultaneously from the army headquarters and from General Eisenhower's Supreme Headquarters, other *Stars and Stripes* reporters gathered the over-all picture of the day's news, of which possibly the divisional attack was the highlight, and sent by courier or telephone to the city room their stories of it.

*"Hello, Desk? This is Russ Jones. Here's the First Army picture . . . Yeah, the Second Division is spearheading. Hodenfield is*

*with them and his story ought to be in pretty soon . . . It's all censored . . . Dictate it to Larsen? . . . Any mail for me? Okay, Carl. First Army Headquarters . . ."*

*"Okay, so you're an MP. So I was drivin' too fast in the blackout. Lissen, Mac, I gotta get this story in to* Stars and Stripes *. . . My name's Blackov, and I'm a courier . . . So press priority doesn't mean anything. You want your goddam paper in the morning, don't yuh? . . . Okay, thanks . . . Every son of a bitch in the German Army shootin' 88s at this lousy jeep and I get back here a hundred miles from the war and some MP says did I know it isn't safe drivin' fast in the blackout? . . ."*

*"Hey, Carl? Take Russ Jones on 23, will you? He's got the First Army story . . . Charlie, Hodenfield's story come in yet? . . . As soon as it does, take that stuff of Jones's, put it with Hodenfield's and wrap 'em up together for the lead, will you? . . . Here's the AP and UP copy if you want to look at it. Same thing."*

Across the war-battered city of Liége, from which the smoke of bombed and gutted buildings has never ceased to rise for two long months of the winter war, sounds a far-off drone, like a big truck speeding down a distant highway on a quiet night.

The drone grows louder, and here and there around the city room of *The Stars and Stripes* a jaw muscle tightens and one or two men look toward the windows. The drone becomes a thunderous roar, swelling in volume until you can feel the desk shake a little beneath your moist palms. A rewrite man steps quickly to the window, peers carefully past the edge of blackout curtain. Straight over the requisitioned newspaper building which houses the army's paper comes a German robot bomb. The Germans have been sending them by the dozens in a steady stream to try and paralyze Liége, supply center of the lines resisting von Rundstedt's desperate winter offensive.

Just as the roar of the bomb seems to enter the very room, it terminates abruptly in a terrible silence. The staffers dive beneath desks, and all over the area everyone who isn't in a shelter is doing more or less the same thing. The buzz bomb's jet engine has cut out and it is diving earthward. A shattering roar which seems to amplify itself in waves of sound shakes the building, and through a slit at the side of the blackout curtain you see an ugly red glow drive away the darkness, surge, then dwindle to the flickering red of a buzz-bomb fire. A block away men and women are dead and others are dying, and even as the rescue trucks race through the debris-strewn streets, another distant buzz bomb begins its horribly impersonal drone over the city.

*"One of those bastards is going to hit this place yet . . . wish we'd published in the basement instead of the top floor."*

*"Okay, Russ, I can hear you again . . . No, a block away . . . Okay, 'push two and a half miles . . .' "*

Downstairs a corporal-sports editor named Charnik takes a look at the page form of type whose inverted letters are carrying to the soldiers news of the sports world back home. There isn't much sports news from the soldiers themselves these days. The soldiers have another job.

In a little cubicle adjoining the city room, *The Stars and Stripes'* own teletype system clatters off an editorial from the main office in Paris and a query as to whether Liége has heard from Ernie Leiser, combat correspondent with the Ninth U. S. Army, who went off to cover a river crossing two days ago and hasn't been heard from since. The query finished, the teletype montonously pounds out a staff story from the Seventh Army front which the paper published in Strasbourg has teletyped to Paris for relay to the other papers.

*"I wish Kenny Zumwalt would stop going up to the lines on his day off. Hell of a way for a copyreader to spend his day off. He goes up there and gets wound up in some scrap and can't get back to the office in time the next day, and then he thinks he ain't gonna get chewed out because he was up seeing what war was like so he can handle the stories more intelligently—he says. He'll find out someday . . . from a German 88. . . ."*

*"Brownie, you got that air story done yet? Well, let's see it and then go downstairs to the composing room and see if you can help Charnik get sports and the editorial page off the forms. We're getting a little late. . . ."*

Under the green-shaded lights around the copy desk, tobacco smoke swirls thick, eddying every time a buzz bomb lands near and the staff dives for doubtful shelter beneath desks. Between explosions the copyreaders' pencils race through typewritten versions of what has happened in the world today, and what the doughboys are doing and how, and what Congressman Zilch said, who had triplets in Keokuk, Iowa, MacArthur's communique, how many miles (the doughboys' favorite reading) the Russians gained up to last night.

As the hands of the clock on the wall spread out toward ten, the noise of the typewriters comes faster and stops completely only for the closest of the buzz bombs. A Belgian youth, who knows eleven words of English all of which end with goddam, and whose expression has never lost the one it acquired the first day he was hired, shuttles between the desk and the composing room bearing copy for the machines below.

One telephone or another almost continually is ringing. Sometimes it is the faint, tentative jangle of an army telephone, routed through an army switchboard, bringing the voice of a soldier-reporter in the field. More frequently it is the brash clanging typical of the Belgian telephone which never again will be the same after the language that has gone into it these past months.

From the Ninth Air Force comes a story of the day's fighter and medium bomber attacks, because the Liége edition services the Ninth Air Force and that news must be in the gunners' and pilots' paper before they go out to fly again tomorrow morning. From Communications Zone headquarters another staffer calls with maybe a story on how many tons of shells and fuel the GI truckers have wrestled over icy roads and through drifting snow to the line troops who are halting the German push. Over the teletype now comes a story of the heavy Flying Fortress bombers based in England, which the London edition has sent out as its contribution to the mutual news service.

The pencils race through the written words. The typewriters chatter. The voices blur into the telephone mouthpieces.

*"There goes that goddam teletype. Busted again. Crandall, call Paris and get the rest of this last story over the phone. That's all we need to lock up. I'm going downstairs to the composing room . . ."*

A buzz bomb lands close enough to crack the windowpanes.

*"If that Nazi bastard cuts the power lines tonight and makes us late to press, I'll . . . I'll . . ."*

*"You'll leave his name out of the paper, huh?"*

*"Okay, Charlie, you sit in while I'm downstairs. And, oh yeah, when Crandall gets Paris, tell them to get some newsprint to us somehow . . . we got two days' left . . ."*

*"Tell 'em for chrissakes to send 32-inch rolls . . . the last six truckloads were toilet paper . . ."*

In the composing room, Belgian linotypers who, before *The Stars and Stripes* came to their battered city, probably hadn't read ten words of English in their lives, turned the typewritten American language into more or less reasonable facsimiles in lead. If they thought the letters "GI" stood for "GONE," and didn't know what either meant, or if they saw nothing wrong in hyphenating the word "this" when they came to the end of the line so that one line ended in "th" and the next line began "is" there wasn't much you could do about it. They punched out the type and it went to the forms.

Carl Larsen—or maybe Charlie Kiley or Bill Spear—searched his memory as the type arrived at the form, said "ici" and pointed graphically to the type and then to the hole in the page where it should go. Somehow the Belgian understood, even when Carl, or whoever it was, varied the routine and said "voici" instead of "ici."

(We had our troubles with foreign languages. Sometimes we found among our civilian help someone who spoke English. Eventually the staffers learned a little of whatever language was necessary, depending upon the locale, and the civilian help learned a little English. In Paris, staffers figured they'd found a gem in a civilian courier who ran uncensored war dispatches from the editorial office to the office of the chief press censor at the Hotel Scribe. He spoke English flawlessly, although with a slightly clipped and faintly guttural accent.

(For two months the efficient, English-speaking courier carried uncensored stories in which frequently there were phrases or items of more or less militarily secret nature, to and from the censor's office.

(There was considerable shock when Lieutenant Colonel Llewellyn, who had employed the civilian courier and had beamed with satisfaction over his "discovery," was informed one afternoon by the Criminal Investigation Corps of the army that the courier would not report for work that evening. He was in prison. The courier was a German army captain who had stayed behind when the Wehrmacht left Paris.)

So the paper went to press, which in Liége meant going to a sleek, streamlined press made in Germany and used throughout the occupation by German forces holding Belgium. Circulation men took the paper as it slid off the rollers, bundled it into jeeps and trucks, and took off in the early-morning darkness toward the flickering red of gun blasts in the eastern sky. In the city room, the noise of the typewriters died away, someone brought in coffee and sandwiches, four copyreaders started a poker game and invited the censor to play. The Belgian copy boy went home. At the city desk an argument began over the relative merits of living in Albuquerque or in Racine, Wisconsin. In the sports department a reporter who had watched Marlene Dietrich putting on a show for combat troops just behind the lines the day before resumed his argument about legs with the sports editor, who once had dinner at a table next to Betty Grable. The buzz bombs droned on.

There were other men and other offices to *The Stars and Stripes.* There were a corporal, Ralph Noel, and a sergeant, Bill Gibson, who kept books on three million dollars; there was Sergeant Jake Riller, who ruled perhaps the biggest circulation area in the world and whose men worked literally day and night that the Joes in the lines might have their papers. But their offices were for business, and were pale with reality; they were full of the neat, orderly sounds of adding machines and coins. People sat at desks in them.

Even in those *Stars and Stripes* editions which had modern buildings, as at Liége or Paris, the editorial rooms somehow were disreputable and dilapidated. It might have been that the first editorial home, in London, was ramshackle and old and lent an aura to all succeeding establishments, or it might have been simply that *The Stars and Stripes* people were the kind of people who made nice gleaming places well worn upon entrance and brought with them an unpressed atmosphere. Not that it made much difference.

Bleak London fog or Irish rain, African heat or Normandy mud, West Front snow or lilac spring in Germany, *The Stars and Stripes* always was so far above—or below, depending on where you stood—its surroundings that the surroundings never made much difference. We moved with the war, and tried to publish as we moved, and when we had run out of Old English letters, and French, and Arabic, and were using Germanic script, we started wondering about how the masthead would look in Chinese or Japanese characters.

But that was afterward. It all started very simply.

# COUNTRY WEEKLY

WARREN FRANCIS MCDONNELL, an easygoing, good-looking kid from Minneapolis who left an administrative job with a midwestern packing house to be a private in the 34th Infantry Division, stared at the sign on the door.

McDonnell was a little puzzled, because he had gone to one office in the big stone and brick building at 20 Grosvenor Square, in London, and a soldier in that office told him *The Stars and Stripes* had moved out of it two hours before and were on the next floor. That was where Mac stood now, and stared at the sign so swiftly applied. He shrugged and opened the door. From the window side of an ornate mahogany desk, Major Ensley Llewellyn lifted his thin, high-cheekboned face, peered a moment, waved bony fingers toward a chair. His voice scratched:

"Hellóooo. Sit down. What can we do for you?"

Mac tried to salute and sit down simultaneously, and just barely made the chair. The major slapped both palms on the edge of his desk, leaned forward and looked hard at McDonnell.

"Why, uh, I'm McDonnell, from the Northern Ireland office, major. When you inspected us last week you told me to come over to London today."

"McDonnell!" The major's voice crescendoed, his eyes dilated and there was as much of a smile as he ever managed on his lips. "Glad you're here. Got a job for you." He stood up and began to pace the room, swinging his thin frame as he pounded one hand in the other palm.

"McDonnell, you're just the man to take over our circulation here. Just the man."

"But, major, I was business manager over in Ireland. I—"

"Oh, yes. Yes. Thinking of someone else. Fellow with an Irish name or Scotch, Mac . . . Mac . . . Oh, yes. Well, take over our business office. That's what you're here for, McDonnell. We'll keep sending the papers to Ireland, but the big stuff's going to be here. Someday we're going to invade Europe from England, McDonnell, can't tell you when, of course; secret. But someday, and right now, *The Stars and Stripes* has to start organizing its business office. Brought you from Ireland to get things straightened out.

"Look around and tell me what you think, Mac. Change what has to be changed. Yes, sir, look around."

The major went back to his desk, on which the calendar said June 20, 1942, and which was to be moved to a dozen offices before that invasion materialized. The major started to write, looked up and saw Mac still sitting there. He didn't see the dazed look in Mac's eyes.

"Okay. Let's go."

Private McDonnell left the office as bewildered as all the long succession of *Stars and Stripes* executives would be for as long as there was a *Stars and Stripes,* anywhere. When he had sat shaking his head and rubbing suddenly fierce fingers through his hair in spasmodic gestures for ten minutes, he went to work resignedly.

He looked at the filing system, which for the first eight issues of the weekly *Stars and Stripes* had been ample; but now the circulation was climbing past ten thousand copies, and Mac knew the filing system had to be something better than a large drawer in a cabinet in Grosvenor Square, London.

He went back to the major's office and said, tentatively, "About this filing system, major. I might as well begin . . ."

"Good boy, McDonnell. Don't think so either. Good. Change it."

Mac left. That afternoon he installed files.

The following morning, McDonnell went back to the major. The method of collecting subscriptions by the year from soldiers whose bases would change constantly was bad.

"Good, McDonnell. Fine. Change it."

Now, the answers to those two problems, other people on the four-man business staff which started *The Stars and Stripes* heard for themselves. The answers the efficient McDonnell, who remained a private for a year and a half while he managed what became one of the largest newspaper businesses in the world, got to his next two questions to Major Llewellyn were heard only by Mac and G. K. Hodenfield, one of the paper's first two reporters, who happened to be there that afternoon. Both of them swear it's the truth.

Back a third time to the major's office went McDonnell.

"Major, the way we handle our records with the army is going to get muddled someday. Let's—"

"Good boy, Mac. Dandy. Know just what you mean. Go ahead, change it, Mac, change it."

Mac went out. It was beginning to lick him. Certainly Major Llewellyn was busy with the daily growing detail of starting a newspaper within the confines of an army. But surely there must be some point at which Private McDonnell (he capitalized the "private" in his mind) would get a "No." Or maybe at least a chance to say . . . Mac sighed. He went back to work for a couple of hours.

He worried about circulation. *The Stars and Stripes* delivered its paper each week to the United States forces in Northern Ireland via army airplane to Belfast, thence by jeep to the divisional training areas. That was all well and good in fine weather, troops got their papers every Saturday. But Mac was worrying about the traditionally bad English weather: what about when planes were grounded and bundles of papers lay at an airfield waiting for clear skies to Northern Ireland? The thing was unsound, and Mac was worrying too much about it to fix the way *S&S* records should be handled or much of anything else.

Twice he started, changed his mind, but finally he shoved out of his chair and strode through the major's doorway.

(Now, McDonnell swears this happened, and Hodenfield, who was in the office at the time, swears it happened, and all there is to do is tell it, adding the parenthetical protestations of truth which are spaced all through the story of *The Stars and Stripes*.)

"Major," began McDonnell, his brow creased in obvious worry, "there's something I've been worrying about. Now, this English weather—"

Mac never finished.

"Fine, McDonnell. Fine. Know just what you mean. Fix it up, Mac, fix it up!"

McDonnell's face blanked. His eyes, which had grown wide in

two days, grew wider. He stepped back half a pace, half lifted his hands as if to ward off a blow—at which the major banged him off a snappy salute—turned and fled. The major swung calmly back to Hodenfield.

And never as long as he knew the major did McDonnell's countenance quite lose the surprise and shock it first acquired when *The Stars and Stripes* was eight weeks young.

That was the way it started out. As a matter of fact, with variations, that is the way it always was. The business office, itself, was pretty sane, but in its connections with the office of whatever major or colonel happened to be officer in charge of *S&S* you always felt there was a sort of weirdness, the kind of liaison that two double-jointed universal joints, never quite meeting, might make.

The weekly, bless it, somehow just grew, and in growing fostered that haphazard, erratic air which always got *The Stars and Stripes* wherever it was going. It was hand to mouth, and a flatbed press thumping away. It was a horse opera, with Don Quixote riding off rapidly in all directions and someone paying the mortgage just as the heroine started into the buzz saw.

Mark Martin, a Des Moines newspaperman turned infantry lieutenant, put out Vol. 1, No. 1 of World War II's army newspaper. With him there were Benny Price, who'd been a cub sports reporter on the Des Moines *Register and Tribune;* Russ Jones, a Minneapolis reporter and feature writer; Hodenfield, another Iowan who had worked for the United Press; McDonnell, and a business office crew which included Einar Eeg, Hal Brauetigam, who took pictures all week and distributed the paper on Saturdays, Dean Hocking, who had to balance the meager income against the major's desire to "buy automobiles," and George Petrakis, who became probably the only first sergeant in the army to be sent to the infantry when, three years later, the cry went up for manpower on the firing line to halt the last Nazi offensive in Europe.

The paper was established under circumstances as vague as those under which it ran. The newspaper business at home was filled with rumors that Bertie McCormick, of the Chicago *Tribune,* was trying to publish an overseas edition of his anti-administration paper. About the same time—according to what spokesmen for the War Department have since said, and it's probably true—the army realized that it was going to send a lot of Americans to Europe who had been used to their own newspapers. That realization coincided with the birth of an idea under the balding pate of Ensley Llewellyn.

The Tacoma, Washington, advertising man had come to England to be a press censor but when he began to espouse the project of an American newspaper for American soldiers abroad, and cited *The Stars and Stripes* of World War I, the idea fell on receptive ears, which already had heard Bertie McCormick's strident demands.

In that eerie sort of coincidence which marks the paper, Mark Martin simultaneously was ordered to start a local paper for troops in Northern Ireland. The plans were unified, Washington blessed, and the flat-bed in the printing shop of Hazell, Watson & Viney began to thump.

It wasn't a very good newspaper. It was a pretty good country weekly, but in the first months of 1942 that was about the kind of army we had in Europe, a sort of country weekly kind of army.

By early summer, however, the manpower and the war-machine power were beginning to pile up, and the paper began to acquire a staff to cover what the growing power looked like. Although Mark Martin lost a lieutenant's argument with the major and left the paper for the Rangers, the paper thumped along with a new man coming in every third or fourth day: Mark Senigo, Bob Collins, Ralph Martin and a couple of fellows from the Canadian Army who'd come over before the Yanks and got tired of waiting for the Dieppe raid which then took place as soon as they transferred . . .

The reporters and editors played blackjack on Monday, went out in the field on Tuesday and Wednesday, wrote on Thursday, set up and published the paper on Friday, and on Saturday and Sunday they joined the circulation men in distributing *The Stars and Stripes* to the soldiers and sailors who already had subscribed to it, getting up in new mess hall tents across England and beginning—

"Fellows, I'm from *The Stars and Stripes*. Er. The newspaper of the Armed Forces in the European Theater of Operations. Now this paper . . ."

That was about as far as it got. Someone mercifully hollered

"How much?" and the staffers took down subscriptions for eighteen shillings, and that included *Yank,* the army magazine. The nascent American Army abroad wanted a newspaper, even a country weekly.

All summer the flat-bed in Hazell, Watson & Viney's Soho printing plant banged away. Soho is strictly Jack the Ripper territory, but the *Yank* newspapermen felt at home; as a matter of fact, they usually slept in their smelly little cubbyhole of an office because by the time they got through playing cards or putting out the paper it was too late for them to catch a bus back to the billets in which the army wanted to keep them.

The first sergeant in charge of the barracks in which they were supposed to sleep grew weary. Every time he tried to discipline a *Stars and Stripes* man for being out of his bunk at night, the man produced, and with injured innocence, the completely valid excuse that he had worked late "at the office." There was no precedent for that in the army in which the first sergeant had learned about soldiers, and finally he gave up:

"You guys don't bother me for nothing, and I don't bother you," he offered. "I'll okay slips for your clothes and whatever army stuff you need, but you feed yourselves and sleep yourselves and stay to hell out of my hair.

"Working late at the office!"

He made a first sergeant's noise and *The Stars and Stripes* staff continued sleeping in the office until the respective members could find small apartments or furnished rooms or friends who had either.

Maybe they were only putting out a country weekly, but the staff of the old paper earned the gratitude of a long line of *Stars and Stripes* men for the precedents they set: they confounded the army by being willing to do more than ordered, they confused it by being individuals, they goaded it into turning them loose to a form of pasture.

The weekly set the basic format of dingy city room, sustenance unto one's self, and confusion to military precedent. It was like that all the long way to Hitler's Germany and then the Pacific.

# PLACES OF BUSINESS

THE *Times* of London is an institution. From the drab and motley cluster of brick and wooden buildings in the dingy shadows of Queen Victoria Street, on the edge of London's old city and just off the Thames, the *Times* does grammatically as it considers right, and in so doing molds an important (THE important, the *Times* is apt to feel and not without a lot of justification) portion of British public opinion. The *Times* does not hurry. Through its intricate, winding hallways linking the buildings which have been expanded with empire and time, *Times* editors walk with thoughtful mien, and they do it in fresh linen, with neckties, and coats. Sometimes, they do it with morning trousers, even in rationed wartime. The editors and subeditors are served tea in their offices at four on silver and china tea sets.

Maybe the *Times* is best summed up: its readers open their paper first to the editorials.

When *The Stars and Stripes* became a daily, on November 2, 1942, it was at the *Times,* the first in a long line of journalistic step-parents to the daily paper of the army.

When the *Stars and Stripes* staff first clattered through their building, the sober editors of the *Times* looked up disapprovingly from under their green eyeshades. *Times* reporters, busy writing out their reports in longhand, lay down their pencils and pens as the unconscious Americans hit the floor, where only toes previously had tread, with heavy GI heels, making more noise than the building or any of its occupants had heard since the last nail (or wooden peg) was hammered in place hundreds of years before. There was a lot of walking to do to get where you were going at the *Times.*

The course from the street, near Blackfriars Bridge, to the *S&S* office in the *Times* led through hundreds of feet of narrow, winding corridors, up and down flights of wooden steps and around little corners.

Strangers groping their way to the office often felt like dropping small bits of paper, Boy Scouts of America-like, so they would be able to find their way out. The second night of the occupation of the *Times,* Bob Moora and Russ Jones started out to find a short cut from the editorial offices to the pressroom, some four floors below, and eventually wound up in a black maze, literally unable to retrace their steps. They stood there and hollered for help until a small, gray *Times* employee came along and, completely unperturbed, led them back to the city room.

The labyrinth, which would have driven any intelligent American laboratory guinea pig insane, was some protection, though, from the thousands of screwballs who tried to get up to the office. Some of the Belgian bicyclists who wanted to insert ads in the paper, the refugee Poles who wanted to find their cousins from Scranton, and the soldier with the self-heating bedroll for tired and cold soldiers got to know their ways to the editorial rooms, but thousands more must have given up, discouraged. We never found any parched skeletons, though, on the way out.

The *Times* got the *Stars and Stripes* daily printing job by underbidding all the other London papers for the job. It was on a reverse Lend-Lease basis, but they were doing it cheaply. It was almost a gesture of goodwill to their American allies. "Sure we'll print your little journal for American soldiers," they said in effect. What they definitely did not understand was that within a year and a half *The Stars and Stripes* would dwarf the *Times'* own circulation and would be published by a high-powered staff from whom "The Thunderer's" own editors frequently borrowed stories.

It probably was a merciful thing that the *Times* didn't realize what was happening until it was too late to stop it. From its venerable presses was coming an American tabloid newspaper, comic strips, pin-up photos of semidressed femininity, black headlines on page one; six days a week, four pages a day except Monday when there were eight and every one of them blatant by *Times* standards.

That first month of November, 1942, full of bold news for

bold American headlines, such as the invasion of North Africa, gave the *Times* an idea of what it was going to be like. Before December, every newspaper in Fleet Street was sending a messenger boy to wait at the *Times'* pressroom, not for a copy of the Thunderer, but for *The Stars and Stripes*. So, too, the American news agencies. The British press picked up leads on stories, and frequently stories intact, albeit injecting into them the unique style of London journalism.

*The Stars and Stripes* was particularly proud of its roundup on the day's bombing activities during that period of the war when there was no fighting in Europe except that in the air; the paper literally was an Air Force trade journal. As such it had to know its business. The air story often ran for 1,500 words and included a meticulous report of heavy and medium bomber missions, their targets, and the background down to the number of tons that target already had absorbed, fighter-bomber sorties, strafings, aerial minelaying and just about everything else. The roundup was so capably handled that most London papers and American news bureaus there waited for it before writing their final stories of the night, sometime along about 11:30 P.M.

The *Times,* from the first day of war, had begun its air story with a simple introductory sentence and then had printed verbatim the RAF communique, later adding whatever the Americans might have done. Its air editor finally got around not only to the *S&S* treatment of the story, but one evening broke down enough over a glass of mild-and-bitter to confess that he was "finding actually more enjoyment these days in treating the subject in your ah American manner. With some reservations, of course, some reservations."

The air war, then, accounted for the reproductions of diving fighters, burning bombers and formations which covered part of the walls of the *Stars and Stripes* office. The rest of the walls were covered with a miscellany of items stuck up haphazardly with paste. The pictures were predominantly "cheesecake," the trade term of Sergeant Ben Price, the Des Moines picture editor, for choice items from his stack of Hollywood girls more or less out of bathing suits.

From the walls the *Times* could have—and probably did—draw its own image of things to come after that first month. The *Times* people were very obliging, but they first began to realize

they were in for real trouble the day the switchboard operator heard a voice from *S&S* make a request.

"Would you please tell the department in charge of knocking down walls that we would like to have the wall knocked down between our two offices?" the voice asked.

The operator, not realizing how surprised she was for a minute, said she would. Fifteen minutes or so later, two grayed men in overalls came into the city room, crowbars, sledges, hammers and saws over their shoulders. The Desk was a little taken aback, but pointed, and they dutifully knocked down the wall which time, the blitz and generations of *Times* men had left standing. That made the *S&S* offices in the building into one large room.

It was about thirty feet wide and twice as long. As you came in at one of two doors—the other was bolted shut and carried a nostalgically huge poster of a dish of American ice cream—there was a small rectangular niche about five feet deep and six feet wide at your left. There, for some reasons, the light switch had been placed conveniently behind a desk and a heavy wooden cabinet. On the far side of the room was the Desk.

The city editor, through whom came all stories other than those from the news wires, sat on one side of the double desk. With the aid of the five telephones in front of him he sent reporters out to cover this largest local news beat in the world—the whole British Isles, the seas around them and the flak-filled sky all the way to Berlin.

The news editor, who handled all the wire copy, the news from home and the stories from other war fronts, sat across from him. Six other desks of varying sizes and states of disrepair were scattered around the room.

On a small shelf, nailed to the wall between the two windows, was the complete office library. There were eight books: a Jane's *Fighting Ships,* a Webster's dictionary, a Tacoma, Washington, telephone book, a 1939 *World Almanac,* Jane's *Aircraft of the World,* a French-English-German dictionary, an *Official Officers' Guide Book* and a volume entitled *The Fox of Peapack.* Over the library, for handy reference, someone had scribbled in foot-high black crayon letters "IT'S ADOLF—NOT ADOLPH."

Running up the middle of the city room was a pipelike affair about six inches in diameter. It served as the office bulletin board although structurally its function was to hold the wooden ceiling off the wooden floor. Toward the top of the pipe, near the ceiling, there was a wicker wastebasket, wired fast. Ben Price tied it to the top of the pole one day when an order came down for all *Stars and Stripes* men to get an hour's exercise every day.

Price and a couple of staffers used to drag out a new case of pastepots every few days and get their exercise by tossing a few of the glass "balls" through the (waste) basket.

The boys got the greater part of their exercise in climbing up to retrieve the glass pastepot-balls until one day Charlie White staggered into the shop and through the thick lenses of his glasses turned red eyes on the basket. Charles was no athlete, but somehow the pastepot he grabbed from Ham Whitman's desk sailed truly through the air and into the basket. Charles was pleased, but irritated.

"Hell of a basket," he grumbled. "It's got a bottom." He climbed on a chair, jerked the basket down and kicked vigorously at its bottom. The kick carried too far. As a matter of fact, it carried Charlie's foot, ankle and knee on up into the basket, and carried Charlie completely off his feet so that he wound up threshing on the floor, the basket jammed up around his waist. In the confusion he lost his glasses, and his myopic eyes spun wildly as he kicked and wrestled with the basket.

At the height of Charles's battle with the wicker waste basket, Lieutenant Colonel Llewellyn walked into the office, and where never in a sober moment would he have thought of saluting, Charles suddenly was seized with a self-martyring urge to stand up and salute. He did, and as he stood there, the basket still around his leg, glasses lost, thin hair mussed, coat up around the back of his neck, eyes glaring wildly, and his balance a precarious thing, the character of Hubert, Dick Wingert's cartoon hero, was born.

The thing had an aftermath. Because Charles had destroyed the bottom of the basket, when it was replaced on the pipe, the pastepots went right through, and, nonbouncing, splattered glue and glass across the room each time the mob exercised.

This, presumably, was the army.

On the walls, finally, in addition to the cheesecake, there were dozens of clippings, memos, pictures, and odds and ends of printed material. There were weekly notices of inspections and various formations, which eventually, as they were disregarded, came to have, you felt, a sort of pleading note in them. Sort of please, fellows, come on up to inspection this week.

One of the staffers' favorite headlines pasted to the wall was:

**YANKS GET**
**ABBEY FOR**
**GI CHAPEL**

It came from the first Thanksgiving in England. For the traditional American services, the friendly Britons gave up their most precious religious symbol, Westminster Abbey. It was a good story; it was worth a top head on page one. That meant thirty-point type, a size that simply doesn't permit the word "Westminster" to be squeezed into one line. The resourceful Desk solved it with their headline describing the venerable abbey as about to become a GI chapel. It shocked a few chaplains, but most of them understood there was no disrespect involved, and there had been a neat job of head writing.

Just behind the desk was the favorite clipping of the city editor. It served as text when anyone turned in a paragraph or more of meaningless copy, and it had been clipped from the November 25, 1941, issue of the very *Times* itself. It read (and there were a couple of staffers who came to be able to recite it by heart):

> With a British Armoured Unit
> LIBYA, Nov. 23
>
> The battle of the tanks in Libya is still going on furiously. At the time of writing the issue is still in the balance. The Germans are fighting furiously to destroy the British tank forces and to break through the ring. The British are fighting with equal fury to prevent them. Both sides have given and taken some very hard knocks. The tank battles are an affair of sudden onslaughts in unexpected places. The battle is joined, broken and rejoined. Sometimes small groups only are involved; other times, large groups . . .

It went on like that.

When the staff first moved into the offices there was just one electric light in the middle of the room. The Desk wanted a low, green-shaded light over each desk. The meticulous *Times* maintenance men obliged with a network of wires and lights.

Suspended from all sections of the ceiling and hanging at ruled heights above the desks, the wires presented a maze too intriguing to anyone who'd spent half an hour in the Lamb and Lark, the pub across the street, before coming back to the office late at night for extra work. You'd start one hanging light swinging in great circles, then another and another and when enough of them were wound around each other, the whole complex structure would come down. Next day the maintenance men would be upstairs, surveying the tangled mess, the chunks of ceiling plaster, and the blown fuses. They would say sadly, "The blast of those bombs is enough to shake down almost anything."

Which was all right and logical on nights when there was an air raid. But sometimes the lights came down after a raid-free night, and they said the same thing, and the staff finally decided they were simply nice, understanding guys who maybe had wanted to do the same thing in the staid *Times* all their lives but hadn't dared.

At frequent intervals, we received a formal announcement that "General Somebody" was coming down to the office to look around. There could have been no more absurd place for a military inspection; but one time the staff was told "for sure" that Lieutenant General John C. H. Lee, one of the army's most inspecting generals, was to visit us. We were ordered to take down the ridiculous display on the walls and clean up the office. Some of the memos and pictures pasted on the walls were part of the office, though, and taking them down was out of the question, even for General Lee.

Ben Price walked over to Fleet Street. He visited half a dozen little bookstores, buying road maps, maps of the canal system in Afghanistan, terrain maps of the territory adjacent to Shanghai, and weather maps showing general pressure areas between Iceland and England. He came back and the staff went to work hanging the maps from hooks or with thumbtacks on the walls.

With straight faces the staff explained to the officer in charge that no one could kick about legitimate maps in any newspaper office. General Lee, of course, like the others, never arrived. Most of the maps came down, and the urgent memos, the cheesecake, and the outdated headlines were visible again in all their dusty yellow uselessness. The weather map of the North Atlantic stayed. Ben said we might need to know someday how the weather was there.

The *Times* people never really got used to *The Stars and Stripes.* They tried, and some of the compositors eventually became as one with the staff. But mostly the *Times* just wondered.

In the first few days strange things happened in the composing rooms with compositors who never had worked for any paper except the *Times.* There was, for example, the mysterious disappearance of a particularly choice bit of cheesecake which had been sent up to the engravers one night. Somehow the picture and engraving disappeared completely, and there always has been an argument as to whether some venerable *Times* worker secretly slipped the picture of the seminude Hollywoodite into his pocket to contemplate in some lonely place or whether the *Times* man was a reforming purist who thought that in the best interests of the soldiers of England's ally the photo should be destroyed. If he simply wanted the picture for his own he was easily satisfied, because after that first week none ever disappeared again, and if he was a reformer he quickly gave us up for lost.

That first week at the *Times* was something English type compositors are going to talk about for a long time. On the sixth night, one linotype operator was carried off screaming mad, and he's in the booby hatch yet shouting about "the language of Shakespeare." Another compositor, setting heads, saw unfilled orders piling up and piling up and suddenly and stiffly fainted dead away; but in general they became familiar with what the editors wanted, and Jimmy Frost, the composing room foreman, and Bill Jolley, a stone man, got to be so expert in the American way of newspapering that they were worried about their postwar return to the *Times.*

Just as the *Times* became a little proud of the army paper it housed, so the army paper was proud of the *Times.* The staff learned the *Times* folklore complete through constant contact with the Thunderer's staff in the building—this was after *Times* editors decided we'd been there long enough for them to stop bowing stiffly from the waist when we passed in the corridors—and in the Printing House Square pub, Alf Storey's Lamb and Lark. There was a great store of *Times* stories, and probably the one the *S&S* liked best was that of the man with the little black bag.

When a new managing director was appointed by the *Times* board of directors, he started a thorough check through the books and offices of every branch of the organization. The new manager noticed an obscure little man in an oversized overcoat and carrying a little black satchel entering the building one Friday, and made a mental note to find out who he was. The following Friday he saw the little man again, and this time started asking who he was. The old-timers admitted they had seen the little man for years, but no one knew exactly who he was or what he did. He came Friday nights, carrying his black satchel, and left Monday mornings.

Over the weekend, the manager was checking some ledgers and came upon a small but inexplicable item. He asked one of the bookkeepers about it and was told the money went for meals brought in Saturday and Sunday from a small restaurant around the corner; the meals went to the little man who appeared each Friday night at the office.

On the third weekend, the manager searched through the dozens of little offices off the rabbit warren of corridors. Beyond one door he found the little man, with a little lunch spread out before him, his little black satchel at his side.

The little man was from the Bank of England. In the little black satchel he had five thousand pounds in cash.

Back at the turn of the century, along about the time of the Boer War, the *Times* wanted to send a man off to cover a big story on the Continent in a rush assignment. He had to leave on a Saturday afternoon, but there were no boats to the Continent that day because of a storm. Charter a boat, ordered the editor. The business office ruefully replied that there wasn't enough money in the place, it had been sent to the bank in the morning.

To prevent that ever happening again, the *Times* had asked that a representative of the Bank of England be on hand Friday evenings and stay until Monday mornings with five thousand pounds in cash.

Long afterward, when the *Times* had its own boats and had fully-manned bureaus on the Continent, no one had bothered to countermand the order, and the little man was still coming every Friday evening.

Stately *Times,* whose subscribers will doubt the world's end until they read it in your pages, institution of British dignity with morals like the collars of your directors, you were very kind; and if you were an old gaffer, the people who came to your house to work were brats, and you were very indulgent. You nodded and smiled when the people in Fleet Street got to calling your musty, cobblestoned old courtyard "Stars and Stripes Square," instead of the Printing House name it had borne so long. You even asked one of the brashest of the Americans to write book reviews for that book review section which is the double-distilled synthesis of *Times* conservatism and backed him up when he lampooned stuffed shirts. You gathered up the pieces when they were broken and you set the precedent for all the rest to come. As it was in the beginning, so always was *The Stars and Stripes,* and so the *Times* was home.

# COMBAT

COMBAT, OF COURSE, is the ultimate expression of war. That's why you're there, to fight. And no matter how difficult, tedious, exhausting any other job of war may be, it's the combat man's task that is most difficult, if only for one reason: his price for failure, or even just for bad luck, is death.

That was why *The Stars and Stripes* was written, edited, and published first for the men in combat, and then for others. And because the *Stars and Stripes* staff was putting out a paper primarily for the fighting men, the staffers themselves went into combat on land, at sea, and in the air.

*Stars and Stripes* reporters felt the necessity of seeing with their own eyes, hearing with their own ears, and feeling with their own viscera what happened to men who were killing and might be killed. The staffers wanted to let the men know, as best they could, that the soldiers' newspaper was really the soldiers' newspaper. It was a moral urge, maybe a little intangible; but it was more compelling than any other. (To be perfectly accurate, the number of staffers who saw and were part of actual combat was not great, chiefly because there was no need for a great number; and there were plenty of deskmen whose jobs did not demand that they go out with the fighting men, and there were plenty of reporters who somehow or other managed to stay clear of the places where men were being killed.)

But for those who went, there was a second, and more obvious, reason—getting stories. The stories were where the fighting was. You could get them by waiting at an air base or at a division command post in the ground war, but the best way, the most certain and accurate way, was to get out there where whatever was happening was happening and get back to tell about it.

Finally, there was a sort of personal issue involved. You wanted to know what it was like, and you wanted to get the stories, and you wanted the guys who were fighting to know their newspaper was there some of the time anyway, and you also wanted to be sure about yourself. You wanted to go there so that you would have the answers, which you wouldn't write anyway, to letters unknown soldiers might send to *The Stars and Stripes* abusing the staff for sitting around the office.

But going out to where the gunfire and the dead were wasn't all there was to combat, and the staff never forgot it:

London, July 18, 1944

**U. S. LIVES PAY THE PRICE FOR "THE HILL"**

**It Had to be Taken, So Yanks Write Out the Check in Blood**

By Bud Hutton and Andy Rooney

WITH U.S. FORCES IN NORMANDY—To the division it was "Hill 192, a heavily defended elevation commanding Saint-Lô from the east." To most newspaper readers it was "a Nazi strongpoint."

But to the dirty, unshaven Americans who peered up at its hedge-bristled slope and knew what waited in the dark-green shadows where the hedgerows met, it was always simply "The Hill."

In the morning the shadows on the hill ran down toward the northern base, in the direction whence the doughboys had come some score of days before. Then the hill frowned, lowering on their new day, souring it even before the rain came, as the rain always did. In the afternoon, the shadows slanted over to their left flank, and if there was enough sun they could see it glint on the ripening cherries of the square orchards which made up the hill. Evening and night were worst; the hill was all black, a lump in the dark, and not even the flash of artillery shells bursting on its brow could make it seem real and part of the war.

The hill was squared with hedges, and the hedges were filled with machine guns and mortars, with snipers and observers who called back to the artillery and heavy mortars on the southern slope. Defending it —part of it is better—were German soldiers in long green jackets which fastened beneath the crotch, and helmets which fitted close and had three straps about the backs of their heads. They were German paratroops, fighting in the line—elite soldiers, tough guys.

Overlooking the valley of the River Elle, commanding the lateral east-west highway from Caumont to Saint-Lô and beyond, covering the avenues of approach from the north, 192 meters above sea level (thus its official name), fortified since D day, an observation point into Saint-Lô and for miles every other way, held by a battalion and a company on the hill proper, 3½ battalions more on the lines forming its east and west flanks. That was Hill 192 to the division and corps and army.

It had to be taken before the advance could go on. On Monday night, the men on the bottom northern slopes of the hill prayed hard.

It was 4 A.M. when the battalion and company commanders, the platoon and squad leaders wakened those who had slept and led them back with muffled footsteps and no words 200 yards from the lines they had held so long. It was 0520 when the artillery began.

All across the Normandy sky the muzzles flared red, and their noise rolled across the wet countryside. The 105s and the 155 hows and Long Toms and some eight-inch hows. They began it, and as the hands of the clock crawled around to straight up and down, the 75s and the three-inchers, the infantry cannon companies and all the mortars joined. Their flashes grew paler against the early sky and the first ten per cent of what would total nearly 25,000 rounds of ammunition were on.

On the easy slope at the base of the hill, out of the orchards and the shelter of the hedgerows, moved the first and second battalions of the division's right-flank regiment and on the left flank, one battalion. In their van went teams of men who had—in the two weeks before—come out of the lines and trained and rehearsed this job until the squad leaders knew by heart every step they would make, every bush they would pass, on the way up the hill—if they got up the Hill.

### Here are the Teams

The teams were a rifle squad, a Sherman tank, four engineers who knew demolition, and in reserve, one hedgerow behind all the way, was another M-4 tank. Behind and around them came the infantry, and the forward artillery observers. Behind them more infantry, and the mortars, and after that the rest of the division—but there was a lot more space between the infantry and the others than the words tell.

The infantry-tank-engineers teams came to the first hedges. The riflemen laid down a fire against the places which hid German strength. The tanks fired their 75s and machine guns. The engineers took explosives from a box on the tank's side, touched them off at the roots of the three-foot thick, nine-foot high hedge and the tank went through, grinding down dugouts that hid Nazi paratroopers, firing on the next hedge row where there were more Germans and more machine guns.

That was the way it started. The artillery churned the hill, its crest and all the slopes and the reserve areas beyond. The shells killed Germans and kept more Germans belowground. That could be planned beforehand. The tank teams went in, the infantry moved up as the barrage rolled ahead. The wire men came in and laid their wire.

### Stuff Roars Overhead

Swoooshswoosh the big stuff went overhead, with a singing and almost a rhythm, although you can't really write the sound, and at 0601 there was the first burping stutter of a German automatic pistol, sharp and clean, like a nervous woodpecker. The enemy guns had been waiting, and almost immediately on the line of the first khaki figures slipping along the hedges they dropped heavy oil shells, which burst with a pillar of orange flame and black smoke and threw blazing oil. From far back, the 105s and the 155s turned to counterbattery, and there were no more oil shells.

At 0631, Private Lester Robbins, 38-year-old man with a Red Cross on his arm, led back the first casualty from A Company of the left center, a man with shell fragments in his shoulder. In five hours one of every twelve men would be a casualty of some sort, by the day's end slightly more than one in ten.

Now the men of A, B and C companies, E, F, G companies to the right, were through the first hedgerows, flattening out in the second of time after the 88s' whistle, taking the silent mortars as they came. The artillery had pushed some of the Germans down into their holes, and the doughboys simply pulled the pins on grenades, held them an eternity and dropped them in the holes.

The light began to break through the mist about 0712 and took away the false feeling of being hidden the infantrymen had when it was darker. On the northwest side of the hill, and on the east slope, about in the middle, the ground was bright with the light of two burning American tanks. Away to the east, one company from a reserve battalion had cleaned up a strongpoint the Germans had ringed with wire and mortars.

### Shells Fall Regularly

On the line of Americans, going uphill, the mortar shells fall regularly, and from there back to the base of the slope they plump down and munch at the hedgerows shielding the khaki forms. At 0912 the report comes to the CP of Major Olinto M. Barsanti, of Tonopah, Nevada, that F Company has a platoon in the little woods to the right crest from which German artillery observers have been pouring shellfire down the division's shirtfronts for days. E Company—also from the battalion on the right—is across the road junction west of ten houses named Cloville. Company A of the first battalion is in the diamond-shaped woods covering the hill's major crest, and B is moving without loss through German strongpoints, taking prisoners and killing paratroops almost as it has practiced.

Now the fighting has spread out not only horizontally, east to west, but up and down the hill, with pockets here and there, and lone paratroopers holding out in trees and holes.

Noon comes and goes, and another stage of the barrage unrolls before the infantry. Time schedules have been altered and realtered today—they were so planned that they could be—because the Nazi paratroops have fought bitterly in spots and have held up the advance.

### The Fight Is Won

In the early afternoon, although you can't see it all, the fight is won. There is enough strength in the woods and along the crest so that the division will roll onward, down the southern slope and across the Saint-Lô road, and the next day it will clean up the pockets and make the Saint-Lô position firm.

All that is because a kid named George Rivers asked an engineer to drag him to a gateway where he stayed with his wounds, firing his BAR, until he died. And because a second looey named Paul Bielic stood up to mortar fire so that the artillery observers could be up with the doughs and direct the fire. It is because Sam Francis, a first lieutenant, and Herb Lindgren, a staff sergeant, were willing to fly through rain almost within slingshot distance of German small arms, to spot resistance. It is because George Hatch, a sergeant, pushed his tank forward until the 88s stopped it. It is because Hugh Lind and Henry Cox have enough faith in something plus the Red Cross on the white bands around their arms to walk among the tracers that wounded men may not die and dying men may do it with less hurt.

The hill is the division's, and no longer frowns with sullen menace on the men below it to the north, because of those names and the things they did, and the scores of others in their jobs for whom they stand. Most of all—all the other branches of the service will tell you, and the look in their faces is the ultimate proof—most of all it is because of the infantrymen, who would not stop.

(*The unit referred to in the above story was the Second Infantry Division. It remained simply "the division" in* The Stars and Stripes *because of censorship restrictions.*)

The staffers who went to the bombers or the infantry always could leave after any one mission, or one battle. The airmen and the tankers and the infantry had to stick. They couldn't decide, whenever they wanted to, that they would go back to an office and write a story. They had to stay for the next haul to Berlin, or the next barrage, or the next attack, and for them there was no surcease until they were hit or the outfit was relieved.

The staff remembered that, to its everlasting credit, and took some of the potential pompousness out of its attitude of "I've-been-there" with, for example, the sign on the censor's desk:

Combat Censor

Or the brand-new, never-used steel helmet which Joe Fleming wore around the office one night which bore the neatly printed legend on the front:

Combat Rewriteman.

From time to time, the policy of sending experienced newspapermen—scarce within the army's personnel—to combat from which they might not return was questioned, but early in the paper's history the Desk settled that argument with the dictum:

"Very simple solution to the possibility of any of you guys getting knocked off and not getting back. Don't let it happen."

Tom Hoge, one-time infantryman with the 29th Division, tried his best to carry out that order during the airborne attack in Holland on the Arnhem bridge, which ultimately failed. Tom flew out to cover the drop from a bomber, planning to write his story on the way back to base.

Over the drop zone, as the British and American paratroopers plunged out toward the ground, flak batteries opened up on the huge air armada. The Fortress in which Tom was flying was hit and plummeted earthward. Four parachutes opened in the wake of the bomber as it screamed into the ground.

That night, when word got back to the office, the city room was maybe a little noisier than usual. *The Stars and Stripes* had lost other men, in the Mediterranean theater, but this was Hoge's first big combat assignment; it didn't seem too probable that Tom could have got to an escape hatch from his position up front in the plane where he was watching the airborne drop. The boys in the office felt badly about it and so they were noisier than they ordinarily were.

Black-haired, grinning, Irish Tom Hoge, however, had been one of the four men in the stricken plane who got a chance to pull his ripcord. In the three months following that morning of the airborne attack, Tom went through one of the weirdest war experiences any Stars-and-Stripeser ever had. The first inkling the office had that Tom was all right came in a January communication from the International Red Cross. It was "believed" Tom Hoge might be alive and a prisoner of the Germans.

The International Red Cross didn't know it, but their use of the term "believed" was precisely correct: Tom did get out of the falling plane, was taken prisoner. But he wouldn't stay prisoner. In machine-gun circled captivity, starving and wretched and cold, the *Stars and Stripes* staffer was just as difficult for his German captors to handle as Stars-and-Stripesers were at any time for the American Army to handle.

Through the long winter months, staffers in Paris or London or Liége occasionally lifted a drink to Tom Hoge. Tom needed their good wishes; he and a thousand or so other American prisoners of war were in a camp on the eastern edge of Germany. Tom told about it a long time later.

"Unfed and with no water," Tom said, "the Germans marched us—or transported us crammed in freezing boxcars from one prison camp to another. Finally we were dumped into a stalag in the far east of Germany proper.

"We existed on what by courtesy was called 'soup;' it was made of boiling potato peelings in water. We got a couple of slices of bread a day. Sometimes we got coffee for breakfast. The coffee was made from the used grounds our German guards had boiled for their own coffee. Maybe it tasted so bad because, in addition to being old grounds, the coffee in the first place had been ground from roasted barley.

"It was the Russian drive of the late winter toward the Oder River which eventually liberated us.

"As the Soviets drew nearer and the sound of their cannon and the rumble of their tanks came through the barbed wire of our stalag, we were ordered to be ready to march out to a prison camp farther into Germany. The first sergeant who acted as leader of our group of American enlisted men PWs told us to fake mass illness. We were all supposed to get dysentery at one time. It worked a little bit but finally the commandant of the camp strode into our enclosure, coldly adjusted the monocle in his eye and said in clipped Prussian accent:

" 'You will be ready to march in thirty minutes. If you are not you will all be shot.'

"We figured he meant business, and our first sergeant advised us to fall in. Hope of escape faded. We trudged off, still freezing, still ill-fed, to the new prison camp. But the Russian advance swept forward, and suddenly the Soviet tanks were almost upon us. The German guards and officers fled. Allied prisoners took over administration of the camp and the little near-by town. Then we found out there were still retreating German forces between us and the Russians.

"Not taking any chances, we organized the defense of the town, using what weapons the fleeing Germans had left. Finally a couple of us set out to try and locate the Russians. We filtered our way through the German units, and those were the longest hours of anyone's life, because freedom was so near but could be gone forever if we made a mistake.

"Finally we located the Russians, or maybe they located us, and from then on it was just a question of waiting to be forwarded to an American area so I could get my story back to the Desk."

And that was the way Tom Hoge came out of captivity. Shifted about behind the Russian lines, he and some of the others eventually wound up in Odessa where they contacted American and British units. Tom figured the best way to get his story back was through the Rome edition of *The Stars and Stripes,* to which he sent it for forwarding to the main office in Paris.

It was typical of the staff's attitude that Tom addressed his first and subsequent stories, as well as his supplementary cables of information and a request for further orders, to the city editor who had been running the paper when he flew off to combat five months before. Tom couldn't know that the man who'd been city editor even then was jumping into action with the paratroops.

Tom's experiences as a prisoner of war, of course, were no different from those of thousands of other PWs. They were the kind of experiences the people back in the United States got bored with hearing after a while. The important thing about the story was that even in the winter bitterness of a German prison camp, *The Stars and Stripes*—though it wasn't planned that way—had a staffer with the guys for whom the paper was written.

Never with the first-person-singular, never with the "I-was-there" attitude, but simply with the self-restricted task of being there so that they could write about what the other people were doing, *Stars and Stripes* men went to combat, to captivity, and even to the lists headed "Killed in Action."

Paul Connors, who covered the Air Force for *Warweek,* the propaganda supplement inserted into *The Stars and Stripes,* was shot down during an Eighth Air Force bomber mission and still is listed as missing in action.

Mostly, though, the staffers went out to the war and got back with their stories. Some held it was good luck, but Russ Jones, who viewed all life with a dim light, held:

"Any sonofabitch who's worked on this paper long enough to draw an assignment covering combat already is too goddamned mean and ornery to have anything happen to him."

There might have been something to that; Russ spent time with the infantry, and once rode into a fortress town on the outside of a tank at which German 88s were shooting "to find out what it felt like to the doughs who have to."

Simply because *The Stars and Stripes* presented, as part of its coverage of the air war news, a daily story on what the Royal Air Force, or the Canadian Air Force, had done in the preceding twenty-four hours, G. K. Hodenfield decided someone from *S&S* ought to fly with the heavy British night bombers. Without any aid from the army he made arrangements, flew with a Lancaster bomber crew one night to Berlin. His story helped the Yanks, who were flying the Forts and Libs to Berlin in daylight, understand what was happening in the rest of the war.

Hodenfield—he kept his first name, Gaylord, carefully concealed—put in a good many hours and days being shot at. He went to Africa in November, 1942, to help set up the African *Stars and Stripes* and in the course of covering that war was with the infantry in the days of Kasserine Pass.

Back again in England, Hod did occasional training stories, flew with the RAF to Berlin and finally disappeared in mid-May, 1944.

It was June 8 before the office heard from Hod again: The Desk got a thousand words signed "Hodenfield" telling the epic of the 2nd and 5th Ranger Battalions' preinvasion assault on the big German coastal guns of Pointe de Hoe which commanded both beaches selected by the Americans for their landing on coastal France.

The Rangers went in from night-riding assault boats a couple of hours before the first waves of infantry debouched on Utah and Omaha beaches.

Hod was with them.

They scaled 150 feet of sheer rock cliff, and when the first Rangers to reach the top of the rope ladders crumpled under point-blank machine-gun fire, others took their places. Inch by bloody inch they gouged a toe hold atop the cliffs, and began their task of neutralizing the fire of the huge coastal guns so deeply set in concrete and steel that they were virtually impervious to aerial bombardment.

For fifty-eight hours the Rangers fought against a superior force which held the advantage of position. Sixty per cent of the kids with the diamond-shaped gold and blue patch on their left shoulders were casualties.

But as Hod said in his first story, "The coastal guns which could have smashed the invasion were neutralized. The Rangers tied down in combat the gun crews who otherwise might have been hurling high explosives into the assault waves on both beaches."

## EVERY RANGER A HERO ON THE FRENCH BEACH

By G. K. Hodenfield
Stars and Stripes Staff Writer

WITH U.S. RANGERS IN NORMANDY, June 10 (delayed)—"Over and beyond the call of duty" is the army description of an act of heroism worthy of a special award. It's hard for an observer with the Rangers to draw a line for "duty" and classify those which are "over and beyond."

There was, for instance, the man whose assault craft was blown up in the water. He managed to swim to shore, picked his way four miles along the cliffs under German sniper fire, scaled a 100-foot cliff, reported to the commanding officer of the Rangers, took a tommy gun and within ten minutes had cleaned out a German machine-gun nest.

He was killed later while exposing himself to give protecting fire for some men moving into a new position.

Then there was "Pops," a staff sergeant just old enough to be called "Pops." He was cornered by the Germans not far from where some of his men were pinned down by a machine gun. The men heard the Germans ask Pops to surrender.

They peeked over the top of their shell hole and heard him tell them to "go to hell." Then he threw a hand grenade that killed three of four Germans. The fourth killed him with his rifle, but he never lived to report it.

Behind the German lines, but within view of the Ranger outposts, was a German ammo dump. It was well dug in and mortar fire couldn't touch it. It was too close to the Ranger line to call for naval artillery.

There was only one way to get it—sneak through the lines, plant a bangalore torpedo and try to get back. A private who had been busted from staff sergeant two weeks before took the bangalore and blew up the dump. To do it he had to jump from shell hole to shell hole for the first 100 yards and then run across open ground for 25 yards more. He was under heavy machine-gun fire coming and going, and how they ever missed him will always remain a miracle to those who saw it.

A Ranger chaplain landed on our beach, one of the hottest landing grounds on the entire front. All during the time his men were coming ashore he walked from one fallen soldier to another, giving first aid to those who were still living and saying a few last words for the dying.

All through the hail of fire that rained down the beaches he did what he could and didn't leave the beach until all his men had crossed it to the comparative safety of the cliff edge.

What is "line of duty" for a company aidman? The Ranger company aidmen were on the go night and day, bringing in casualties, treating men in the field, carrying litters from one outpost to the other. Because they were aidmen they were unarmed.

The captain was standing in a pillbox, trying to spot a German artillery position for the navy. He had radio contact with a destroyer and was giving the co-ordinates when a German shell struck the pillbox. The captain was heard to say, "The co-ordinates are right, they check." Then he toppled over.

Two men came back together. They had been out trying to get a German sniper, but he got them first. One had a bullet hole through his elbow, the other a bullet through his knee. Both refused to be taken back to the CP. They knew they were needed on the line. They knew they could still fire their rifles. So they stayed on the line, that thin line of riflemen, until the Rangers retired from the position.

With the Rangers—and of this I am positive—there is nothing "over and beyond the call of duty."

* * *

Hodenfield fought with the Rangers and to him fell the lot of being the first *Stars and Stripes* man to kill a German in ground warfare.

For what they did on Pointe de Hoe, Hod's Rangers received the gratitude of the infantrymen who stormed the beaches; they also received the gold-edged blue ribbon of a presidential citation.

Phil Bucknell, however, had beaten Hod to the first *S&S* decoration of the invasion of the Continent.

Earl Mazo, Rooney and Hutton had won Air Force decorations up to D day, but Bucknell, an American who had spent twelve years on British papers, enlisted in the U. S. Army and was assigned to *S&S,* collected the first award an *S&S* man won on the Continent. It was the Purple Heart, for injuries in action.

"Bob, we ought to have someone with the paratroops when invasion starts," Buck said to Moora one day in the early spring of '44.

"Bud and Andy will be with the bombers, and Llewellyn says he's picking a force to go over and start a paper wherever we land on the Continent, but there's no one for the paratroops, so I'll have a crack at it."

Moora looked at Buck's solid two hundred pounds, thought about the thirty-four years Buck's frame had been aging, and wondered aloud whether the reporter could make it, and although he didn't mention it there was the additional fact that Buck was married to a very lovely girl in London.

"Too heavy, Buck, and too old."

"I don't think so, and anyway, Bob, I've already completed arrangements to go to a jump school and get qualified with the paratroops who are here in England now."

Which seemed to settle it. Bob and the staff admired Buck's guts but they wondered if the paper would get a story back.

Buck went off to jump school, which Bob Reuben, of Reuter News Agency, and Bill Walton, of *Time* and *Life,* also attended. On his first practice jump, Buck splintered a bone in his right leg, and Colonel Fred Sink, the grizzled paratrooper running the school, said he was washed up for the invasion.

Buck limped back to London, splinted up, and saw a civilian doctor, who agreed with the army medics' decision. Bucknell sadly told the desk, but it already was too late to get another man trained

It seemed likely that *The Stars and Stripes* would not be covered on the paratroop action whenever invasion started. Buck went about morosely for two weeks, limping a little less each day and spending a lot of time at the bar's edge of the Lamb and Lark, "getting his strength," as Alf Storey, the publican, put it.

About the 20th of May, Bucknell disappeared from the office, even as Hodenfield a few days later. No one could find him, not even Lois, his wife.

Just after one o'clock on the morning of June 6, Phil Bucknell spilled out of a C-47 transport along with other men of the 82nd Airborne Division toward the blackened countryside of the Cherbourg peninsula.

He went down through the flak and the small-arms fire. Men were hit in the air. Planes burned and plunged earthward to explode with great white sheets of light. Bucknell dropped in the darkness through tracer fire from machine guns.

The ground rushed up at him and Buck landed. His 34-year-old right leg, its shin bone already splintered, snapped.

All through the fierce night, menaced by German patrols seeking the paratroopers and in danger even from fire from his own men, Bucknell lay in a Normandy field, trying to gather notes. At daylight, the Americans found him and took him to the command post, where he gathered the story of his division's attack.

When the land forces hit the beach, and a corridor to the sea was opened, Buck went out with the other wounded, and was taken back to England through the gantlet of Nazi bombs to a general hospital.

They started him toward the operating room.

"Not me!" roared Bucknell. "I've got a story to do for my paper, for *The Stars and Stripes*."

The doctors and nurses tried to argue with him, but Private First Class Bucknell lay there and hollered until the colonel commanding the hospital was called. To him, Buck told his story, and the colonel understood.

Before he was operated on to have the fracture reduced, Buck dictated a story of the paratroopers. A lieutenant was ordered to mount a motorcycle and get that story without delay to the news desk of *The Stars and Stripes* in London.

(The story got there, a couple of days late, but it was a full, colorful account which, most important of all, gave credit to the airborne for their part and gave it from a *Stars and Stripes* reporter who was there.)

Then Bucknell lay back on a stretcher and was wheeled to the operating room while a clerk filled out the papers which made him the owner of a Purple Heart medal for injuries received in battle before the dawn of D day.

*The Stars and Stripes* was pretty well covered on that D day morning for which the world had waited since Dunkerque. Hod went with the Rangers, Buck with the paratroopers, and Hutton took off before daylight with the Marauder medium bombers to blast open a way for the land forces on Utah Beach, along the eastern shore of the Cherbourg peninsula. The bombers that morning left their fields in pitch blackness, in a driving rain which blotted out the running lights of the other ships in the formations. Ice formed on the wings, and bombers plummeted to the English countryside.

As day broke, the bombers were flying above the thousands of assault craft which churned across the English Channel to France. Wave after wave of bombers and fighters roared against the coastal fortifications of Fortress Europe, blasted holes for the doughboys nearing the shore.

Hutton and Bede Irwin, Associated Press photographer who was killed in action at Saint-Lô, a month and a half later, were with Wilson R. Wood's Marauder group which was fouled up in bad weather and was late for its bomb run. The other groups had struck and left when their group came down the Cherbourg coast at 3,500 feet, with Jerry throwing up everything he had, including small-arms fire.

Because they were late on their run, Wood's group hit the coastal guns back of the shore just as the first American infantry actually swept ashore, giving Bede Irwin a picture scoop as he worked his camera from an open bomb bay, and Bud the first story of the actual landing.

The bombers flew back to base, and Major General Sam Anderson, the medium bomber chief, provided a liaison plane for Irwin, Frank Scherschel of *Life* magazine, and Hutton. The three of them shuttled to London, with pictures and stories.

Bud had no orders to go to France, but it was noon by the time he reached the *Times* offices and since there was no word yet from the beachheads, he decided to go to France. He called

Llewellyn at the business office, said he needed two hundred dollars in fifteen minutes.

"Can't tell you what for, colonel," Bud shouted. "Got to have it in fifteen minutes."

In fifteen minutes the money was ready in American Express travelers' checks, Hutton grabbed it and raced for a London airport. There the Ninth Air Force was paying off for the missions Bud had flown in their planes and the stories he had written; waiting for him and another liaison ship, which ferried them to the south coast.

Three hours later they were on an assault craft heading for the Continent. It worked out well. Pinned down to the beach for 58 hours and battling for his life even into the third day of the invasion, Hodenfield had no chance to get out copy. Bucknell had been injured.

Hutton's first story, scribbled in pencil as he touched the beach and handed to the skipper of the assault craft, who headed back to England for another load, was the first story back from the Continent itself. The next day the Air Force had a single emergency landing strip on narrow Omaha Beach, and with his connections with people who flew Hutton had virtually a direct courier service as long as he wanted it. Hod and the Rangers on D plus 2 fought their way out of Pointe de Hoe and he was able to start sending stories back to the fevered city room in Printing House Square.

## PIANO IN BATTERED VILLA DIMS WAR—A MOMENT

SOMEWHERE IN FRANCE, June 17 (delayed)—The communiques can tell only of battles, of men and material in mass, of places taken and lost. War is more than that—it is little things you remember, which will have no bearing on the red and blue lines shifting across the maps. War is quick glimpses, like scenes on an old stereopticon, that sometimes wake you in the night and bring their own music, like an old violin, or the wind in the Normandy trees. . . .

There was a villa, behind the lines near Isigny. The windows were broken, almost all of them, by the shells and the bombs of the first five days, and the fighting which had left dead gray bodies, and some khaki ones, on the web of trenches near the house. The slates of the roof had been torn away, and dust had settled through the broken floors onto the old furniture of the salon, onto the walnut stain of an old piano.

A man came out of the lines and took a detail back in a car to get rations for the rest of the Rangers dug in near a wood. He was twenty-four; he came from Maine; he had busted out of OCS to join the Rangers. His name was Dick Barrows, and he should have been a boy, but because things had been the way they were he was a man, with tiredness in his blue eyes and even in the heft of his burly frame. They stopped at the battered villa and the Ranger wandered into the room where the piano was covered with dust.

"Jesus," he said, "it's been a long time." He sat down at the piano, placing his rifle against the last of the keys in the bass, and his rough, cut fingers began to play.

There was "Madelon," the song of the poilus in another war. He played that, and then "Chattanooga Choo Choo" and "Bye-Bye Blues," "Lady, Be Good" and "Blues in the Night." He played a hymn, three choruses of it, and the lilting French nursery rhyme which goes, "Sur le pont d'Avignon . . ."

The tiredness went out of his eyes, and his body sort of slumped in the stained clothing. Sometimes he looked away from the keys, out the broken window, and sang softly against spaced chords. The piano was all the tinny pianos that ever were in honky-tonks or bistros, and maybe it was better than it was, because there all the sweat and hate and blood and fear were gone and the man was a kid for a little bit.

Some soldiers stopped when he played "Begin the Beguine." They listened awhile and went away quietly. Frank Scherschel, the *Life* photographer, heard the music and came with his camera. He took a picture and couldn't see to focus for another, so he went away. Bede Irwin, the AP photographer, and another fellow listened as long as they could, watching the kid at the piano, and then they looked at each other and went out.

Barrows played some more; once in a while you could hear the tunes come through the other noise. Finally he came out of the villa, through the broken glass around the doorway. He shoved his hat back on his head and laughed a little and went down the road to find his detail and get the rations for the Rangers.

When invasion became a not too distant certainty, Lieutenant Colonel Llewellyn announced he was planning to send a force into the continent "with the third or fourth wave." He picked Charlie Kiley, Earl Mazo, Rooney, Morrow Davis, and a few more to go along. About the first of June, they were ordered to a British southwestern port to wait.

They waited, and waited. D day came and the colonel came to the port to join them in waiting. He called a meeting and said they were going "on a great ambiguous landing." He called on them to do their best. But the first wave of combat troops went, and the second and the third and a good many more.

"Somebody," declared Llewellyn finally, "has slipped up."

Finally, about D plus 12, they sailed, landed on Omaha Beach and went into Carentan, which the 101st Airborne Division had captured.

Llewellyn found the local sign painter and had a big banner painted for the front of a flat-bed printing shop he took over. It read:

STARS AND STRIPES—CONTINENTAL EDITION

On the second day of occupancy, with the German lines still only a mile or so south of the little town, the presses weren't working yet. Llewellyn said any day now, any day now.

As Llewellyn finished speaking, there came the unmistakable scream of an 88-millimeter shell inbound. The staff flattened on the floor just as it came through the skylight and exploded in the two-story print shop. The roof caved in, a wall buckled.

Covered with debris and rafters, one staffer felt someone tramp across his back, and a voice shouted, shrill and high:

"We move to Saint-Mère-Eglise in the morning!"

There were other invasions covered by *The Stars and Stripes*, from Africa to Germany, but no one ever did a neater job of getting an exclusive story than Jack Foisie, sergeant reporter on the Italian edition of the paper.

In the Mediterranean Theater, *Stars and Stripes* men had a tougher job than those in the ETO. There the officials insisted they always must be treated as enlisted men, and they thus found it difficult to attend briefings and get other information with civilian correspondents, who were treated as officers.

Came one of the amphibious operations up the western shore of Italy, before the Fifth and Eighth armies there had settled down to their first winter, and Foisie was selected to go along for *The Stars and Stripes*.

He and the civilian correspondents went to a staging area on the beach where the attacking force was, to await time and tide and moonless night to embark. The question of the status of an enlisted man correspondent came up, as it always did, and Foisie, not caring very much except that it made his job harder, found himself separated without ceremony from the correspondents, who were staying in officers' quarters, and dumped with the enlisted men on the sands.

Jack shrugged his wiry shoulders; he'd be happier living with the EMs anyway, but it might make him lose a valuable briefing on what the operation was to be like. Oh, well . . .

With a couple of sergeants and a private, Jack slept on the sand.

The civilian correspondents and the public relations officers were quartered off to one side.

During the night, the weather turned and was right for the amphibious attack. Quietly sentries slipped among the sleeping combat men on the beach and awakened them to board the assault craft. "Come on, this is it," Jack heard a voice whisper as a hand shook his shoulder.

With the combat men, Jack went down to the shore, waded out to the assault craft and at daylight made the attack, while the correspondents, awakened in the morning by the public relations officer, found the attack had gone off and left them to come along with the rear echelon units.

Jack took the trouble to thank the PROs later.

Sometimes *Stars and Stripes* men went off to battle with task forces or special assault units and had such a fine time doing it that they forgot (or simply didn't bother) to file a story. Morrow Davis got his name of "Two-Gun" from such an episode.

When the American armies burst out of Normandy and cut off the Brest peninsula before dashing on across France in the route of the Nazi forces in August and September, 1944, Davis, a 39-year-old veteran newspaperman who'd spent most of his life on the sports copy desk of the New York *Herald Tribune,* shoved a .45 in his belt and headed for Brest.

The Yanks were besieging the great Breton port, with elements of the Second, Eighth, Ninth and 29th divisions gradually battering the Nazis there into surrender. It was a terrific story, full of color and action.

Davis went in with the assault troops. He fought isolated German detachments, grabbed a bag of prisoners, and generally had a hell of a time. But back at Cherbourg there was not a line of copy from Davis. Finally, there weren't even reports about his activities. No one heard from him.

After two weeks, three rumors came out of the Brest fighting about Morrow Davis:

(1) He had been badly wounded and was homeward bound in a hospital ship.

(2) He had been killed in action.

(3) He was fighting with the doughs, captured German pistols completely encircling his waist, captured German watches covering each forearm to the elbow, captured German combat knives thrust in each boot.

Two days later, Morrow staggered into the Paris office a bottle of wine under each arm, his waist encircled by some seven German pistols and belts, four watches on each wrist and a German knife in each boottop.

"Wasn't much of a story there," Morrow hiccuped as he toppled onto a cot, still clutching the wine, "so I didn't bother to write anything."

The newly renamed Two-Gun Davis—he always held it obviously was a gross understatement—had a lot of fun at Brest. Thereafter, he was chary of accepting rear echelon assignments.

A new division came to the Continent, and when it failed to get much of any publicity after a few weeks, its commanding general, a two-star hunk of genial brass, came to the second floor of the Paris *Herald-Tribune* building at 21 Rue de Berri, Paris, where *The Stars and Stripes* was setting up its principal offices for the Continent.

The general wanted to know if he could get a *Stars and Stripes* reporter assigned to his outfit. The division was moving, and was going "to see some action, it appears."

Bob Moora, who was on the desk, looked around the shop. Two-Gun Davis was the only unoccupied reporter.

"Two-Gun, how about going up to the general's division and seeing what they got there?" asked Moora.

Morrow slid his frame off a desk and ambled with his lazy stride over to the major general.

"We'll see you're taken good care of," the general said. "Keep you along with me, as a matter of fact, if you like, and get you back here when you've got your story."

Morrow's face was unchanged.

"General, I don't care what kind of quarters you've got or anything like that. All I want to know is this: Are you a fighting division? Are you really on the ball? Because I'm not going to waste no time fooling around unless you're gonna go like hell!"

The general's countenance changed half a dozen times during the address, but he finally allowed they might do some fighting, so Two-Gun went off with him and brought back half a dozen top-flight stories.

From the day in January, 1943, when Andy Rooney took off with the B-17s for Wilhelmshaven, there always were staff men ready to go into combat for stories. The office never gave them any undue treatment.

The night before Rooney left the office in London to go to a bomber base, Ben Price, Moora and Charlie White borrowed from one to three pounds each from him, and it was only after they had the money that one of them pointed out to Rooney that he'd better get back alive to collect. Rooney couldn't see that it was very funny at the time, but he laughed until the tears rolled down his face when Tom Kelly, a gunner who had finished a tour of combat, measured Hutton for clothes sizes just before Bud went on his first mission with the Forts; Kelly was figuring on what he could wear if Hutton didn't get back from Bremen.

Sometimes staffer reasons for going to combat were pretty thin.

There was the time that Rooney, Kiley and Hutton, who liked to be together, decided they ought to have a week's vacation. They couldn't figure out any way to manage it together until Rooney suggested casually:

"Why not all three of us make a bomber mission from the same group? We could go out to some base and lie around for a week, fly the mission, do a story, and then go back to work."

Kiley and Hutton looked at him quizzically, and Irish Kiley remarked dryly, "You wouldn't want us to go to extremes or anything for this vacation, would you?"

There was a catch: how to figure out a story which the Desk—which Hutton had left for the fun of covering the air war—would approve as worth sending three men into combat.

The three reporters finally worked out a deal, and enlisted the aid of Earl Mazo, then a public relations lieutenant for the 385th Bomb Group of the Eighth Air Force, who later transferred to *The Stars and Stripes* on the recommendations of Hutton, Kiley and Rooney.

"Why don't you get some new crew with a new Fortress to name their plane 'The Stars and Stripes'!" demanded the reporters. "We'd give it a good story, with pictures, and it probably would get a good play in the papers at home as well."

Mazo liked the idea, sold it to his colonel and a new crew headed by Lieutenant John McElwain. Dick Wingert, who was just in the process of developing his character, Hubert, went out to the 385th and painted a screaming eagle holding the Stars and Stripes on the fuselage of McElwain's plane. Kiley won—the others said he lost, because it was a green crew—a toss and was to fly in The Stars and Stripes. Rooney was to go in a plane on one wing, Hutton on the other. Thus, they assured the office, even if one of them got shot down, the chances were good the others would be back with the story of the baptismal flight of The Stars and Stripes, which certainly should be well covered.

Reluctantly the Desk agreed, having been outmaneuvered by The Stars and Stripes promotion scheme, and the three reporters had a week of loafing around the bomber base, eating four meals a day and relishing the Indian summer sunshine.

Unfortunately, when the day of the christening came, Hutton's plane had engine trouble and turned back. Rooney and Kiley flew on to report the baptism under fire of The Stars and Stripes, and then stayed on the base almost another week until the next mission, when Hutton flew to Bremen with what was until then the greatest force of bombers ever sent out in daylight to Germany.

Hutton and Rooney continued flying with the bombers, and eventually Andy totaled some ten missions and Bud twenty-odd, which was more than the average gunner lived to amass. Charlie flew the thirteenth—the air crews call it the 12B—mission with The Stars and Stripes, and when the ship and crew were ready for their twenty-fifth mission he went back to make it with them.

The weather was bad. Day after day there was no flying, and this at a time when the office was shorthanded and Charlie was needed there. Finally, he decided to slip back to London over the weekend, help in putting out Sunday night's big paper and come back to the base early Monday morning.

On Sunday morning, while Charlie was in London, the weather cleared and McElwain and The Stars and Stripes flew off to Germany for what was to be their last mission. They lost an engine to flak over the target, deep in northeastern Germany, and on the way out, over the Baltic Sea, Luftwaffe fighters caught the crippled plane.

Two of the crew baled out to drown or freeze in the sea, the others apparently were caught in the plane as it hurtled off into the mist out of sight of the rest of the formation.

Charlie heard about it Sunday night, at the office.

It was more difficult to do a first hand coverage of the fighter planes; they were built for one man, and the *Stars and Stripes* staff didn't believe in going to war as passengers or spectators; it wasn't fair to the others, who had to play the game for keeps. Staffers went as gunners with the bombers, but there was no room for them to do a useful job in a fighter.

Eventually Earl Mazo, who had transferred to the paper by then, and big, lumbering lovable Pat Mitchell flew fighter sorties in P-38 Lightnings which had been converted to carry an observer for reconnaissance. The staff felt that, since the planes had been altered anyway to hold an observer, there was some point in going along and no added risk to the pilot who was doing it as a job.

In time, the *Stars and Stripes* reporters became aware of a distinct difference between the attitude of the airmen about having reporters along and the views of the ground forces, particularly the infantry.

Both groups were glad to have someone from their paper with them. The airmen were glad to have you along but thought you were crazy for sticking your neck out when, as they viewed it, you didn't have to do it.

The infantrymen were glad to have you along and wanted you to stay around and get shot at and endure the misery of their lives. It was a natural feeling on the doughboys' part, because only those who have been with them not only under fire but through the miserable and filthy days and nights of a ground soldier's existence can understand well enough the bleak futurelessness of their lives to write about them.

Everyone who is fighting in a war has a tough job. But the staff figured the paratroops and the glider men had the toughest. They not only went into battle in a hazardous manner, but if they lived through that, they then had to take up as ordinary infantrymen and endure what the doughs had to endure. Possibly that was one of the chief reasons *Stars and Stripes* men jumped when the paratroops jumped in Normandy, Holland and across the Rhine.

When the 82nd and 101st Airborne jumped at Nijmegen, Holland, while the British were striking up the road at Arnhem, Herb Palmer jumped with the 101s. Palmer was an extracurricular member of the editorial staff, but for absolute pinwheelness he qualified with the most veteran.

"Tired of doing this office work," Palmer complained one day. He was in his late forties, was a second lieutenant. "Oldest second lieutenant in the world," he claimed, a little proudly.

Palmer's record of World War I certainly entitled him to the softest job available—he was a major in the British Army at twenty, had won the Military Cross, the French Croix de Guerre and a handful of other decorations—but he didn't want the soft job.

"Going to be a parachute jump," he breathed eagerly down Bob Moora's neck one day in Paris. "Better have somebody on it, and I'm the guy."

No one else was available, so Bob said sure, and the London office said sure, so Palmer, who knew nothing of writing or pictures, was briefed on what to ask for a story, was shown how to run a camera, and bidden a Godspeed which was a little fearful as the staff contemplated the age of his joints and remembered what happened to Bucknell.

Palmer made the jump, had a hell of a time, and some two weeks later turned up casually in the London office, long after half a dozen reports of his death had been received.

"Where are your pictures?" wrathfully demanded Bill Spear, the ex-Associated Press man who was on the London desk.

"Forgot 'em; left 'em back at the airport," Palmer replied, grinning.

Before Bill could ask, let alone scream, Palmer added:

"Didn't get any story. But I'll go back to the airport and get the photos—and—can I go on the next one?"

The staff eventually quieted Spear, and coaxed Palmer into writing a story of sorts, which was only two weeks late.

Palmer went back to his business office job, but he was unhappy, and finally coaxed Hutton into arranging for him to go to Air Force gunnery school. He passed his tests and the next thing the office knew, he came limping in from a mission to Germany on which two engines of his ship had been shot out, one crewman killed, half a dozen, including Palmer, wounded.

"Had a crash landing too," Palmer said. "But I got the name of every man in the crew and what happened on the mission. Where do I write it?"

The thing reduced Pete Lisagore, who had succeeded Spear on the London desk, to weeping, because it was a rule of censorship that no wounded man's name might be used until two weeks had elapsed, giving his family an opportunity to be notified officially of the casualty.

"You," he glared at Palmer, "have picked a hell of a time to start remembering to get a story."

From time to time thereafter, Palmer would come into the editorial rooms of the paper in Paris, or Liége, or Strasbourg and try to wangle an editorial assignment, "like going with the dive bombers bang! crash! beat the hell out of the Krauts! Do you think I could, huh?"

He eventually got into trouble for taking off from Paris without orders and going up to the line just to visit with his airborne friends in the 101st.

Ed Clark, who spent most of the war covering the activities of the Seventh Army, in the south of the Western Front, and Hutton were the other two *Stars and Stripes* men to make an airborne invasion. Clark flew in a glider and Bud jumped with the 513th Parachute Infantry Regiment in the biggest airborne attack of all time, the jump across the Rhine which opened the way to the rout of Nazi Germany's last defenders.

Bob Capa, the *Life* photographer, and Corporal Bob Krell, of *Yank* magazine, also went in with the paratroops. Krell became the second *Yank* man killed in action on the Continent—Peter

Paris was the first, on D day—when an attempt to ambush a Mark IV tank failed and the enemy gunners cut him down.

Clark and Hutton found themselves fighting instead of writing for the first twenty-four hours after their landing as the airborne bled to smash one big hole in the inner west wall of Festung Europa. Ed went into action as soon as his glider touched down amid the wrecks of blazing carrier planes, colored parachutes and smashed gliders. With Don Pay, public relations captain of the 17th Airborne Division, and the divisional chief of staff, he fought through German-held woods toward the little clump of trees which had been picked beforehand to be the command post. Ed, Pay and the chief of staff routed half a dozen Nazis from the trees, dug themselves in and waited for the division to reach them.

Finally the chief of staff went off on a reconnaissance to try and find the division commander, Major General William Miley. Don Pay went off in the other direction, and was replaced by Lieutenant Desser, a censor who had landed in a glider to handle the correspondents' copy.

Suddenly, Ed saw a figure coming fast across the open field in front of him. He raised his tommy gun and hollered, "Halt!" The figure stopped. It looked like an American, but there had been scores of instances in which Germans put on American uniforms to infiltrate the lines, and Ed wasn't taking any chances.

"Who are you, a GI?" he called.

"I'm General Miley, and stop this damn foolishness!"

Neither Ed nor the censor ever had seen Miley.

"You'll have to do more than say so," Ed roared, and menaced swiftly with the tommy gun when the "general" started to walk toward him.

"Who the hell are you, stopping me this way?"

"I'm Ed Clark of *The Stars and Stripes.*"

"Well, by God! let me in there so I can show you the two stars on my collar and then get and keep to hell out of my way!"

There was no doubt about the authenticity of the verbiage, peculiar to American airborne generals. Ed let him come closer, saw the two stars denoting major general's rank, and grudgingly said, "Well, all right," completely unperturbed by the five-minute dressing down he got from the general.

The formation of carrier planes in which Hutton was flying missed their target a short distance, and the 513th Paratroops came down across a cluster of buildings which housed a Nazi regimental command post. All the way down in their chutes, men were hit by the storm of small-arms and light antiaircraft fire the Germans put up.

Bud had gone out of the plane unarmed, the better to do his job of getting pictures and stories, but as he hit the field and men he knew started dropping all around him, he grabbed a dead man's tommy gun and for a while was a combatant paratrooper, remembering only occasionally to take pictures.

For twenty-four hours, the battle was a thing of horror, touch-and-go as to whether the move would succeed, but then tank destroyer units broke through from the land forces which had crossed the Rhine simultaneously with the airborne strike, tanks followed with heavy artillery, and the jump was successful.

Bud came out of the lines after five days, having sent back pictures and stories daily, and *The Stars and Stripes* had been covered again where the fighting was.

From *The Stars and Stripes*.

WITH 17TH AIRBORNE DIV., GERMANY—Benny March and Charlie Krupp, Keith Leech and all the hard-dying who stayed in the red snow on Flamierge Hill that January day in the Ardennes—this is for you. You who charged tanks with bayonet and grenade, and died earthbound on a wintered Belgian hillside and never had a chance to go to battle as a paratrooper should—this is the way it was when the time came. This is the way it was when the airborne jumped across the Rhine.

* * *

All through the spring evening, until the darkness came, the paratroopers sat by the fence and watched the French plowman move patiently up and down his field. It was a little cold, after the sun was gone, but as long as the farmer would plod his furrow kids with the high boots and the side-pocket pants stayed there and watched him. They didn't say much; they just sat there, inside the barbed wire that would cage them until it was morning and time to go to Germany, and watched the green field turn brown under the plow, and it was a good thing to watch because it was not like anything would be the next day.

In the dark, Colonel Jim Coutts, the West Pointer from Philadelphia, sat in a small tent and by the white light of a gasoline lantern read the last of the battle order, read it into his memory before he went outside to walk through the camp a last time.

The 513th Parachute Infantry Regiment was still in its blankets as Jim Coutts walked along the company streets. Ward Ryan, the West Point lieutenant colonel from Fort Atkinson, Wisconsin, came and walked with the Old Man. Sometimes they would pause when there was the low talking of men in a tent, and it was long dark when they went to get a little sleep.

"They're ready," Jim Coutts said.

In the morning the sun was red through the mist, and we felt colder than it was. We drank coffee and marched over to the airfield where the round-bellied Curtiss Commando transports waited. We went to Germany.

All that part you will understand—the waiting and the getting in the planes, the way the chute harness cuts into your shoulders because it's always a little tighter than you figured. You will understand about how our hands were too wet and our throats had no moisture at all, and how everyone smiled when they looked at someone else as we sat there going to Germany because more than any time in life things had to be good.

You will understand how that was, you who stayed on Flamierge Hill when the regiment was slogging with the doughs, because you knew how those men were; you know why dark-haired Jim Hedges, the corporal from Cold Spring Harbor, Long Island, would turn and say, "Nice day for a ride, isn't it?" and why everyone who heard him laughed harder than the thing was funny.

Over the French countryside we flew, and above Belgium, north of the Ardennes where you stopped Rundstedt's tanks with your bodies. Planes from other fields came to join, the transports towing the gliders. Just ahead of us in the long stream pouring toward Hitler's Reich were the men of the 507th, with veteran Edson Raff in their first plane. Behind us were the glider guys, the 194th. Sid Johnson, the lieutenant from Hillsboro, North Dakota, turned in his gear and looked out a window.

"Where's the Rhine," he said.

After that it was different than anything had been before. Because you could not be there, you will want to know.

The flak came up from German soil 500 feet below us. The air began to smell of cordite as Ward Ryan stood to the right-hand door, snapped the lock of his static line to the overhead cable. His voice roared out, and it's hard to tell how it sounded like a trumpet calling above the noise of the flak and the thunder of the engines.

"Stand up and hook up!" Ward Ryan's voice called, and we got out of the seats where we had waited in sweat and fastened the locks of the static lines.

A new man, a man who'd never jumped before, but who'd seen a bit of flak when he was flying with the bombers long before, said, "They're laying that stuff in here," and Les Taylor, who used to coach boxing out at Fort Sill, said in steady tone, "Not for us."

There were two sticks of us, because the new Curtiss transports have doors on each side, and we shuffled tight together and no one even cursed as flak came through the plane.

"Ready, men," Ward Ryan roared again, and it was good to be there with him because everyone was scared but no one was afraid, you understand.

The bell rang (we never looked for the green light, too) Ward Ryan shouted again and the slipstream tore his voice away as he went out. There never was time to make that last check you always thought you'd make because it was to the door and shove with the left foot and let the slipstream turn you and it was done.

Now here belongs a part that was not us, yet it belongs here because it is about the first of the brave men that Saturday morning. There were a great many of them, and some lived and some died, but you will want to know about Bob Reeder. He was the pilot of the ship. He came from Fairmount, Indiana. When we started our drop run, maybe two minutes from the time we left the ship, the first flak hit us, and more after that. The right engine caught fire. The fire spread to the wing, burning hot inside the metal. Bob Reeder saw the fire, and he knew what could happen. But our job was to drop where we could fight, so he held the ship on the course and checked his navigation as the fire burned toward the gas tanks. He never said a word, he never told us about it. He took the thing to himself, and when we were where he thought we should be, we went out the side and Bob Reeder stayed with the burning ship, because when he had held it there long enough for us to jump there was nothing else for him to do.

Out of the burning plane we went—and there were others that burned—into 500 feet of broad daylight nightmare.

Even before the mottled green chutes flipped out of the back packs and cracked the harnesses, the nightmare began. Freak flak hit a transport's cable, and the men jamming out the door never knew there was nothing there to yank their static lines and open the parachutes. Only a couple of reserve chutes opened. The rest plunged straight in.

From the squared clumps of woods we had studied in the sand-tables came the flak. Twenty-millimeter stuff, a lot of it, that started up like a long chain of lazy orange balls, just loafing along until they got close, when they went past whooshwhoosh like that.

The next man in the air was carrying grenades. Flak hit him and he exploded. There was another man, penduluming a little farther beyond, and each time he swung thick white smoke trailed behind; he was carrying white phosphorus grenades, and flak had hit them. They burned off his leg in the air.

From farm buildings and hedgerows there came the old familiar sound of the Schmeissers, the burp guns with their ugly sharp clatter. Almost straight down, a German soldier stood in a wagon and lashed a horse to a wild gallop. Sergeant Curtiss Gadd, from Cleveland, fired his tommy gun as he dropped and the German sprawled across the traces while the horse galloped away.

The troopers pulled the pins on their harness as they neared the ground, and cleared the shroud lines when they hit. German mortars began to fire on the men in the open fields.

Some of us landed on top of a German artillery regiment's command post, a cluster of farm buildings. Some died where their chutes collapsed, and some got to fight a little bit.

The German fire came out of their command post buildings. Fred Stauffinger, the supply chief who'd worked through the last night loading supplies to be dropped to us, died where he hit. A new kid, a replacement who'd only heard of Flamierge Hill from the others, went across the farmyard firing from the hip. He killed some Germans, but there will always be a little red in that barnyard sand that came from the hole in his head when he fell.

The noise grew louder. There were more mortars and machine-gun fire. Here and there the Nazis had placed 88s, and the 88s fired on open bore sighting as the gliders began to come in behind us. There was a screaming of all the winds in hell and a big transport, the whole left wing bright with red flame, dived into the field and exploded.

Captain Jim Cake, the artillery observer who jumped with us, stalked through the farmyard firing his pistol, and even as he fought he called to the others with never a hurried note in the soft Virginia drawl.

Lynn Vaughn, the Pfc, from Georgetown, Kentucky, took the first two prisoners. He left them in a clump of trees with a trooper who had been hit and went back to get some more.

The troopers got in close, and the Hun didn't like that, and he began to quit. Some of the mortars were silenced, and some of the men who'd landed with Colonel Jim Coutts charged the 88-mm. gun emplacements with gun butts and the knives they carried strapped to their legs. The 88 fire stopped.

Long before he'd collected a battalion, let alone the strength of the 513th, Colonel Coutts molded what he had into a striking force and headed south toward our objective. He lost men on the way, but he destroyed German forces, companies at a time, and when nighttime came the 513th had counted 1,100 prisoners and maybe half again as many killed and wounded of the enemy.

But before that could happen, the troopers one by one and in clumps of two and three fought their way into solid units, oriented themselves on landscape they had studied so long, and went to the job of clearing their bloody island in the middle of the German Army.

Ward Ryan was the regimental executive, you'll remember, and it wasn't the way you'd think a regimental exec would be. He led us in taking the command post we'd dropped on, and then he grabbed what men he could and headed south for a linkup with the main body.

"Task Force Ryan," we called it, and we never had more than forty men but we took more than a hundred prisoners. Up and down the length of the little battleline we put through the pine woods and across the railroad tracks Ward Ryan stormed; when the mortars came he walked upright and everyone felt good he was there. When they pinned us down for a little bit, he did what was right, and Jim Cake got his radio set up and four hours after we hit we were receiving support from our own parachuting artillery which Lieutenant Colonel Kenneth Booth and his gang had set up after they'd fought to win positions for their guns.

The glider pilots got out of their craft and took the tommy guns they'd been given. They joined us. Flying Officer Billy Hill, from Brewton, Alabama, fought like a paratrooper.

"They went an' got my lovely ol' glider with their damn' mortars," he said as he knelt behind a tree and reloaded the tommy. He stood up and ran firing toward a farmhouse, and the Germans in there fled.

Sometimes it was a little funny. A jeep from a glider drove up in the middle of machine-gun fire, and a young captain, John T. Stewart, of Memphis, leaned out of it. You could tell from his voice how surprised he was.

"Maybe it's hard to believe," he said, "but we're the Quartermaster Corps!"

We fought to the end of the woods, and then our supplies arrived.

Just above the treetops in thundering V formations came the Liberators, lower maybe than they'd ever flown. They held their course through the flak that was left and over the open fields their bellies dumped bundles which swung to earth on green and red and blue parachutes.

"Now we can lick anything they got," said Pappy Edwards. He was thinking of the antitank stuff in those bundles for which some of the Liberator men paid in flaming wreckage littered across the German land.

That was the way it was, then, through the first day, and through the night when the glider men beat off a counterattack just like veteran infantrymen; and through the next day until British tanks broke through from the Rhine to the island in Germany the paratroopers held.

It was like that through the next morning, when Herb Sieben's Item Company—every man in it had shaved his head to an Iroquois scalp lock—pushed across the Issel Canal and the rest of the regiment went with them and knew the German defense in the West was cracked wide open.

Toward noon the tanks arrived, big British Churchills, and we knew then there was a corridor open westward to the Rhine, and that our supplies would move in overland and knew it was an infantryman's war once more.

That's the way it was, then, except for one thing: the brave men.

There were some who were brave and died, and the rest who were brave and fought and lived. The men who charged 88s with knives and gun butts or who landed and fought in the heart of a Nazi command post will tell you, though, that the bravest of all was no man who died nor who fought and lived.

The bravest was old Doc Meir.

He came down in his chute and began his task. He went to the wounded and helped them. He made it easier for the dying to do what they had to do. He walked out there through the fire, never bending, never hurrying; deliberate and sure of his strength. Where men were hurt, Bill Meir went, and he never tired.

Sometimes, when it was real bad, he'd pause, and he'd take off that tin hat with the red crosses on the white circles. He'd mop the sweat from his head, and look a little like a Dominican monk with his fringe of hair around the bald spot, which was a kind of funny thing to think about then.

You remember Doc, all right. You know how he was. He knew about machine-gun fire. He got a Distinguished Service Cross learning about it in Africa, when the first American paratroops jumped into battle.

These were the same kind of machine guns. Of course, they give Doc Meir and all the medics these red crosses on the white patches, and it says there in the Geneva Convention that medics won't be fired upon; "protected personnel," it calls them.

Doc Meir knows how many bullets those things will stop.

But there were people hurting out there. There were men with pieces of German mortar in them, and with holes exactly 7.65 millimeters wide in their bodies where the machine-gun slugs had passed. There were the wounded and the dying, and because there were, Doc Meir walked among them and through the fire; never paused and never hurried, except to help the hurt and make the ones he couldn't help go away easier. . . .

But you will understand about that without being told, you who stayed at Flamierge Hill. About the burning planes, and the things that happened on the way down, you would want to know. About the men and how they were you will understand, because you knew them in the red snow then, and they are no different now.

Maybe the strangest combat correspondent *The Stars and Stripes* ever had was Larry Riordan; "strangest," because Larry not only didn't have to go where he could get shot at, but he was not a member of the *Stars and Stripes* staff, and finally, he wasn't even in the army. He was a civilian.

Riordan, 30-year-old ex-photographer for a paper in Newark, New Jersey, was a top-notch cameraman for the Office of War Information branch in Paris. The OWI, however, couldn't get clearance to get Larry up to the front for the kind of pictures they needed and he wanted to take. The *S&S* Desk and the OWI chiefs eventually worked out a strictly sub rosa deal whereby Riordan was lent to *The Stars and Stripes,* which would provide him with transportation, get him to the front and back, and also get first crack at his pictures. OWI was to get all the negatives next, and so would have the photos they needed. OWI was to continue paying Larry's salary, which was more than any two men or maybe three on *The Stars and Stripes* made, and was to provide film and cameras.

Larry went off to the war, crossed the Roer with the assault troops, wandered across the front under fire or wherever he felt his job might take him. He looked more like the average Joe in a line outfit than any other *Stars and Stripes* man, and when someone asked him whom he represented, the answer never was "the OWI;" it always was "*The Stars and Stripes.*"

Frequently *Life* magazine or some other pictorial outfit would marvel at the excellence and the split-second battle quality of Larry's photos and would offer him four or five hundred dollars for a particular assignment if he would do it. Larry never took the jobs.

"Too busy for *The Stars and Stripes,*" was his answer.

Some of the officers in charge of *The Stars and Stripes* had their taste of combat, too.

Arthur Goodfriend, after he got to be head man of the paper, spent some time with infantrymen. You might not agree with the conclusions his orientation-bent mind reached but you admired the earnest little propagandist for his willingness to go through the grim routine of an infantry replacement system to see how it worked.

Just before the Roer River crossing, in March, 1945, Goodfriend adopted a pseudonym and the rank of private and went from a replacement depot to a line outfit, joined a squad as a rifleman. He spent nearly four days with the squad and came back with a Combat Infantryman's Badge and half a dozen or more editorials using a squad's esprit as an example of how and why soldiers should deport themselves toward ultimate victory in both war and peace.

Ensley Llewellyn, the other officer in charge in *The Stars and Stripes* history, had had most of his combat experience before the paper was formed.

"I put in two hitches with the Chinese, fighting the Japs, long before America got into the war," Llewellyn revealed to some forty business and editorial office men who had been unable to produce any valid reason for avoiding an inspection one morning.

Lieutenant Colonel Llewellyn had led an active life before the war, and in the course of his fighting in China, he told the staff, he'd picked up so much of the Japanese language that he was one of the few experts on it in the American Army.

"Trouble was," the colonel explained, "I was so well known to the Japs from fighting them in China that there was too much of a price on my head to send me to the Pacific when America got into the war. So they sent me over here, but someday I'll get out there and make the little yellow monkeys pay for that gas in China."

The colonel, however, apparently managed to get in a little combat with the Air Forces in the ETO. He never would tell us where, or just how, but twice after he had taken a week off for a rest, he came back to the office looking satisfied and exhilarated.

"Been off on a couple of missions with the Air Force," the colonel explained to staff questions, but he would say no more, although one night he hinted he knew enough about the inside of an RAF Mosquito "to take over as navigator any time it was necessary."

The paper basically was, for a major portion of its existence, a paper for the combat men first, and after that a paper for everyone else in the overseas forces. The staff felt from the beginning that men in combat had first choice as to what should constitute their newspaper.

With that view—in which, unfortunately, some of the brass did not always concur—the paper always essayed to publish as close to the fighting as was feasible.

When the first paper was printed in Cherbourg, there was no transport, or virtually none, and for nearly two weeks, as the Yanks fought to break out of the Normandy beachhead and into the whole of France, the paper went up to the troops in captured Nazi vehicles, Cub liaison planes, and any other vehicle.

Wally Newfield probably hit the all-time high—or low. As circulation man for a corps area, Wally distributed the paper from the back of a little donkey he "liberated" from a Wehrmacht service corps.

The shaggy little donkey grew to be a common sight just behind the lines, Wally spraddle-legged on its back, a bundle of papers slung over his shoulder. A civilian war correspondent took a picture of Wally and it went out with a caption explaining how *The Stars and Stripes* was utilizing all methods of locomotion to get the paper to the troops. One copy of the photo came to the *Stars and Stripes* office, and although we didn't normally publicize the doings of our own, Bob Wood thought of a caption for the picture too good to pass up. It read:

Circulation Man Gets His Ass Up to the Front

It was one of the most popular pictures, other than the cheesecake, ever run in the paper.

The night the picture of Wally and his quadruped transport system went into the paper, Llewellyn sat in the dingy editorial rooms at Cherbourg and fell to musing on horses.

"Any of you fellows ever ride a bronc?" he asked. The staff hadn't.

"Greatest sport in the world," EML declared, swinging a chair around so he could straddle it backside front. "Greatest sport in the world. Cossacks out in Russia probably are the greatest horsemen. We probably could use some of their tactics in this hedgerow country today."

He referred to the thick hedgerows which divided and screened all Normandy fields, and made tank warfare almost impossible on any scale.

"Used to do a lot of bronc busting myself, strictly amateur. Rode the whole rodeo circuit out west for years and the papers out there claimed I was the best bronco buster in the country.

"Some of the more sensational papers said 'the best in the world,' but that wasn't really true. When I went to Russia to study cavalry tactics with the Red Army, I saw Cossacks there handling horses and doing stunts I never figured I could do.

"I hear Hutton's been covering the front on a horse. Great idea! Might get horses for the whole staff. In fact, think I will. MacNamara, make a note of that. Get horses for the reporters tomorrow."

"But, colonel," objected the administrative officer, "the jeeps just got in today, and there's a jeep for every two reporters."

"Well, in that case," decided the colonel as the staff meeting broke up and the staffers headed hastily for the nearest café, "just mark it down that if we ever run out of jeeps again, we'll get horses and I'll teach the staff to ride."

It was a strange thing that the editorial department, which never had been practical about much of anything except the editorial end of a newspaper, was alert thence onward lest some catastrophe befall them and they lose their jeeps.

Getting the morning's paper to its soldier readers was a circulation man's nightmare. A pair of staff sergeants, Jake Miller and Jack Melcher, whose pay for handling something more than a million in circulation was in the neighborhood of $125 a month each, saw to it that the Joes got their papers.

Some of the stratagems to which Melcher and Miller had to resort to obtain transportation will not be told until the two of them are beyond the army's grasp. It's safe to say, however, that when a *Stars and Stripes* car or truck was stolen—and in France and Germany soldiers and civilians alike seemed to feel any army vehicle momentarily unattended was a perfectly legitimate object of requisition—a jeep or another truck took its place within twenty-four hours, whether or not the Quartermaster Corps would authorize such an issue.

One *Stars and Stripes* transportation man (whose identity was completely forgotten when the authors of this story were simultaneously afflicted with amnesia) came up with a classic solution to the lost circulation truck problem in his area.

Finding that French thieves and temporarily transportation-less soldiers were grabbing *Stars and Stripes* trucks or jeeps unattended for even a few minutes, this completely unidentified staffer went to the French underworld in the city in which he was stationed. It took him some time to convince the French gang boss that he was there on legitimate illegitimate business, but he finally did.

"I want to hire, on a per job basis, the four best car thieves in the city," the staffer told the underworld chief.

The gangster ultimately and with great French logic saw what the staffer was driving at and assigned four car thieves to the *Stars and Stripes* man.

The other staffers who knew about it always felt it was a coincidence of considerable magnitude that thereafter that particular circulation office always had exactly the right number of jeeps and trucks on hand, and as a matter of fact could provide, on demand, a spare vehicle or two for any other area that happened to be short.

The editorial department could put out an extra on the Schweinfurt raid, or the landings in Southern France, or anything else that was news to the Joes, but that was no good unless the paper could get to the men in the lines. The circulation department got the paper up there.

At times delivery of the paper involved all-night drives across two or three hundred miles of the snow-covered Western Front, in blackout, with no lights, and strafed now and then by marauding German planes. The paper used soldier drivers for as many of those jobs as possible, but the demand for news at the front was so great that we had to employ civilian drivers as well.

French drivers picked up truckloads of papers at two o'clock in the morning, as soon as the paper started coming off the press, and raced them over French roads, which had been thoroughly ruined by months of rough treatment under the treads of American tanks and heavy supply trucks, to main distribution points all over the country.

The French are, without qualification, the world's worst drivers. French armored divisions, equipped with American tanks and trucks, drove their vehicles until they stopped for lack of gas. They refueled and went on. That was the only maintenance they knew. They had more vehicles wrecked because of reckless driving and lack of mechanical care than an American division had due to enemy action. The French civilian drivers for *The Stars and Stripes* were no exception. A week seldom passed when Jack Melcher, our transportation expert, didn't have to report a dead French driver to the French Labor Ministry.

The French seemed to take it as a matter of course that in the hazardous occupation of car driving some people simply would be killed. That was all there was to it and nothing could be done about it.

In May, 1945, a French driver overturned the weapons carrier he was driving and killed the French assistant in the seat next to him. The accident occurred near Pfungstadt, Germany, and not knowing what else to do the driver righted the vehicle, piled the body of his dead friend in the back of the truck and headed back for Paris. It was a two-day drive and he made his routine stops on the way back.

The driver finally pulled into the *Stars and Stripes* garage in Paris late on the night of the third day. He parked his truck, put out the lights and went home. He was not due to work again until six o'clock the following night.

Melcher was there when he came in.

"What shall I do with Monsieur Renaud?" the driver asked Melcher.

"What do you mean what should you do with him?" Melcher bellowed, always impatient. "Take him with you. Assistant driver, isn't he?"

"Yes, but—"

"God damn it, I have more trouble with you Frenchmen than you're worth. What's the trouble with Renaud?"

"Monsieur Renaud is dead," the driver said. "I had a little accident in Germany and I thought—"

"Dead?" Melcher said. "Where is he?"

"He is in the back of the truck, sir."

Melcher was hard to surprise but that did it.

The driver took Melcher to the truck and pointed to the body crumpled in the back. His head was smashed and by now he had been lying there four days.

Since the day Lieutenant Colonel Llewellyn hired sixty Frenchmen, Melcher had had all sorts of problems on his hands but never a body in the back of a truck neatly parked in line in the dark corner of the garage.

He immediately called a French funeral parlor and explained his problem. Please, would they come and take the body away.

They would come and get the body, they told Jack, immediately upon receipt of either 10,000 or 12,000 francs, depending on whether we wanted to give the man their class A or class B funeral. In no event, however, would they or could they consider undertaking the job until payment was made.

Jack did not have 10,000 francs and by nightfall the body was still haunting the dismal corner of the garage, which was being avoided by one and all by this time.

Melcher went to the home of the man's family for the unpleasant job of telling them of the man's death. They were quite poor and a very religious family. Jack said that when he saw so many crucifixes hanging throughout their little house he knew then and there that for a very religious funeral he would have to pay the funeral director for the special 12,000-franc ceremony.

In the morning he called the French Labor Ministry, hoping that they would pay the funeral parlor so that they would come and get the body. The Ministry told Melcher that they only allowed "up to 1,000 francs" for burials although they would pay for transportation of the body from place of death to Paris.

Seeing that he could only get 1,000 of the 12,000 funeral costs from the Labor Ministry, Jack quickly figured the angles.

"Who do you pay the transportation charges to?"

"We pay the person who transported the body. Who brought the body from Germany?"

"I did," Melcher said quickly, "and my charge is 11,000 francs."

They would not pay it, however, and by noon that day the body was still haunting Melcher's garage.

In desperation Melcher called the funeral parlor and told them if they would come over he would have the money and the body for them. Then he typed out a touching little note about the man's poverty-stricken family, about his wife and three children (which he did not have), and sent three of his drivers through all *Stars and Stripes* offices to collect what he called "a flower fund."

By the time the undertakers got to the garage he had enough money rounded up to satisfy them temporarily and they took the body to a Paris cemetery and put it in a mausoleum, pending funeral ceremonies the following day.

Finally, after the funeral director once more refused to bury the body on the following day until the final payment was made, Melcher scraped together enough to pay him and the French driver was buried with full 12,000-franc honors.

That was the last trouble Melcher had with French drivers until one turned over a jeep loaded with thousands of papers near Nice, along the Riviera road, and smothered to death under the load three days later.

To help Jake Miller's circulation men do a better job, the various editions moved frequently. A couple of times they had to retreat when American retreat in the face of enemy counterattacks became necessary.There was one time, however, when the army retreated, but *The Stars and Stripes* stood firm and with a few stray GIs held a city. That was Strasbourg.

Two affable characters, who had done their share of pinwheeling for the most part in the African and Mediterranean campaigns, were running the *Stars and Stripes* edition at Strasbourg: soft-spoken Ed Clark, who had volunteered with the British Navy before the United States entered the war, and brilliant, affable Vic Dallaire, the managing editor.

They, with John Kearney, the lieutenant from New York who was fired for printing the story of how rotten the Maginot Line concrete had been found by the Yanks when they arrived, were putting out a paper in Dijon, southeastern France, when the armies pushed to Strasbourg and the Rhine.

Vic promptly took off on a reconnaissance of Strasbourg's printing facilities, found the plant of the largest local newspaper untouched. Without further ado, Clark and Dallaire moved their edition to Strasbourg, and asked permission from the Seventh Army authorities after they were moved and had the new plant safely occupied.

Their living quarters were pretty fair, too. When the fighting was moving through the town, Ed Clark was caught in machine-gun fire in a street. He threw himself against a doorway. Surprisingly, someone inside opened it, and Ed grabbed for his gun, suspecting Nazis were hiding there. It was a good-looking young woman who opened the door, and the place turned out to be a modern small hotel. Ed and Celline got along well, and when the paper moved to Strasbourg, the staff moved into Celline's hotel.

"It's a swell plant," Vic used to tell people from other editions if they dropped in. He would take them through the modern composing room, into the gleaming pressroom, and inevitably the visitor would ask, "What are those sort of explosion noises I hear outside?"

"Well, that's one of the drawbacks to the place," Vic would admit with a rueful grin. "Those are German shells busting into the town. You see, the Germans are just across the Rhine bridge, down at the foot of the street."

Nonetheless, *The Stars and Stripes* stayed in Strasbourg, putting out a good paper that was in the hands of the doughs early in the morning.

However, in mid-December von Rundstedt started his last great push, striking in the Ardennes, far north of Strasbourg.

American forces were rushed to the breakthrough zone from wherever it was felt they could be spared. Some of them pulled out of the Strasbourg area and during the subsequent weakening of the line the Germans began a push across the river, threatening Strasbourg. The High Command felt it would be easier to hold on a line farther west while the main effort was put in the north eradicating the Ardennes bulge, so all the French and American forces in the Strasbourg area were ordered to pull back.

Someone, however, neglected to notify the *Stars and Stripes* office when the move was made. Dallaire and Clark awakened one morning early, very early for them.

"You hear a lot of traffic in the street, Vic?" Ed demanded.

"Sounds like it, but guess it's all right," was Dallaire's sleepy answer. They went back to sleep.

Toward nine o'clock, they awakened again.

"It was kind of a foreboding, I guess, that awakened us," Ed Clark said. "Something was too damned quiet for a town with troops in it."

They looked out the window and saw citizens taking down the American and French flags which had been put up on their houses when the Boches left.

"Something stinks!" yelled Dallaire, grabbing for his clothes. As he went out the door, Madame Celline, the hotel owner who had befriended the Stars-and-Stripers, greeted him with, "The Boches are coming. All the Americans and the French soldiers have gone!"

"That was a hell of a note," Vic recalled later. "There we were with two typewriters, two Colt .45s and a jeep to defend the town of Strasbourg. We were damned if we were going to leave if we could help it, because that plant was a sweetheart, and we knew there was nothing as good back at Nancy or Besançon, the only printing towns to which we could retreat.

"Ed and I talked it over and decided to stick as long as we could."

They went out on reconnaissance, and gambled that while German forces had crossed the river north of the city, it seemed unlikely they would be able to cross a canal on the city's edge in the face of the French rear guard defending it.

The two enlisted men spent the day urging French citizens of the town to stand fast, assuring them everything was going to be all right, "although be damned if we believed it ourselves." With a few straggling American soldiers, the newsmen walked around the town, appeared everywhere they could to give the civilians a sight of United States uniforms and try and make them feel they had not been abandoned, although the Yanks knew full well they had been.

In the evening, they coaxed a couple of French linotype operators and a handful of pressroom workers to the plant. All of them spoke some French, and they wrote their stories in American and French and sent them to the composing room.

The next morning's two-page edition of *The Stars and Stripes* certainly was the first trilingual newspaper the American Army ever published.

The extreme left-hand column of page one was in French.

It told the story of the situation on the Western Front and more or less left readers with the impression—although it wasn't actually specified—that Strasbourg was a very safe place indeed. That column was for the French-speaking citizens of the city.

The next column was in German, because a large number of the border cities' civilian population were of Germanic descent. That column, too, told the news of the Western Front and subtly left any doubting Fritzes with the impression that no matter what it looked like this wasn't the time to come out with any repressed "Heils!" they might have been hoarding in their systems.

The rest of the paper was in English, not because there were any soldiers left in Strasbourg to read it but simply because the first two columns had exhausted the Clark-Dallaire French and German vocabularies.

It probably falls within the realm of complete candor to report that there was at least a minor further motive in publishing the trilingual paper. Even as *Stars and Stripes* staffers all over the world, from the paper's inception, Clark and Dallaire were behind in their pay. Their military records were still in Rome, or some place, and it had been a good many months since the soldier-newspapermen had seen a paymaster who was interested in seeing them.

They felt that, since they hadn't been paid, it would be proper to sell the paper on the streets, thus bolstering the Allied cause and also very incidentally providing Clark and Dallaire with sufficient funds to carry on their assigned military job of putting out a paper in Strasbourg.

Armed with this philosophical justification, Ed and Vic went out onto the streets in the morning and sold their papers for five francs each to the civilians, therebly acquiring enough capital to maintain the "American Army" in Strasbourg.

When they found they had papers to spare, Clark and Dallaire coaxed an army truck into town to get a load of papers at the plant for distribution to "the front-line troops," all of whom were considerably behind the printing plant.

Eventually the situation was stabilized, and civilian newspaper correspondents discovered that a couple of GI newspapermen had held Strasbourg against the Nazi Army and told the story over the wires to America. The boys felt it was a little ironical that only publication of the story in the civilian press and the attendant favorable comment for their action saved them from the disciplinary action which was threatened for having stayed in Strasbourg when the army withdrew.

Not only in Strasbourg was *S&S* published under fire. It happened in a good many towns, including the long nights of air raids and the thundering days of the V-weapon attacks against London. It was so in Liége, Belgium.

On the morning of December 16, 1944, a handful of staff men set out from Paris to reconnoiter Liége, just behind the First and Ninth Army fronts, as the site for a forward paper. The paper was too far from the war; the troops weren't getting their paper on time.

Charlie Kiley, Al Ritz, Joe McBride, Charlie White, Bill Spear and Hutton were the advance party in two jeeps. Max Gilstrap and Fred Mertinke were due the following day. We knew Liége was being pounded unmercifully by V-1 robot bombs —Peter Hansen and the circulation men who used the town as a distribution point phoned back that news—but if we could find a plant undamaged by the bombing we would risk printing there; the paper was getting out much too late from Paris.

As the jeeps rolled through the early winter twilight, the boys could see sudden red glares filling the sky to the east, and later would hear even above the clatter of the jeep the rolling boom an exploding V bomb had made. But it was when they began to pass frequent westbound convoys, jamming through the darkness without lights, that Charlie Kiley said, "What the hell! These guys look like the mob I saw on the road back in Normandy once when we had to retreat!"

At Huy, a little Belgian town about twenty miles west of Liége, the jeeps stopped and the staffers located an army ordnance headquarters to find out why the westbound roads, away from the front, were jammed with traffic.

"Germans have broken through just south and east of here," an ordnance captain said, looking up from the papers he was getting ready to burn in a stove. "Nazi paratroops dropped all over the whole area. Army's withdrawing and they hope to stop them somewhere before they get here and cut the big supply lines."

Bill Spear, who was coming as close to the war as a series of desk jobs ever had permitted, sighed patiently.

"Only a *Stars and Stripes* crowd could pick a time like this, without even trying, to open a new paper. Maybe we can publish it in German and call it *Der Stars und Stripes.*"

The staffers looked at each other.

"Well," said Kiley at last, a grin on his Irish face, "we started out to set up a paper in Liége. Let's get going."

The jeeps drove on to Liége, and as they went into the city twisted and turned through blazing masses of wreckage where a series of robot bombs, aimed at crippling the Liége railway yards, had just smashed and set afire a convoy of army trucks. They pulled into town just as jet-propelled bombers of the Luftwaffe streaked across the city spreading more flames and death before the antiaircraft guns could open up or the sirens sound.

"We are sure opening this joint with a bang!" Joe McBride remarked enthusiastically.

For nine days, the editorial men scoured the burned city for printing facilities. They discovered that the plant of *Le Meuse,* a Belgian newspaper, was one of the most modern in Europe, and arranged to take it over and print there. They dug up a garage, arranged living facilities, but on December 24, while Hutton was off with the 2nd Infantry Division, on the north shoulder of the bulge a few miles down the road from Liége, they got orders from the head office at Paris to abandon the city.

They grumbled, but packed their personal gear, locked up the offices, which were ready for business, promised *Le Meuse* management they would be back, and headed for Paris on roads now almost deserted for thirty miles westward.

The following day, two *Stars and Stripes* couriers, bringing copy back from Hodenfield and Russ Jones at First Army press camp, which had just been bombed out, traveled the same road out of Liége and wound up in a fight with a German armored car.

The couriers were Morris Blackov and Tom Dolan, both veteran infantrymen who had fought in Africa, Sicily and Normandy with the old 1st Division and had been "retired to pasture" in supposedly noncombatant jobs with *The Stars and Stripes.*

"We were coming down the road, and it was deserted as a skunk's picnic," Blackie told later, "when Tom saw an armored car pull into a crossroads up ahead. We'd both seen that kind of armored car before. For a second we didn't know whether to turn and get the hell out before that 37-millimeter cannon on the car opened up, but they hadn't seen us yet.

"We drove the car off the road, grabbed the tommy guns we've been hauling ever since we left the line, and started stalking the sonofabitch. And was he dumb!

"The guy in the turret apparently figured he was all right, or maybe he had seen us and was trying to locate us, but anyway he unlatched the turret and stuck his head and shoulders out just as we got within gun range.

"Tommy cut loose on the guy and just about chopped him in two while I made a dash to get in close, under the gun. It worked, and even better, the other Kraut in the car got so panicky he opened the escape hatch in the bottom of the car and started to crawl out. I was waiting for him and that was that."

Blackie and Dolan got back to Paris with new watches, two Lugers, and each had a fancy German winter-issue fleece jacket when they delivered their copy.

A month later, when the Nazis' winter push had been stopped and then driven back, the Brass gave the order and *The Stars and Stripes* went back into Liége and began publishing, even though robot bombs smashed the garage and half ruined the circulation office with a near miss. Within three months, however, the Allied armies had smashed across the Roer River, raced to the west bank of the Rhine, jumped across the Rhine, and were plowing so far into the inner Reich that the Liége edition was a rear echelon paper and was discontinued in favor of a plant on the edge of Frankfurt, in the heart of Germany, which less than a year before had been one of the toughest aerial bombardment targets in the world.

# CHARACTERS

MEN WENT OUT of the old London courtyard that was labeled Printing House Square and set up *Stars and Stripes* editions in Africa and Rome. They went across the dank old cobblestones and down the worn stone steps to the Embankment and sailed to Normandy, and made *The Stars and Stripes* there and across Europe to Germany.

Those men began to come to *The Stars and Stripes* as it started, and as it expanded there had to be more and more of them. They came in fantastic fashion, from infantry outfits, from the Air Force, from replacement depots, from armies in which they had served as expatriates. Two of them were native-born Americans who had lived all their lives in England.

Of them, there were better newspapermen, there were better soldiers, younger men and a few older, but none more the double-distilled essence of *The Stars and Stripes* than Charles Worthington White, of whom you can recount only as he was and swear it is true.

Hubert, the little beer barrel of a man who hefted his battered, khaki-clad carcass from one bitterly absurd soldier pose to another on the sketching board of Sergeant Dick Wingert and thence in the editorial pages of *The Stars and Stripes,* was a less genuine Charlie White. Wingert patterned Hubert after Charlie White, and since the artist was a Hoosier too, he gave Hubert some of Charles's dry Indiana philosophy. But no inanimate character, no matter how well done, could be as was the pride of Bean Blossom, Brown County, Indiana.

Charlie, as were a handful of other *Stars and Stripes* men, was a transferee from the Canadian Army, and it was always a tossup in the minds of those with whom Charlie lived as to which had the harder time of it, the Canadian or the American army.

A winter day at the beginning of 1941, Charles sat in the office of the Bean Blossom *Bugle,* a weekly publication which carried a hunting and fishing column, by Charles W. White on page one; a "Brown County Notes" column by CWW on page three, "Court Proceedings, by Our Court Reporter," on another page, and small advertisements scattered here and there throughout the paper listing variously "Learn Shorthand in Ten Simple Lessons. Charles W. White, accredited court reporter" or "Be a Newspaper Reporter! Learn the Most Fascinating Business in the World! Journalism Class Starting January 15. C. W. White."

Charles had the simplest and, he maintained, the best system in the business for getting material for a hunting and fishing column.

"Trouble with most of these fellows running a hunting and fishing column," Charles would explain in his flat, dry-hay tones, "they go buy a whole mess of fishpoles or guns and tents and stoves and stuff, then when the season gets around they go a-hellin' off into the woods, get all bit up by flies and snakes and such things, chop their toes, catch cold, and come back and write very authoritative pieces about how the trout are rising to Royal Coachmen this year, or the deer are running to low ground. But by the time they get back and get it written, hell, everybody's already found out for themselves or they're getting ready for the next season anyway, and all it does is start arguments.

"Now on the Bean Blossom *Bugle,* I had it figured out differently.

"Take off about eleven o'clock the first day of trout season, after a fellow had a decent night's sleep and breakfast, and just go straight out the road to the last tavern out of town. Sit down there, there was a fellow named Sykes run this one tavern and he just had the walls filled with deers' heads and big stuffed trout and hell! he'd never lifted a fishin' pole and was scared to death of guns, well, anyway, stop there at the tavern and just sit.

"Fellow'd get a chance to pass a decent few hours that way, just sitting around, you know, talking and so on, and pretty soon you'd look out the window and you'd see the first of the fishermen coming down the road.

"Well, they'd be all soaking wet, and cold, and they'd come in and half of 'em wouldn't have two minnows between 'em but they'd all sit around there getting warm, you know, and lie about everything, and all a fellow had to do was sit and listen to them and then walk back to town just as nice and go write his column.

"Lot of stuff and nonsense, most of it."

When *The Stars and Stripes* had gone to press for the night, Charles the soldier, would sit around the office and talk for hours about country people. He liked 'em. No cities near 'em. He liked Canadians too. From the day he left the Canadian Army, and in directly growing proportion to his service in the American Army, he liked Canadians better. Charles would sit at a desk, his big GI shoes up in front of him. His little blue eyes would twinkle with a light that had been kindled by watching people and so grew in delight and inward joy every day of Charles's life.

He wore glasses, thick-lensed ones, which framed the graying fringe of his thin, sandy hair. Mostly, Charlie needed a shave, not very much, but the sort of light, two-day whiskers your grandfather always used to have. There were cigarette ashes on the lapel of his jacket. His shoelaces always had been broken and tied time and again.

"Bud, we gotta get back and get to farming," Charles would say. He would stretch and you could almost see his mind wandering across some Indiana field, looking at the wheat and wondering if there would be many pheasants that fall, after the wheat was harvested and the corn cut and the work done. "Get a place with a house on a hill, where you can see everybody coming and go hide in the cellar with the cider if you don't want to be home. Gotta get back to that, Bud, so let's you go hurry up and win the war. These young fellas ain't doing it right."

Both Charles and Bud had been Canadians, and they would sit for hours in the Lamb and Lark, or at Chez Charley's in Paris (which always amused Charles's Indiana instincts), and swap great lies about their respective army careers.

It was no lie, however, that Charles told about how he transferred from the Essex Scottish Infantry Regiment of the Royal Canadian Army to the Calgary Tanks. Bud knew Canadians from those outfits, and they swore Charlie's story understated the case, if anything.

At a little town near the Canadian Army camp of Borden, in Ontario Province, Charles went to an auction. He came back to the Essex Scottish huts at Camp Borden that evening carrying a magnificent chamber pot, a porcelain affair with pink and violet roses painted around its sides.

"Beautiful, eh?" Charles demanded of his hutmates. "Bought it at an auction. Ten cents, I bid, and I'd 'a' had the cover too, but some damn-fool woman started bidding for the cover—guess she wanted it to put over a potato dish or something—and when she put the cost of that cover up to fifty cents I said to hell with it, I'd have a chamber pot for under my bunk without a cover."

Ted Spay and the other old Essex Scottish men, before they went to Dieppe and didn't get back, liked to tell about Charles shaving in bed of a morning when they were in huts at Borden.

"Charlie'd lie there after reveille blew," Ted recalled, "gradually opening his eyes. Some of us would be late to parade sometimes just sitting there watching him.

"He slept with a turtleneck sweater on, and a knitted wool balaklava helmet, and when he woke up he was something to see. Finally he'd step out of bed with this long sweater hanging half to his knees.

"Charlie'd go rinse out his big fancy pot at a water tap outside the hut door, fill it up and bring it back to bed. He'd put his pack at the head of the bed, and climb back in, leaning on the pack. He'd roll down the collar of his turtleneck, roll up his balaklava. Then he'd reach around for his shaving gear, prop a mirror up on his knees there in bed, reach down to the floor and wet his shaving brush in the pot of cold water.

"Lying there like a kind of an ugly Buddha with glasses, Charlie lathered his whiskers, shaved and finally washed, all the while in bed. He was a great guy to be in the army with."

Charlie about that time began a mysterious series of acts which involved having his hair trimmed almost every other day, and in view of the original sparsity of hair on his then 34-year-old pate, the Essex Scottish were a little puzzled. It seemed an extravagant length to go to please some female, the obvious first suspicion, but a check on Charlie's whereabouts in the evenings found him at the regimental canteen pouring away Black Horse ale and singing, in due time, "Fisherman, Fisherman." No female.

Finally, they discovered the reason for the hair trimming.

Across the dirt street in Camp Borden from the Essex Scottish were stationed the Calgary Tanks. Almost opposite Charles's hut was the Calgary Tanks' barber. In front of a fly-specked mirror in which the customers could vaguely see him work, the tanks' barber kept three white bottles labeled, left to right:

Eau de Cologne . . . Water . . . Tonic

The middle bottle really had water, but the end bottles were filled each morning with medical alcohol from the dispensary and water, in equal portions.

Charles had stopped at the Calgary Tanks' barbershop for a haircut, his rural Indiana conversation had impressed the Alberta tanker who was doing the barbering and Charles had been admitted to the secret of the two end bottles. Thereafter, Charles had his hair trimmed almost daily.

The rest of the boys found out the reason for the tonsorial meticulousness just as Charles announced he was transferring to the Calgaries: Haircuts at the Calgary Tanks' barbershop, it seemed, were twenty-five cents to men from other units in the camp, ten cents to soldiers of the Calgary Tanks, and at the rate he and the barber were going on the two end bottles Charles was continually broke paying for haircuts he didn't need. He transferred, but the Essex were laughing so hard at his reasoning that they forgave him and welcomed him to their pubs when they met again in England.

Charles, as a matter of fact, had occasional trouble arising in pubs after he reached *The Stars and Stripes,* but he had it, too, when the Tanks got overseas. The story the tankers liked best was how Charles received twenty-eight days in the digger.

Near the tankers' camp, on England's south coast (the English name doesn't come back easily now, but it was the next town west of two communities called Little Dean and Rotting Dean, and the tankers called their town Dizzy Dean, to the bewilderment of the English), anyway, in the town of Dizzy Dean there was a pub, the White Queen, and Charles did a lot of drinking there. One night he rolled out of the White Queen drunk beyond speech. He started for camp via a short cut which crossed the Brighton electric railway lines.

Reeling over the high-tension third rail, Charles fell, struck his head on a cross tie, gashed his scalp and collapsed unconscious across the tracks, his legs a scant foot from the power rail.

In the late summer twilight, the motorman of the Brighton Limited just barely saw Charles's prostrate form and stopped the train. A hospital was called, the military police and the local constable. Charles reeked of mild-and-bitter fumes when they picked him up, but fortunately just as the military police arrived the sympathetic publican came out with a glass of old brandy and Charles nearly took his arm off downing the brandy. It was found he wasn't hurt, but that he couldn't walk very straight, so they took him to camp and a summary court-martial was called for the next morning.

When the trial judge, however, began to question the military police he found they had seen Charles given a glass of brandy to revive him, so that took care of the alcohol fumes and Charles could claim innocence of drunkenness.

They thought of charging him with obstructing traffic on the rail lines, but obviously he had fallen and been knocked unconscious.

He had come reeling into camp with the MP escort, but the officer knew his Trooper White and could foresee the defense against drunkenness: he was dizzy from the blow and/or the brandy.

Charles began to relax as the trial judge checked off the charges, but even today Charles will tell you he admires the man for his resourcefulness in the decision.

"On charges of drunkenness and disorderly conduct, Trooper White, you are found innocent. And so on a charge of having obstructed the rail line and His Majesty's Posts.

"But questioning of the military police who apprehended you reveals you were improperly dressed, so you are sentenced to twenty-eight days confinement at Aldershot military prison for appearing in public without a respirator gas mask."

Charles admired that judge's resourcefulness all the way through the twenty-eight days in the digger.

Charles went through the usual vicissitudes in transferring, and eventually wound up as a secretary in the office of the Supreme Commander of the Allied Expeditionary Forces, Dwight Eisenhower, and spent most of his time handling correspondence for Captain Harry Butcher, the general's right-hand man.

When *The Stars and Stripes* was ready to turn daily, however, Charles had a burning desire to get back into the newspaper business. Coincidentally, this desire was born simultaneously with a bit of military police trouble in a London pub, and the transfer was made without trouble.

Charles became successively a rewrite man, a feature man, Northern Ireland bureau reporter, editorial office expatriate for more pub trouble, and finally member of the public relations staff of the Services of Supply. To a man who had started the war in the fighting Essex Scottish, the last was unbearable, so unbearable that Charles eventually took the pledge and returned to the fold when the fold reached Paris.

In the couple of years it took for Charlie to get on the *Stripes,* off it and back on, Dwight Eisenhower was busy after a fashion. There was Africa to invade, Sicily, Italy, the Continent; the Luftwaffe to defeat, the Wehrmacht to defeat, and the direction of the Allied forces. While Charles White wasn't the sort of individual easily forgotten, it would have been understandable if the name didn't stick with General Eisenhower. Not so, however.

After the paper reached Paris, and before it expanded to Strasbourg, Liége and Frankfurt, Hutton was recalled to the city desk he had left a year before to cover the air war. In the process of straightening out the setup for covering the war, Bud was called out to see General Eisenhower, one of the two or three times the Supreme Commander ever felt he had reason to be concerned with *S&S* policy.

Bud walked into the general's office and was just a little taken aback when the general, after greetings, said, "Well, how's White these days?"

"White? You mean Colonel Egbert White? That colonel we had with us and *Yank* for some . . ."

"No. Private Charlie White. How is he?"

Apprised later that the Supreme Commander had inquired about him, Charles, with only a small light in his eyes, observed, "That was sure nice of him. How's he doing these days?"

* * *

It wasn't very curious, when you knew them and considered what they were, that *The Stars and Stripes* of the two world wars were as wholly unlike as their staffs.

*The Stars and Stripes* of World War I, a full-size weekly, was a stylized publication, full of literary pieces about the army and the doings of its components. It was leisurely, and had a whole week to be leisurely before each issue.

*The Stars and Stripes* of World War II was a tabloid daily newspaper. Its only style was a straightforward account of the world at war, the home front, and anything else that was news in civilian papers.

Whereas the paper of World War I was intended to supplement the daily English-language newspapers available to the soldiers—the Paris *Herald* and the Paris edition of the Chicago *Tribune*—*The Stars and Stripes* of World War II was all the troops had other than the weekly magazine, *Yank*.

There was little in common between the papers of the two wars except the name; there was less between the staffs.

The soldiers who put out the weekly of the first war were full of literary talent, and from the soldier paper came Alexander Woollcott, Harold Ross of the *New Yorker*, Grantland Rice, Steve Early, and a dozen more to fame in the postwar literary world.

The staff of the daily newspaper of World War II was apt to get pretty peeved if someone suggested there might be anything literary about what they wrote. There wasn't a line of prose in the paper, the staffers swore.

Since the soldiers who were putting out *The Stars and Stripes* of World War II had dedicated themselves to a straight job of reporting with no first person singular about it, it is entirely reasonable that they should have become as zany a collection of eccentrics as ever gathered in what at best is a pretty zany profession: their personal eccentricities, which became legendary in the army, were a counterbalance to their self-imposed limitations of straightforward recounting of the news.

Little Joe Fleming typified the zanies, and when the staffers charged him with it, he cackled in that thin, harsh laughter, waved his left hand above his head in an empty gesture and, looking at eye level but in a direction about three feet to one side of his vis-à-vis, demanded "Do you mind? DO YOU MIND?" and cackled some more.

Fleming was a little guy. He was thin to the point of being scrawny, not much more than five feet six, and his big brown eyes peered out suspiciously at the world through thick glasses. He had stringy black hair, spoke with a New York accent marred by a couple of years as a newspaperman in England, and Charlie Kiley swore his facial features were those of a dachshund, particularly when he was being verbally chastised and adopted an air of injured dignity.

But Joe Fleming could write. He was a good reporter, could handle a feature story, and had a flair for satire that seemed especially born to take the hide off pompous personalities, especially those tinged with khaki and brass. Joe was under no illusions about his role in the war.

"Goddam collaborator, that's what I am!" he swore. "Waited for the draft, think armies are fascist and I'm against fascism, and if I had the courage of my convictions about liberty and freedom I'd make them lock me up for refusing to be part of an army. But I don't, so I'm no more than a goddam collaborator with the American Army, and come the revolution I'll deserve to be shot, especially by the Communists I'll deserve to be shot because I hate them too much even to collaborate by voting for the Democratic party."

It was typical Fleming illogic. He worked as hard as any man on the staff to turn out a good paper as his share of the war effort, flew several missions with the Air Force so that he'd know what he was writing about as air war editor.

There were a great many stories about Fleming, but none of them ever topped his arrival in France.

It was some two months after D day, and *The Stars and Stripes* already was set up in Cherbourg and getting out a daily paper for the troops when Fleming was ordered to leave London and report to the Continental office. In full field gear, he was magnificent.

His uniforms always were too large for him, and the smallest jacket he could get draped around his sparse frame like a Russian winter overcoat. His canvas-web belt wrapped nearly twice around his waist, and Fleming was the last man in the world to be accoutered with martial gadgets such as canteens, first-aid kits, compass, trench knife, and ammunition for the carbine which was fantastic on his shoulder. His helmet settled over his head, down over his forehead and eyes so that he was continually twisting his head to the side so he could peer out at the world through eyes more hurting from life than ever.

Thus Joe departed for the war.

The Cherbourg staff was sitting around the office, laying out the night's paper, when there was the noise of someone coming upstairs with a staccato gait. Kiley lifted an eyebrow: that pace sounded familiar. In the office at the time were two French cleaning women who had seen the Yanks arrive two months earlier, and it must have been a shock to them when the door burst open and in careened Joe Fleming in field gear.

Slanting across the room in a Groucho Marx-like walk, Fleming waved one arm to the staff, blew a kiss to the wide-eyed charwomen, and repeated rapidly:

"Je suis american! Je suis american!"

Even the French charwomen went out and got drunk.

Joe was a wow in France. He teetered through Continental life with a wild gleam in his eyes and time and again confounded the French with a typical Fleming gag.

Almost anything can and does happen on the Champs-Elysées, and it's a tossup as to whether the Parisians who walk there in the heart of their city are more correct in their appraisal of "zose crazee Américains encore" or the Yanks who swear "those screwy French." Joey had them all stopped.

Walking down the Champs, on a Sunday afternoon, Joe and Kiley watched the passing crowd. At the corner of the Rue de Berri, before they turned off for the office, Joe saw two Frenchmen in earnest conversation. Both of them were quietly and well dressed and one wore a most dignified beard. Without a word, Kiley reported later, Joe stepped over to the Frenchmen who seemed deep in some argument. He tipped his head sideward, cupped one hand behind his ear and listened until they stopped in astonishment and looked at the little Yank. Joe straightend up, beamed and said:

"Vous parlez tres bien français."

He wheeled with a leering smile, twisted his hand in his usual gesture and walked away while the two Frenchmen stared in amazement after the American soldier who had paused to tell them they spoke French very well.

Joe's method of landing a job on *The Stars and Stripes* was typical Fleming—and typical *Stars and Stripes,* for that matter.

A draftee, Joe was sent to England after basic training and dumped, as were thousands of other basics, into a replacement center there. It is from such centers that all branches of the ground forces draw new personnel, but while they are there the soldiers go through the same old day-after-day routine close-order foot drill and the rudiments of handling small arms.

After a week of trying to teach Joe the rudiments of infantry drill, the sergeant grew understandably weary and Fleming was transferred to the clerical section of the permanent staff at the depot, where he seemed stuck for the rest of the war.

"Concentration camp," Joe mutters today when he thinks about it.

One morning there passed through his clerical hands a buck slip from *The Stars and Stripes,* requesting the replacement depot to hold for an interview the following Monday all men it had on hand with newspaper experience.

"It was my job to find the guys and set 'em up," Joe confessed later, "so I did a pretty good job of digging out their specification cards but I made sure there weren't any there with better records of experience than mine, and when Lieutenant Colonel Llewellyn came loping into the joint Monday, looking for newspapermen for *S&S,* I was a lead-pipe cinch."

Joe arrived at the *Times* office when Hutton, for whom he was to work, was away for the day, taking pictures on kind of a busman's holiday. Moora was too busy to learn much about him, and all Joe found out about his new place of army residence was an overheard conversation in which a couple of staff members speculated on what degree of sonofabitch Hutton was. When Bud got back the next day and walked into the office, he was in a bad humor after an encounter with some photo-reconnaissance colonel who thought he knew better than Bud what security was and had refused to allow pictures already approved by the Air Force.

Hutton came into the room and found Fleming unfortunately sitting in his chair at the city desk; Joe was just waiting around for something to do. Hutton glared.

"What the hell do YOU do?" he demanded at length. Joe blinked and started to answer, but couldn't.

"Look like a goddam school of journalism type to me," Hutton snarled. "Get to hell out of my chair and go sit down and read back issues of the paper for a week. Gonna have one bastard around here who knows *S&S* style before he starts writing."

Joe did as he was told, and before the week was up had been moved into a spot on rewrite, just at Hutton's right elbow where he caught, literally, not only the copy to be rewritten but the full bitter measure of Hutton's comments about every man on the staff as copy was turned in and read.

To this day, Joe will flinch a little if someone sitting beside him suddenly turns and starts talking. Sort of combat reaction, Joe says.

Fleming's cackle, his friendly manner, and a curiously unbelieving attitude about life made him a staff favorite. He was wacky enough to be a staffer almost upon arrival, and when he went to share an apartment with tall, good-looking Ben Price, he embibed some of Price's fresh young wackiness and gave Ben, in exchange, a degree of balance. Sometimes they would go out after work and get drunk together in Alf Storey's Lamb and Lark, and sing, although neither of them could carry a tune, "Fisherman, Fisherman," with Charlie White who was sure to be in the L&L before them.

One such night they stayed long after closing time, and when Alf threw them out went back to the *Times* offices.

"Benny, I think we ought to do a story on the speech today," Joe said as they entered the city room. Art White and Bob Moora, who sat quietly in a corner for the next ten minutes, told the rest of the staff what happened.

"Yerse?" hiccuped Benny. "What speech?"

"The speech of Dr. Whoshowhosho to the students of Ling Poo," Joe replied gravely. Abruptly his voice changed to an order.

"Price, get your lead ass over on rewrite and take a story from Fleming. He's out at Ling Poo University."

Benny stared for a moment, then sat down, a little hesitant, at the rewrite desk where there was a telephone with a headset receiver. He put them on, slipped paper into the typewriter and waited.

Joe strode across the room, picked up a telephone on the far side of the room and waited for the staid, decorous old gal who was night switchboard operator on the *Times* board.

"Give me extension 138," Joe ordered.

"No, you just think that's right in this room. It isn't, though, as any fool can tell you. I'll tell you. It's in the *Stars and Stripes* editorial rooms.

"Where am I? I'm calling from Ling Poo, naturally."

Finally, the poor gal connected Joe with Benny's extension across the room and Fleming began:

"Hello, Price. Guess I'll dictate this. The Desk wants it to run and have a lot of names in.

"Dateline it Ling Poo University, Feb. 12. Okay?

"Dr. Whoshowhosho, speaking to two thousand undergraduates of Ling Poo University, today told them that Fascism (capitalize that, Benny) was a threat to Democracy (that too, Benny). After the address, in which he soundly scored high-altitude daylight precision bombing by the Japanese, Dr. Whoshowhosho distributed diplomas to the two thousand undergraduates who gave their names as, semicolon. No, make that colon."

At that point Benny had had enough, and he spoke back into the phone.

"Joe, better hold it down. The Desk says we'll do a feature story on their names sometime later. So that's all. 'Bye, Joe, and thanks."

They hung up and walked out of the office together after Benny had carefully folded and placed in the "in" copy basket the photographic print on the reverse side of which he had typed the story.

Moora and White said the best thing about it all was that, although Joe was shouting—he claimed the connection was poor—Benny never once listened to the shouting; he got the whole story over the phone.

Not all the eccentrics were limited to reporters or editors. One of the prides of the old staff at the *Times* was George Popham, Llewellyn's chauffeur, a Canadian too before the Yanks came into the war.

Popham first came to the notice of the city staff over a matter of pins.

The staff was hammering toward a deadline one evening late in December, 1943, when Popham walked into the city room and stood quiet for a time long enough to cause Russ Jones to look up.

He saw Pop contorting his face as he reached his big fingers into his mouth.

"Pop, what the hell you trying to do?" Russ demanded.

From the burly Popham's mouth came a series of grumbling jumbled sounds.

"What?"

Popham took his hand out of his mouth and said, understandably but still with twisted speech, "Grot blins in m' mouth."

"Pins in your mouth? Where the hell did you do that?"

By that time the staff was looking up and the Desk was torn between irritation and intrigue. Popham jammed his fingers back into his mouth, fished again and triumphantly came out with two straight pins, reached in and got two more. The whole staff sighed with relief and Moora asked, "Pop, how did you ever do that?"

"Putting up maps for the major in his office and forgot to take the pins out of my mouth I'd put in there so I wouldn't drop them," Pop answered, his speech still a little thick.

The office roared with laughter and went back to work. In about ten minutes, Jones had a feeling something was wrong and looked up to see Popham with his hand again jammed inside his mouth.

Russ's roar of laughter and astonishment brought everyone back to Popham. "Well . . ." said Moora menacingly, letting his voice drift off.

"Blore blins."

Bob said: "Well, Pop, you go out in the hall and try to get them out and if they're still there when I get this head for page one written I'll take them out for you."

Ten minutes later the head was written, Bob went out to the hallway. Popham was still there, groping in his mouth, growing red in the face. Bob shoved him under the light, found four more pins and extracted them.

"What," he demanded in ultimate exasperation, "is the explanation for those pins after the others?"

"Lot of maps," Popham said sadly. "Lot of maps."

Pop had his troubles with Major Llewellyn. (E.M.L. only became a lieutenant colonel after Pop left him.) He became, for one thing, probably the only man in any army anywhere who ever was court-martialed for going to the toilet.

Llewellyn stormed into the city room one day looking for

Popham. "Where's that crazy chauffeur?" he demanded. Gene Graff, the sports ace, said he'd seen Pop going into the toilet.

"He can't do that," Llewellyn screamed with one of his bursts of sudden and illogical anger which the editorial staff had grown used to brushing off and forgetting as meaningless. "He didn't ask permission."

That was funny in an establishment such as *The Stars and Stripes,* but Llewellyn didn't see it that way.

"If he isn't here in five minutes, I'll court-martial him," he shouted and went back into his own map-lined cubbyhole. No one thought any more about it; just the major going off the deep end again and he'd forget it in a minute.

Ten or fifteen minutes later, Popham walked into the city room and someone told him the major was looking for him. Pop went into the major's office. Half an hour later there came to the desk a telephone call.

"Hey, Bud. This is Pop. I'm under arrest and the major is going to court-martial me. I told him I was only in the can, and he says that's why he's giving me summary punishment and fining me ten bucks and I have to stay in my quarters every night for the next month."

The editorial staff protested to the major that this was rank injustice, and wanted to carry the appeal further when he was unmoved, but Popham said to hell with it he was past thirty-eight years of age and had applied to get out of the army and join the Merchant Marine.

Within a month he had his discharge. He stopped at the *Times* the same day and the staff learned for the first time that his father had been a law partner of the great Clarence Darrow, that Pop had gone to Notre Dame Preparatory School, finished two years at the University of Chicago and then had decided he had heard too much about being a lawyer and so went off to sea. Ben Price rode uptown in a taxicab with Pop the day the ex-chauffeur left London for the States.

As the taxi passed Grosvenor House, the swanky London hotel which had been partly taken over by the army for an officers' mess and in front of which pink-panted officers always were crowding, an army car with a major in the back seat pulled out in front of Pop's taxi. There was a traffic snarl.

Pop, Ben said later, reached swiftly into his pocket, pulled out his formal discharge papers which had separated him from the army, and then gripping them tightly stuck his head out of the taxi window.

"You," he roared at the officer lounging in the back seat of the offending olive-drab car. "You! Get that goddam car out of the way and do it in a hurry! Yes, you!"

The startled major jerked erect. He blanched and looked at Pop's angrily red face, saw Pop's new civilian clothes, but couldn't see the discharge papers Pop clutched in his hand.

"Yes, sir. Yes, sir. Right away," answered the major. He turned on his chauffeur and gnattered at him until the GI, whose countenance wore a happily smug expression, moved the car away.

Pop leaned back in the seat as Benny prepared to leave.

"Benny, tell the boys about that," Pop said dreamily. "Tell 'em about it, will you?"

The word "fabulous" is apt to get a bit overworked in telling of the staffers and what they did. Nonetheless, it is a most proper usage in that connection.

*Stars and Stripes* men always were turning up in the strangest places—in one week toward the end of the war in Germany not only were there *Stars and Stripes* men filing dispatches to the Paris office or to the Rome office from every zone of the fighting front, but Earl Mazo and Larry Riordan were in Norway, Pete Lisagore was in Copenhagen, Charley Kiley was with General Eisenhower, Andy Rooney was in the air somewhere on the way to China in the plane of a general with whom he had bummed a ride, Corporal Phil Bucknell was talking to the morning-coated statesmen—and mowing them down with his British accent—at San Francisco, Tom Hoge was in Odessa on the Black Sea, Ernie Leiser was in Berlin, and there were a handful more scattered around.

Ed Clark and Vic Dallaire were riding through the Alps on a flatcar.

Ed and Vic had started out from Germany in a jeep, planning on driving down through the passes of the Alps to join the Fifth Army in Italy. They found one pass blocked by a landslide. The only route southward was the railroad line through a long tunnel. Driving up to the switching tower at the tunnel's northern entrance, Vic managed in his bad French and Ed's worse German to convince the civilian towermaster that they were railroad experts from the United States who were going to supervise the railroads through the Alps.

Immediately at their demand, the towermaster halted the next train south, ordered a crew of workmen to shove their jeep aboard a flatcar and the two staffers rode triumphantly through the Alps to Italy.

As was pointed out, Stars-and-Stripesers were always turning up in the strangest places. And virtually every time they were wiring shortly thereafter for money. The soldier-reporters never seemed able to stretch their army pay until the next time they had a chance to collect any. One reporter, whose name somehow cannot be recalled, once was farmed out to the public relations section of the Supply Forces for a period of six months. Even with the PRO, the reporter couldn't make his money last. Finally, in the alcoholic throes of despair the reporter "borrowed" an army typewriter and went to a hock shop.

"That typewriter belongs to your army," the pawnshop proprietor admonished.

"No, it doesn't. I own it."

"You get a slip from your commanding officer saying it's your typewriter and I'll lend you six pounds on it."

The reporter was back in the pawnshop half an hour later. He had the slip which said the typewriter was his personal property, the signature on the slip read: "Colonel Joseph Zilch." The pawnshop proprietor squinted, seemed satisfied, took the typewriter and handed over six pounds.

Two days later when the army had missed its typewriter and the military police detectives had finally traced it to the pawnshop, a friend found the reporter guzzling the last of the six pounds in a pub.

"The MPs are on your trail!" the friend warned.

Red-eyed and unsteady, the reporter nonetheless was competent to meet the threat to his personal liberty. With a hurried "thanks," he sped out of the pub and raced away in a taxicab just as the MPs arrived in their jeeps.

There ensued a veritable cops-and-robbers chase through London streets, with the reporter directing his taximan along an escape route he obviously had planned, with commendable military foresight, well in advance. A scant two blocks ahead of the MPs, who missed his final turn and never caught up with him until twenty-four hours afterward when it was too late, the reporter's taxi swung into a United States Army military hospital, where he turned himself over to the Psychopathic Ward as an obviously mentally ill GI, and had with him the unpaid taxicab driver to describe the flight across the city—from pursuers who apparently never had been there, since they weren't present now—to substantiate the reporter's slyly insinuated intimation of a persecution complex.

When the police got there a day later, the reporter was ably and successfully defended by the hospital psychiatrist. He was obviously suffering from a temporary derangement, was not responsible for his actions, and should be given a rest from duty under hospital care for at least two months.

On the fringe of *The Stars and Stripes* organization there were always individuals who somehow became associated with the paper either officially or unofficially. Some of them worked for us, some of them with us, but whatever the connection most of them sooner or later whirled off on some strange tangent because of the association.

A New York *Times* correspondent, Fred Graham, always a favorite of staffers, started traveling with Earl Mazo and Jim Grad when he was assigned by the *Times* to Patton's Third Army.

One night Fred ran a little short of clean shirts and borrowed one from Grad. Grad, a sergeant, had only one shirt left, a GI wool one on which he had had stripes sewn when he was with a line outfit before joining *The Stars and Stripes*. It didn't bother Fred, he put it on and covered the stripes with the field jacket he always wore.

After he finished work that night, Fred wandered over to the elaborate headquarters officers' bar the Third Army had set up. With another correspondent he sat around for an hour or so, drank and talked. The barroom began to get warm and finally Fred stood up, took off his field jacket and sat down again, forgetting about the stripes on his shirt. No one said anything until he started out the door with his friend.

A brusque old colonel bolted across the room and grabbed Fred by the striped arm.

"What the hell do you think you're doing in here, soldier?" the colonel bellowed.

From behind him Fred heard the voice of his friend whisper over his shoulder, "Don't tell him."

Graham, realizing he was wrong, decided to give the colonel a rough time anyway. After two or three minutes' bellowing, the colonel, blue in the face with rage by then, called for military police.

Deciding he had carried the gag far enough Fred told the colonel he was actually a war correspondent. He had the sergeants stripes on by mistake, he told the officer. It was too late, though, and the colonel demanded his identification papers.

"The hell with him," the voice behind Fred whispered, "Don't show them to him."

"Nope," said Fred, "I'm afraid you'll have to take my word."

By that time a crowd had gathered and the MPs had arrived. Fred reluctantly started reaching for his correspondent's War Department pass. First he went into his breast pocket where he usually kept it, while the colonel, the MPs and the crowd stood around waiting for him to produce evidence that he was not a sergeant in the officers' bar.

A little faster his hands moved from his shirt pockets to his pants, then his back pockets.

"Gee, I had it here when I came out—I think."

Fred got away that night but the colonel, fully aroused, filed charges against him. He wanted the New York *Times* correspondent tried. Grounds? "Impersonating a noncommissioned officer."

Fred never was tried but he left the Third Army and has since been careful about borrowing shirts from *Stars and Stripes* staffers.

Graham's experience, unique in itself, was typical of the things that seemed to happen to what we often referred to as "our civilian staffers."

Not all of them got into trouble but certainly one of them was the most arrested individual in Europe for the few months after the Seventh Army drove into Strasbourg.

He was a 14-year-old Alsatian named Lucien Detière, black-haired and black-eyed. Lucien on rare occasions smiled at the world with a brightness that was sad to see because it shone through a very bitter and very troubled young soul: Lucien lost both his parents to the war.

Lucien most assuredly was the most efficient fighting man on the unofficial *Stars and Stripes* roster of civilian staffers. For a year before the liberation of Strasbourg Lucien was with the French Maquis, harrying the Germans who occupied their Alsace and Lorraine. In the fighting during which Ed Clark and Vic Dallaire found Lucien—or maybe it was the other way around—the American forces drove up through southeastern France and into Strasbourg. When the last German fled out of France's two last provinces, 14-year-old Lucien Detière had four notches in the butt of the rifle he carried.

Clark and Dallaire may have been the best-natured and most inherently kind staffers *The Stars and Stripes* ever had. Both of them had been combat men before coming to the paper. They were also competent newspapermen, and when the army took Strasbourg they moved the *Stars and Stripes* edition they had been publishing at Dijon into the newly liberated city. Lucien became the paper's copy boy, armed guard and instigator of endless clashes between the staff and the military police until eventually all the MPs in the Strasbourg area knew him. Most of the MPs liked Lucien nearly as much as the *S&S*ers, and the few who resented his somewhat proprietary air about Strasbourg, *The Stars and Stripes,* and the American Army let him alone if only by virtue of the fierce step-paternity Clark and Dallaire exhibited about their orphaned protégé.

But eventually Ed and Vic left Strasbourg for another edition and Lucien of course went with them. They couldn't always take him when they went out on trips so Dallaire wrote out an official-looking document for the kid.

"This is Lucien Detière," Dallaire began his letter. "He is on official or unofficial duty for *The Stars and Stripes* in the central and southern portions of the European Continent. He is an Alsatian who speaks French and some English with a German accent.

"The clothing he wears," the letter continued, "has been given to him by the paper's staff and by various other American units he has met. He is 14 years old and will get into about as much trouble as a good 14-year-old boy will."

While the letter continued to cover almost any circumstance the boy might find himself in, he nevertheless spent most nights away from Clark and Dallaire in some American MP brig.

During the siege of Cologne, Ed Clark took Lucien to Terry Allen's 104th Division with him. Ed used to go up front every day and he left Lucien at division headquarters. Finally, when he dashed back to Liége with a story, he left Lucien there in care of 104th headquarters men.

Lucien was not the boy to stay where he was put. Three days later, after he had upset the whole 104th Division MP corps, he hitchhiked to Liége himself. Lucien loved American soldiers, so, attired in a complete American uniform, the little fourteen-year-old went to the places in Liége where he would find his friends. While he might conceivably have got by in any other place, Lucien, in a bar, looked like just what he was, a four foot eight inch, 14-year-old kid. During his stay at the 104th Division he had collected insignia as he always did when he stayed with a unit. He had sewed the Timberwolf patch on his arm but the extra-special item he had acquired was a blue and white MP brassard.

Because he liked it and because he thought he might get into less trouble with the police if he posed as one of them, Lucien put the MP armband on in Liége. The kid with the .45 automatic slung at his hip, the American equipment and the MP brassard couldn't have been more conspicuous if he had been riding an elephant. In two days the MPs from the various military police units in Liége picked him up seven times. Each time Lucien pulled out his now dog-eared letter signed by "Staff Sergeant Victor Dallaire, Editor, Strasbourg Edition, *The Stars and Stripes.*" And eventually, each time, the police would call the office and get someone over to vouch for him.

Lucien Detière, like thousands of French, Belgian and German kids in towns American columns passed through, worshiped American soldiers but, unlike most, he did something about it—he insisted on being with them. Kids, even German kids, don't like losers. They backed the winners and American equipment rolling by their doorstep was better evidence than Hitler had ever presented.

While Fred Graham and Lucien Detière's association with *The Stars and Stripes* were typical of a hundred civilian staffers unofficially attached to the paper at one time or another, neither of them or any of the others were so permanent on the exofficio roster of Stars-and-Stripers as Alf and Gert Storey, great friends and, incidentally, proprietors of the Lamb and Lark, the Printing House Lane pub.

Printing House Square was a dank, cobblestoned little thoroughfare around which the motley buildings of the *Times* clustered to keep out the sun. In the quiet, friendly half-gloom, you could hear the dignified noises of *Times* presses, an occasional rattle of a typewriter, and, in the proper hours, the comfortable clink of ale mugs from the Lamb and Lark.

The Lamb and Lark traditionally was the pub in which men from the *Times* gathered for their favorite mild-and-bitter. Its dingy, brown, two-doored front was the first thing on your right as you came up Printing House Lane to Printing House Square. You stepped over the worn threshold, walked past the public bar, where generations of *Times* teamsters had been replaced by lorry drivers, and came to the inner bar, which eventually was as much a part of *The Stars and Stripes* as the paper's very masthead. In the white light of a gas lamp—and a gas lamp was exactly the sort of illumination the Lamb and Lark should have had—you saw a table with four chairs, an eight-man bar on your left, and Alf and Gertie.

Two items should explain the relationship between Alf and Gertie and the noisy American soldiers who came to shatter the quiet of Printing House Square. First, in the rack of pigeonholes which served as the staff's mailbox in the editorial department, there was reserved for all time one compartment labeled "Storey, Alf and Gert." Of course, they never got any mail, but that was the way the staff felt about them. And, secondly, before the army paper had been at the *Times* two months, Alf was answering the Lamb and Lark telephone not with "Storey here," as he always had done, but "City Desk," as the *Stars and Stripes* deskmen always answered their own phone across the square. That's the way things were between us and Alf and Gertie.

The Lamb and Lark was the staff's YMCA, pool hall, bar and recreation lounge. It was sort of a *Stars and Stripes* USO. Stocky, blue-eyed, cockney-accented Alf was the director. Gertie, the publican's wife, dealt with Alf and the staff in a slightly sardonic tone belied by the little smile at a corner of her tight-lipped mouth and a twinkle in her gray eyes. They were completely at home in the lunatic fringe atmosphere of *The Stars and Stripes.*

Eventually the Storeys got to be a little American, and the staffers, naturally, got to be a little of whatever kind of English the Storeys were. By the time we'd been in Printing House Square six months, Alf was accompanying his good-bye wave to customers, not with the historical "Cheerio, Jack," but with "Don't take any wooden nickels, Mac." And the staffers were hoisting their drinks—despite wartime rationing, there was always a drop of something for them at the Lamb and Lark—with "Cheerio" or "Chin chin."

The intimacy of *The Stars and Stripes* staff and the Lamb and Lark's publican served a practical purpose: It circumvented the law which decreed that City of London pubs should be open to the public only from 10 A.M. to 2 P.M., and from 5:30 P.M. to 10:30 P.M. Inasmuch as Alf and Gertie fed fundless staffers who missed meals elsewhere, or put to bed long-drinking staffers who missed the last train home, and quite as much because staffers occasionally had to put Alf to bed, or if he had stayed too long on the wrong side of the bar took him home with them to avoid Gertie's displeasure, all concerned held that it was a purely family relationship, and *Stars and Stripes* men thus were able legally to be in the Lamb and Lark whatever the hour. Usually the hour was very late.

It was fitting that in the well-worn, slightly cobwebby atmosphere of the Lamb and Lark there should be a rough and burly Airedale named Prince. Prince on rare occasions managed to catch one of the foot-sized rats which made their way up from the Thames docks to run around the walls of the Lamb and Lark on quiet nights. Every time Prince caught a rat, one resourceful staffer or another somehow managed to wangle a piece of steak for the dog despite rationing.

When Prince died, the staff quietly assessed its members for £60, which was the price of a very pedigreed Airedale from Britain's very best kennel. No one on *The Stars and Stripes* would have been caught dead being sentimental, so that night the staff simply took the new and very pedigreed pooch with them on a leash when they went to the L&L after presstime.

When Gertie finally threw everyone out about 1 A.M., Ben Price handed Alf the other end of the pup's leash and said:

"Here's a dog we brought you, Alf. Maybe his name ought to be Deacon."

He hurried out for the subway with the rest.

At Christmas, 1943, the staff bought Deacon a collar with a

silver name plate, and sometime that winter also opened a mailbox compartment for him in the editorial room, just ahead of the one reserved for Lieutenant Colonel Llewellyn. Everyone concerned felt that a dog of Deacon's standing shouldn't go around wearing the same collar every day, so for Christmas, 1944, we bought him another one. That same Christmas, most of the original *Stars and Stripes* staffers were across the Channel in France and Belgium and Germany, but as the Yule evening settled on Printing House Square, the telephone rang in the Lamb and Lark. In answer to Alf's "City Desk," there came over a network of army and civilian telephone wires a *Stars and Stripes* voice from the Continent, wishing Alf and Gertie, their daughter Joyce, and Deacon a merry Christmas.

Alf maybe was the man in all England with the best sense of humor. He participated in more *S&S* escapades than any other civilian staffers. He was never left out.

When Bill Dunbar, one of our messengers, married an English girl, everyone went to the wedding in Shepherd's Bush, one of London's outlying districts. Of course Alf was invited, but because he had to work until two o'clock, Alf missed the actual wedding. The bridal party left the church in the only kind of automobile you could hire in London besides a taxi—a huge, black, nine-passenger limousine, the kind with a liveried chauffeur who can communicate to his passengers only through one of those silver-belled speaking tubes. The sergeants and privates and corporals, and the handful of civilian-garbed in-laws, rode from the church to the in-laws' house, with the staffers hoping all the time that Alf could get there before they drank up the precious bottles of Scotch Alf had managed to dig up for the occasion.

When the reception really got going and became a boiling little party, the staff tried manfully to maintain a pleasant teatime conversation with Bill's new in-laws and at the same time throw down glass after glass of good Scotch. In the middle of the party Ben Price decided it was time to get Alf. The only available transportation was the hearselike chariot. The Lamb and Lark was seven miles from Shepherd's Bush and to get there it was necessary to pass through the heart of London's West End, through the parts of the city where the Americans were thickest and down into the drab businesslike area of Fleet Street.

Benny volunteered to go for Alf, and for Gert, if she would

come. He stepped out the door and had the stripe-panted chauffeur open the door of the Rolls-Royce limousine for him. The chauffeur's mouth dropped open when Benny gave him the address he wanted.

"Printing House Square!"

The great black hearse took off with Ben sitting there like a little king.

When the limousine pulled into Printing House Lane, there was barely room on the narrow street for it to get in. Ben went into the L&L. got Alf and a few more bottles and came back to the car with him.

So the English publican and the American sergeant started back toward Shepherd's Bush in the back seat of a car not unlike the big limousine the King and Queen of England used in their tours.

As Alf passed friends starting up from Printing House Lane he nodded condescendingly and passed a slow studied wave to them. Farther along, Alf continued the performance as he passed American soldiers and, with Ben in his American uniform sitting next to him, a lot of United States soldiers must have walked off with the impression that they had just seen either the King or his second-in-charge of the realm with a Joe in his car.

Except that Bill eventually wished he had never asked any of the staff to his wedding, the rest of that party was relatively uneventful. The staff had never been one to be invited to sacred events.

Once before one of the photographers on the staff had been married and his wife had a child. When it was time to baptize the kid, the staffer thought it would be a nice gesture to ask a few friends to the church for the function. Realizing, just as the ceremony was about to take place, that a godfather was a customary thing for a well-baptized child to have, he walked down the aisle of the church to one of the rear pews where Sergeants Ralph Noel, Bill Gibson and Herb Schneider were sitting.

"I would sure like to have one of you fellows as the boy's godfather," he said hopefully, looking at them. "How about it?"

At that point he was called back down in front by his wife, who beckoned to him.

While the minister started saying prayers over babies and touching their foreheads with water from a baptismal font, the three men in the rear pew huddled together trying to decide what the functions of a good godfather were and which one of them would be it. None of them wanted the job but, not wanting to offend, they decided to toss for it.

Because they realized it was a responsibility not to be lightly considered, they made it three out of five, eliminating the odd man each time. They were careful not to drop the coin during the prayers.

When the happy father came back they had picked him a godfather from among their group.

Despite Alf's occasional sortie into the world, neither he nor any of the *Stars and Stripes* people in London went far from the Lamb for their recreation as a general rule. There was a shove ha'penny board and an American pinball machine in there. A pinball machine was totally out of character in the Lamb and Lark and to present an accurate picture of the place it should be left out, but nevertheless it was there.

The shove ha'penny game was played on a board about eighteen inches long and twelve wide. It had nine grilled grooves an inch apart up and down its length. The object of the game was to knock five ha'pennies, with the heel of the hand, so that they stopped in the center of the grilled lines, without touching the lines. When each grill had had three ha'pennies land in it—they were marked with chalk at the edge of the board each time—the game was won.

Alf was the master of the game. He could spin ha'pennies, twist them, seemingly, around curves to hit others into place, and generally do what he wanted with the heel of his hand. Ben used to play him several times each night for the first six months and became expert at the game himself, although he was never able to beat Alf.

Occasionally Alf and Benny would wander along Fleet Street on Saturday, a staffer's day off before the paper published seven days a week. Ben would eventually wander over to the shove ha'penny board in whatever pub they happened to be in and after watching the Englishmen play the game for a few minutes, he would express casual interest. That was in the days when Americans were still somewhat of a novelty in London and more often than not some Englishman would offer to show Price how to play. Playing the role of the contemptuous American, Ben would sneer at the game, saying it didn't look very tough; as a matter of fact, he could probably pick it up in one game.

Before long there would be a beer bet on a game in which the Englishman usually offered to give points to Benny. He always refused them contemptuously and then, starting like a beginner, "learned" in three or four shots and invariably beat all comers, to the utter amazement of all regulars of the local. It was a filthy trick which he and Alf thoroughly enjoyed.

Alf always took the worst end of any dealings he had with staffers. He was their Bank of England. At one time the staff was into Alf for £300, which, to a man managing a small pub, is more than pocket change. Still Alf never refused anyone. On Fridays he was always asked to cash two or three checks. The staffers figured, knowing Alf, that they wouldn't be cashed that day anyway and wouldn't clear the bank, where their funds were insufficient to cover the amount of the check, until Monday. Monday morning they hoped to rush to the bank and make a deposit before the check cleared.

More often when Monday morning came they would head worriedly for Alf's and ask him whether or not he had sent the check to the bank. He almost never had. If he had, he lent them the money to cover it.

If one of the boys came into Alf's with a stranger and wanted to buy a drink, Alf always seemed to be able to tell when the fellow was broke. He would set the drinks on the bar and then hand the fellow change for a pound note—which he hadn't received.

One mad night after the rest had left, Alf got into a crap game with one of the boys. By three o'clock Alf was in debt £200 and he would have paid the debt if it broke him. They continued playing though and by dawn the staffer was owing Alf £75.

Into Alf's at one time or another there wandered the strangest collection of characters who ever walked the streets of London. A quorum which very often held out until two and three in the morning consisted of Bob Moora, a "Mr. Alf Barrum," Alf, Gert, Benny, and Jim King, an AP man with the London bureau.

Rolypoly Jim King shared an apartment with the only completely conservative *S&S*er, Len Giblin. The two once had worked together on the Associated Press in Boston; Gib came into the army and wound up in London, and Jim stayed with the AP and wound up in the same place. (Through all his long association with *The Stars and Stripes,* Jim King was periodically tormented by the thought that he could probably have even more fun with the soldier-reporters if he were in the army; but he was 4-F and stayed a civilian.) In addition to being one of the customary quorum at Alf's, Jim had a date with the staff to play baseball in Hyde Park every Friday morning.

Fridays were inspection days for the staffers and after inspection there was a baseball game at seven o'clock. In old gray pants, red sweater and a skullcap, Jim arrived at Hyde Park corner each Friday just before Llewellyn ordered, "Fall in for baseball." At that Jim came to attention, swung into the tail end of the formation in step with Joe Fleming. It would, in passing, be nice to say Jim could march better than the soldiers, but he couldn't. He was just about as good, or as bad, as the rest; but he didn't wear a brown suit. The *S&S* staff always figured that it worked out pretty justly—that Jim King couldn't march any better than we could.

Anyway, Jim marched over to Hyde Park and when they reached the baseball diamond the Yanks had laid out on the age-old green grass, Llewellyn dropped his Friday morning pretense of soldiering and *The Stars and Stripes* and its civilian staffers played baseball.

When the ball game was done, the majority of the staffers went off and deliberately got drunk in protest against inspections and baseball and Jim went with them. (As this is written, it is two years since we stopped the baseball games, and to be perfectly candid our exact reasoning for getting drunk in protest against inspections and playing baseball is forgotten. It must have been a valid reason.) At any rate, on one such Friday Jim, Ben Price, Bob Moora, Joe Fleming, and Hutton took off for a pub crawl through Chelsea, London's Greenwich Village.

In the center of Sloane Square, Chelsea, there was a large steel emergency water tank for use against air-raid fires. It was Jim's misfortune that he passed the tank after the group had had five or six at the Queen's Head. As a sign of their affection, the staffers threw Jim into the water tank. After a great deal of contorting he emerged soaking wet, and they went on to the next pub. In the midst of his second drink at the pub, which was a sedate sort of place frequented by the nicer people of the neighborhood, Jim suddenly stepped away from the bar, twisted his torso and kicked lustily with his right foot. He kicked again. Out from his pant leg came one half of a pair of green- and orange-striped shorts. The shorts sailed over the bar, to which Jim turned and finished his drink. He spun about and kicked with his left leg. The other half of the shorts, less like the Associated Press than almost anything anyone could wear, arced gracefully across the room and settled in a corner.

Somehow the group of Americans simultaneously had the same idea. With one gesture they emptied their glasses and, brazen faced, bowed deeply to the astounded patrons of the pub and strode out.

It was some time later that Jim, for obvious reasons, won even more of the staff's undying admiration for a bit of haberdashery legerdemain.

Late one evening Ben Price, Len Giblin and King left a Mayfair cocktail bar and, the worse for wear, headed toward Clifford's Inn and their apartments in a taxicab. In the blackout they rode drowsily across the city. When they arrived at Clifford's Inn, paid off the taxicab, and went into the apartment house, the staffers got their first look at King since leaving the cocktail bar.

Jim had on his gray fedora, his pants, shoes and the coat of his suit. Neatly tied around his bare neck was his necktie, and he wore no shirt.

The staffers caught the taxicab before it got away, but there was no shirt in it. Jim giggled and said he didn't know how it happened; he guessed maybe it was the same thing that had separated the legs of his shorts that time in the Chelsea pub.

Ernie Pyle was probably the paper's best-known civilian staffer, since we printed his daily column, and to *The Stars and Stripes* there came regularly letters for Ernie from soldiers all over the world. So, too, in a considerable measure were other civilian war correspondents whose writings we occasionally felt covered a particular subject better than our own staffers. Among them we had a handful of friends almost as close as Jim King. One such was Homer Bigart, one of the New York *Herald-Tribune's* ace reporters who covered the air war with Stars-and-Stripesers, went to the Continent with them, and whose office sent him to the Pacific about the same time as the vanguard's skeleton staff of the army paper. Homer was a close enough friend so that he and the staffers could laugh together about his occasional difficulties in telephoning his stories to the *Herald-Tribune* bureau in London. Homer stuttered.

Covering the story of the raid over Wilhelmshaven by Eighth Air Force heavy bombers, Homer and a *Stars and Stripes* man talked to the returning crews at their base and together walked over to the Administration Building to telephone their respective stories to London. *The Stars and Stripes* man was talking on one phone as Bigart finished writing his piece, and heard the bespectacled *Herald-Tribune* man speak to the public relations man in the office.

"W-w-w-will you p-p-please t-t-t . . . t-t-telephone my s-s-story f-f-for me?" Homer asked the PRO.

The public relations man replied offhandedly, "Sure, if you want me to. But there's another telephone. You're welcome to use that, yourself."

With a straight face, Homer replied:

"I c-c-can't h-h-hear very well over the t-t-t-telephone."

There were all sorts of individuals, whose sole common denominator with the staff was a lack of a common denominator with normal people, who came to *The Stars and Stripes,* the Lamb and Lark, or any of the far-flung offices across the world and their auxiliary barrooms.

Inasmuch as Charlie White, George Popham, Ralph Noel, and a few others had come to the American Army as transferees from the Canadian Army, there usually were two or three old friends from the Canadian Army wherever *The Stars and Stripes* was. After one visit by Canadians to the Lamb and Lark, Alf Storey put up a sign which read:

Out of bounds to Canadian and ex-Canadian bagpipe players.

Some of the boys from the Canadian Essex Scottish and Calgary Tank regiments had dropped in to see their old comrades on *S&S.* Charlie White and Hutton adjourned their nostalgia to the Lamb and Lark.

The legal afternoon closing hour came and the patrons of the Lamb and Lark left. Charlie and Hutton, as members of the family, stayed on to tell Alf for the several hundredth time about what fine people the Canadians were and, oh boy, couldn't a fellow march to bagpipes. Alf should have known better. He confessed to a liking for the skirl of the pipes.

Immediately, the nearly tone-deaf White and his equally so companion began to drone the pipe band marches to which they had trod many a Canadian mile. It was "remember this?" and "remember that?" and the Scotch flowed on as Alf joined in the droning.

Outside, Printing House Square and the lane were quiet, but on busy Queen Victoria Street, onto which the lane opened, the late afternoon rush was just beginning.

Suddenly, as the trio finished a particularly moving (to them) vocal version of "The Road to the Isles," Hutton could stand it no longer. He seized the bar towel, tucked it in the fashion of a Scottish sporran beneath the belt American soldiers wore at the time over their blouses, and with a swift motion removed his khaki pants. Firm in the belief that he now resembled a Scot in kilts, which Charlie a second later verified by emulation, the sergeant seized one of the tall wooden bar stools, upended it and somehow managed to drape it over his shoulders and around his torso. One leg of the stool was at the level of his lips, and pumping lustily with his left arm as he stopped imaginary holes in an imaginary pipe with his fingers, the half-clad Yank stalked stiffly out of the Lamb and Lark, droning with all his might:

> "The Essex Scottish sailed away
> And left their girls in a family way . . ."

At this point Charlie White grasped the worn old club with which Alf used to pack ice in the cooler, raced after the departing pseudo piper and fell into step going down the street with the club carried Canadian rifle-fashion over his left shoulder.

> "And they won't be back until Judgment day,
> To put them back in the same old way."

Across Printing House Square, shattering the afternoon calm down Printing House Lane, and out onto Queen Victoria Street went the two ex-Canadians. They droned, "What'll We Do With the Drunken Sailor" and as that ended, Charles roared:

"The company will retire in a column of twos! A-boooout TURN!"

They had finished half a dozen skirling Scottish tunes, Charles had taken his company through a series of Canadian foot-drill maneuvers impeccably, if with a slight stagger, ordered and carried out, when the imploring Alf finally caught up with them, and before a laughing throng of Englishmen—who, as a matter of fact, had cheered lustily at each well-done maneuver and strangely done pipe tune, Alf begged:

"Please come back to the pub. It's after closing time, and you'll have the bobbies down on us all! Come back and you can march all you please inside the Lamb and Lark."

Magnificently Charles turned his head as they marched up the street.

"Storey! Fall in!"

With a despairing groan, Alf fell into step just to the rear of the piper, and Charles carried out his part of the unspoken bargain with a final order:

"The company will retire . . . to the Lamb and Lark . . . a-booooout TURN!"

The crowd cheered.

## THE BRASS

MAD AS *The Stars and Stripes* was, it somehow never outpaced its first officer in charge. There were half a dozen of them on the road to Tokyo via Berlin, but no one on the staff ever felt that the commanding officer ever should really be anyone except Ensley Maxwell Llewellyn, of Tacoma, Washington.

Llewellyn, who started *The Stars and Stripes* as a major and became a lieutenant colonel before he left the paper in Paris and went out to the Pacific, treated every problem that arose to block publication just as he treated McDonnell's half-voiced plea about the English weather. With a wave of his bony hand, a shrill "Okay! Let's do something!" and a bland obliviousness to the fact that no sane man would do whatever it was he was going to do, EML, as he signed himself, set the paper going. He picked up a nickname early.

Walking past the circulation office, Llewellyn overheard Bob Collins, the private who was production boss for the paper, ask someone "What is The Brain going to do about no newsprint?"

Llewellyn, back in his office, asked Harry Harchar, the major who had come into the army from a job as assistant executive of the Bethlehem, Pennsylvania, council of the Boy Scouts of America and who had been assigned to be executive editor of *The Stars and Stripes,* "Harry, who do they call 'The Brain' in the outfit?"

Harchar already knew. "That's you," he said, not knowing whether to smile.

Llewellyn beamed. "Figure the Old Man's pretty smart, eh," he mused. "Not bad, not bad at all, Harry."

The following day he sent Collins a memo about newsprint, and signed it "The Brain."

Staff relations with Llewellyn were not as with other army brass, but more on a basis of hired hands and the boss's son who was holding down a director's job. You could argue with him, and we always did. We broke about even.

The Desk, as the heart of the paper, was a professional function. Professional newsmen, turned soldier, ran the Desk, and as such spearheaded the staff's arguments with all outsiders; and the term "outsiders" included Ensley Llewellyn as far as the newspaper business was concerned. Sometimes the EML-Desk conflicts ended with EML retreating down the halls of whatever plant we were in to lick his wounds, and sometimes it ended with the personnel of the Desk being banished to Northern Ireland, or Belgium, or whatever place was most remote from where the chief paper of the chain happened to be at the time. Usually, Llewellyn managed it so that he never banished both city editor and cable editor at one time.

The first such conflict between Llewellyn, then a major, and the sergeant and the corporal who at the time made up the Desk ended in a sort of Mexican stand-off.

For the first month of the daily's existence in London, the major tried valiantly, day after day and by every ruse he knew, to keep the editorial content of the paper directly under his will. But it no longer was a country weekly, it was a daily, big-time and getting bigger every morning, and there was no time any more to fool around with arguments which mattered not at all. After a month of slugging every night to get out a good paper with a seven-man staff, including copy boys, and slugging every day to keep E.M.L.'s amateur touch out of a professional paper, the corporal and the sergeant collapsed in weary sadness one evening against the bar of the Lamb and Lark. Tom Bernard, the Los Angeles yeoman who, with Seaman Jack Foster, of Chicago, covered the navy's doings for the paper, joined them.

A few Scotch-and-sodas and the commiserating sympathy of Alf Storey only sharpened the woes of News Editor Bob Moora and his companions. A street minstrel came in and played "Danny Boy" on a violin and the three newsmen really began to pack away the Scotch. Sometime about midnight they lurched forth, and by mutual understanding headed for the office. As they surveyed the scene of their sweatings (which was the best fun they'd had in years although they wouldn't admit it) the three grew sympathetic for themselves and bemoaned the callous army that was trying to stifle them.

Somewhere during the next half hour of self-pity, the urge to do something about it swept the trio.

When morning came, the editorial offices were a battlefield. The telephones had been ripped from their connections, the ever-delicate complex of hanging lights rested in a tangled mass of desks, wire, typewriters, chairs, smashed pastepots, torn paper and charred ashes of what had been stories piled atop the city desk.

The simple, unsuspecting cleaning staff that found the mess in the morning could think of only one thing: Nazi spies had broken into the offices of the paper. They called their chief and he called the general manager. Major Llewellyn was called from his breakfast. A little checking showed it could have been only the two men on the desk. (Somehow, Tom Bernard never was connected with it, which was poetic justice; he spent the night in the apartment the two deskmen shared in one of London's most exclusive apartment houses, and en route home Moora and the other half of the desk, after fighting with each other, turned united on Bernard when he tried to stop them and blacked his eyes, cut his lips, and put a two-inch gash in his head with a bottle before tucking him with great care to sleep in one of their beds.)

Llewellyn was faced with a problem. What had happened to the office (for days we sent salvaged stories to the composing room whose members greeted the charred edges of the copy with wide eyes) called for punishment. On the other hand, the job was to get out a daily paper, and a professional one. There simply weren't any other deskmen available.

"I ought to court-martial you two," EML told the deskmen when at his phone call they had dragged themselves red-eyed down to the office that morning. "But, frankly, I'm not going to. Part of it probably is my fault for any number of reasons. If it happens again, though, or anything like it, you'll both stay here as copy boys if we never publish a paper!"

A couple of weeks later, for Christmas, he gave the Desk four bottles of Scotch.

The battle as to editorial authority finally resolved itself, with the Desk running the news end of the paper without question, and EML writing the editorials. He wrote about the value of the Japanese yen in conquered Borneo, about Russian cavalry, about Jap naval tactics, about the Luftwaffe, and for all his editorials he could describe a background to justify his opinions. It was just as the daily began to get under way that the major decided he'd known some of the boys long enough to tell them a little of that background.

The Luftwaffe was giving London a light going over, and the antiaircraft batteries in the scarred old city were putting up a fantastic flak barrage when Llewellyn walked into the blacked-out office one night and swung his loose-jointed frame onto the end of the desk. Price, Moora, Senigo and a handful of the others were laboring over the page proofs and looked up to see the major's deep-set eyes bright with excitement, and across his narrow, bony face that not infrequent expression of some eternally hidden and never wholly understandable joy. He ran fingers through the thin fringe of hair which sat Dominican-friar fashion on his high domed skull.

"Lot of flak out there," he observed. "Lot of flak. But their predictors for the antiaircraft guns aren't the equal of what we have back in the good old U.S.A."

Benny, who would turn his mind to any argument and especially with the major, put down his copy pencil and observed that the British antiaircraft predictors ought to be pretty good in view of all the combat they'd had for developing them.

"Not like ours though," the major insisted. "I was National Guard Coast Artillery before the war, and I know. We've got a predictor that . . . why . . .

"Listen, a month before Pearl Harbor our G-2 figured there might by spy planes over the West Coast. You know how it is on the West Coast. Some of us who were in the confidence of the Big Brains in G-2 were put on special gun sites with those new American predictors. Well, not many nights before Pearl Harbor we were on duty, right on the coast it was, when our predictors showed there was a plane coming in from the sea, high and fast, and a check showed it wasn't American.

"Well, sir, we turned our guns to the course and height the predictors said, fired, and there was a blinding flash way up there in the sky a few seconds later. Just one round apiece, that was. The flash had hardly died away in the sky when kerr-thump! right outside our gun site there were two terrible sounds, right close together, and we went outside to find the smashed bodies of two Jap aviators. They were dead."

When he finished the story, Llewellyn got up and strode from the office, triumphantly, as a man who has proved his point. The following morning there was a note on Price's desk, although such matters were none of Price's concern.

"Price: Any technical stories dealing with antiaircraft fire will be edited by me. EML."

Llewellyn finally admitted he was no authority on editorial problems. (He never claimed he was; he simply wouldn't admit he wasn't, at first.) But he found newspapermen who were, and when the army said it wanted a daily newspaper to replace the country weekly, Llewellyn took a quick whirl and said he could deliver in three weeks. He set out to find the men for the job.

Bob Moora, one-time night city deskman on the New York *Herald-Tribune,* was the first man Llewellyn needed to round out the Desk. Moora, a sergeant, was in England for *Yank,* the army news magazine. *Yank* had a hot tip that the Allies would invade Europe within a few weeks, a month at the outside. That was in July, 1942. They sent Moora to England, and he waited through the summer. Nothing happened, until it seemed there was to be an invasion of North Africa, anyway. But Llewellyn asked his staff what they needed and the staff said another deskman to go with what it already had, so Llewellyn sold Moora on the idea of setting up a daily. Moora got a transfer by cable from *Yank,* which felt kind of silly about the whole invasion business after such a long wait. From replacement depots, Llewellyn filled out his staff, and on November 2, 1942, two days less than the promised three weeks, he delivered the daily paper to the army. Llewellyn could pay off.

There was the time, for example, long afterward, when we had come to France, that *S&S* needed transportation; specifically, jeeps. Over a telephone, EML found that all new jeeps coming to the Continent arrived at the port of Cherbourg. Another call got him the authority to obtain all the transportation he could find. A third call, to Cherbourg, used the results of the second call to obtain a promise that, if he could drive them away, he could have sixty jeeps any time the following day, but that they would all be gone the day after.

In the next twenty-four hours, EML went out onto the

Parisian streets and grabbed every Frenchman he saw who looked as if he could drive a car. With a wild gleam in his eyes, Llewellyn stalked from newly liberated French garage to newly liberated French garage, an interpreter tagging along and trying to translate and explain to pre-eminently logical Frenchmen why this wild-eyed American wanted to hire their services for two or three days as chauffeurs, although admittedly he had no money with which to pay them a retainer, and non, ce n'était pas absolutement certain combien, mais . . . and the interpreter would gesture and point to the lieutenant colonel (he'd been promoted by then) who stood impatiently waiting for the Frenchman to say yes, and with his gesture and shrug, the interpreter said all he had to say.

Pinwheel or no, the colonel collected forty Frenchmen to be chauffeurs, recruited twenty more staffers, copy boys, editors, photographers and accountants, and headed for Cherbourg in two big circulation trucks which also carried three meager K ration packs for each man as the sole sustenance. He and his caravan got there in time, took over the jeeps from an astounded but promise-bound colonel, and headed for Paris, a couple of hundred miles away.

They made it without an accident, without the loss of a single jeep or Frenchman, with everyone fed, somehow, from occasional messes along the route, and the papers went out from the Paris circulation office as soon as the presses rolled out the first copies. No one was sure how, but it had been done, and Llewellyn was the man who did it, even if it did take two weeks of maneuvering afterward to get the money for the French chauffeurs.

That was the kind of guy who promised there would be a daily paper within three weeks of October 15, 1942. Having his staff and little else, The Brain whirled dizzily in his office, sometimes holding (by Warren McDonnell's sworn count) three telephones and a sandwich at one time, and called for bids from London papers, got a clearance on payments by reverse Lend-Lease, got shipments of newsprint started from the United States.

So the daily came out, and set the precedent. Some of the other papers in what grew to be the *Stars and Stripes* chain occasionally outdid the *Times* and "its little American army paper," but they did it on the format set up at the *Times*.

When the army landed in North Africa, a force of about ten business and editorial men was shipped there to start publishing a paper. The editorial office eventually got to look like the London office, but the mechanical problems never did resemble the London mechanical problems.

Russ Jones, G. K. Hodenfield, Dean Hocking, Bob Neville, Harry Harchar (a captain) Ralph Martin, and a handful more who didn't speak much more than the have-you-seen-the-pen-of-my-uncle type of high school French started working in Casablanca to publish the first *S&S* in Africa.

The typesetters and compositors spoke French only. The type was French. There were no letters W and S. The presses were bad. But, all things considered, it was not a bad paper and it got better.

As a matter of fact, from that early beginning the southern edition of the paper grew to print in several towns and within a few months it no longer was a London edition subsidiary. It picked its own staff from the army units in North Africa and eventually, under Lieutenant Colonel Egbert White, a New York advertising man, became one of the best and probably the most honest of all the *Stars and Stripes* editions.

Generally, on its way across Africa, through Sicily and Italy, it got into more serious trouble than the northern editions, and that, in an army newspaper, often was the criterion of honesty.

Coming into Southern France from Italy with a mobile printing press, the southern paper was better organized for an invasion than the one that came to be known as Llewellyn's Ambiguous Force.

Llewellyn's ambiguous force took the original *Stars and Stripes* out of England and Ireland, where for two years it had been virtually the Air Force's own, and to the Continent with the Allied invasion, where it became the doughfoot's paper, or as much so as the staff could make it.

"Won't tell you what you are going to do," announced EML to the staff when it was growing obvious that invasion was near. "I've got my plans and they're locked in a safe and there they stay until the first waves go ashore on the Continent, and then we go too."

Three weeks before D day, Llewellyn suddenly jerked half of the editorial staff and a good hunk of the business staff out of town. They disappeared into secrecy for two weeks, when a couple of them got back to London. "We're billeted down in the port of

Bristol," they revealed, "and what we've done so far to get ready to publish the *S&S* on the Continent is to learn how to run motion-picture projectors."

They told of EML's disclosure to them of their task. On the train down to Bristol, he talked to them three or four at a time, in a furtive whisper.

"We're going in with the second or third wave," he said, looking sternly at his listeners who began to figure, well, The Brain really has the deal taped, this time anyway. "We're going to put out a newspaper on the beaches, and the rest of the time we'll run motion pictures for the troops behind the lines. We're all set, equipment all ready. We're a regular ambiguous force."

The boys protested that the idea of running motion-picture projectors was fantastic. What was that all about? It was a long time afterward that a slip by the colonel revealed that at the last minute he had been unable to obtain passage to the Continent for *S&S* personnel, and only by agreeing to run motion pictures for the Special Services people had he been able to get room for the staffers in the Special Services section of a trans-Channel boat in something about the forty-fifth wave, along about D plus 10.

Llewellyn's ambiguous force swarmed ashore on beaches littered with rear echelon supplies, and while the colonel led the others in a search for a printing plant, reliable old Charlie Kiley, the one-time Jersey City sports writer, dug up a mimeograph machine and a portable typewriter and began putting out a beachhead edition of *The Stars and Stripes.* It was mimeographed, it was sketchy, and it was only two sides of ordinary copy paper, but the troops to whom he could get it ate the paper up and hollered for more. They got more: Every day, as the big C-47 transport planes winged across the Channel with supplies vital to sustain the beachhead, they brought copies of the London *Stars and Stripes,* and circulation men picked them up at the hastily constructed airfields and rushed them out to the men in the line.

After picking a plant in Carentan, a little town at the base of the Cherbourg peninsula, which the Boche promptly smashed with an 88-mm. shell through the roof (the front lines were less than a mile away), Llewellyn moved his ambiguous force to Cherbourg when the big French port fell, and there published the first Continental edition of the paper since World War I.

It was published in the bomb-damaged plant of the Cherbourg *Eclair.*

The presses were relatively undamaged, but the linotype machines needed repairs and parts, which weren't available. Maybe the most pressing need was a roof; the compositors and staff labored over the forms with raincoats each day it rained until they found enough tarpaulins to make temporary repairs.

From England, four soldier-linotype operators were selected and flown to France, where they went to work on the battered lines with rubber bands, hairpins and the traditional American bailing wire. Somehow they got them operating, but when the mechanical troubles were solved, there were personnel problems.

The French typesetters, always up in the air and shouting at each other about something, usually politics, refused to work for anyone but their original shop foreman. Military Government officials, however, had him under arrest as one of the most active collaborationists in all Cherbourg, although that per se was no great crime, since at one time or another almost every Frenchman in Cherbourg accused almost every other Frenchman there of having been a collaborationist.

The paper lurched out daily, though, and the plant began to look like other *S&S* plants. The staff lived in a house formerly occupied by the Germans, and Llewellyn found a couple of maids and a cook to run the place. When the loyal French of Cherbourg got around to cutting the hair of all women known to have been friendly with the German occupiers, one of the first bald heads belonged to Paulette, the boss cook the colonel had hired.

About the time the paper got settled—settled except for the mines which blew up every other day or so in the harbor and spilled type all over the composing room—the colonel started to worry about inspections and the staff cheered when Rennes fell and the paper moved to keep up with the troops.

At Rennes, which was only a stopping point on the way to Paris, *S&S* took over, naturally enough, the plant just vacated by the staff of the German Army magazine *Signal,* a color production not unlike the U. S. Army magazine *Yank.* The day Paris fell, August 25, 1944, a task force of *Stars and Stripes* men who, well armed, could almost have taken the city by themselves, moved into the French capital and headed for the plant of the Paris *Herald,* the New York *Herald Tribune's* Continental edition.

* * *

The paper, of course, hadn't been published since the German declaration of war on the United States, but a fiery, red-haired Frenchwoman, Madame Brazier, who managed the business end of the paper for the *Herald Tribune,* had loyally stayed with the plant and had managed to keep the Germans from destroying any part of it and even from occupying the premises, a fine modern building. The Germans in Paris, as the Yanks found out when they got there, had been, officially, very polite in many instances. They seldom had taken over any building which was used or wanted by the French official governmental agencies. Madame Brazier pulled a deal with the French Ministry of Agriculture, the terms of which called for them to occupy the building. When the Wehrmacht came to see Madame Brazier about taking over the American-owned building at 21 Rue de Berri, she showed them the papers she had signed with the French Agricultural Ministry. There was some argument, but the Germans never pushed the point, and a couple of days of oiling and dusting after August 25, 1944, and the presses were ready to roll.

The French linotype operators and compositors, who streamed back to work from the Resistance movement, from hiding and from their normal lives, immediately bound themselves for all time to the staffers with the declaration of one veteran printer.

He had been a linotype operator on *The Stars and Stripes* of World War I, which was printed in Paris. The staff waited for the the inevitable comment that came from oldsters—well, this was a good paper, and probably it was modern, and yet it printed every day and all that, but by golly there never would be a paper like the OLD *Stars and Stripes.* After about two weeks, the veteran printer declared himself, to the satisfaction of a staff which had heard too much about Alexander Woollcott, Grantland Rice, Steve Early, Harold Ross et al.

"They were all right, but they didn't know much about the newspaper business," he declared.

Regardless of whether the statement was true, everyone was happy to hear one clear derogatory voice lifted against the memory of that goddamned first war *Stars and Stripes.*

For a while, the staff of the Paris paper lived in a luxurious hotel. The army moved them out when a circulation man arrived home from an all-night party just as a general, who also lived there, was going to work. The general might have passed it off if the circulation man hadn't leered at him, hiccuped and remarked, "High time you were up."

Before the staff was kicked out—and wound up in barracks in which the staffers refused to sleep as long as they could find cots enough to bed down in the editorial offices—two of its officers staged an epic feud.

Bob Moora, the news editor and a first lieutenant, had taken issue with the proffered opinions of Rader Winget, a former Associated Press man who as a captain was in charge of the paper's communications—four telephones, a teletype, and two radios. Finally, their argument reached such a stage that they sat down one night in the lobby of the hotel and started describing what should be done to the others.

"Moora, if I had a knife, I'd cut out your heart!" declared Winget with feeling.

"Well, get a knife," replied Moora.

Apparently both of them got to thinking over their threats before they went to work the next day, and Moora came into the office toting a 45-caliber automatic in a holster, which he slapped down on the desk with a flourish.

Someone went looking for Winget, to tell him that Moora was going to plug him if he entered the editorial offices, and found the communications officer upstairs beside the teletype, grimly grinding an edge to a vicious-looking fighting knife.

Neither of them got hurt, chiefly because Moora never went near the communications room and Winget didn't come to the city room, and after a while they both got tired of carrying around their weapons and quit.

Moora's resentment of criticism of the editorial office by an outsider was only a logical outcome of the first line of defense set up against the army by the staffers when the paper was young. From the first day, the Desk and with it the city room staff had fought against the dictation of news policies by people who were not professional newsmen.

Eventually, the attitude of the Desk and the staff became reflexive: An order from the army which in any way, according to our thinking, jeopardized our ability to exercise our best news judgment brought an automatic "No," and after that we'd see what we could do to defend the "no." The whole thing certainly was at odds with all military precedent, but so was the very paper. The army ordered publication of a good, honest, daily newspaper within the army's framework. That was the job handed us, just as other soldiers were given the tasks of shooting rifles or flying planes (although some of us did those things too).

It happened that in addition to being the task assigned us by the army, the publication of a good, honest, daily newspaper also was the thing we could do best and that a good many of us had been doing for most of our working lives.

Eventually, not only the brass connected with the paper but a good share of the ETO command realized that here was a collection of professional people doing a highly professional job far better than it ever could be ordered done, and they were helpful about it. Aside from Dwight Eisenhower, two men in high commands were among the best friends the paper had. They were the late Morrow Krum, a professional newsman who became a colonel and chief public relations officer for the European Theater, and the late Lieutenant General Frank Andrews, who succeeded General Eisenhower in command of the theater when "Ike" went to Africa in the fall of 1942.

Half a dozen times when some colonel or general along the line started throwing the weight of his brass around the *Stars and Stripes* pages, the corporal who then was city editor went to Morrow Krum for help. They'd talk it over, and if it looked to Krum as if he could help, he'd take the corporal in to tell General Andrews about it; and the brass-throwing would cease.

One night the paper was waiting for an official announcement on some policy or other affecting the troops in the ETO, and it was unaccountably held up. The Desk phoned Colonel Krum, and asked if we could get the story before our 11 P.M. deadline. Colonel Krum said he'd try. Eleven o'clock came and passed, and no story, but during the early morning hours it was released, and the British papers in the morning had the story and we didn't. At 10 A.M., the phone rang in the apartment shared by the two men on the Desk.

"Morning. It's Old Man Krum. Guess we're on the top of

your unpopularity list for the way that story was released, but there'll be another one up tonight that we'll make sure you get."

Which from a colonel to a corporal was all right.

When, several months later, the plane carrying Morrow Krum and Frank Andrews crashed in Iceland and hurled them both to their death, *S&S* lost a pair of good friends. There was never another theater PRO who'd call up as Old Man So-and-so and be sorry for something he couldn't help anyway.

The public relations officers—and their generals—of the Eighth and Ninth air forces were our friends, and we liked to feel it was not just because the paper could do things for them. The two air forces were doing all the fighting that was to be done in the ETO before June 6, 1944. The land war hadn't crossed the English Channel, and it was the bomber crews and the fighter pilots who made war news. Sometimes their problems of morale, especially in the early days when American losses frequently were fantastically high, maybe as much as 30 per cent a mission now and then, must have made the air force public relations officers want to ask *The Stars and Stripes* to slant the day's air story this way or that, to play up this battered bomber group or this scattered fighter group. But they held the belief that the army newspaper was trying to do an honest job, and they never asked. Hal Leyshon, a veteran newsman who was a major and public relations executive for the Eighth Air Force, summed it up this way: "If what we're fighting for, the so-called system of freedom, is right and should win out, then the honest telling of the news, which is an integral part of that system, isn't going to hurt us in the long run."

Despite the lack of official pressure for certain stories or particular treatment, the job the paper did on the air was such as to bring from Major General Frederick Anderson, commander of the Eighth Bomber Command, which was sending the heavies out to Europe every flying day, a letter expressing thanks for the accurate, authoritative stories of the air war and declaring that "between the *Stars and Stripes* story of one day's combat against the Luftwaffe and the results of the bombing on the next mission there is a very real and positive connection."

That was enough for *The Stars and Stripes;* if the kids who were flying out to German skies were benefited by our self-imposed task of battling short sighted persons in order to maintain an honest newspaper (for every "must" story of somebody's special service band playing somewhere there was that much less room for the story of a kid in a warplane), then we would battle and damn the regulations.

Ensley Llewellyn fitted right in with the conditions which made *S&S* for so long the Air Forces' newspaper. He was an old airman, himself, the staff learned. We first heard about his aerial background the night of February 27, 1943, when Andy Rooney came back from the second Air Force mission against a target in Germany.

The office had decided that if we were to cover the war in the air, we couldn't do it from a desk. To be accurate and knowing, some of the staff had to fly with the big bombers. That was a fair assignment in the days when a combat crewman's useful life was figured at a maximum of fifteen missions, but Andy wanted the first crack at the job and went.

Andy came back from his first mission, on which Bob Post of the New York *Times* also flew and was lost in action, and entered the office in usual Rooney fashion: he came into the noisy city room panting and red in the face.

"Made it," he gasped, sinking into a chair breathless.

"What?" asked the man on the desk.

"Held my breath all the way from Charing Cross subway station to Blackfriars," Rooney panted. "Been trying for a month."

Ensley Llewellyn walked into the office just as Rooney finished speaking. He shouted when he saw Andy: "Hey! Good work, Rooney. Glad to see you back. Heh heh. Come along for a cup of tea and tell me about it. Want to hear."

Over a cup of tea in the old *Times* cafeteria, where you frequently looked up to see a rat snatching a crust off the floor and racing for a hole in the ancient woodwork, the major asked, "Well, how was it?"

"Oh, all right," Andy began. "We flew—"

"Bomb at about four miles, don't you?" broke in Llewellyn. Rooney said yes they had and . . .

"Wish I could have gone with you," EML said, banging the table and shaking his head. "You fellows don't know it, but I helped to set the world altitude record for Flying Fortresses, and I'd like to have been there today. Of course, in the early days, when I was flying, the Fortress was a new thing, very secret. But we set out one morning from a field near Tacoma. War Department sent me along to take pictures and broadcast, so they'd have a record right up to the last minute if anything went wrong.

"Well, we took off and I focused my camera on a bush in a fence row. Got higher and I focused on a tree, but right off I was switching to a whole clump of trees. We were climbing! First thing I knew I was focusing on a lake. Needed something bigger as we climbed. Finally, we got so high—set the world's altitude record of 46,600 feet—that I had to focus my camera on a mountain and I was half afraid the next thing would be the edge of the sea!"

The major took a gulp of tea, and one of the circle of staffers drawn around to hear Andy's story of the raid started to ask a question.

"Great airplane, though," the major continued enthusiastically. "Used one to fly an expedition I was with into the Arctic Circle. We dropped by parachute from the bomber and set up a camp. Lived there for nearly six months. Land of the Midnight Sun, you know; studied weather conditions. Had pretty nearly nothing but blubber to eat toward the end, and by the time I got back to the States my system was so used to blubber that it seemed I couldn't get enough of it. Had a terrible time getting used to civilized food again."

The major drank the last of his tea and shoved his chair back from the circle of staffers. No one else moved. The major made a lunge for the sixpenny check.

"No, sir," heh-hehed the major, "this one is on me. Well, you certainly had a time, Rooney. Good work, my boy. Sounds exciting."

He strode off whistling, "Off we go into the wild blue yonder . . ."

The cafeteria at the *Times* was about the only place in the whole building, except the composing room and possibly his own narrow little office down the hall from the editorial rooms, where an officer in charge of *The Stars and Stripes* ever dared whistle. Whistling being verboten in the editorial rooms, to staffers, visitors and officers alike.

The no-whistling rule was particularly hard on Max Gilstrap.

In civilian life, Max had been a Forest Ranger, then a lecturer on wild life and finally a reporter-columnist on the *Christian Science Monitor*. As a sort of newspaperman, however, Max continued his lectures about the flora and fauna of the United States, illuminating his lectures with remarkably good bird call imitations. He brought his whistling into the army, where he became a censor and a captain, then was transferred to *The Stars and Stripes* as an executive editor, the official title of the administrative officers in charge of the various editions.

But before he joined the paper, back in his censor days, Max was assigned once a week to come to *The Stars and Stripes* in London to check the night's paper for matters of military security. Through his first five or six visits to the paper, the good-natured, kindly Gilstrap found the staff a little reserved in their acceptance of him; suspicious of brass per se, the staffers were inclined to feel that his air of camaraderie, which was genuine, was maybe a little faked. In addition, he was called down by the Desk for whistling in the city room, and that made Max cautious, but finally the boys began to talk to him and he made up his mind he had been accepted.

That night as Moora, Ben Price and Hutton finished making up the paper in page form and turned away from the composing room, they took up their usual practice of whistling "The Road to the Isles" as they strode through the long corridors, because with the paper gone to bed everyone naturally felt better and whistling would disturb no one.

At the first note, Max Gilstrap checked off the last story on a page proof and raced across the composing room after the whistling trio. He pushed himself between Price and Moora, threw his arms around their shoulders and with a beaming smile said:

"Say, fellows, that's great whistling. But do you know the 'Washington Post March'?"

The three newsmen looked surprised.

"Because if you do we could have a great time. I know the oboe part and we could have a quartet."

And all the way down the winding halls, Max whistled happily the oboe part to the "Washington Post March."

Max Gilstrap's whistle got him into a lot of grief with the staff, eventually. Not serious grief, from the staff's viewpoint, but Max seemed unhappy about it.

During the Battle of the Bulge, in the winter of 1944-45, the paper opened a new edition in Liége, Belgium, better to service troops in the First and Ninth armies on the northern flank of the Bulge. Max was appointed administrative officer there (the charts always said executive editor, but everyone concerned understood). The appointment came just after Ensley Llewellyn had been booted upstairs because he squabbled with the Special and Information Services of the SOS, which tried to inject orientation into the news columns of the paper. Arthur A. Goodfriend, a major who had some newspaper and considerable advertising experience in civilian life and who was chief of the orientation and propaganda section of the army, was named to be officer in charge and editor in chief of all *The Stars and Stripes.* The staff, while acknowledging his honesty of purpose, challenged Goodfriend's right to try and tell the fighting men how to think through the medium of a paper the Joes had come to trust, and, consequently, everything Goodfriend did for a long time was wrong in the minds of the old staffers. Goodfriend appointed Gilstrap, which automatically made Max non grata with the city room.

Max went to Liége, lived through the buzz bombs with the boys and tried manfully to erase the curse of the Goodfriend appointment by being a regular guy. Eventually, the boys readmitted him to their circle as such, but not before he was tagged with the most damning phrase any brass ever got from *S&S.*

Every time someone from the outside, usually a newspaperman from one of the civilian papers, would ask a staffer what Gilstrap's background was, the answer was the same:

"He used to be bird call editor of the *Christian Science Monitor.*"

It was a beautifully wicked damnation. There was just enough truth in it—Max wrote the nature lore and wild life column and had lectured and sounded off with his bird call imitations—to make it pretty tough denying. After two or three weeks of that, it got so that people would be introduced to Gilstrap and then say, "Oh, yes, you're the chap who used to be bird call editor of the *Christian Science Monitor.*"

It was murder.

Max would say, no, he wasn't the bird call editor, honest he wasn't. But he was too honest to deny he could and did imitate wild birds, that he had written a nature lore column, and the more he denied the more people nodded their heads and said mmm-mmm.

Finally, Max asked the boys to lay off, and because he'd been very much of a help in organizing the Liége edition, never complaining and never attempting to find refuge in the brass on his shoulders, the boys did lay off; but Max spoiled the whole thing by blurting out the very next afternoon, as they sat around the office listening to the buzz bombs crash around the city, that the whistling business was "a lot of fun."

"I worked out one whistle while I was living out in the woods," Max told the boys, "that you couldn't hear if you stood next to me, but you could hear it perfectly plainly a half mile away.

"Called it the 'silent half-mile whistle.' "

Max never understood the mad laughter that elicited.

### SAID A PVT. TO A PRINCESS–NOT MUCH

**Brass Wall Comes Between the S&S And Royalty**

By Gene Graff
Stars and Stripes Staff Writer

AN EICHTH BOMBER STATION, July 7—Princess Elizabeth and I inspected some U.S. bomber stations yesterday—and some other people were there too, including her mother and father and a general or so and innumerable aides and custodians.

That last part is important, because somehow they seemed to put a crimp in conversation between a princess and a private, although there were no barriers to conversation with King George VI and Queen Elizabeth themselves.

Shortly after the royal party arrived, Princess Elizabeth was standing in front of a fireplace, looking at pictures on the wall and occasionally glancing around to study faces in the room.

#### She Enjoys Visit

"Is this your first visit to an American camp?" I began.

"Yes, it is," she replied, "and I'm enjoying it very much."

"Do you ever have American guests at your hou . . . er, palace?"

"Not unless they attend state parties or are being decorated by Daddy," the pretty but shyly aloof young lady replied. "If you mean at my parties and dances, Americans never have attended—probably only because I haven't met any."

Further conversation was interrupted when a British general edged purposefully between us.

Three hours and two Fortress stations later, Princess Elizabeth was eating ice cream with three American Red Cross girls while the rest of the party was off discussing aeronautic engineering or something. It looked like a perfect opportunity to renew the brief acquaintance.

"Does a trip like this tire you?" was the open shot. One eye noticed that Elizabeth was a pretty girl with effervescent expression. The other, of course, was peeled for interrupting officials.

"I've been enjoying myself too much to think of being tired," the Princess said with a pleasant smile. "You know, I don't get to meet so many people very often.

"Those hats [canvas caps with jockeylike brims worn by ground crews] certainly are funny. And I never realized a pilot has to wear so much equipment."

She seemed to grow more cordial at this point and was about to volunteer further information about the mental ponderings of a princess when an RAF uniform, housing a wing commander, loomed.

Someday here I'd like to complete the interview, because there won't be any princesses in Chicago. But when the RAF officer politely asked, "How long have you been in England?" I launched a strategic withdrawal in nothing flat.

That was the way a general opened his dissertation the day I breezed by without saluting. And what I heard then convinced me I didn't want to hear it again.

# SOLDIERS FIRST

MOST NEWSPAPERS have a dictator somewhere in their organization, and most newspapers get hundreds of complaints; but maybe no newspaper ever before was in the absurd position of having half its complaining readers in a position to dictate. *The Stars and Stripes* was.

*The Stars and Stripes* was an army organization and had for its reading public virtually no one but army personnel, and most of its readers were, by virtue of their army rank, in a position they had always hoped for in relation with their morning paper back home: here, by God! was a newspaper they could tell.

In Paris, in the early days just after the liberation of August 25, 1944, a colonel who was vaguely associated with the paper well up toward the top of the Special Service pyramid, walked into the editorial rooms in the Paris *Herald* building. In his hand he carried a slip of paper carefully lettered in pencil:

IKE'S ARMY STRIKES!

"I want you to use this as your headline tomorrow," the colonel said as he handed the paper to Bob Moora, who was running the paper at the time. "I have an appointment with Eisenhower tomorrow, and I'd like to have that on his desk when I come in."

It was not run, of course. Patiently Bob Moora explained to the colonel that (1) Ike's armies had not struck that particular day, (2) headlines were tailored to fit a story according to size type used, and (3) even if Ike's armies had struck and even if the headline had fitted the story he wanted to use, that would not be the head which would appear in the paper.

Just after the German breakthrough in the Ardennes had been stopped, the colonel (by then a brigadier general) came into the office bubbling over with enthusiasm for a new idea he had just conceived.

The general, it appeared, had been mightily impressed with the Hearst slogans back home which advised readers to "Buy American" and with the catch phrases such as "Buy Bonds" which some civilian papers were using. He felt he had a humdinger of an idea for helping to end the war with a slogan. Again he had printed his message clearly on a slip of paper, and he slid it across the desk to the man making up the paper:

HAVE YOU KILLED YOUR GERMAN TODAY?

That phrase, he thought, should be inserted at every break between stories in the *Stars and Stripes* columns.

"I think we ought to use that as little fillers in the paper," the general said. "That would make it easy to fill up those little holes in the columns. A good catchy saying, something to help win the war and show the fighting men we're behind them.

"Have you killed your German today?"

The general stood waiting, smiling happily at his contribution to the paper. No one in the editorial room had a word to say.

There were men there who had flown more bomber missions than most bomber crewmen ever got to live through, who had spent more time in foxholes than a good many generals had spent in the ETO; the staff looked around at them to see what they thought, and it was all right there in their silence.

The thing was so absurd it was funny, but a little too bitter to be as funny as the usual dictates of the brass-shouldered readers. It might have been interesting to watch the reaction to its use by the couple million service troops, up to five hundred miles behind the front, who read the paper daily; not to mention the reactions of the combat troops who were killing Germans just so they themselves could stay alive.

Finally, the general left the room, trying pretty hard to smile.

The only idea of his which he pressed to a point that officers in charge and the enlisted editors could no longer refuse was one he professed to have one day after reading the New York *Times*.

The *Times,* he noted, ran on its front page a brief digest of the day's important events, listed as a sort of table of contents. The *Times,* he reasoned, was a great newspaper, and because he felt a paternal interest in *The Stars and Stripes,* he wanted that, too, to be a great newspaper. He sent down an order that we should run about six inches of type daily containing a digest of the news. That was about what the *Times* used.

*The Stars and Stripes* then was only a four-pager, and was at its most voluminous a brief digest of selected news sent us by the *S&S* bureau in New York and a specially culled glossary of news from the press agency wires. We tried to explain to the man that such a feature would be a digest of a digest, but he insisted and it ran, for a while.

The staff always marveled that we weren't ordered to run the Macy advertisements the *Times* used, too, and that was always good for a laugh until we finally did run a full-page advertisement disguised as a plug for a war bond contest.

As the war in Europe drew to a close, and it appeared that some of the staff would stay with the paper for occupational troops and some others would head for the Pacific to put the old *S&S* out there, the powers-that-be ordered a War Bond Contest sponsored by *The Stars and Stripes* to aid the Seventh War Bond Drive. It was a good idea, would help interest the troops in salting away a little of their spare cash. The idea was to write an essay on one's postwar future and plans and send it to *S&S,* where it would be judged on merit alone for one of ten Chevrolet automobiles, postwar models, or one of ten Frigidaires, postwar models.

How General Motors Corporation came into the picture with two of its products that way no one ever explained. In the Paris edition, most nearly under the eye of Lieutenant Colonel Arthur Goodfriend and Lieutenant Colonel Frederick L. Eldridge, who were officers in charge at the time, the first announcement of the contest used the term "Chevrolet" or "Frigidaire" half a dozen times, advertising priceless to General Motors. Some of the other papers used the trade names, too. The Nice-Marseille edition refused point-blank, figuring it was immoral and anyway citing an old order from the brass which chewed at one editor for having referred to Coca-Colas in the news columns. There was no comeback from Paris, but the following week, *The Stars and Stripes* in all editions except Nice-Marseille carried a full page purporting to be contest rules and terms that featured huge engravings of Chevrolet sedans and Frigidaire iceboxes, and labeled them as such.

Finally, the editor of the Nice-Marseilles edition was summoned to Paris to explain his failure to comply with a direct order to print the contest stories verbatim, including trade names and engravings of the prizes. He was threatened with court-martial if he continued his refusal. With enough combat credit to be discharged from the army within a few months, the editor figured what the hell and said he'd print them.

It was cowardly, but by that time *The Stars and Stripes* had become in fact just what the thousands of special service officers, public relations officers and various other noncombatants always had wanted it to be: an organ of the army completely under their control. The fighting in Europe had stopped, and the combat men no longer were combat men, so the paper's staff had no moral grounds on which to fall back.

Despite hundreds of little incidents similar to, if not quite so absurd at all times, as these, the paper's staff in London and on the Continent only once seriously considered refusing to put out the night's paper.

*The Stars and Stripes,* along with the rest of the world's newspapers, had printed a sensational story from the Mediterranean Theater of Operations. The story was negative, an official denial by the army of a statement printed in Drew Pearson's Washington column that Lieutenant General George S. Patton Jr. had struck an American private recuperating from combat fatigue in an army base hospital. Every correspondent in the Mediterranean had known about the incident, but all of them withheld publication at the request of the high command there, who feared the news would hurt army morale. It probably would have. However, Pearson broke the story in the States, and there was nothing for the army to do except make some kind of statement. The army denied it, and *The Stars and Stripes* put down what the army said. There was no complaint about that.

The following day, Associated Press copy came into the office with an army confession that the denial was a phony. Patton had slapped the convalescent soldier because he thought he was goldbricking. Patton, the army said, was sorry. Then the details of the story came out, whether or no the army wished. It was learned that all the correspondents in Africa knew of the story but were prevented from filing it. The whole thing made reading for every soldier in the army. A high-ranking officer was in plenty of trouble. That was readable news for soldiers at any time.

The Desk of the London *Stars and Stripes*—the only paper in the ETO, then—let the story run, shoved it to the composing room and had it in type slated for a prominent spot on page one.

About six o'clock that evening, the officer in charge of the paper dropped in, as he occasionally did. He took one look at the Patton story and said it would not be run.

"That's an order!"

The phrase became famous around the office.

The staff, however, was faced with a problem. If the people who put out the paper quit right then and there, no *Stars and Stripes* would be on the streets or at the mess lines in the morning; but a mutiny such as that would bring serious charges and courts-martial against all concerned in the strike. Some of the staff felt that if we refused to put the paper out minus the Patton story the incident would get so much publicity at home that it would be associated with the Patton case and the thing would be too hot for the army to grab and handle in army fashion.

The more sober soldiers of the staff voted against a strike in protest of brass censorship, and reluctantly the paper was put to bed, without the full story of the Patton incident.

The following day, the staff regretted that it had turned yellow. No *Stars and Stripes* man could walk through Grosvenor Square, where most of the army headquarters were housed, without getting a knowing smile from everyone who recognized him as a staffer.

"Missed a little story this morning, didn't you?"

Everyone bought the London dailies in addition to *The Stars and Stripes,* so the Patton story was no secret. Even on the most remote airfields there were half a dozen copies of the British papers, with the Patton story splashed around page one in glee. The fact that we had run the original denial and then no more made the paper look that much more like a dictated army house organ.

The third day after the story broke, there was another story stating that Eisenhower had officially reprimanded Patton. The

London papers threw it across their pages. We did not run it, again by order.

All those little incidents served to underline the army's original and oft-repeated pronunciamento: soldiers first and newspapermen second. Sometimes we'd escape that a little bit, but sooner or later a khaki sleeve whose upper end terminated in brass reached out and grabbed.

Sometimes, though, it worked out in just as ridiculous a fashion as it should have.

Back in New York, *Yank* was putting its staff through daily foot drill under the watchful eye of several hundred service command colonels and an occasional *Life* photographer. It was an absurd waste of time, but the army felt that the uniform alone was not enough, and eventually in the spit and polish London Base Command sector *The Stars and Stripes* was caught in a net of the same weaving.

The brass sent down an order, and it was pasted up on the iron pipe in the city room which was the bulletin board. What the order had said in effect was that once a week, at 7 A.M. on Fridays, the *Stars and Stripes* staff would be soldiers first, and after that they could go publish a newspaper.

That made Friday night's paper maybe the best in the week. Compounded of resentment at what was palpable nonsense and discouragement that the army could thrust itself upon us when it wished, the paper on Friday night was tossed together with an air that usually made it the brightest, most sparkling of the week, even though we didn't realize it at the time. But how that mob of individualists, nonconformists, quasi-sedentary newspapermen suffered before they could leave the inspection and drill behind and sneak off to the sanctuary of the smelly old offices in the *Times!*

In London, the staff had been for some time on a very special and desirable status known as "per diem." That meant simply that the staffers received from the army one pound ($4, more or less) each day for food and quarters, and the individuals could live and eat where they pleased but got no further help from the army. It was a sensible arrangement, and it didn't take a day more than nine months of arguing with the army to bring it about. The staff worked until one o'clock most mornings, and it was obviously impractical to put men who didn't get up for breakfast in a barracks.

On per diem, then, the staff was scattered all over London, and some even found themselves suburban homes an hour's train ride from the city. They may have been the army's only enlisted commuters. It's just about certain that the staff was composed of the only men who went to the army in taxicabs.

In order to reach a given point for an inspection at seven it was necessary for the men, who had gone to bed only a few hours earlier after putting out the paper, to get up any time from 5:30 on to 6:45, depending on how far they lived from the little alley back of the business office off Grosvenor Square.

Ordinarily, on normal workdays, they were not a bad-looking lot of soldiers, or newspapermen. They were neatly dressed, for the most part; some shoes were shined and pants and blouses almost always well pressed. A couple of them, particularly two who lived just off Belgrave Square in the heart of London's most fashionably dignified district, had valets and were very well pressed.

But on inspection days they were a crummy-looking lot.

Low shoes, oxfords, could not be worn. We had to wear high army shoes, and none of us had worn the army shoes enough to get the grease out of them so they would take a polish.

Neat and clean khaki shirts had to be replaced by regulation army issue heavy wool shirts, which, being worn once a week, always had collars which pointed in all directions except down.

Stripes, which privates first class and corporals found they did much better without when trying to be newspapermen, had to be worn, which meant a quick sewing job by probably the least proficient group of seamsters in the world.

In short, it took a different wardrobe to stand an inspection.

Thus once a week, from musty barracks bags stored in polished London apartment house closets, staffers pulled out the necessary pieces of soldier suit. In the early hours of the morning they rubbed a little metal polish on tarnished buttons and scrubbed quickly for a few minutes, leaving speckled evidence of their work in the form of metal polish all over the fronts of their clothes and scraping just enough tarnish from the brass to make the high spots gleam and the dull spots duller. They clambered into the strange garb and raced for their apartment house doors where early-rising porters waited with already summoned taxicabs. The taxi drivers, under rush orders, careened through the bleak streets for the soldier's appointment with the army.

En route the staffers tugged and twisted at their army suits to try to look like soldiers. Since their ideas were liable to differ from the army's, the results, what with the unfamiliar garb and all, were not startlingly spectacular, and it was a motley crew that drew up in front of the alley, paid off the taximen in the fashion of newspapermen and then turned around to be soldiers.

(There were two or three taxicab drivers who used to wait especially at staffers' homes on Friday mornings so they could take them to the army and then hang around and watch the fun.)

The inspections in London never were discontinued, although most other staffs of the far-flung chain managed to defeat them. Maybe the Algiers staff did the best job. Bob Neville, then a captain, was officer in charge when he got an order to "get the men in top physical shape; make them soldiers." Bob ordered calisthenics. He said he would lead the exercises himself.

The first morning, the staff piled into a courtyard in the early African sun, and waited for tall, balding, quiet Neville, whose carriage and demeanor are the antithesis of athletics. Finally, he came out, with big Bill Estoff, who, nearing forty, was a long way from being a physical training director. Bill did better in the Kasbah.

"All right, men," began Neville, "we'll start this program today and keep at it as long as the army demands. First exercise, the deep knee bend, with hands outstretched. To the count, ready.

"One . . . two . . ."

Bob never got past two, which was the count at which the group squatted on haunches, arms outstretched. He couldn't reach three, because try as he would Bob couldn't get himself back upright.

"Estoff, fergawdsake take over. I can't get up."

The Algiers staff rolled on the courtyard in laughter, but it wasn't funny to Bill.

"Take over, hell! I couldn't get that far down, myself!"

The Algiers edition found that morning exercises were better marked down on the schedule as performed, and nothing further said.

* * *

Not so in London, under Ensley Llewellyn's soldierly eye. The editorial staff might look like something from an Abbott and Costello movie and the business office staff as bad, but E. M. Llewellyn was in his glory. As he told us, he'd been a National Guardsman for years, he'd soldiered in China and a lot of other places, and Friday morning was the time when he could appear in resplendent pink riding breeches, gleaming boots and O happy day white gloves. White gloves in Hyde Park on Friday morning, where are you now?

"Attention! Forward march!" My stumbling friends, stragglers from a lesser Coxie's army, where do you march?

"Hup two three four" and yesterday two of you were sweaty in the subzero altitude as the Focke-Wulfs made their run on the Flying Fortresses, but today you will make noises like soldiers in the rear echelons.

"Names will be taken." That was the way the weekly notice of inspection always ended. If we were not this or that, and if we looked the way we had looked the last week, "names will be taken." We were always threatened, ominously, that "anyone who does not meet inspection standards will have his name taken." The staff took it just as it was said, and that is all the procedure ever amounted to, except it was a hell of a lot of fun to stand there and tell Acting First Sergeant Corporal Ham Whitman (on *The Stars and Stripes* it seemed the most natural thing in the world that the first sergeant really was a corporal; naturally) your name and rank when you knew all the time that he knew it, and Llewellyn, who was listening, knew it, and anyway all three of you knew that nothing would ever come of the affair anyway.

Sometimes the sun was bright on those inspection mornings, and the buttons didn't look too bad. On cloudy days, though, there wasn't any shine to them and John Cornish Wilkinson, the South Carolina captain who was the paper's writer of jokes, shone less than any, so he led the punishment detachment.

That was a euphemism of the sort in which *S&S* abounded; egregiously First Sergeant Corporal Whitman. Colonel Llewellyn would look at buttons, decide they didn't shine, and with a gesture of his white gloves snarl "Hammersmith." When the inspection was done and Whitman had saluted very properly and said that all were "present or accounted for," the punishment detachment set out.

Wilkinson tried not to laugh and to sound very stern at the same time and failed miserably on both counts as he ordered the "following men to fall out, fall in and march to Hammersmith," some five miles across London.

For five or maybe six steps, as the unshining group started out from the alley, they were as close to being in step as a *Stars and Stripes* unit ever was. After that, it was the usual straggling, meandering, abstract group of staffers. Before they had gone a mile, all remembered they had eaten no breakfast. The course to Hammersmith led them past the Hans Crescent American Red Cross Club in Knightsbridge, well, anyway, pretty close to it, a matter of five or six blocks out of the way, and a detour and coffee and doughnuts made a break in the punishment. Second, by cutting then over to Kensington, the detachment could pass the Milestone Red Cross Club, and have more coffee and doughnuts. The fact that these side marches totaled an extra couple of miles made no difference; the staffers got breakfast and, without mentioning it specifically, there was a feeling that thus the army was finally and almost completely foiled in its effort to control them.

By the time they left the Milestone Club, it was almost ten o'clock in the morning, and that was the hour at which the pubs opened. The punishment march, led by the captain with the dull buttons and the coffee stains on his necktie, at 10 A.M. was turned into a rout.

There was one thing about it, though. Driven by some strange sense of honor—which could make itself unaccountably compatible with the detours and the pub stops—every man every time managed to stagger the complete distance to Hammersmith before boarding a bus for home and a return to his ordinary, noninspection-day clothes in which he again was a fairly presentable citizen soldier. None of the marchers, however, ever were able to come to work that day. Even if they never felt better in their lives, part of the staff which marched to Hammersmith couldn't come to work; the whole office decided that if people who marched to Hammersmith didn't work it would show Llewellyn the whole thing was a farce.

In the course of three years of such inspections, all that gesture ever managed to accomplish was to make more work for those who didn't do the Hammersmith march. Pressed about the advisability of that type of punishment for men who had a day's work to do, Llewellyn told a harrowing tale of his experiences on the march, with which the staff hardly could argue.

"I remember when I was a private in the National Guard in Washington," the colonel related.

"We had a mean first sergeant, and sometimes for no reason at all he'd wake us at three or four in the morning, line us up in our underwear and start us on the run over a ten-mile road of sharp stones in our bare feet. Our bare feet, mind you.

"If I could stand that, I guess you fellows ought to be able to take a little walk to Hammersmith—*with* shoes on."

There were what Llewellyn came to describe as "incidents" every time there was an inspection, and especially when inspection was followed by military drill or instruction.

There were bound to be incidents when the colonel tried to teach the copy-desk men and the reporters about grenade throwing and used for his grenades six wooden practice grenades which the previous week had been painted yellow, green, pink and blue by the *Yank* staff artists for an Easter cover illustration.

But when it was decided to introduce sports into the curriculum—because it was so hard to keep the staffers from going over the hill to a pub or their flats when they were out "drilling" in spacious Hyde Park—the army was completely routed. It was decided to let the staff play baseball. We were all going to get healthy, including the ones who jumped with the paratroops, the gunners and the reporters who were combat infantrymen. They were to be made tough and healthy by a sports program, playing baseball.

The colonel played in the first game, sprinted for second base in the second inning and was tossed some five feet in the air when Private Charley Kiley blocked the base line. In the next game, the colonel said he would umpire. There came one of those arguments that no army, no order, no martial discipline is ever going to prevent when American kids play baseball. The colonel called a man safe who was out by ten feet, and the side in the field descended on him screaming "robber," "blind man," and no "sir" about it, either. The colonel tried to argue. He was shouted down. He drew in his breath and roared.

"The man is safe. That's AN ORDER!"

Even Jim King, the civilian reporter for the Associated Press who showed up at inspections some mornings because he liked to play baseball so well, decided that was enough, and baseball as a body builder for the staff of *S&S* became a thing with grenade throwing.

For all of the fact that he was the direct cause of our unhappiness on inspection days, the colonel brightened them too. From his stories, we knew he had soldiered all over the world, had led a life of one adventurous incident after the other; and if the allegedly military training (for the rewrite men and copy editors and other such martial characters) that followed the inspection became dull, the colonel always was good for a story of a campaign or an exploit somewhere to brighten the day and sort of illustrate the point involved. There were the lectures on chemical warfare, for example.

(Bob Moora used to do a pretty good job of brightening military lectures, too. Assigned "Chemical Warfare" as a topic on which to lecture to the staff, Moora began his talk to a leering staff with "Chemical warfare is making war with chemicals.")

Llewellyn, however, chose to tell some forty members of the business and editorial staffs about his campaigns in the Chinese hinterlands, when he was "fighting the Japs long before our war. They used gas on us, and a lot of people were killed, died in terrible agony, but just because I'd attended lectures such as this and knew what to do, I got out of it with hospitalization. Twice, that happened.

"So, you fellows, pay attention, especially you people from down at the editorial offices who always are so sure you know more than anyone else. Maybe you'll get gassed."

He brushed his white-gloved hands together briskly, said "dismissed" with an arch smile so that we never knew whether we were being ribbed or not, and strode away.

One man, however, really stopped the good colonel cold at an inspection. That was Herb Palmer, the wild-eyed 49-year-old second lieutenant, who was supposed to be an administrative officer in some vague way connected with the business office but who always turned up aboard some bomber that limped back to base on two engines, wandered off with a bunch of Joes and stayed with them when they turned out to be paratroops on their way to jump in Holland, or something equally odd.

Colonel Llewellyn started a "Wear-Your-ETO-Ribbon" campaign. The ribbon was a multicolored affair denoting service in the European Theater of Operations. It seemed kind of hard to understand why anyone should wear, while stationed in the European Theater of Operations, a ribbon which denoted that one was stationed in the European Theater of Operations. The staff figured you could almost certainly tell a fellow was stationed in the ETO by looking at him if you both happened to be standing in the ETO at the time, and that maybe the ribbon was just a little superfluous.

Llewellyn's first trouble came when one staffer, a corporal, showed up wearing an ETO ribbon on each shoulder as officer's shoulder bars. Palmer came to inspection with no ribbon at all. "You," shouted Llewellyn, "are a fine officer. Next week, you wear every ribbon you're entitled to." He glanced down quickly at his own pre-Pearl Harbor and ETO ribbons.

Next week, Palmer stood in line, shining, polished and pressed beyond anyone's belief. Llewellyn strode down the ranks and came to the grayhaired second lieutenant, looked at his shoes, his buttons, his chest, his hat, and then jerked his gaze swiftly back to the chest in a magnificent double-take. On Palmer's left chest there were almost three full rows of ribbons, every one of them strange to the colonel's eye except the ETO affair.

"What," demanded the colonel, suspecting broad satire, "is the meaning of this? What are those . . . those ribbons?"

In his softest tones, Palmer answered:

"This is the ETO ribbon, sir. After that, all from the last war, except the last ribbon, are the British Military Cross, the French Légion d'Honneur, the French Croix de Guerre, with palm, the 1915-16 campaign ribbon of the British Expeditionary Forces and the Mons Star, the 1918 victory ribbon and the Medal of Honor of the Spanish Loyalists."

Llewellyn was taken aback but hung on grimly to his original assumption that it was a hoax. "And how did you get them?" he asked.

"I've been fighting Germans for some time, sir," Palmer answered, still in the soft tones, and the colonel moved on.

The colonel, or any other brass connected with the paper and its staff, should have known better than to try to make the privates and corporals and sergeants of *The Stars and Stripes* look like privates and corporals and sergeants of the army.

To begin with, Private Joe Blow, for instance, of the Umteenth Messkit Repair Company, has his life all laid out for him by the army. Private Blow's job is repairing messkits and the army, maybe starting somewhere along with Baron von Steuben's time, has concerned itself with the best way to repair messkits. The army has written a little book which says how messkits will be repaired and since that is Private Blow's only job the army does not have much trouble ordering Private Blow to repair a messkit, as per Field Manual B1005. When he is through work Private Blow has to dig ditches to maintain the camp in which he lives, or the station; he has to make beds or wash dishes or pick up cigarette butts or do whatever it is the army says he should be doing according to some other field manual.

But neither Baron von Steuben nor the army ever had the temerity to try to write a field manual about publishing a newspaper within the army. In World War I there had been the first *Stars and Stripes.* Then it was published hand to mouth just as the newspapermen connected with it figured out it should be. So with the paper of World War II. And still unlike Private Joe Blow, of the messkit repair battalion, *The Stars and Stripes* lacked, in addition to an army manual on how to publish a newspaper, any other directive from the army on what to do with its spare time, because *Stars and Stripes* staffers didn't live in camps or stations and anyway most of them at one time or another had a maid or a valet to pick up cigarette butts or make the beds.

Somehow, maybe just because that happened to be the format for everything the paper touched, even the personal military records of *Stars and Stripes* personnel were in arrears, mixed up, wrong or lost. A careful check of the hundreds of personal service records which moved their mysterious ways through the *Stars and Stripes* administrative files, once failed to reveal a single set of records complete and correct. Bill Esthoff, the sergeant from Syracuse, went to Africa from a job as circulation director in Scotland, and for seven months went without pay until his service records finally arrived at Casablanca. Bill got paid regularly through 1943, but then he went to Italy and in turn to Southern France and Paris, and it was April, 1945, before Bill collected his soldier's pay for June of 1944.

There was one master sergeant on the editorial staff who transferred to the American Army from the Canadian forces. In three years on *The Stars and Stripes,* the sergeant never received a single hour of the basic military training through which, in theory—and in practice everywhere else in the army—all soldiers must pass. As a matter of fact, that same sergeant spent three years as an American soldier without receiving a single medical inoculation, and if there are twelve million Americans in the forces, then there are twelve million Americans that will swear it's impossible. He never signed a payroll but collected his pay every month through some alchemy the process of which he never dared question; never had a set of dog tags, never heard an official reading of the Articles of War, and never had a physical inspection, all army procedures normally as automatic as putting on a khaki suit in the morning.

The staffers who went out to the war from the editorial offices in search of news carried with them their own particular little aura of disorder. One staffer, who flew twice as many missions with the bombers as the average gunner lived through and in the course of doing it became more or less of an authority on aerial gunnery, did so although he never had gone to the gunnery school through which all aerial gunners must pass, never had taken the rigid physical examination without which the army insists no one may fly. There were three *Stars and Stripes* men who jumped into action with the paratroopers, but of the three only one went to any sort of a jump school in preparation for the task; the other two simply arrived more or less unannounced at airborne units, climbed into the carrier planes with the paratroops and made their first jumps in combat. Neither of those two, incidentally, could have passed a physical examination for a third-grade rear echelon typist's job.

No fighting unit, nor its officers, ever seemed to be disturbed about the impromptu, unheralded fashion in which *Stars and Stripes* men arrived, gathered their news of the fighting and departed. The only objections came from the rear echelon organization.

Four hundred miles behind the war, surrounded by files in a Paris office the Wehrmacht administrative section once had used, sat an officer and his staff whose duty it was to see that travel orders sending one *Stars and Stripes* man or another out to do this job or another were properly filed. Because they loathed argument with the paper-work people, the staffers tried once in a while to go to the places their orders specified but frequently it was impossible.

For one thing, a corporal or a sergeant might know of an impending military move of such consequence and importance that few outside the General Staff knew about it. The staffer then informed the city editor—who was maybe a corporal or a sergeant, too—and received an assignment to cover the offensive or retreat or whatever it was.

At that point any attempt to carry out the prescribed routine of having the Army issue travel orders became absurd. Obviously the corporal or sergeant could not reveal to some captain or major what only the General Staff and the reporter knew about. So the staffer took off on his own without orders, got his story, brought it back and received the inevitable reprimand from the administrative people. Sometimes the reprimand was hard to take.

In the blow that opened the way for the Allied armies into the heart of Germany, two army newspapermen jumped with the paratroops. One of them was a *Stars and Stripes* man. The other was Corporal Bob Krell of Brooklyn, New York, young, laughing, curlyheaded combat correspondent for *Yank*. The airborne attack was prepared in highest secrecy and neither Krell nor the *Stars and Stripes* man for a moment considered informing the travel order people so that they could carry out the assignment in "proper" military fashion.

The troopers jumped and started fighting when they hit the ground in the midst of Germany's last-ditch line of resistance. The two army reporters fought with them. In the heart of a black German forest, Bob Krell and three troopers fought a German tank holding up the attack. German infantry surrounded the four Americans, killed them just before help arrived.

The *Stars and Stripes* reporter, who had had his share of the fighting not far away, heard about Krell's death a day later when he went to divisional headquarters to radio out the story of the airborne assault. Some two weeks afterward, wearied from the swift attack that had cut deep into the Reich, the *Stars and Stripes* man got back to Paris. After he turned in some other stories and pictures, he was ordered to report to the officer who sat in the midst of the filing cabinets of the administrative section.

"What's all this paratroop business?" demanded the officer. "I see in the paper you've been away, but you didn't have any travel order."

"Look," replied the reporter, who was too tired to worry about discourtesy, "I'm sure you can understand how secret that thing was—I couldn't come around here and tell you about it."

"You could be court-martialed for going off without orders like that," growled the officer. He sighed and slumped in his chair. He had been working very hard seeing that the papers were filed in all the service records for which it was his army task to care. "That Corporal Krell from *Yank* got killed, I see," the officer continued in an even wearier tone. "Now we've got all his papers to try and straighten up because he wasn't on travel orders when he got killed. You can't understand the amount of trouble that causes us."

The *Stars and Stripes* reporter looked at the officer a long time. The reporter had a notoriously bad temper, but at length he shook his head slowly, turned and walked out of the office and an hour later was in a transport plane going back up to the front. He didn't have any orders, either.

The *Stars and Stripes* records, travel orders, inoculations and pay were confused and mixed up but their state of military disorder never approached the nightmare quality of *Stars and Stripes* uniforms.

In the course of searching for news in infantry regiments, bomber squadrons, engineer battalions, the occasional navy warship—to say nothing of the same sources of news in other Allied forces—the staffers collected and wore a pretty motley assortment of clothing, footgear and headwear. Had a quartermaster supply officer stood in the doorway of the *Stars and Stripes* office at Liége or Frankfurt, Paris or Rome for three days, and tried to identify those who entered as to rank or branch of service, he probably would have become crazy enough to get a job on *The Stars and Stripes.* As a matter of fact he probably would not have been able to tell which of the United Nations they represented.

Russ Jones, the quiet combat correspondent from St. Paul, used to cover fighting in the First Army sector in garb that began at the bottom with high leather Ranger boots over British Army gray woolen sox, and proceeded upward through a pair of American officer's field pants, a civilian shirt, a German captain's wide leather belt, a vest of Russian rabbitskins, which had been captured by the German Army and then captured by Jones at the fall of Aachen, a Canadian infantryman's olive-green battle jacket, and an American Air Corps flying cap. (On his monthly two-day sojourn in Paris—during which he wore clothes of the same type—Jones stayed at the apartment of a White Russian refugee who before the invasion had been the group leader of a Maquis unit composed entirely of Spanish Loyalists.)

Sometimes, if there happened to be enough resemblance to an American Army uniform to arouse suspicion, *Stars and Stripes* men were stopped in rear echelon areas by well and correctly dressed rear echelon officers, and required to explain, unless they they could evade the issue, why they were improperly dressed. There was at least one red-faced old Colonel Blimp of a colonel who probably never again asked a strange enlisted man about his uniform after the fine Parisian spring day on which he stopped a *Stars and Stripes* reporter and demanded an explanation for military undress.

The reporter was a sergeant, although there were no visible signs of the rank. He wore a pair of paratroop boots. Tucked into them were ordinary khaki trousers. His shirt was a dark-green officer's shirt. Over it was an Air Corps leather flying jacket. The shirt was open at the neck and the flying jacket was open all the way down. The pants were grease and mud spattered and unpressed, the shoes hadn't been shined at all during the month of combat from which he had returned not ten minutes earlier. Most heinous crime of all, however, was the sergeant's lack of a hat. For no reason that any quartermaster can explain, the army insists that its soldiers wear hats of one prescribed sort or another. The sergeant wore none. Finally, as he strode up the Champs-Elysées, there was the sergeant's walk, a loping, hands-in-pockets bounce which any parade ground would have opened and swallowed.

Hurrying along the Champs at the same time was the multitude of vari-clad Allied personnel, soldiers, sailors, marines, airmen, civilians, and here and there, it will be noted because it became important to the colonel and the sergeant, the odd American civilian technician. Throughout the war large American manufacturers of munitions and weapons sent civilian representatives abroad to advise in the use of their products such as airplanes, guns, tanks, trucks. The technicians were apart from army discipline although they wore, when they wished, a uniform which was khaki and which at least vaguely resembled a soldier's uniform. It was among that crowd, then, that the sergeant jounced along.

The red-faced colonel was coming the other way. He was two steps past the sergeant before a magnificent double-take relayed to his colonel's brain that, by God, that must have been a soldier!

He whirled and roared, "Soldier!"

Naturally the sergeant didn't think that was meant for him. He walked on. Purple gilled, the colonel leaped after him, grabbed him by the arm.

"Give me your name, rank and organization!" roared the officer.

The sergeant didn't need a double-take to recognize the situation or the cause of it, nor to classify the colonel.

The corner of his eye saw the vari-uniformed crowd passing by—the soldiers, the sailors, the civilians, the American technicians. Before the colonel's question had scarcely thundered away, the *Stars and Stripes* man turned on a beaming Rotary-Club-welcome variety of smile, thrust out his right hand. In an elaborately overcordial gesture, he banged the colonel on the shoulder with his left hand and said in a tone as jovial as the colonel's had been thunderous:

"Why, I'm Thomas—Bert Thomas—of Republic Aviation! Who're you?"

The colonel sagged through every inch of his jowls, flustered out a rank and some sort of name, limply and hurriedly pumped the sergeant-reporter's proffered hand, turned and fled into the vari-uniformed anonymity of the Paris crowd.

The "soldiers first" dictum was injected into *The Stars and Stripes* regularly. And the staff failed miserably, as a matter of candid reporting, to offer any reasonable grounds as to why it should not be comprised first of soldiers and secondly of newspapermen, until almost the end of the war against Germany. The staff fought the dictum, and fairly successfully; but never, even to itself, on any other grounds other than that it was too much bother to dress up like a soldier.

Just before the first elements of *The Stars and Stripes* began to drift out toward the Pacific, however, one staff member was cornered by a brigadier general. The general went through the usual routine about the staff man's state of improper dress and concluded with the timeworn cliché which the army had been addressing to *The Stars and Stripes* from the day the paper was founded about "You know, just because you men are putting out a newspaper you don't want to forget you're still in the army. You're soldiers first and newspapermen second."

The staff man's reply was inspired, but it should have been made three years earlier (although all concerned would have missed a lot of fun if the army had taken up his suggestion).

"General, in all seriousness," the staffer asked, "since we put out a newspaper and that's the only thing we do in the army, why shouldn't the *Stars and Stripes* staff be newspapermen first and soldiers second?"

To a brigadier general the query was fantastic, and he said as much. He said it for quite a while and finally concluded "and anyway, you're in the army and you are soldiers, so naturally you have to be soldiers first."

There wasn't any argument about that; there couldn't be. When the army pulled that line on the staffer he was licked. But let the army get one inch over onto civilian ground . . .

There was a time a staff writer, a corporal then, was going from London by train to a West England port. Rail transportation in England, as in America, is divided into classes corresponding roughly to Pullmans and day coaches. The British army officers ride first class; all other ranks ride third, or day-coach, class. (There is no second class for some reason no one ever seems to have inquired about.) The American Army in England sent its officers and all enlisted men above the rank of buck sergeant by first-class coach; buck sergeants and below traveled third class.

The *Stars and Stripes* corporal, as did all other *Stars and Stripes* men, bought a first-class ticket out of his own pocket, boarded the train and entered a first-class compartment. Already in the six-person compartment were four civilians and a British major. The major, who was reading the *Times,* looked up as the American soldier entered the compartment. He saw no insignia of rank on the soldier's sleeves, and in his best old-school-tie manner demanded:

"See heah, soldiah, aren't you out of bounds? This is a first-class carriage."

The *Stars and Stripes* man looked at the major stonily, sat down and began to read the morning's issue of *The Stars and Stripes.* The major rustled his *Times* fiercely, leaned forward and barked:

"I say, have you a first-class ticket?"

The reporter eyed the major again. "I think that is a matter between me and my conductor."

British Army enlisted men do not talk to British majors in that fashion even if the major has asked a stupid, impertinent and irrelevant question. The major leaped to his feet, threw open the door of the compartment, disappeared down the corridor. Almost immediately he returned grasping the train conductor firmly by the arm.

At the compartment doorway the major pointed a stern finger at the *Stars and Stripes* man. "This man's a common soldiah—he has no right in heah."

The expression on the conductor's face obviously said, "Yank, I don't like it but regulations, you know," but the trainman's voice asked, "Do you have a first-class ticket?"

The American stood up and on the British major's countenance there grew one of those righteous expressions of vindicated virtue as the Yank, apparently flustered, began to search with mounting haste through his pockets, fumbling in his billfold with apparently nervous fingers, even searching the seat on which he had sat. The major's cup was almost running over when the Yank snapped his fingers, reached in his watch pocket and produced a first-class ticket. The conductor accepted it, was more polite than necessary in thanking the American soldier as he punched and returned the ticket, and left. The *Stars and Stripes* soldier sat down and resumed reading. The major, his day spoiled, returned to his *Times* with the air of a man who has found the worm in the apple. The major's face was red, and after staring stonily at his paper for long minutes during which it might have been a snicker that came from behind the papers the civilians in the compartment held, the major drew from his pocket a package of Players cigarettes, selected one, tapped it impatiently on his wrist watch, lighted it.

Quietly the reporter across from him stood up, and slipped

out into the corridor. In the second car ahead he found the conductor. In a few moments they were back. The reporter's countenance was serene as he entered the compartment door, silently pointed a reproving finger at the smoking major, then lifted his gaze and finger toward the sign on the window, which said: "No Smoking—Five Pounds Penalty."

There was joy in the conductor's eyes as he said to the major, "I shall have to have your name and rank and service number, sir. You will be notified when to appear in court by the proper authorities."

The reporter sat with downcast and modestly flickering eyelids as the major left the compartment, tried vainly to argue his way clear in the corridor, and finally surrendered his name, rank and service number.

# FOXHOLES AND FEATHERBEDS

THE staff always seemed to find themselves a pretty good place to live. Even the combat reporters, who slept with the men at the front in what the folks at home seem to think are always foxholes, usually managed to do pretty well. Just like any other combat man in the line, the staffers slept in abandoned houses in the battle zone when they could, in barns which weren't too obviously the targets of enemy fire, and sometimes best of all in one of the elaborate dugouts which Jerry somehow always found the time to construct and live in until we chased him out.

Most *Stars and Stripes* reporters carried their shelter halves (one half of a pup tent, which the army provides each soldier as his home in the field) all the way from their first London apartments to the requisitioned German castle just outside Frankfurt, which was their eventual halting place on the Continent, and after that some of them toted the same shelter halves across the Pacific to the war against the Japs.

But there is no known record of a *Stars and Stripes* man unfolding one of those pup tents and hammering the little wooden pins into the ground. And more frequently than abandoned German dugouts, barns, houses or foxholes, the average *Stars and Stripes* place of temporary abode was apt to be pretty luxurious, as luxuries go in the war. Russ Jones, one of our First Army correspondents, summed it up:

"There's no use in wearing a hairshirt if you can find a linen one, and if I'm getting shot at all day, by God! I'm gonna sleep as well as I can, eat as well as I can, come night."

Most of the boys did.

## THE 4TH—IN A FOXHOLE, BUT A MEMORY

WITH THE U.S. FORCES IN NORMANDY, July 3—When he got back to base there was a message. The office wanted a piece on how the guys were spending the Fourth of July in France. He went down to the side of the road and sat on a broken German antitank-gun frame, and he said, "What the hell."

Five or maybe ten years ago most of these guys would have gone to bed this third of July night knowing they could get up tomorrow and wake up the neighborhood with maybe a couple of cannon crackers, and put torpedoes on the trolley car rails, and tomorrow night there'd be Roman candles all over the sky, and you could watch skyrockets arc over the town.

Tonight they crawl into foxholes, if there is time, and tomorrow they'll do the same things they've been doing today, and some guy, dirty with Norman mud and red-eyed with waiting for this Fourth of July, will make a sour crack about firecrackers before he picks up his M-1 for the day.

The fellow by the roadside said he didn't know of anybody who would have the gall to write a story contrasting that.

A long time ago, it was a day for picnics, and the kids turned the ice-cream freezer in the morning and spilled rock salt all over the back porch. Grandma made a batch of cake, with frosting, and there were pickles from last fall's cucumbers, and fresh raspberries on the ice cream. You met a lot of aunts and uncles you only saw once a year, and one of your cousins was a wise guy who took apart some 12-gauge shotgun shells to get the powder and fire it from an iron pipe.

Tomorrow these guys'll have good old Ks again, or maybe in some places they'll get some Cs. Not an awful lot of ice cream in a can of Cs, nor cake in the brown wax paper marked K.

The fellow by the side of the road figured anything anyone had to say about that was better unsaid.

Sometimes there would be a concert in the octagonal wooden bandstand in the square on the afternoon of the Fourth, and then one at night too, with the council spending 20 bucks or so on giant sparklers that were pale in the early dusk and only bright when it was almost time for you to go home.

The fellow by the side of the road scratched a beard grown three days long and listened to 155 hows, banging away toward the lines beyond Carentan, and thought of the noise of screaming meemies, which the infantry had heard up ahead for two days without end. If the infantry people thought about bandstands in a town back there somewhere, all right; but how could anyone else try to tell the contrast between those other days and what the infantry was having this day before the National Holiday?

In the little towns behind the lines in Normandy people were planning with the officers of the civil affairs sections to observe the Fourth of July, and they asked would the Americans in turn help them ten days later to celebrate Bastille Day. In Grandcamp-les-Bains and Isigny, in Cherbourg and at the bomb-scarred communities all along the beaches there would be little speeches by M. le Maire, who knows a few words of English, or maybe the civil-affairs guy would translate. There would be fresh wreaths placed in the cemeteries where civilians and American soldiers were buried side by side.

There would be maybe—it wasn't certain—a simple parade or two, and all across the Norman countryside which had been freed the Tricolor would fly with the Stars and Stripes. To the east, it would fly with the Union Jack and the Maple Leaf.

The fellow got up from the roadside, caught a ride in a jeep and went back to the beach. He talked to an MP, Ed La Due, who came from Utica, in upstate New York, where they have Fourth of July picnics, and there are bandstands in the town squares.

Ed said "Yeah, a hell of a way to spend the Fourth of July." He watched a truckload of sober-faced men going toward the place where the sound of guns had been in the air all day. "I bet a lot of guys will make a lot of speeches over on the other side."

The fellow said, "Yeah," and walked away, down to a stretch of sandy shore where there was no work. At a place where the Channel had left a scum of oil on the sand there was a piece of khaki webbing, part of a soldier's gear. There was salt rime on it and the water had run the purple of an indelibly penciled ASN into a blur.

The fellow looked at it awhile and remembered he had to do a piece on the Fourth of July, which used to be a holiday a long time ago.

In Paris, the editorial men lived in a comfortable little hotel on the Rue du Faubourg Saint-Honoré (where the landlady wanted only one thing from the American soldiers: a pair of rubber overshoes). In Rennes, the French city at the base of the Breton peninsula, the small staff lived in a lovely little brick house hurriedly abandoned by the Gestapo chief for the entire area when the Yanks came down the road. Possibly it was in Nice, the Riviera rest area for American troops, that the *Stars and Stripes* staff achieved its ultimate collective luxury. There, as soon as the fighting swept through the town and settled down to a war of position some five miles to the east, toward the Italian frontier, the staffers ensconced themselves in the Francia Hotel, a room to each man, a bathroom to every three, a maid to every three, a civilian chef who once had run the kitchen of the Sands Point Bath Club on Long Island, one waitress to every six soldiers, and the whole fabulously expensive Blue Coast of the Mediterranean in which to swim and sunbathe. All the soldiers not on leave but working in the Riviera district were billeted in regular army fashion. The *Stars and Stripes* staff got its own hotel when the area commander asked one thing of them: a good newspaper published on time every morning and delivered daily at six A.M. beneath the door of every combat man spending a seven-day leave in Nice. Most of the staff on the Nice edition had had a plethora of combat and came to work there because *The Stars and Stripes* felt that its own combat men deserved a rest as well as anyone else —although they might as well publish a paper as long as they were there.

It was of living quarters in London, however, that most of the staff thought with fondest memories. Perhaps that was because most of the original staffers lived there for more than two years.

The fondest and most fantastic memory by far was the home—and it was literally that—which Charlie Kiley, Ben Price and Charlie White rented in Beckingham, Kent, some thirty miles outside London. It was a fine old house with four bedrooms upstairs, good kitchen, baths, and a backyard complete with flower garden and grape arbors. At a time when a good many officers in London below the grade of general were living two to a hotel room, Sergeant Kiley, Sergeant Price and Private White decided they wanted "a country home." They had lived a year in metropolitan London—one enlisted man to an apartment—and figured there was no reason why two sergeants and a private shouldn't commute to work.

The three hired a maid and a gardener and at one time started with elaborate plans to grow their own vegetables on their day off. (On the other six days of the week, the gardener grew the vegetables, and eventually on the seventh as well.) Their Beckingham house quickly became a *Stars and Stripes* rest home all by itself.

The life of the country gentleman had one drawback: train fare to and from London was one shilling thruppence each way, about twenty-five cents. Kiley, who settled easily into the temporary luxury of country life despite an occasional interruption to go off and spend a month training with the Commandos or a couple of days flying with the bombers, somehow always had his train fare. Ben Price nearly always had it.

With Charles Charles Worthington Worthington White, however, it was different. (When you start remembering stories about Charlie White, you invariably find yourself thinking of the stubby, myopic, 39-year-old ex-Canadian tank trooper in the manner by which he always referred to himself: Charles Charles Worthington Worthington White, which wasn't exactly the way his name went, but it should have.) Charles Charles occasionally had enough money to get out to the country, and if he didn't he usually could borrow enough. There were times, however, when he couldn't make it back to work.

After one long night in the Lamb and Lark, old Trooper White climbed aboard a train at the Blackfriars Station with just enough money to buy a one-way ticket. He got home all right, but neither Price nor Kiley came home that night and the following morning White called the office and in a lonesome voice told the Desk he was stranded.

"I got no money to come to work on," he said plaintively.

It was a busy day for the Desk and Charlie got little help and no satisfaction, so he hung up and looked around for another source of funds. There was Vicky, the maid the three had hired when they rented the house. Charles waited until she arrived for work at one o'clock and approached her. It was a delicate job because Vicky received some three pounds—about twelve dollars—a week. Also, she hadn't been paid for seven weeks.

Charles, however, made the touch successfully and walked out of the house with two pounds tucked in his pocket. The railroad station was a mile from the house and while Charles Charles may have started out with good intentions of catching the 2:12 to town, he never got past the Running Horse Tavern.

Anyway, by pub-closing time, Charles Charles had drunk his way through all of Vicky's two pounds, and he returned dolefully to Cheesecake Manor, so called because Ben Price, who made the arrangements for renting it, was the paper's art editor.

At home, Charles went to bed and when he awoke the next morning, almost noon, Price and Kiley had been home and gone and the trooper was right back where he had started the day before—no money to get to the office. Vicky arrived for work, and calling to her from his bed Charlie asked her to go down to the Running Horse and bring back a few pints of ale. To pay for the brew he gave her an odd four pennies from his pocket and told her to trade in some empty ale bottles under the kitchen sink. He gave her his musette bag to carry the bottles, because Vicky wasn't very strong. When the maid returned with the ale, Charles Charles drank it, felt better and began to wonder, once more, about getting to work. Once again he was penniless and thirty miles from his place of business.

Finally, as a last resort—Charles was afraid to call the Desk—he telephoned the local taxi driver with whom he had done a small amount of business and a considerable amount of drinking, and asked him to pick him up in front of the house in ten minutes. The cabby, happy to have business at an unexpected hour of the day, drove around promptly. Charles Charles stepped out of the house and briskly walked up to the cab.

Charles turned the handle to open the door, paused, seemed to consider something that had just struck him and swung his head toward the cabby, who was waiting for the destination.

"Say," Charlie said confidentially, "uh . . . I wonder if you've got a couple of quid you could let me have?"

The driver apologetically explained that, because he had just come out of the hospital where he had been ill for two weeks, as Charlie knew, he only had ten shillings to his name. With a wife and kids at home that wasn't much money for a man.

Charlie said yes he reckoned as how it wasn't very much at that, but somehow he would make out with it all right. The cabby reluctantly and with a sort of mesmerized expression turned over the last ten shillings he had. Charlie shoved the note into his pocket, stepped into the cab and said, "Well, let's stop first at the Running Horse."

The cab drew up at the tavern and, since Charles was a kind and generous American, he did not merely hop out and say "Charge it" to the cabby, nor was he going to spoil a beautiful friendship by tipping the man with money he had borrowed from him; he invited the driver inside to have a drink.

The two drank several mild-and-bitters. In the course of the second glass, there was some discussion during which Charles Charles allowed he thought it was immoral for one man to treat another with money he had borrowed, so he had the publican of the Running Horse put it on the cuff.

At half past six, the cabby took Charles back to Cheesecake Manor, put him to bed, and went off presumably a sadder but wiser man. The next morning, Ben and Kiley, on orders from the Desk, got Charlie out of bed, made him eat breakfast, and marched him off to the train and a return to work. It is poetically just that Kiley made Charles Charles buy all three tickets with the borrowed ten shillings.

Most of the staff on the original paper in London couldn't see their way clear to commute daily between the office and England's flowered coastal counties. For one thing, some of them were going from one training area to another across the United Kingdom, getting ready for D day and writing about the combat men who were getting ready for D day, and they weren't in London enough to make it worth while. So the rest of the staffers satisfied themselves with apartments of varying degrees of luxury in metropolitan London. Especially those men who were flying, or were getting ready for the eventual invasion of Europe, had some conscience about living so well while the rest of the army was in the field or at best billeted in requisitioned and thoroughly "army" houses in cities. But since they were doing their job, and since those who flew possibly might not come back to the paper or London or anything else in any given week, most of them figured that Russ Jones was right about the hairshirt business and settled themselves to utilizing what luxury their sergeant or corporal or private's pay, the per diem allowance for subsistence of £1 a day which the army paid, and their newspaperman's wits could provide.

Maybe Dick Wilbur, former *Yale News* editor (who continually had navy lieutenant commanders dropping in on him) had the best apartment of the lot. Dick, who came to the paper from a hospital unit as a sergeant, rented the spacious flat belonging to a lieutenant general in the British Army. Dick shared the flat with Ray Lee and George Maskin, and from time to time with half a dozen other staffers. In the eight months they occupied the British general's flat, they could never get the gas and electricity bill straightened out with his Majesty's gas and electric organization, and had it not been for the rank of the apartment's rightful occupant, the trio would have finished their tour there by candle-light. Eventually the lieutenant general returned from the wars, North Africa probably, and took over his flat again. Wilbur, Maskin and Lee had to find new quarters. They complained bitterly for some time that they came down in the social scale when they eventually could find vacant only the flat of a British Army lieutenant colonel, who also was away to the wars.

One *Stars and Stripes* staffer lived in one of the most exclusive buildings in one of the most exclusive neighborhoods of London—just off staid, dignified, old Belgrave Square. The sergeant took great delight in the doorbell name plates at his apartment house. The chaste engraving above the polished bells read: "Lady Simonds, Apt. 4," "Colonel the Hon. H. Ramsey Tweeding, Apt. 6," "Mme. the Princess Raspigliosi, Apt. 2," etc. Under Apt. 12, just below a brigadier general, was a finely engraved card bearing the sergeant's name and the carefully spelled-out preface, "Sergeant."

The sergeant, in addition to living in a pretty exclusive kind of foxhole, belonged to the near-by expensive and exclusive Cadogan Gardens Tennis Club, whose membership was by invitation and limited to four hundred. Saturday mornings the sergeant used to put on an old pair of army pants and play a few sets of tennis, usually with a major who worked in the Censor's Office, and once in a while with one of the British Foreign Office's bright young men whose great-something-or-other had been one of the founders of the club. One afternoon, the sergeant went back to his apartment after a strenuous tennis game and was luxuriating in his bath when the very valet-looking sort of valet, whom the sergeant shared with a lieutenant from *The Stars and Stripes* who had moved to the same house, knocked on his door and handed him a card from a Czechoslovakian diplomat who lived downstairs.

The Czech, the valet explained, wished to discuss world affairs with an American newspaperman and had, seeing the sergeant's valet in the hallway, sent his card with an informal but quite correct verbal invitation to a drink. Without giving much thought to it, the *Stars and Stripes* man took a pencil and scribbled a brief note on the reverse side of the Czech's card saying he would drop down someday when he had more time, maybe Saturday.

The valet returned the card to the foreign diplomat in his

flat below and the sergeant heard nothing more of the incident for several weeks, when the lieutenant from the same building, Earl Mazo, who became one of the paper's top combat correspondents despite the handicap of being an officer, eventually revealed what happened when the Czech received back his card.

The Czech diplomat, after the fashion of his country's etiquette and oblivious to the fact that Americans normally do not put too much store in the varied forms of Old World courtesy, considered the return of his card and the writing and faint trace of bath water and soap on it the equivalent of a slap in the face with a pair of gloves. In the valet's presence (which the Yank later decided was a breach of etiquette itself on the Czech's part), the Czech speculated aloud to a friend who was visiting him on whether he should challenge "the rude American" to a duel.

Frake, the valet (who, incidentally, never got over an involuntary frown when his American employers called him Bill and suggested he have a drink or maybe breakfast with them), got off a discreet cough in the direction of the Czech and said:

"I trust you will forgive me, sir, for intruding in a gentleman's affair, but unless I am mistaken, were you to demand satisfaction from the sergeant, his would be the choice of weapons, and the last time a gentleman demanded satisfaction from the sergeant—it has gone this far several times—the sergeant's choice was 50-caliber machine guns at a hundred yards, and the sergeant in addition to being a newspaperman is possibly the foremost gunner in the American Air Forces."

The Czech's desire for satisfaction, according to the story which Mazo gleaned from the valet, forthwith was dispelled.

Considering the number of bombs which struck London at one time or another while the staff was spread through the city, it was surprising that no one was ever bombed out. Russ Jones, G. K. Hodenfield and Herbie Schneider used to live with Robin Duff, the BBC news broadcaster, in his comfortable St. James flat, and Robin's home was hit shortly after D day by a buzz bomb, but the three staffers had moved out by that time. Other than that, the Clifford's Inn home which Joe Fleming, Ben Price and Charlie Kiley inhabited before and after Cheesecake Manor had the closest call. Clifford's Inn was a fine apartment house on Fetter Lane, just a few steps from Fleet Street and close to the *Times* office.

During February, 1944, the Germans made their last effort to bomb London on anything like a major scale with conventional airplanes. Fleming and Price were sitting around in the apartment about two o'clock in the morning talking when the sirens sounded. Planes droned overhead and within thirty seconds there was a crash in the open courtyard behind Clifford's Inn and through the blackout curtain came a brilliant burning light.

They put out the lights in the apartment and threw back the curtains. Outside white-hot lumps of phosphorus were burning where a basket of German incendiary bombs had scattered over the area and nestling neatly in the open-topped, towerlike spire of St. Martin's-in-the-Fields Church was an incendiary fire which shone magnificently through the unbroken stained-glass windows.

Price ran downstairs, grabbed an ax from a stupefied fireman and ran out into Fleet Street prepared to chop almost anything down rather than see it burn. After a few minutes of putting out lumps of the inflammable metal which had fallen on Fleet Street's block-wood surface, he ran back upstairs and helped the fireman on top of Clifford's Inn itself, where several of the small basket incendiaries had fallen.

Back downstairs again, he found that by now the church behind the apartment house was flaming. The pews inside had been set on fire by burning timbers that had fallen from the ignited roof. Across the street Benny (who, it must be remembered, was the paper's picture editor) saw that the Acme photographic agency offices were burning.

At that point a little man in clerical robe came running up to him.

"Don't you see? St. Martin's-in-the-Field is burning! St. Martin's-in-the-Field is burning!"

There was no doubt about that, but every man to his own in times of stress. Benny turned from the beseeching pastor of the church and made for the picture agency building, ax in hand.

While both the picture agency building and St. Martin's-in-the-Field were almost completely gutted, the Clifford's Inn home of the staffers was almost untouched.

By the time Benny finished his night's work with the ax he had endeared himself to every last one of the proud members of London's Fire Department present by comparing them unfavorably, constantly, and in loud oaths, while he worked, with the fire department in Des Moines, Iowa.

After the invasion, when both Price and Kiley eventually returned to work in the New York office of *The Stars and Stripes* for a few months, Joe Fleming took over the flat by himself.

Kiley had always attended to the little working details of the apartment, while Ben took care of lease problems with the agency that handled the place.

When they left, Joe was helpless. He found he did not know where to send laundry or to whom he should pay the monthly bill. When the three of them lived there together they often ate a late meal in the flat at night and for that purpose they had one loaf of bread delivered to the door every other day. The maid used to bring the bread in and put it on the shelf in the flat's little kitchen.

Joe never ate there himself and after a week alone he noticed that there was an extraordinary lot of bread on the kitchen table but gave it little thought until later that same week.

There was no longer room for the bread on the shelf and the maid was putting the accumulating loaves on the stove.

Joe realized that something should be done. Charlie Kiley had made the bread arrangement and Joe had no idea where to go to have the order stopped. He left a note in the apartment but no one seemed to read it and Joe, of course, was always at work by the time the bread man came in the afternoon.

Finally, when the loaves had overflowed the tiny kitchen and were beginning to pile up in the luxuriously furnished living room of the flat, the maid, who hated to see the food wasted, decided to have the order stopped until Joe ate the bread he already had.

Openhanded hospitality and a sort of communal share-the-bed policy were integral parts of *The Stars and Stripes'* feather-bed-and-foxhole existence. Especially if you didn't have a bed and could get into the bed of someone who did have one before they did, it was a share-the-bed policy.

The two *Stars and Stripes* men who lived in the exclusive apartment house with all the colonels and ladies and so on ran open house for the Air Force crews with whom they occasionally flew. When the members of the crews came into London on a 48-hour pass they knew that above the doors of flats 8 and 12 at 17 Chesham Place there always would be the keys, that inside the flats there might or might not be someone before them, that in any case they always would be welcome. The gunners and pilots came, drank whatever there was in the liquor closet, ate whatever there was in the icebox, gave Frake the valet their clothes to be pressed, and at the end of their leaves went back to base. (It was no particular philanthropy that prompted the open house; bomber crews especially, but all other kinds of combat soldiers as well, welcomed *Stars and Stripes* reporters and invariably went out of their way to see that the staffers were as well fed as possible, had the choice beds or corner in a hayloft or captured German dugout, as the case might be.)

In addition, there came to the sergeant's flat in Chesham Place periodic visitations of burly, tough Canadian infantrymen with whom the sergeant had served before America got into the war, and even long after the sergeant had gone to the Continent with the invasion, succeeding occupants of flat 12 were apt to be awakened at two or three o'clock in the morning by a thunderous pounding on the door and a strident Canadian voice demanding:

"Slim, you old son of a bitch, since when did you lock your door?"

The *Stars and Stripes* staffers all had patchwork uniforms but certainly the military wardrobe of those correspondents who made their apartments available to the soldiers with whom they flew or fought were the strangest. Canadians, airmen, and infantrymen alike would find themselves wearing soiled shirts after their first day on pass in London, would select from the bureau clean shirts, socks, underwear, and meticulously put their soiled linen in the dirty-clothes basket. The next time the size-15-neck staff writer got home and went to put on a clean shirt he was equally liable to find himself putting on a size 16 garment that had an Air Force patch on the shoulder, or a collarless Canadian shirt of the variety his Majesty's troops were required to wear beneath their buttoned-up battle blouses. It was just barely better than no shirt at all.

But it was at the Hotel Haussmann, a couple of blocks away from the Arc de Triomphe in Paris, that the *Stars and Stripes* mob reached its ultimate in a communal existence. The *S&Sers*

at the Haussmann eventually got to be communal with a Frenchman, who kept two motorcycles in his bathroom, a beautiful brunette Latvian accordion teacher, a professional French prostitute, who claimed that during the Occupation she had done her bit of sabotage by deliberately contracting gonorrhea and spreading it in fulsome fashion among unsuspecting officers of the German Army.

When *The Stars and Stripes* established its main office in Paris, the staff was handed the comfortable little Saint-Honoré Hotel, which had been requisitioned by the army as its billet, and did very well until some rear echelon feather merchants decided that the hotel was much too luxurious for a bunch of "ordinary enlisted men" and *The Stars and Stripes* was assigned a barren army billet in an old series of lofts in the Champs-Elysées. It was a frigid, dirty building, and its furnishings consisted entirely of wooden bunks more or less covered with straw mattresses; which would have been all right if it were necessary, but it wasn't. The staff called the place "Pneumonia Manor" and as soon as the individual reporters, editors, and other hired hands could find a little capital or a little blonde, they moved out. Armed with their cigarette ration, whatever money the army offered, and whatever else they could find, most of the boys moved into cheap hotels near the office. Five packages of cigarettes was the standard week's rent.

The Hotel Haussmann became the most notorious unofficial *Stars and Stripes* billet. Although only six or seven of the staffers ever rented rooms at the Haussmann at the same time, almost everyone slept there sometime or other, occupying either the floor, extra army cots they brought along with them, or comfortable chairs. Bob Moora proudly hit the high point in sleeping arrangements when, bedless one night, he went through the darkened hotel jerking pillows from under the heads of already sleeping staffers, and then dumping the pillows into Ben Price's bathtub where he spent what he claimed was an exceedingly comfortable night until Ben, indignant in the morning because his had been the first pillow taken, awakened and turned on the water in the tub where Moora slept.

Most of the rooms in the Haussmann were double and one of the occupants, without warning the other, was likely to bring home two or three or four guests to spend the night.

Ben Price went to the hotel one night planning to sleep in a room shared by Joe Fleming and Gene Graff, the sports editor. Joe told Ben he could use his bed. Price walked into the room and saw a black-haired form already in the bed Fleming had promised him. Thinking it was some other staffer who beat him to the mattress, Benny tore the covers off the bed and loudly threatening mayhem, started to roll the occupant out onto the floor.

The sleeper woke, yanked himself free of Benny and stood up in bed, glaring. It was Billy Conn.

Graff had brought Conn home and given him Joe's bed. Benny smiled weakly, indicating he was really only kidding about the beating he had just threatened to hand out, and walked out of the room leaving the man who almost beat Joe Louis to sleep in peace.

Among the occupants of the Hotel Haussmann—that is, the normal citizens who slept in their own beds and paid the rent with money—was Gay Orloff, blonde, lovely Russo-American, one-time mistress of "Lucky" Luciano, the New York gangster.

Gay considered herself, eventually, one of the *Stars and Stripes* mob and, although she never had any amorous dealings with any of the staffers, she was as apt as any copyreader to sit on the edge of a bed until dawn arguing with staff men about the stories in the morning's paper they had brought home with them.

Jimmy Cannon, a latecomer to *The Stars and Stripes,* whose claim to fame on the paper lay in a masterful capacity for telling dialect stories, gave Gay a bad time one evening when he telephoned her at the hotel and whispered confidentially that he had just come from the States and had seen Luciano the gangster.

"Gay, he has a picture of you, a picture of you over the bed in his . . . his . . . that place up the river he's at now. He said did you need any money. I'll stop around tomorrow at three o'clock and see you. Right now I'm hot . . . these French dicks are on me."

The blonde Orloff never did find out the phone call was a hoax, and while Luciano may have continued to hold a place in her affections he had to share it with the *Stars and Stripes* man who jumped with the paratroopers for stories. Bob Capa, the *Life* photographer who also jumped with the paratroopers, sent to the *Stars and Stripes* office a negative of the soldier-correspondent in the paratroop uniform. Gay got hold of the negative, had it enlarged to maybe a quarter life-size, and hung it on her bedroom wall. She called the staffer her "pin-up boy" and certainly felt more kindly toward him than the professional prostitute in room 17, who also used to join the informal midnight discussions of the staffers.

The prostitute's name was Madeleine and she plied her hoarse-voiced trade between the Champs-Elysées and a dirty little side street hotel each afternoon. Her evenings she kept free for one of the *Stars and Stripes* editors with whom she was completely and, in her own lights, truly in love. (Let's call that particular editor Luigi, since that wasn't his name.)

Luigi didn't reciprocate Madeleine's love but he had a warped sort of affection for the little whore. Madeleine, who had thriftily saved tens of thousands of francs while spendthrift Germans were in Paris, eventually became a sort of unofficial banker to the perennially impoverished soldier-newspapermen, but the fine entente was shattered when Madeleine was unable to collect a loan she had made to a reporter who went back to the United States. Madeleine apparently felt she had avenged herself by coming to the *Stars and Stripes* office about seven o'clock one night, demanding to see "my luffer, zat Luigi, who have made me wiz baby, also zat journaliste who have made my sister wiz baby, zose peegs!"

The unabashed staffers simply threw Madeleine out and they should not have been surprised when they got back to the hotel that night and found every room rifled of cigarettes, which were the next week's rent, candy and every other thing barterable on the black market.

## SECRETS

EVERY TIME some major general from somewhere withheld a story from a *Stars and Stripes* man on the grounds that is was secret information, the staffer might be annoyed, but he could not help reflecting on the absurdity involved.

Because the paper was the army's paper, and because its staff members were in the army, and because from the very beginning the really big brass of the army opened all its files to the paper, and because *Stars and Stripes* men continually were moving across the theaters of war, because some of them went into action with the combat troops wherever the fighting was and knew at first hand far better than the major general what we were doing and how, there were few secrets which sooner or later were not unfolded to the soldier-reporters.

We never knew whether the German High Command's Intelligence Section tried, but if they didn't do everything within their power to plant a spy on the staff of *The Stars and Stripes* they weren't as smart as we knew they were. (Of course, it is possible they tried and succeeded and that one of the men who made *The Stars and Stripes* what it was originally was a German spy, who got on *The Stars and Stripes* and after a couple of weeks of looking around and seeing what the paper was and who the staffers were, decided there wasn't any use in trying to get his information back to the German High Command because the high command of no army as sensible and sane as the Wehrmacht ever would have believed the things that made up *The Stars and Stripes* and its people.)

Most of the secret stories that *The Stars and Stripes* knew and didn't print remained a secret because the military censors, whose word was ultimate with the army newspaper, just as it was with civilian newspapers, forbade their publication.

## NAZIS DID ATTEMPT TO BOMB NEW YORK—BUT FAILED

(The following story was written by a *Stars and Stripes* correspondent who was on TD with the paper's New York bureau in November. It was withheld by *The Stars and Stripes* until after Germany's defeat.)

by Andrew A. Rooney

A German attempt to bomb New York City was made last Election Day, Nov. 7, according to sources considered reliable.

The bomb, presumably a jet or rocket propelled projectile, was reported to have been launched from the deck of a German submarine lying off the Atlantic Coast. The attempt failed when the V bomb either fell short of New York or was shot down by fighter pilots alerted to watch for such projectiles.

Soldier operators at Mitchell Field said they detected the projectile on its course toward the city and determined that it dropped into the sea.

No confirmation or denial of the story was given by tight-lipped Mitchell Field G-2 officers to a *Stars and Stripes* reporter at the time. In Washington, on the following day, Nov. 8, high-ranking officials in the War Department refused to comment.

Later that day a joint statement was issued by the army and navy, warning the people along the Atlantic Coast that a German V-bomb attack on the United States "is entirely possible."

The official statement said that the robots might be launched from long-range bombers guided across the Atlantic by radio control from submarines.

Soon afterward strong fighter reinforcements were moved into the Atlantic Coastal Area.

Rear Admiral Jonas Ingram, soon after his appointment as commander in chief of the Atlantic fleet, told a press conference on Jan. 8 that "it is possible and probable the Germans will attempt to launch bombs against New York or Washington within the next 30 to 60 days."

He said the opinion was based on his own experience with the enemy and not on intelligence reports. He added, "There is no reason for anyone to become alarmed. Effective steps have been taken to meet this threat."

The same day the Navy Department said, "There is no more

reason now to believe Germany will attack with robot bombs than there was Nov. 7, 1944."

Public relations officials told the *Stars and Stripes* reporter that within a few hours after Ingram's statement there had been a rush for reservations by air and rail to get out of New York and Washington, and it was deemed advisable to issue a comforting statement.

Actually, the bombing incident has never been officially confirmed or denied.

Sometimes we didn't tell a story because its merits as news were not enough, in the opinion of the people of the Desk, to outweigh some harm it might have done to the soldiers' morale. We undoubtedly made mistakes on some of our self-imposed censorship, but they didn't happen because we weren't trying.

Maynard H. (Snuffy) Smith, a staff sergeant gunner in the Flying Fortress bomb group at Thurleigh, in East Anglia, was the Eighth Air Force's first Congressional Medal of Honor winner. Snuffy almost singlehandedly put out a raging fire in the fuselage of his bomber on the way back from attacking German submarine pens on the Bay of Biscay coast of France. He saved the life of another gunner in his plane, and pretty much by himself was responsible for the bomber's return to England through swarms of attacking Luftwaffe fighters.

An alert public relations officer sensed that this was the time, if there was going to be one, for Eighth Air Force men to start winning Congressional Medals of Honor. Snuffy's heroism was duly recommended and approved, and a couple of months later when Secretary of War Henry L. Stimson visited the United Kingdom on an inspection tour, he brought Snuffy's Congressional Medal of Honor with him for personal presentation.

But Character Snuffy Smith was enough of an eccentric to have been a *Stars and Stripes* man, and when the secretary arrived to present the medal at a full-dress parade ceremony, Snuffy Smith was on KP because he and his first sergeant couldn't agree on how many hours away from the post Snuffy Smith could stay with a pass that was good for twenty-four hours for anyone else.

Those things Andy Rooney's story in the army paper duly chronicled. Snuffy objected, when he read the story in the paper, but the Desk had felt that the news value outweighed the consequences of any possible effect on morale that Snuffy's un-Congressional Medal of Honor job on KP might have had.

Snuffy had been a hero on his first raid.

What *The Stars and Stripes* didn't print about the gunner they took off KP to receive a Congressional Medal of Honor was that after he managed to get in four more missions, thus qualifying for the Air Medal, an award infinitely inferior to the CMH, he was taken off flying status and went no more to the war as a gunner because all concerned felt that his experiences that day over France had taken too much out of Smith to make him an efficient member of an air crew.

The self-censoring staff of the army paper felt that other air gunners, who might read that Snuffy Smith, the Congressional Medal of Honor winner, was through flying after only five missions, might find their morale lowered in that knowledge, and that such a reaction was worth far less than the story's value in a purely newsworthy sense.

Even aside from the Snuffy Smith story, the greatest single bunch of yarns *The Stars and Stripes* knew but couldn't tell stemmed from the Air Forces. There were those wonderful tales of Air Force men shot down over the Continent who, through the French, German, Belgian and Dutch underground movement, made their way back to the British Isles.

Figures are difficult to get but it is estimated that 50 per cent of all the men who parachuted safely to the ground in German-occupied countries eventually made their way safely back to England. Every one of them has tales to curl the hair of his children.

If the flier could escape being caught within the first few hours after he reached the ground he was almost certain of contacting some underground leader who would start him out on the road back. The road back was through the houses of hundreds of French and Belgian patriots who were willing to risk their lives to house an American for the night, in hiding from the Germans. That part of the story is an old one but the experiences American boys had—boys who a year previous were comfortably settled at home attending high school—were fantastic.

One Fortress ball-turret gunner finally showed up back at his station with a mouthful of stories, none of which he was supposed to tell because of an oath he had taken. There was one, however, which was too good to keep to himself.

"I'd been wandering around for about four hours after I landed," the gunner told the fellows crowded around him.

"Jesus, was I thirsty. Funny, but that's what was bothering me most, thirst. Couldn't find any damn water anywhere.

"I walked down this dirt road into a small town. Nobody said anything to me because I'd picked up some old civilian clothes.

"I walked a little ways into town, worrying mostly about finding some place to get a drink of water where I wouldn't have to talk the language.

"Finally I see this little place where they are selling beer, so I walked in. There were a couple of Frenchmen sitting around but I wanted to be careful so I just pointed to the beer tap when the fellow asked me what I wanted.

"He drew me a glass and I drank it down. Really thirsty. Just as I finished the glass, this German officer comes walking into the place and I figured I'd had it. I just stood there sort of stiff without turning, but he comes up, stands there next to me and orders a beer.

"I really wanted to get out of there quick. I reached in my pocket for money to pay the guy with and, Jesus, I pretty near turned green. I had nothing but those big new notes they give you in the escape kits. I didn't know how much the beer was, how much any of the money I had was worth, but I knew if I pulled this wad of brand-new money out of my pocket and start fumbling through it, this Jerry next to me is gonna get wise.

"While I was standing there trying to figure what the hell to do I must have put my hands in all my pockets.

"I see this Jerry officer eying me and figured there wasn't much sense trying to kid him any longer.

"All of a sudden this guy smiles. He reaches in his pocket, pulls out some change, figuring I am broke, and throws it across to the bartender to pay for my beer.

"I give the guy a weak smile like I meant 'thank you,' and walked out."

Americans will never know how many of the French, Dutch, Belgian and even a few German heroes harbored American fliers but certainly when the boys begin to tell their stories Americans will at least hear, at first hand, of the great underground movement, which couldn't be mentioned while it was in operation. The Germans knew of it, of course, but feeling that every line which appeared in print was unnecessary advertising, Allied authorities closely guarded any reference at all to the underground.

Many American families must have experienced the strange sensation of having their sons reported missing in action one month, only to have them show up in the States the next. Fliers were honor bound not to discuss their experiences, and many of them did not explain their mysterious disappearance even to their families.

A *Stars and Stripes* reporter ran across an amazing story of an American woman who married a French count. She lived in a large château in Normandy and while she secretly kept eighteen to twenty American and British fliers between the false floorings of her home, she billeted five high-ranking German officers with a highhanded hospitality that fooled them for months.

The fliers who lived in the garret-like space between the two floors had to live in their stocking feet for fear their footsteps would be heard below by the German officers. At night the fliers crept downstairs after the German officers had retired and ate like kings from the fat of the rich Normany countryside. The countess had to buy a cow or several lambs each week on the black market to feed her hidden guests and with the meat she gave them Wehrmacht wine to wash down the fare fit more for kings than hideaways.

The other side of the story—and it may or may not have been the same countess in the same château—was discovered when the 2nd and 69th Infantry divisions cleared the German city of Leipzig almost two years later.

An American-born countess was freed from her Nazi captors there and she told the story of how she had been taken as a political prisoner after the Gestapo had been tipped off that she was harboring Allied fliers who had been shot down.

The woman said that twenty Gestapo agents had entered her house one night unexpectedly. She had twelve American and British fliers hidden at the time, she said, and while the Gestapo agents searched the house thoroughly for an hour, they failed to discover the double-floor hideaway. Later, however, they returned and arrested her anyway on someone's word that she was helping Allied fliers.

Even after the invasion of the French coast what were known in the business as "escape" stories were not released by censors. The American First Army, and later the Third, Ninth and Fifteenth, ran across thousands of Americans who had been living with French and Belgian families. United States tanks would trundle unexpectedly into some small French town and while the French civilians went noisily mad with joy, invariably four or five healthy-looking specimens in ill-fitting clothing would saunter over to an American tank.

Tank crews, expecting the usual "Cigarette pour moi?" were always startled when the first of the approaching boys spoke:

"Fer chrissake it's about time you guys got here."

It is a great mystery how the Germans missed spotting the Americans who lived almost openly in French towns. When the 3rd Armored Division rolled into a small village just outside of Liége in Belgium there were three "Frenchmen" leaning up against a corner store watching the tanks roll by.

Two of the boys were tall, good-looking fellows of about twenty-three, and the third was shorter and probably not more than twenty. The two tall fellows wore unpressed blue jeans which came to a point on their legs just below the calf muscle. They wore old brown corduroy coats which fitted so tight across the shoulders that the arms were pulled up almost to their elbows. Perched on top of this sartorial camouflage were two of the most un-French-looking berets that ever went on anyone's head.

The short one in the trio wore brown tweed trousers which he had rolled up at least four inches at the bottoms, a tattered blue pinstripe coat and a silly Tyrolean hat which he had cocked over one eye.

The three of them were standing there against the building and all that was missing was the Coca-Cola sign. One was leaning with his elbow against the wall bracing his head with his hand. The second was standing, or half standing, slouched against the front of the building with his hands jammed down into his pockets, and the little fellow had planted one foot against the wall behind him while he stood on the other.

They were three American Joes who had been living in the town for five months waiting for the army to get to them. How they, and thousands others like them, escaped the watchful German eye is hard to explain.

Those three had a great story to tell *The Stars and Stripes* but even then it could not be printed.

Many Americans like them had chosen to wait with their French or Belgian hosts rather than risk their own lives and the lives of those willing to help them, by moving through the underground channels back to where they could be shipped to England. There were thousands of Americans who chose to lose themselves in the Paris crowds for months, and some even years.

Two years before the invasion the bomb group at Chelveston, the 305th, had a favorite story they liked to tell about one of their pilots who, they were sure, was living in the lap of luxury in Paris.

It fell in the category of those stories we knew and couldn't print—and even now his name better be Joe Doyle.

The 305th used to have the same great heartache that everyone of the original Fortress bomb groups used to have. The notorious Luftwaffe Abbeville Kids were in their prime in those days along with the famed Goering Yellow Nosed Circus. They were the crack fighter pilots of the Luftwaffe and they sent more than one—and more than a hundred for that matter—four-engined American bombers down in flames over France. And Joe Doyle was taking no chances.

Every time the 305th was scheduled for a mission you could see Joe over in his Nissen hut packing up a little overnight bag he had bought for the purpose. He put in pajamas, some underwear, shaving kit and tooth paste, and other odds and ends of articles he wanted to have with him.

When the briefing was over Joe Doyle would trudge out to the hardstand where his Fort stood, dragging his parachute and all his flying paraphernalia with him. And his overnight bag.

Everyone laughed at Joe for it. It was one of the station gags, Joe Doyle and his little bag.

Finally Joe got it one day over Lille. Joe made sure the rest of the crew cleared the ship and then he jumped from the burning bomber before it fell to pieces. The rest of the group got home and they sadly told the story of how Joe finally got it. Some of them got out of the ship, they knew, but the pilot, Joe, probably didn't have time.

It was three weeks later that the real story came home to Chelveston. Three of Joe's crew had been taken in by the underground and had been shipped through in a hurry. When they were asked about Joe Doyle they could only laugh and tell the tale.

They had made contact with an underground man just a few hours after they hit the French soil.

He took them to his home and made contact with another friend farther along who was going to escort the boys along the road in the right direction.

As the three fliers and their guide walked down a dusty French road they came to a small intersection. A quarter mile down the side road there was a figure gaily swinging along and at his side he carried a little bag—an overnight bag.

The three crewmen couldn't have been happier to see anyone than they were to see Joe Doyle.

They looked around carefully to see that there was no one to see them then they dashed up to Joe and told him what a good thing they had run into.

"This guy's gonna take us back, Joe!"

Joe was glad to see his boys, glad they were safe, but when they wanted him to go along with them he smiled and tapped his bag.

"I didn't pack this for twenty-two trips for nothing. I got three addresses in Paris and that's where I'm going. Been wanting to go there all my life. I'll be standing on the curb waving when the army comes marching in there."

And that was the last the boys saw of Joe Doyle as he picked up his bag and started down the road toward Paris with his peculiar swinging gait, whistling as he went.

And when the First Army finally reached Paris a year and a half later, Joe Doyle probably was standing on the curbstone, waving like mad with the rest of the Frenchmen.

Jack Foisie, ace combat reporter for the Mediterranean edition of *The Stars and Stripes,* revealed during a furlough back to the States in 1944 one of the best-kept secrets—and one of the most terrible errors—the army ever had. It was the destruction of a score or more American transport planes and their burden of battle-bound American paratroopers by American and Allied antiaircraft guns during the first morning hours of the invasion of Sicily.

Jack came home from the war for a brief vacation and a tour of duty in the *Stars and Stripes* bureau in New York. On a tour of the States, Jack submitted for a local army public relation officer's approval the typed manuscript of a talk that included disclosure of the Sicilian fiasco. For God knows what reason, the PRO passed it. Jack talked, and the news service wires hummed with the revelation that made page one of virtually every paper in the world. Everyone in the Mediterranean Theater of Operations had known about the slaughter when the low-flying C-47 transports came in over the Sicilian beaches as the invasian was starting by land, sea and air, but there had been a tight censorship "stop" on it, and the home front hadn't heard a word about the kind of military mistake everyone should know about so that there won't be so many of them.

Jack was censured for what he had to say, but one way or another the paper had managed to tell one of the secrets it felt shouldn't be secret.

Now it can be told that the airborne assault which eventually cracked the Rhine barrier and opened the way to the guts of the Nazi Reich originally was scheduled for November or December of 1944. As *Stars and Stripes* understood it, the airborne were to leap into action at the Rhine bridges as soon as the course of battle some forty or fifty miles to the west along the Roer River had forced the Germans to commit their Sixth Panzer Army, which the Germans—oblivious to the American connotation—called their "Salvation Army," because it was their last undefeated, unimpaired reserve of any magnitude. The idea was for the paratroopers and the glider men to hold the Rhine bridges against retreat by the Nazi panzers while the Allied forces destroyed the enemy west of the Rhine.

A *Stars and Stripes* staffer who eventually jumped with the 17th Airborne Division across the Rhine at the end of March, 1945, was scheduled to jump in the ambitious plan to destroy the Nazis at the close of 1944. Even today that staffer gets acute attacks of the shakes—and probably the Allied High Command does too—when he realizes that von Rundstedt's unleashing of hoarded and secret German power in the Battle of the Bulge on December 16, 1944, delayed by three months the plan to cross the

Rhine. Neither the staffer nor anyone connected with the operation likes to think of how affairs might have gone for the airborne troops had the Rhine bridge jump come off when scheduled with the Germans holding all the power they had built up for the Bulge offensive.

It was a relief when the German strength was worn out in the Ardennes campaign, but the bonds of security, and of patience, were stretched long and thin in *The Stars and Stripes* during the wait for the attack, which eventually occurred on March 23.

Just before the jump across the Rhine, a *Stars and Stripes* staff man stumbled onto another story which ranked with the most intriguing of the war but couldn't be told for reasons of military security. That was the yarn of the so-called Nazi Suicide Corps "human torpedoes" of Remagen bridge.

The German human torpedoes who tried and failed to destroy the one steel and three pontoon bridges across the Rhine where the 9th Armored Division had seized a bridgehead on the east bank early in March, 1945, were seven members of a highly elite group of Nazi volunteers organized to carry out missions of usually suicidal nature against the Allies.

For a long time the Allied High Command, some intelligence operators, and two or three *Stars and Stripes* men were aware of the existence of the Suicide Corps. There was nothing to be gained by boasting of the knowledge of its existence, even had the censors permitted. An even better story whose publication would have militated against the possibility of his capture was that about the leader of this German corps, fabulous, scar-faced, Hungarian Stefan Skorzeny.

When the Americans seized the bridge at Remagen and the little wedge of ground on the Rhine's east bank, the Wehrmacht's high command shot the bridge's defenders for failure to do their duty and called on Skorzeny for a detachment of human torpedoes to destroy the Remagen bridge and the auxiliary pontoon structures which the American engineers had erected to supply the forces across the river. Skorzeny sent seven men.

"Destroy the bridges," he ordered them before they boarded the plane at their training school in the Austrian Alps and flew to the German lines upriver from Remagen. "After you have destroyed all the bridges there, swim on down the river, reconnoiter the American positions on the west bank, and then swim across to the east bank opposite Bonn where our patrols will be waiting for you."

That was one of the things that made Skorzeny one of the great soldiers of the war, friend or enemy. Of the Suicide Corps he demanded and frequently got the impossible. Most commanders would have been content to say to their men, "Try to destroy the bridges."

The human torpedoes came down the Rhine with the current, but there was no negligence at Remagen as there had been seven or eight months before when a similar detachment played an important role in thwarting the abortive Allied effort to seize and hold the storied bridge at Arnhem, in Holland. Vigilant guards at Remagen spotted the Nazis in the water. The Yanks opened fire, killed three Nazis by exploding the demolition charges with which they swam, and captured the other four.

As it had happened before—so often that the Desk almost came to count on at least a measure of "*Stars and Stripes* luck" in any emergency—so this time a staffer happened to be on hand as the human torpedoes were taken and led in for questioning.

The four Germans, whether one liked to admit it or not inasmuch as they were of the enemy, were as brave men as there are in the world. They weren't fanatics; they simply were the type of thinking, adult fighting men that recognizes what happens to people in wars but isn't afraid of it.

Interrogation of the human torpedoes and a close inspection of their equipment provided a top-notch story. Over heavy underclothes they wore a thin garment coated with a chemical which, activated by the extreme cold of the Rhine River waters in late winter, generated heat to keep the swimmers from exhaustion or death due to the near-freezing temperature of the water. Their outer garment, which conjured up thoughts of warriors from Mars, was a completely enveloping rubber suit with webbed hands and feet. With simple oxygen masks the swimmers were able to traverse long distances underwater, coming to the surface only infrequently to get their bearings, and hauling with them semibouyant containers of explosives which traveled just beneath the surface of the water. Even the explosives were a story: They were of a fantastically light, pliable plastic, to which almost anything could be done safely except giving a sharp jolt.

Interrogation of the prisoners revealed they were part of Skorzeny's corps and that it was from him they had their instructions.

Eventually parts of the story could be told and the paper carried all the details the censor felt would provide no knowledge to the enemy. But by that time the Allies were closing on Berlin and the story had lost much of its significance.

That was the way with many such stories, among them another one in which the fabulous Skorzeny figured.

*The Stars and Stripes* and a good many people on the Allied side knew but didn't tell for obvious reasons the gravity of the situation in the first three days of Germany's desperate, last-throw offensive in the Ardennes, which began December 16, 1944. To maintain that secret until long after the Battle of the Bulge was won was an obvious case of self-imposed and military censorship. The story we would have liked to tell, but couldn't at the time for censorial reasons, was the never-substantiated whisper in high military and intelligence circles that Stefan Skorzeny and a suicide squad had parachuted to earth behind the Allied lines and were playing a deadly hide-and-seek with Allied counterespionage while they sought an opportunity to assassinate Supreme Commander Dwight Eisenhower, British Field Marshal Montgomery, and other ranking Allied leaders.

It had been Skorzeny and a picked band of Nazis who parachuted into Italy and kidnaped Benito Mussolini. Every soldier knew that had been a magnificently conceived and carried-out exploit. It was not beyond the realm of possibility that the Suicide Corps could get away with a similar feat against the Allied command.

Maybe Intelligence knew whether the whispered conjectures had a basis in fact and maybe it didn't, but *Stars and Stripes* staffers felt fairly certain through information gleaned from various sources that the story was a skillfully planted bit of disquietude from German espionage agents. We would have liked to tell the story, listing all possibilities and probabilities as to its authenticity, but the censors held, and quite possibly rightly, that such an article would only serve to fray even further the nerves of troops long in combat.

Sometimes, though, censorial "stops" on yarns the Stars-and-Stripers had turned up were the results of flat orders by some undoubtedly thin-skinned individual much higher up than the echelons of command who had maybe made a mistake, been caught in it by the enemy, and wasn't going to have anyone rattling the skeletons in his officer's foot locker if he could help it. Such, we always felt, was the case with the failure of an American secret weapon, the YB-40 super-gunned version of the Flying Fortress.

The first few American heavy bomber raids on Nazi targets in Europe revealed, in addition to the fact that enough of such raids with enough planes could do a lot toward winning the war, at least one chilling conclusion: Somehow the bombers had to have even more protection from German fighters than the admittedly great gun power provided by the thirteen heavy machine guns in each Flying Fortress. The army had to provide single-engine pursuit planes with a range long enough to escort the bombers to their target and back. The army set about doing that, and eventually succeded.

In the interim, however, it was decided to set aside a number of conventional Flying Fortress bombers, eliminate their bomb racks and install 50-caliber machine guns and 20-mm. aerial cannon everywhere on the plane that room could be found. The resultant gun-bristling aircraft was designated the YB-40, the "Y" symbolizing the experiment, the "B" that it was a bomber and the "40" that it was the fortieth basic bomber design the Air Force ever had attempted.

"We'll blow the Luftwaffe out of the skies!" declared one public relations officer to his *Stars and Stripes* staff man who had stumbled onto the existence of the YB-40.

Eventually the American Air Forces did just that, but they didn't do it with a YB-40, which flopped with almost as loud a noise as the explosion of one of the bombs it should have been carrying.

The YB-40s did fine on the way to the targets, scattered through the formation of conventional Fortresses. The heavy armament of the experimental craft took a big toll of Nazi attackers. But most of the success of the American bombers' defense lay in their tight formation, whence all ships could bring to bear on attackers a concentrated fire power far greater in total volume than the scattered YB-40s.

When the target was reached and the conventional Fortresses dropped their 6,000 pounds of bombs, they turned for home three tons lighter and thus considerably faster in cruising speed. The only weight the YB-40s had got rid of—and they were at least as heavy as a bomb-loaded plane since their armament tacked on roughly some three additional tons—was the couple of hundred pounds of ammunition they had used up. The YB-40s fell behind the formations, and the Luftwaffe, although not without a fight, played hell with the stragglers.

In a short time the Air Force abandoned the YB-40s, but right up to the end of the war somebody way up the chain of command refused to permit lifting of the original censorship embargo on the story.

Sometimes the reason for reticence about confidential matters by people below the very top echelons was the time- and army-honored stand that any officer could be trusted with a confidence but not the most intelligent enlisted man. With two or three exceptions, *Stars and Stripes* reporters were enlisted men. And after all, as they invariably put it, the assistant public relations lieutenant in a port somewhere on the French coast couldn't be expected to hand over to an enlisted man the tonnage of supplies handled through that port in, let's say, the last fifteen days.

Not that the enlisted man was a spy or anything, but it said "secret" at the top of the page in the assistant PRO's drawer and these fellows from *The Stars and Stripes,* after all, were enlisted men and enlisted men weren't supposed to see secret documents unless they had the written permission of the general commanding or something. No one on *The Stars and Stripes* ever bothered to find out just what kind of permission one had to have because when you ran up against something like that you did one of two things: you either went to the general commanding the area and asked him, and he told you, or you said unh-unh to the assistant public relations officer and walked next door to the enlisted man chief clerk and he gave you the figures or whatever it was you wanted because the reason he was chief clerk was that he was a level-headed individual who knew his job and had sense enough to know that the army's newspaper probably wasn't going around collecting port tonnages for the Wehrmacht.

One of the reasons you got the information—from the general or the chief clerk—was the *Stars and Stripes* patch on your shoulder and another was the khaki uniform. The staffers were Joes in a citizen army of Joes, and most of the time you can tell a Joe even if he wears a gray suit and a fedora. The Joes talked to the staffers.

In October, 1942, the American forces in the British Isles were getting ready for the invasion of North Africa, and because it was their first invasion, the getting ready was a fairly obvious thing, *The Stars and Stripes* was about to become a daily, and the newly forming staff was anxious that its first big story be covered successfully.

Charlie White, who had joined the staff only a week before, took a couple of men and started out to do what he called "a plain ordinary police reporter's job on this invasion."

One of them walked into the public relations office and spent the bigger share of the day just sitting around, inconspicuous in khaki, and listening. The others perambulated through the maze of headquarters offices, talking to clerks in this office or that, stopping to chew the fat now and then with the odd colonel who happened to be a personal friend.

By simply listening and comparing notes afterward, Charlie and the others were able to come to the city desk, a week before the paper became a daily, and tell the story of what the invasion would be, when it would be, give or take forty-eight hours, and who was going.

"People like to talk," Charles said in explanation. He said it a little sadly, because Charles always was finding out that most of the things he suspected about people really were true. "We didn't steal no secret papers or anything like that. We just stood around and listened and once in a while asked questions with a dumb look. Great system. Especially in armies."

There were guards with fixed bayonets, and multi-steeled safe doors, and very complicated secret ciphers, all guarding the details of the North Africa invasion, but *The Stars and Stripes* covered it.

There was some dispute as to who was going with the invaders. Everyone wanted to go, but they also had a sneaking desire to stay in England and help make the weekly a daily, a newspaperman's dream job. Charlie White and his "police reporter" collaborators had first choice, and they made it in a taxicab on the way to the office one day.

"We'll flip coins," Charlie said, "odd man going to Africa. The other two make him go."

In a cold light, however, it seemed as if putting out a daily paper would be more fun than going to Africa, especially since the big show would be the invasion of the European continent; in October, 1942, everyone was sure that the invasion of Europe was only a matter of months away. So the Desk cast around for a good reporter to handle the job.

Bob Neville, nervous, capable one-time foreign editor of *Time* magazine, no tyro he, had been sent to the European Theater by *Yank,* the army magazine for which he worked as a sergeant correspondent, to do a series of stories about the Canadians in the war. He had run into the *S&S* crowd even as Moora had earlier in the summer, and with his consent and help he was stolen from *Yank* in a quick double-shuffle about extraordinary orders, top secret, and emergencies. The Desk assigned him to the Africa invasion, and he sailed right behind the first wave.

A week or so later, on the morning that the German radio just beat the Allies to an announcement that American troops had landed in Nazi-held North Africa, the daily *Stars and Stripes* was ready.

In the musty old library of the *Times,* which was still drawing in its breath at the arrival of the Yanks in its quiet hallways, no one ever would have noticed the plain pieces of white paper which inconspicuously marked pages in a dozen travel books. There was nothing on the paper markers, and if you opened the books to the pages so marked you found only some paragraphs about Abyssinia, or maybe prune plantations in California. However, if you looked at the number of the page, and multiplied it by two and turned to the page number by the product of that multiplication, you found maybe an engraving of the harbor at Oran, or a picture taken in 1929 of the fortifications at Casablanca, or a page of documentary material on the French colonial army, or even, in one pamphlet, a post-1941 summary of what the Nazis had taken over of the French colonial empire.

It was all kind of Boy Spy in the White Houseish, but it paid off when the flash came. *The Stars and Stripes* simply turned to the library references which had been so carefully prepared on the basis of the findings of what he called the Charles White Commission and each night was exactly abreast of the news with a well-documented background story of what was happening.

We made one mistake, although the staffers always held with some smugness that the mistake was not *The Stars and Stripes* at all, but rather that of the army, which was forty-eight hours behind on some of its plans.

In the original schedule, the French West Africa city of Rabat, with its high-power propaganda radio station, was to be taken on a particular day, possibly four days after the first landings. *The Stars and Stripes* adhered meticulously to the schedule it had managed to learn, but as the paper went to press that evening there still was no official announcement that Rabat had been taken, which was news of some import in those days.

"The announcement probably will come after we've gone to press, and we'll look bad," the staff decided finally, "so we better just go ahead and assume it's been taken."

Thus, the next morning, the interpretive article with the news story went into a fairly detailed description of the propaganda radio station at Rabat which was now in the hands of the Americans and which could be of immense help in getting the North African French around to our side.

All the next day, Rabat radio was exhorting the people of North Africa to resist the invasion, and it wasn't until the following evening that the American forces moved in and made *The Stars and Stripes* truthful.

*The Stars and Stripes* made plenty of mistakes in the war but we tried very hard not to make them where the fighting men were involved. For that reason long after *Stars and Stripes* reporters had known about and flown on the secret series of raids against the German rocket-bomb sites in coastal France, and long after the second medium bombardment attack from bases in Britain resulted in a 100 per cent loss, long after three groups of Liberator bombers made a mistake in navigation and wiped out a harmless Dutch town, long after a staffer had flown with and watched in operation the secret device by which American bombers accurately aimed their explosives through clouds—long after those things and many more, just as long as there were men fighting who might be harmed by premature stories, the paper did its best to keep the faith.

## D DAY LANDING IN BRITTANY IS REVEALED

### Isolated French Paratroops Battled on for Two Months Waiting the Big Break

VANNES, Aug. 17—A French paratroop battalion dropped near this city on D day and its remnants fought savagely for two months to disrupt German communications and to organize the French resistance army in Brittany.

Its story can be told now that U.S. Forces have broken through the German resistance to free the isolated paratroopers roving, hitting and hiding, fighting all over Brittany.

From June 6 until the day the Sherman tanks showed up in Vannes on Aug. 3 the French paratroopers armed loyal Frenchmen with Sten guns; they took up miles of railroad tracks, tore up cable lines, and generally played havoc with German communications and transport.

The battalion was divided into squads, each led by one officer. The men had light machine guns of all descriptions, Sten guns, Bren guns, tommy guns, pistols and carbines. They had mortars and bazooka guns when they landed and it wasn't long before they had captured more mortars.

Whenever possible the paratroopers avoided pitched battles with the Germans. Their assignment was not to fight, or they would have had no time for their important jobs.

Their biggest battle came June 18, more than six weeks before they hoped for help from the beachhead landing force. The paratroopers had been living on a large French farm. The Germans began to notice that Allied planes circled over that particular farm regularly and frequently and they soon discovered that supplies were being dropped in the fields near the farm.

The German commander assumed that the farmhouse garrison was a routine gathering of parts of the French resistance army. Underestimating the size and strength of the force, the German commander proceeded as usual. He rounded up a large force of Georgian soldiers and ordered them to march on the farmhouse and wipe out the group there. It was 4 A.M. when they first attacked. They came forward singing and marching in open file, unaware that behind farmhouse walls waited one of the world's toughest fighting units.

The paratroopers waited. Finally, with the upright, marching

German soldiers only 20 yards from the muzzles of their machine guns, they opened fire. The withering burst cut the German ranks in two and the remainder retreated in disorder.

There were 120 paratroopers and about 400 French patriots in the farmhouse garrison, and when the German commander realized its strength he reinforced his attacking party until there were 3,000 German soldiers with him. The battle continued with wave after wave of German infantrymen attacking. Each time they fell back, badly beaten. At ten o'clock the following morning the paratroopers took advantage of the confusion in the German lines to launch a counterattack. For the loss of only two paratroopers the counterattack further depleted the German force by almost a hundred men.

That midnight, after the paratroopers had killed 500 Germans and wounded 600 more, they withdrew with the patriots and vanished into friendly Brittany, where the Germans couldn't find them.

The cruel Georgian troops were offered a standard price of one million francs for every French paratroop officer they captured and fifty thousand francs for every enlisted man.

One of the Frenchmen wounded in the battle was hit in the throat, in the stomach and in the thigh but he managed somehow to crawl to a near-by woods. A Frenchwoman helped him with his wounds and while he lay helpless on the ground a party of German soldiers discovered him and filled his dying body with slugs from their machine pistols.

The philosophy of the Georgian troops, according to the paratroopers, was that if they were captured by the Allies the Russians would make sure they were shot as traitors; if they were abandoned by the Germans, the French people would kill them; if they did not fight, the Germans would kill them.

Of the French fighters who are left, most plan to settle down in a free France after the war. But one Frenchman who spent fifteen years working in a restaurant in Los Angeles plans to return to the United States.

# PUBLIC RELATIONS

IF EVERY CIVILIAN in America held a rank or rating, as every soldier in the army does, and if the publicity manager for a Fifth Avenue fur shop was a colonel while the managing editor of the New York *Daily News* was a corporal, there probably would be a lot of fur flying around the pages of the *News*.

Although very few fur merchants wanted to insert advertising in the columns of *The Stars and Stripes,* we were roughly in that sort of position. Every special service public relations officer (PRO) outranked every *Stars and Stripes* deskman, and every time the PRO's little unit put on a show for a few hundred men he wanted the rest of the army to know about it. Releases which started like this came in by the thousands to *The Stars and Stripes:*

AT THE FRONT WITH THE UMPTY DIVISION—Five hundred delighted GIs tonight listened to the syncopating rhythms of Fred Shmertz and his all GI band of the 101th Special Service Command, commanded by Capt. Arthur Emlyn of 1010 Hollywood Boulevard, Gloversville, N. J., who formerly played with Glenn Miller's band, etc.

The facts of the show usually were that it was put on in front of a hundred soldiers of a trucking company fifteen to twenty miles behind where anyone was mad at anyone else by a bunch of special service soldiers who did a pretty good job under the leadership of someone who had heard Glenn Miller's band and may have lived at 1010 Hollywood, etc.

Not only special service PROs approached the Desk with that sort of thing, but PROs from every outfit in the army.

*The Stars and Stripes* regarded every PRO as a frustrated newspaperman, which was not actually true. There were a lot of PROs who were better newspapermen than some of the staffers themselves, but they were in one of the war's most unenviable jobs.

Most of them considered that half their job was getting their unit, whether it be a bomb group, an infantry division or a special service unit, into the *Stars and Stripes* pages. At best, the paper was an eight-page sheet while the war was being fought, and if in any given week *The Stars and Stripes* had decided to print the name of every unit in the ETO, it could have filled the eight pages for seven days without mentioning every unit there. That, of course, would have left no room for L'il Abner or the Russia story. Here, then, were hundreds of public relations officers, all with great heroes and honest to goodness top-flight newspaper stories on their hands, and their commanding general on their necks, trying to get something in the four- or eight-page army daily in which there simply was not room.

Time and again PROs would approach reporters in the field, point to a story in the paper and then point to one they had sent in.

"Mine is a better story. I think you'll admit it. Why wasn't it run?"

Usually the reporter had to admit it. What the PRO seldom could understand was all the little things which, haphazard as they seemed, put the other story in ahead of his. Maybe it didn't get held up so long by the PRO headquarters through which all such stories funneled to us; maybe his story had trouble in the censor's office, but more probably it was still buried in a mound of stories, every one possibly as good, in the *Stars and Stripes* office.

Sometimes the corporals and the sergeants didn't even have time to read the material which the lieutenants and the majors who were the PROs sent in to them. In a way it was criminal negligence. The stories represented hard work for the PRO and his staff and more often than not they involved men's lives. It was not right for the army newspaper to toss them off without notice but it was the only way in an eight-page paper.

Some of the fur merchants tried the forceful approach. Often a major from some artillery outfit would storm into the office and demand to see the officer in charge.

"The sergeant just sent him out on an errand," someone invariably remarked, maybe truthfully.

"I want to see the man who edits this paper," the irate PRO would continue.

"I put out the paper," another stripeless soldier sitting at a desk would say. "Can I help you, sir?" The "sir" was double-edged.

Realizing that the man was an enlisted soldier, the major would start laying down his demands. Depending on who was on the desk, he was handled with varying degrees of firmness but always the deskman talked as a man with the authority of *The Stars and Stripes,* not his authority as sergeant or corporal. Staffers always figured the paper held the rank of something equivalent to a grade between a major general and a lieutenant general.

Along with all the other good but sad things in the world, it always seemed that the best PROs represented the best outfits; the saddest, the saddest outfits.

The 4th Armored Division, the Flyaway 4th, had, for a long time, a good PRO named Ken Koyen. Koyen, a first lieutenant while he was with the 4th, probably submitted more copy to *The Stars and Stripes* during one three-month period than any other man ever did. It was at a time when the paper was first being printed in Paris for distribution to the First and Third armies to the east, and to the Ninth Army back in the Brest peninsula. The paper was only four pages at the time because of serious newsprint problems and every day literally tens of thousands more words than could be used came to the Desk.

The man handling all the PRO copy noticed that for every four releases he handled from all the divisions put together, one was Koyen's. The staffer saved all Koyen's unused releases for one week and then added together all the words the PRO had sent in to *The Stars and Stripes.* In more than 500 stories sent in by that one division alone there were about 70,000 words.

At that time, the type size and column width allowed about 500 words in the average printed column. In four pages, five columns to a page, that left room for about 10,000 words jammed together without headlines or pictures.

The rewriteman made a note to that effect to the Desk and

the following day *The Stars and Stripes* printed a boxed story in the form of a memo to Lieutenant Ken Koyen of the 4th Armored Division. The story stated, for his information, and for the information of other PROs who did not understand why few of their stories were printed, that if we used all Koyen's releases we could have just filled the paper with nothing but them for seven days each week.

The crack infantry divisions in France and Germany had crack PROs. Captain Lindsey Nelson, for example, agent for the great 9th Infantry Division, was first interested in seeing that American people at home got the right story on what American boys were doing in the war and how they were doing it. Second, he was interested to see that his own outfit got the credit it deserved.

When the Ludendorff Bridge crashed after First Army troops had captured it intact and used it for their initial crossings of the Rhine at Remagen, Lindsey Nelson, a *Stars and Stripes* reporter, and Howard Cowan of the AP happened to be around. The 9th Infantry Division had little to do with the bridge's capture, but the heroism of the engineers who dropped into the Rhine, and their companions who swam out to save them, was a great story of American heroism. Lindsey and two of his assistants worked for five hours getting the full story, with hundreds of names and home towns. When they had collected and written their material they had it mimeographed and handed it to fifty correspondents who, through a stroke of bad luck, were not at the scene when the bridge went down. All those men wrote stories, and the pieces appeared under their by-lines at home, but it was Lindsey Nelson who actually was responsible for every one of the thousands of words they wrote.

Nelson is credited by correspondents with having designed the original PRO Kit, M1 (M-1 being the official quartermaster designation for the first design of a new piece of equipment). The PRO Kit, M-1, consisted of Scotch, bottle, one ea., gin, bottle, one ea., copy paper and carbons for correspondents who have forgotten same, and three soft lead pencils.

The 1st Infantry Division, the Red One, had a good PRO. He was Captain Maxie Zera, zany, calypso-singing Slapsie Maxie, who probably knows more stories of American heroism than any other in the army just because he has been with the fightingest division in the U. S. Army. Some may have fought as hard, but none longer.

Maybe the most unfortunate PRO in the business was Major Haynes Dugan, 3rd Armored press relations man. The 3rd Armored, always with the First U. S. Army, and one of only two heavy armored divisions left in the entire U. S. Army, had a great gripe directed against *The Stars and Stripes* and every American newspaper at home. What editors could not seem to get straight enough to satisfy the 3rd Armored Division was that it had nothing to do with Patton. It was not Patton's armor, it was not even in Patton's army, and the fact that its official name was the 3rd Armored Division and that Patton's Army was the Third U. S. Army was only an unfortunate coincidence.

All across France, Belgium and Germany the 3rd Armored led the way in their sector and all the time newspapers seemed to give credit to nothing but "Patton's Third Army."

The 3rd Armored, together with the 2nd Armored Division and two infantry divisions, the 1st and 9th, made the breakthrough at Saint-Lô. It was the turning point of the war on the Continent and the four divisions were proud of the job they did that July 26. Four days later, General Patton's army, which had been coming into France on the beaches secured by the First Army weeks before, was committed. The breakthrough was made and Third Army armor raced through the hole torn in enemy lines like a halfback in the open. General Omar Bradley planned it that way and it worked to perfection—but when the 3rd Armored started getting their home-town papers through the mails all they could find was Patton's Third Army in the columns and in the headlines.

As months rolled by and *Stars and Stripes* deskmen changed, some of them got a little hazy on the background of the great breakthrough and several times, in reviewing the situation, *The Stars and Stripes* made the grave error of crediting the Saint-Lô breakthrough to Patton instead of the First Army and the 3rd Armored Division and its cofighters.

It was not from those good PROs and those good outfits that the beefs and the pressure were always coming to *The Stars and Stripes*. The paper had more trouble from the London and Paris PROs, the brass, than from all the line outfits combined. The line outfit's beefs were usually legitimate, the others almost never.

In London a high-ranking PRO, a fur merchant, came to the offices one afternoon with a request that bordered on being an order. The provost marshal wanted to put American soldiers in London on their toes, he wanted to enforce stricter saluting discipline, he wanted the GI better dressed, and he was worried about organized vice.

Realizing that MPs alone might not be able to accomplish the job the way he wanted it done, he had come to the PRO, who, in turn, came to us. We were to start a campaign against poorly dressed soldiers and soldiers who weren't acting the way the army thought they should.

Without being for or against poorly dressed soldiers or soldiers who didn't salute every one of the thousand officers they could pass in five minutes along Piccadilly, the *Stars and Stripes* staffers rebelled at the idea of preaching anything to the GI. Maybe that was the start of the longest argument *The Stars and Stripes* ever had with the army. Was the paper strictly an organ through which news was to be presented to the soldiers or was it to be "used"? Was it an army house organ, or was it a newspaper?

The PRO didn't know or care about the morals of the thing, all he understood was that *The Stars and Stripes* reached more soldiers and had more influence than any other single thing he had access to and he planned to use it.

The Desk, while not accepting the half-order, made a compromise. They told the ranking PRO that if there was a news story in it, *The Stars and Stripes* would run it. That is, if the provost marshal wanted to announce a new enforcement campaign aimed at arresting soldiers who were out of uniform, that was a legitimate news story. The outcome was that Charlie Kiley got together with Sergeant Bruce Bacon, one of the Army Pictorial Service's ace cameramen, and together they did a story with a picture layout on vice rampant in London. It was a good news feature and in an honest, moral way, an editorial. It presented the facts, it did not preach.

From that time on, the PRO who felt he failed in what he set out to do, seemed to lay for staffers. The PRO was in a position where the *Stars and Stripes* staffers often had to call on him for information.

On one occasion a reporter called in a routine fashion.

"This is *The Stars and Stripes* calling, colonel, I wonder if you could tell us—"

"Who is this on *The Stars and Stripes*?" the colonel interrupted angrily.

"O'Shaugnessy," the reporter replied, giving one of the staff's favorite pseudonyms. (The by-line Pfc Luigi O'Shaugnessy was used on St. Valentine's Day and St. Patrick's Day stories usually.)

"O'Shaugnessy, huh, what's your rank?"

"Private, sir," the sergeant reporter answered.

"All right, Private O'Shaugnessy, hang up, call this number again and start your conversation with a superior officer in the prescribed manner."

The *Stars and Stripes* man hung up. Then he dialed the number again.

"This is Private Luigi O'Shaugnessy, of *The Stars and Stripes,* sir!"

"That's better! Now what do you want?" the colonel at the other end of the pipe said.

There was a ten-second silence.

"Well," the colonel repeated, "go ahead, what do you want?"

"I'm sorry, sir, I have the wrong number."

The *Stars and Stripes* reporter hung up.

Generally the PRO's attitude toward *The Stars and Stripes* enlisted men was much the same as the staff's own. And the staff got away with some very unarmy encounters with brass simply because they would talk to generals and captains exactly as though they were enlisted men.

One night after the paper had gone to bed the phone rang and Charlie White, who was sitting nearest at the time, picked it up.

"Hello, White here."

The staff, which had been sitting around the office talking, listened because there was nothing better to do until Charlie, one of the principles in the bull session, was through on the phone.

"Yeah, yeah," Charles said, nodding. "Yeah."

There was twenty seconds while the party at the other end explained what he wanted.

"Just a minute until I get the headset on," Charlie said.

Charles Charles Worthington Worthington White prepared

to take a dictated story on the typewriter. Then he picked up the phone and spoke again.

"Okay, general, whattya got? Shoot!"

The staff, which never became immune to the humor of its own attitude toward brass, broke out in a loud laugh and picked up the conversation without Charlie while he took the general's story (which was probably not used).

The most consistent source of trouble emanating from the PRO high command came as a result of cartoons *The Stars and Stripes* ran. In London Sergeant Dick Wingert developed a roly-poly soldier whom he called "Hubert" into one of the best, and least advertised soldier cartoons of the war. Hubert was the caricatured prototype for all inept, out-of-uniform soldiers in the army, and the army, which thought its left hand should know what its right hand was doing, did not think that the Hubert-type humor was funny. The official army thought it was not right for one branch of its organization to laugh at a little man who did almost everything a soldier shouldn't, while another branch issued stern warnings that there was nothing funny about being out of uniform, etc.

Down south, Sergeant Bill Mauldin and the Mediterranean edition were having similar trouble with "Willie," the cartoon character of Mauldin. Mauldin always played his "Bill," prototype of the front-line infantryman, against rear-line SOS soldiers. There was already enough friction there, the army felt, without having an army publication make pointed jokes about it.

Bill Mauldin's cartoons were the most popular because, from a front-line infantryman's viewpoint, he laughed at top brass, poked fun at outdated training programs and at all the other things the army held sacred.

After Mauldin came into Southern France with the Seventh Army, his cartoons began to appear regularly in the Rennes, Paris, Liége, Besançon, Dijon, Strasbourg, Pfungstadt (Frankfurt), Nice and Nancy editions of the paper. The Liége paper was servicing the First and Ninth armies while the Nancy edition was circulated in the Third and Seventh. Mauldin himself wandered through all army territories in a jeep.

*The Stars and Stripes* with Mauldin's irreverent cartoons began to reach the army commanders, and finally Lieutenant

General George S. Patton, Jr., informed a *Stars and Stripes* representative that unless Mauldin's cartoons stopped appearing in the paper he would bar it from Third Army territory.

Typical of the Mauldin cartoons Patton did not like was the one which made fun of the Patton posters in Third Army territory which warned men along the roads and in the towns that if they were out of uniform or disorderly in any way they were subject to fines running up to $50. There were, for instance, signs one hundred miles behind the lines threatening soldiers who failed to wear their steel helmets. Soldiers who walked the same streets with women pushing baby carriages felt a little silly with steel helmets on. The Mauldin cartoon depicted Joe and Willie stopping before one of the signs in a jeep.

Headed "YOU ARE NOW IN THIRD ARMY AREA," the sign was a list of offenses with their fines. Mauldin added a few of his own to reduce the thing to complete absurdity.

No helmet .......... 20 dollars
No shave ........... 30 dollars
Buttons unshined .... 40 dollars
Windshield up ...... 50 dollars
Pants down ......... 60 dollars

The sign listed fifteen or twenty items and was signed:

By Order of
Old Blood and Guts

Willie was saying to Joe in the caption:

"Joe, you better radio the old man we'll be a few days late because we gotta detour around an area."

After a few such had appeared, Mauldin got a call to appear before Patton himself. The genial general just wanted to "talk it over."

Patton told Mauldin that he did not appreciate his character, Willie, and thought he was not typical of the American soldier in the Third Army. Mauldin presented his view on the subject and they departed, not friends, but sergeant and general. Soon after, Mauldin packed up his jeep and the army let him go back to Italy, where he had a little more freedom to draw what he saw.

Dick Wingert ran into the same kind of trouble in London

and later in Paris. From time to time, after some cartoon lampooning the army or the officers in it, the editors got a direct order from very near the top that no more Wingert cartoons were to appear. Somehow, after a few weeks and new promises to be good, or better at least, Wingert's great cartoons with Hubert waddling rampant through them were reinstated.

Somehow those orders from on high always seemed to come through the public relations office, and the initials "PRO" became a little phrase in a category of disrepute all its own in the *Stars and Stripes* office. There is little doubt that the words "The Stars and Stripes" were more spit out than said in most PRO offices. The lack of affection was mutual.

The paper generally prided itself in the early days on its coverage of the air war. Staffers flew in the war, they lived at the bases, and complete files were kept of raids and bomb tonnages. At any given time, the *Stars and Stripes* man writing the air story could go to a card file and find out how many times Saint-Nazaire or Bremen or any other target had been bombed, by how many bombers and the number of what size bombs dropped while gunners were shooting down how many Luftwaffe planes. It was information no one but the people in the business cared about, for the most part. At any rate, when it came to air statistics, a few of the staffers carried a chip on their collective shoulder. They figured they knew more about Air Force statistics than anyone else except the official statisticians and were ready to argue about it. It was the cause of one of the nastiest little wrangles the paper had with a public relations office.

The Eighth Air Force started flying P-47s as fighter cover for its own B-17s and B-24s some time before the Ninth Air Force came up from Africa. The Ninth, when it came, was to be the invasion air force, or, as someone called it, "the infantryman's air force." When the invasion finally came on June 6, 1944, it was just that, but until invasion its fighters escorted Eighth heavies.

For a long time Colonel Hubert Zemke's Fighter Group, an Eighth Air Force outfit in Thunderbolts, led all other fighter groups in enemy planes shot down. For some reason that was not easy to explain. Zemke's Outfit (as it was known) just seemed to run into more of the "fun," meaning German planes, and always shot down more than other groups. It was a red-hot fighter mob and others became envious of its knack of running into and shooting down so many German planes.

Before long, twenty of the twenty-five "aces," a tag applied to a pilot who has shot down five or more enemy planes, belonged to the Zemke Outfit. The other five American aces were scattered through a dozen other fighter groups.

Meanwhile another group of pilots flying from the old RAF field at Debden started to come along. They were all transferees from the RAF and many of them had flown with the famous Eagle Squadron, the all-American outfit that fought with the Royal Air Force during the Battle of Britain. They were just slightly different from any other group of American fighter pilots. Before the United States came into the war they had volunteered to fight with the RAF or the RCAF, something the average American boy wouldn't, or at least didn't, do. Ipso facto, they were that kind of guys—not quite average Americans.

With the RAF they had been flying the highly maneuverable little Spitfire. They liked it. They knew it well, they knew what it could do, and it was the plane they liked best to fly. When they made their transfer to the United States Air Force they were given the then new P-47 Thunderbolt. The P-47 was a high-powered juggernaut as unlike the Spitfire as one fighter plane could be from another. They didn't like it.

For several months they did their job of escorting the bombers but they did not shoot down many German planes. They were a little bitter about it. They accused the Zemke Outfit, all of whose pilots thought the Thunderbolt was a great airplane, of leaving the bombers uncovered while they chased German fighters.

When the P-51 Mustang began to appear in England, the old Eagle Squadron pilots were the first to get the new plane. The group liked the Mustang. It was more like the Spitfire they were used to, and almost immediately their batting average began to improve. Slowly they began to creep up on the Zemke Outfit, which by this time was nearing a record of four hundred German planes destroyed in the air.

As time came closer to the invasion date there was more low-level strafing to be done by fighter planes. With the air almost cleared of German fighters it was safer than it had been for our fighters to race at low altitudes over French and German terrain, shooting up locomotive engines and flak towers without so much fear of being "bounced" from above by flights of German fighter planes.

Because the P-47 of that period was at its best at high altitudes and the P-51 Mustang was good on the deck, the Eagle Squadron group did a good deal more work close to the ground than the Zemke Outfit. While they went out with the bombers and then came down close to the ground to shoot up what they could find on the return trip, the Mustang group went in low all the way for the specific purpose of shooting up Luftwaffe airfields.

As time went on it soon became evident that someone was going to top the record of twenty-six enemy aircraft destroyed by Captain Eddie Rickenbacker in the last war. Zemke's Outfit had Walker Mahurin, Bob Johnson, Francis Gabreski, Dave Schilling and Zemke himself with records of about twenty destroyed.

The Eagle group had two men, Duane Beeson and Don Gentile, both pushing up around the same mark. The only other contender seemed to be Charlie Beckham, from the 353rd Fighter Group.

Everyone became conscious of the race among the fighter pilots, although it was officially discouraged because Fighter Command insisted that the fighter pilots' primary job was to protect the bombers, not to shoot down German planes.

After every raid the big question was "How did Mahurin make out?" or "Did Gentile get another?"

PRO releases read "Twenty E/A [enemy aircraft] destroyed, ten probably destroyed and thirty damaged."

The problem arose when fighter pilots started strafing German airfields. The communiques were changed to read "Fifty E/A destroyed, thirty on the ground, twenty in the air, etc."

Finally Bud Mahurin, Beeson and Beckham were forced to bail out over German territory, eliminating them from the race, but Bob Johnson of the Zemke Outfit and Don Gentile, with the Eagles, each passed his twentieth victory and headed for that goal of twenty-seven.

Gentile went out and, while strafing a German airfield, set fire to one or two German planes. He repeated the performance on several days during that month and Air Force PRO credited him with another enemy plane destroyed.

On the first night it was released this way, *The Stars and Stripes* printed it with the statement that Gentile had forged ahead of Johnson in the race for the record. When the staffer writing the air story found out the next day on what the claim was based the argument, which was never satisfactorily settled, began.

Should planes which pilots destroy on the ground count toward the record? *The Stars and Stripes* thought not. PRO claimed that a plane destroyed on the ground was just as definitely out of the battle as one shot down out of the sky, and some of the pilots said it was even harder to get them on the ground than in the air. If they were not going to count on the ground, what about the ones destroyed as they were taking off? Should they count?

It seems insignificant now, but it was big news in America and in England at the time and, while it was strictly a newspaper record, it meant a lot to the boys flying.

In the course of the argument it was discovered that one of Rickenbacker's "planes destroyed," was actually an observation balloon. Some claimed that was a ringer; that the record should be cut to twenty-five.

The whole argument was settled when Major Richard Bong, way over on the other side of the world, shot down another Jap plane and passed all ETO contestants to become the first American fighter pilot to hit Rickenbacker's record. Gentile at that time had twenty-three destroyed in the air and seven on the ground. All of Bob Johnson's twenty-five were shot out of the air. It was a petty argument but *The Stars and Stripes* and Fighter Command never got along well afterward.

## HEROES COME WHOLESALE

Here, briefly, is the story of one Fort Group, one of many units making air war history fighting the Germans

By Andy Rooney
*Stars and Stripes* Staff Writer
Thursday, April 27, 1944

If gallantry came in cans, there would never have been enough shipping space to get all the Eighth Air Force has used to England.

Heroism has been buried by heroism here. Heroes have come wholesale and there have been more than America could digest. Stories which in normal times would be headlined in every paper in America end up as two paragraphs in someone's home-town paper.

In U.S. military history no fighting unit the size of the Eighth Air Force ever performed with a higher percentage of workaday heroes; not heroes in name, but men who have actually been warmed by comradeship to do more for their fellow men than they need have; men who have unnecessarily risked their lives to save others and men who have performed with an intelligence and a courage to save their own lives when it would have been easier to die.

Had the men of any one of the ten United States heavy bombardment groups operating from fields in England performed with commensurate heroism in battle actions which caught the imagination of the American public as did Guadalcanal, that group would be the most celebrated in American military history.

Here, briefly, is the story of one Fortress group which has been operating against the Germans for a year and a half. It is a story of American boys which could be a book: there are other groups with the same story and people don't want to read that many books.

The group has never had a name that stuck. The boys know it as a number or by the name of the small town near the field. Both are restricted information.

Its first haul was last October 9 when it went into Lille, France. From that day on the group was at war and it didn't take the men long to find out that heavy bombardment of targets on the Continent was no picnic. Principal objectives in the early days were German U-boat pens. Again and again they struck at Saint-Nazaire, Lorient and La Palice. On the second trip into Saint-Nazaire, the one of November 9, the group participated in one of the Eighth Air Force's most successful experiments—the experiment proved to everyone's satisfaction that medium level was not the altitude at which to send in Flying Fortresses. They got the hell shot out of them.

The group went in that day at about 8,000 feet and the ships that did come back came back looking like colanders. There are still a few veterans left in England as gunnery instructors who will tell you about that raid. They may have been to the heart of Garmany since that day but when they have bad dreams it is the flak that day over Saint-Nazaire they dream about.

The group has completed 135 missions and dropped about 6,000 tons of bombs in Germany and on German targets in occupied countries. Like too-short or too-long artillery fire, some of the 6,000 tons fell in kraut fields and potato patches, but a lot of it has fallen in the middle of some of Germany's best industrial plants.

The group is made up of four squadrons. The Eager Beavers, the Clay Pigeons, Fitin' Bitin', and one which has never adopted a name that stuck. One they picked held too much blood and thunder and was forbidden. In anger the fliers dubbed themselves "The Buttercup Boys."

Of the four, Fitin' Bitin' and the Clay Pigeons squadrons gained most of the early fame. A story appeared in the *Saturday Evening Post* dubbing the one squadron as "The Clay Pigeons" because in those early days they had lost so many men. Time after time they returned, and while squadrons on each side of them would be lossless the Clay Pigeons would have lost two or three ships.

What made the thing even harder to understand was that flying in the same group with the bad-luck squadron was the Fitin' Bitin' outfit. The Clay Pigeons set up an attrition record at the same time Fitin' Bitin' was starting a lossless streak that was to extend to 43 raids. Today the Clay Pigeons have been 20 raids without a loss.

There were heroes in the group. First of the long line was a young lieutenant by the name of Bob Riordan. Riordan piloted the first really famous ETO Fortress named Wahoo and on three successive occasions he brought the ship back under circumstances which when set down on paper set the style for the thousands of wing and a prayer stories that have come out of the Eighth Air Force since.

Riordan went on to finish a tour of operations. Now, more than a year later, he is several years older and a lieutenant colonel who shows no signs of stopping at that rank. Last week Riordan went home for a 30-day rest.

Because of its early start on operations the group had the first officer and the first enlisted man in the theater to finish. Mike Roscovich was the first man in the ETO to complete a tour. He was a tech sergeant radio gunner at the time with a penchant for cutting off people's ties whether they were colonels or corporals.

Rosky went a long way toward being one of the happiest men who ever lived and his was almost a completely happy story. He was commissioned soon after he finished his ops and assigned to a near-by station as gunnery officer. As a nonflying officer he made more trips than anyone knows of and possibly completed more than any other man in the Eighth Air Force. Unofficially he had 33.

The colorful Rosky came to a tragic death last February. In Scotland on furlough he was in a plane taking off for home. For reasons which are not altogether clear, the pilot was trying to take his B-17 off with three motors. The plane crashed and all were killed. After 33 missions over the most dangerous enemy territory in the world Rosky died in an ordinary accident.

The first officer in the ETO to finish a tour was First Lieutenant Eugene J. Pollock, of New Orleans, Louisiana. Pollock was a navigator.

The group's most popular legend and hero is Arizona Tempe Harris. Arizona Harris was a gunner's own gunner, a hero's hero.

He hated the army and at the same time he was one of the best combat men in it. In the States the boys in the group knew him as a spirited redhead who was afraid of nothing and who didn't want to do much but get back to his home in Tempe. Once in England, Arizona was one of the most conscientous gunners of the war. No armorer touched Arizona's guns or the guns of any man in his crew.

Returning from a haul to the U-boat pens at Saint-Nazaire, Harris's plane with Charley Cranmer at the controls was forced down in the Bay of Biscay. German fighters kept up the attack as the plane eased down to the water. In another ship Bill Casey, pilot of the famous Fort, Banshee, pulled at his stick and wheeled the Banshee out of formation to help protect Cranmer.

The ship finally hit the cold waters of the bay but in the tail of Casey's ship P. D. Small could see Harris still firing away from the top turret. As the plane settled and the water crept up over the wings they could still see Arizona Harris at his guns in the turret firing away at the FW 190s which dived in to strafe any possible survivors. The last thing they saw of the ship was Arizona's smoking guns as he drowned at his post.

That story and Arizona himself are a legend at the base and when the story comes up there is always an old-timer who will swear that if any man ever deserved the Congressional Medal it was old Arizona Harris.

In the first days Colonel Frank Armstrong was the group CO. He was promoted to brigadier general, and Colonel Claude B. Putnam, a tall, slim pilot with a brain like a whip, moved in. The present CO is Colonel George L. Robinson.

Like men from any bomber outfit, the boys are proud of theirs. Talk to any one of them for ten minutes and he will be listing for you the things the group has done first, most and best. They'll tell you:

"The Eager Beavers were the first squadron in the USAAF to drop 1,000 tons of bombs on the Germans—or on anybody. They passed that mark the last day of 1943."

"Fitin' Bitin' went 43 missions without a loss in the days before fighter escort."

"We have the only enlisted man who ever got the Congressional Medal of Honor here, 'Snuffy' Smith."

"This base was the first in England to be turned over to the U. S. from the British . . . we had the first aero-club."

"We had the tallest tail-gunner Hank Cordery. Used to be a first sergeant. He was six feet five inches.

"Only ship in ETO which shot down 11 planes and had them

confirmed. Lt. Bob Smith's crew got them May 21 over Wilhelmshaven."

The three-man awards and decorations section at Colonel Robinson's station have done a lot of work. They have handled the paper work for one Congressional Medal of Honor, four DSCs, 18 Silver Stars, five Legion of Merits, 467 DFCs, 200 Purple Hearts, 4,500 Air Medals and Clusters, and four Soldiers' Medals.

The station's heroes today are men like Gilbert Roeder. Roeder's got 25 in now and he's come back on one, two and three engines more times than he's come back on four. He's got a knack for flak. The boys will swear, though, that there's not a better pilot in the Air Force than Roeder. He and his crew could have been living in Switzerland, Sweden, France or Germany now if they'd chosen the easy way out, but instead they chose to fight it the hard way, take a chance of going down in the North Sea or blowing up in mid-air, or of crashing over England. They've taken chances and they've paid off.

One of the group's favorite wing and a prayer stories is the one they tell of Captain Purvis E. Youree and Le Roy C. Sugg his copilot. Their Fort was badly damaged in the best tradition of flak-riddled Fortresses. It was in danger of spinning out of control any minute because the cables on one side had been completely shot away and Youree had little control over the ship.

Sugg looked the situation over and without a thought for his personal safety stripped his parachute off and used the harness to tie to one end of the frayed control cable. The other end he gave to Youree and that way the pilot guided the plane home—pulling on one end of his copilot's parachute harness.

Two of the station's favorite characters were Jewish boys. The story of one was a happy story. Captain Arthur Isaac was a character from Brooklyn in every sense of the word. He ditched once, crashed once, and came home on countless occasions in a ship full of holes, but always he came home. Now that it's over the secret of Isaac's dog tags is out.

He carried three pairs. On one was his right name. On another he had printed "Otto McIsaac." That set was in case he was shot down over Germany.

On a third pair of dog tags he had stamped "François d'Isaac," to be used in the event he went down in France. The Brooklyn bombadier always swore that the first thing he would ask for if he was shot down in Germany was the nearest church where he could hear a Catholic mass said over him.

The other Jewish boy was Eric Newhouse (nee Neuhaus), an

Austrian gunner whose family owned a little chocolate shop in Vienna when Hitler began making European Jews uncomfortable.

Eric joined a band of kids—he was fifteen in 1937—and with them slugged German police and tore up German rails. He made his way from Germany to Yugoslavia, to Greece, to Palestine, to Syria. Still fifteen, he convinced British authorities that he was nineteen and joined the British Army there, where he fought with the Kent regiment against the Arabs. At Jaffa, Palestine, he paid a German consul a bribe of three pounds for a visa and finally got to Gibraltar in his fight to get to America.

Newhouse was broke, but on the boat he met an American nurse. As a souvenir the nurse gave him a dime, and when he got to Boston that was all he had. He didn't speak a word of English but he was so thrilled with America that he spent the dime on two trolley rides. He went to the end of the line for one of the nickels and came back with the other.

On December 7, 1941, Newhouse was not yet a citizen. The minute he heard of the Jap action he volunteered for the army. He was rejected and for 120 consecutive days he heckled his enlistment office at Wausau, Wisconsin, until they finally took him. He was assigned to the Air Force and became a gunner.

Once in London he met a French refugee girl and became engaged. The day before he was to be married, Newhouse was shot down. Dave Scherman, *Life* photographer who had planned to picture the happy ending to Newhouse's story, was left with a tragic finish and no pictures.

Men on the field will tell you that Newhouse was the only man in the group who ever hated the Germans with the intensity that drove him to kill and kill. Emanuel Klette, a pilot on the base, finished a tour of operations and crashed at his home field after his 28th raid. He has been in the hospital recovering for several months and has recently been put back on operations at his own request, but Klette loved flying more than he hated Germans.

Captain Raymond Check, of Minot, North Dakota, was one of the group's great heroes, and the circumstances of his death were tragic. Check was on his last mission. Colonel James Wilson, air executive, flew with Check as copilot and Ray's regular copilot, First Lieutenant William P. Cassidy, refusing to miss Check's last haul, went as a waist gunner.

Check was killed instantly. A 20-mm. shell struck him in the head. A fire started in the cockpit and Colonel Wilson stayed with the controls until the rubber of his oxygen mask melted on his face. His hands were so burned that he could not let go of the wheel. Finally, Cassidy came up from the waist and helped Wilson. In the ship that day they were luckily carrying a flight surgeon who wanted practical experience, and had it not been for his work Colonel Wilson might not have lived.

There had been a party planned that night at the officers' mess and Check was to have been the guest of honor. A cake was baked and his name was inscribed on the top. When Check's ship flew into the field with Cassidy at the controls there wasn't a man on the field who felt like eating cake or having a party

The ground personnel at the field was unsung as is the tradition and knowing that they would live to tell their own story they had no objection. Major Thurman E. Dawson and his crew of bomb loaders have put into the bomb bays every last pound of the 6,000 tons the group has dropped. In addition they have done the work that hurts. The work that has to be undone a few hours later when the report comes through that the mission has been scrubbed—bombs must be unloaded.

That doesn't tell all the group's story. It doesn't tell about the officer whose greatest delight is to take a Very pistol and a pocketful of assorted green and red flares and chase the old white horse in the pasture next to his Nissen hut around in circles; it doesn't tell about Harold Rogers and his dog "Mister," who went on eight missions with his gunner master who used to be a Hollywood stunt man, and it leaves out completely the hundreds of ordinary Joes in crews who have stood around their potbellied stoves at night worrying and throwing 50-caliber shells into the fire for excitement. It doesn't tell any of that; it would take a book.

You can tell, though, from these few people, why the Germans haven't got a chance. You can tell why the U. S. Air Force can make a lot of mistakes and still somehow struggle to the top of the heap of world air forces.

Generally you could generalize about public relations officers: all but a small minority of PROs in combat outfits were pretty reasonable people doing a pretty unreasonable job, and all but a small minority of rear echelon PROs didn't like *The Stars and Stripes.* The conflict between the paper's staff men and demanding public relations characters went back to the very beginning of *The Stars and Stripes.* A photographer-reporter who was a corporal and might as well be called Slim, went to northern Ireland in July of 1942 to cover the first inspection of American troops overseas by the King and Queen of England.

Some fifty civilian war correspondents, and the corporal,

waited on the docks of a North Ireland port for the royal ship from England. A lieutenant colonel cautioned the correspondents.

"You are not allowed to come closer to their royal Majesties than fifty feet," the colonel told the newspaper people, capitalizing every letter. The photographers groaned. Pictures of British royalty talking to American privates wouldn't be much pictures at fifty feet.

The corporal-correspondent suggested that when he had been a photographer in the Canadian forces, a year or so before the Yanks got into the war, he had taken a good many pictures of the King and Queen and that the specified distance always had been fifteen feet.

"Fifty feet, corporal!" the colonel roared. He turned and added, "and gentlemen."

Their Majesties arrived. Down the gangplank came a British brigadier, as formidably correct as British brigadiers are. He was the King's equerry and had handled this sort of thing scores of times. He knew some of the newspapermen and nodded. His eye went over the soldier-reporter, paused.

"Hello there, Slim. Changed armies?"

"Yes, sir, and we're having a little misunderstanding here."

"Oh?" with lifted eyebrow.

"A rule has been made, sir, that we can't take pictures closer than fifty feet. Would you mind fixing it up?"

The King's equerry was not unmindful of the situation: the corporal was straightening things out. That happens in armies all the time. Among the reasons the brigadier was the King's equerry were good sense and better taste, along with a not overinflated sense of proportion, even in time of war and royalty. He turned to the American colonel:

"The photographers may take pictures at fifteen feet, colonel," he said. Everyone thought he said the word "colonel" pretty firmly.

The pictures were taken at fifteen feet.

At the end of the three-day inspection tour, the corporal was broke. He needed steamer fare to cross the Irish Sea with his pictures and story and told Bob Vining, the genial lieutenant commander who got United States Navy public relations off to a good start in Europe. Vining searched his pockets as the rest of the party headed for the ticket window.

"Broke myself," he said. "But I know where to borrow it. Five pounds for you and five for me."

Vining stepped across the dockside, spoke low and brief to the lieutenant colonel, who pulled out his pocketbook and handed over two five-pound notes. The colonel stood graven, a little slump beginning in his shoulders, as Vining recrossed the dock and handed the corporal half the money.

It was a little thing and petty, and didn't help much to win the war or lose it—fifty feet or fifteen feet. But it set some sort of gauge by which the long lines of privates and corporals and sergeants who passed through *The Stars and Stripes* in the years to come could judge their own responsibilities.

*The Stars and Stripes* was to be an enlisted man's newspaper, published and written by enlisted men lest it lose the soldiers' viewpoint; and the army wanted a good newspaper, something that would be to the soldiers what their morning papers had been at home; and if there was difficulty in compromising the two basic tenets, the *Stars and Stripes* staff would work the thing out as best could be done en route, but no one—not even the army itself—would balk that staff from doing their primary job in the war, publishing and writing that good newspaper.

It was a little mixed up.

*The Stars and Stripes* always was a little mixed up. Even on the occasions when everything connected with it had been momentarily straightened out it was mixed up, because the condition was so unusual that it was confusing, maybe a little frightening. The original purpose and setup was simple enough on paper. To make it clearly simple and direct, General George C. Marshall, the American Army chief of staff in Washington, put it down in the form of a letter, printed in the first issue of *The Stars and Stripes* of World War II. He wrote:

Like any other veteran of the AEF in France, I am delighted to welcome the new version of The Stars and Stripes.

"I do not believe that any one factor could have done more to sustain the morale of the AEF than The Stars and Stripes," wrote General Pershing of this soldier-newspaper. We have his authority for the statement that no official control was ever exercised over the matter which went into The Stars and Stripes. "It always was entirely for and by the soldier," he said.

This policy is to govern the conduct of the new publication. From the start The Stars and Stripes existed primarily to furnish our officers and men with news about themselves, their comrades, and the homes they had left behind across the sea.

A soldiers' newspaper, in these grave times, is more than a morale venture. It is a symbol of the things we are fighting to preserve and spread in this threatened world. It represents the free thought and free expression of a free people.

I wish the staff every success in this important venture.

Their responsibility includes much more than the publication of a successful newspaper. The morale, in fact the military efficiency of the American soldiers in these islands, will be directly affected by the character of the new Stars and Stripes.

There were quite a few interpretations placed on General Marshall's declaration over the years. Folks used to spend no end of time interpreting what General Marshall must have meant when he said no official control ever was exercised over the matter which went into *The Stars and Stripes* in World War I and that it would be the same way this time. A lot of people figured they could interpret that and make it plain. They knew just what the general meant.

Twice in the years that followed, General Dwight Eisenhower, supreme commander of Allied forces in Europe, talked to members of the staff and recalled for the army what General Marshall had written.

The interpreters got busy both times figuring out what General Eisenhower must have meant when he quoted General Marshall.

*The Stars and Stripes* relations with the military press censors weren't quite like its relations with the rest of the army.

At the outset, wartime censoring of press copy for policy and security was a comparatively new thing in the European Theater, as it was everywhere for the American citizen army. It had been done in World War I and not since. It was a tough job, for even the very word "censorship" is mild anathema to the average American who has a vague feeling that somewhere back there in the Bill of Rights or something like that there is something that says nobody is going to tell American newspapers what to print and what not to print.

The military censors who came to the ETO to see that no breaches of security or policy were committed in the tens of thousands of words written daily about the growing United States war machine in the United Kingdom had been fitted as best the army could for their task, but it was largely a case of learning as they went along. *The Stars and Stripes* was in roughly the same position, and the two groups learned together. Yet despite the misunderstandings traditionally supposed to exist between newspapermen and censors, *The Stars and Stripes* felt it had friends in the office of press censorship, and the censors felt that, strained as it might occasionally be, there was friendship between them and the soldiers who put out the newspaper.

The straining came in various ways. If the *S&S* Desk thought a cut in a story to be unjustified, there was no hesitation in calling the censors and arguing it out.

Someday, maybe, Lieutenant Colonel J. D. Merrick and the lieutenants, captains and majors who worked for him as censors will know how gratefully the *S&S* accepted their reasonableness.

Not that it was all one long honeymoon. The *Stripes* staff prided itself on the authenticity and background knowledge which went into its stories of the air war. The censors had to get their air war knowledge by remote control, as it were, and not infrequently a censorial cut would be argued, and bitterly. Sometimes the paper won; more often the censor, but unhappy his lot if later events proved the cut unjustified.

Then there were the pastepots.

Somehow, when the paper was a couple of months old, a vast shipment of paste arrived at the editorial offices, gross upon gross of pint-sized bottles of paste, whereas normal consumption would have been about a pint a month in that office. The staff didn't believe in clipping stories from other sources.

One evening, Phil Bucknell, an American-born staffer who had been a top-flight newspaperman in England when the war broke out, was having trouble with American verbs. Phil had been writing English verbs so long ("The RAF HAVE done so and so" or "His Majesty's Government HAVE . . ."). Plural verbs with collectively singular nouns were a red flag to the Desk. Phil committed four of them in two paragraphs and the tough guy-city editor could stand it no longer.

"Damn it to bloody hell, Bucknell! You limey so-and-so!"

The city editor grabbed the nearest pastepot and heaved it

in a flat trajectory across the room at Bucknell's head. Fortunately it missed.

"Will you ever learn [another pastepot crashed against the wall] to write the American language?"

Bucknell, like the rest of the staff, operated on the theory that if they were going to set up the Desk as a sort of terrestrial god (albeit two-headed) they'd put up with what the Desk did as long as the Desk was right, and raise hell if the Desk was found wrong, a fair arrangement. However, the pastepots seemed a little beyond even terrestrially godlike prerogatives, and Buck, too, grabbed a pastepot. The first one smashed on the wall just behind the city editor, and with a fine show of justice splattered Bob Moora across the desk with broken glass and the city editor with paste.

The flurry ended when the immediately handy supply of paste was gone, and then Mark Senigo, the sports editor, started to laugh and pointed. Beneath his little table which had been exactly in line with the flight of the pastepots was the censor for the night, a Lieutenant Bennett. He had slid into his walnut foxhole at the first salvo and stayed there until it was over, each passing pastepot drizzling a swirl of gooey liquid across his uniform.

That set the measure of the Desk's displeasure. A staff man relating in the Lamb and Lark how mad the Desk had been at him counted the anger by the number of pastepots hurled before he got out of the office.

Victor Meluskey, lieutenant censor from Philadelphia, however, was no man to take refuge when a pastepot war started. Mollie was a burly customer and was willing to stand up for himself. (He became more proficient than any men on the staff itself at starting fires under Joe Fleming's chair without being detected.) Mollie alone of staff or censors held a pastepot decision over the Desk.

A warm spring evening, when the paper had gone to press early, the staff sat around the office drinking Coca-Colas. Meluskey was wearing a new pair of pink officer's pants, which the staff, sweaty and tired from three straight sixteen-hour days, had eyed disdainfully all evening. Suddenly, Hutton picked up a half-full pastepot and hollering "Meluskey!" tossed it at the censor.

Mollie had been waiting for that, a long, long time.

Sidestepping the missile, Mollie reached swiftly into the drawer of his censor's table, pulled out a full bottle of paste and heaved it at Hutton, who caught it carelessly with one hand. Mollie came up with a second pot and heaved that. Hutton caught it with the other hand. With a fierce howl, Meluskey triumphantly brought out a third pastepot and pegged it straight down the middle.

Unable to move, Hutton instinctively brought together his two hands already holding pastepots. There was an explosion of glass and glue as the three factory-fresh containers smashed together. Paste flew all over the city desk, over feature stories typewritten for the next day's paper. Paste streamed from Hutton's chest and face, and in a couple of seconds blood began to follow from a cut in his shoulder where flying glass had lodged.

The staff cheered, Meluskey bowed gracefully and stalked out, while for the next two or three days copy sporadically appeared in the composing room smeared with the blood Hutton had shed that night.

Meluskey's opinions on security and policy were valued as long as there was a paper, not only because he was a competent censor and knew his business, but because he was pointed out to each new man on the staff as "the censor who licked the Desk at pastepots at five paces."

Some of Lieutenant Colonel Merrick's censors never caught the *Stars and Stripes* assignment, and would have felt they were fortunate except for the telephone calls from staff members who wanted to thresh out a point of censorship. Long-standing relationships were built up thus over the telephone and the censors and staff members frequently never saw each other, although from their arguments they achieved a pretty accurate mutual insight into character.

One censor, Lieutenant Charlie Desser, talked for months with the staff of the Paris edition without ever seeing a single *S&S* man, and it was not until he went in a glider on the airborne invasion of Germany itself that Desser found a staffer. At a press headquarters, which was a foxhole in a clump of German woods, Desser looked up the second day of the invasion and was handed copy by an individual who from his dress obviously had jumped with the paratroops. At the top of the first page the copy read:

TO: Stars and Stripes, Paris.

Desser groaned. "I'll censor it," he said finally, with a wry grin. "But if you want to argue about any cuts I make, you'll have to call me on someone's telephone or I won't know how to talk to you."

Lieutenant Colonel Merrick insisted to civilians and army alike that *The Stars and Stripes* was entitled to exactly the same treatment as any other publication, and he did his best to see that we got it. More than once he stuck his silver leaves as well as his neck way out beyond the dictates of duty or conscience to see to it that the army's newspaper wasn't forced through any censorship to degenerate from the honest publication it set out to be.

Such treatment from censors had a beneficial effect on the *Stripes* staff, too. Inclined anyway to put accuracy above everything, since its readers were the people who had made the news and would know where mistakes were written, the paper was doubly careful because of the obvious trust imposed by the censors. Consequently, some of the paper's stories became sources of precedent, particularly the air stories.

The greatest compliment that the censor's office paid *The Stars and Stripes* happened one afternoon in early 1944.

An editorial phone rang. Hodenfield answered.

"This is the censor's office," a voice said. "Lieutenant So-and-so. Look, we've got a story here from an American correspondent to censor. He's writing about the new B-17 Fortresses. He's referring to the B-17G, and we don't know whether we ought to pass that or not. We figured you could tell us."

Hod called a conference of the other air people—he was the first staffer to fly to Berlin, and did it at night with the RAF bombers—and it was decided there no longer was good reason for keeping the designation B-17G secret, since Jerry had knocked some down, so the story was passed.

It was Captain, later Major, Eugene Nute, who summed up the censors' attitude toward the duty trick at *The Stars and Stripes.*

"It's all right to go there, and they're a good bunch," Nute explained to a new censor. "But we've been thinking for a long time of getting the army to award a censor an Air Medal or an Oak Leaf Cluster, which is what you get for five missions to Germany, to every censor who makes five missions to *The Stars and Stripes*."

The censors packed their blue pencils and went across to the war wherever the fighting and *The Stars and Stripes* went. Lieutenant Colonel Merrick never would admit it officially, but as the relationship continued, the *Stars and Stripes* staff began to have a sneaking suspicion that Merrick occasionally farmed out new censors to a *Stars and Stripes* job so that they could get the worst over with first and also maybe learn a little more about their jobs than they would have ordinarily. Some of the favorite censors from London turned up again in France and Germany. Happiest, perhaps, were the staffers of the Liége edition to censor whose paper Lieutenant Colonel Merrick sent Meluskey, the hero of the pastepots.

All through the bitter winter war of 1944-45, while the buzz bombs droned regularly into Liége and shattered buildings and lives all around but never in *The Stars and Stripes,* Meluskey stuck with the Liége staffers, censored combat stories as they came back from the front, and contributed greatly to the staff's financial condition. Maybe that was the index of how *The Stars and Stripes* thought of Vic Meluskey: He was the only outsider they ever would admit to their poker games. To be perfectly fair about it, however, Meluskey's lack of skill as a poker player may have had something to do with it. While he was at Liége, Vic became a captain and drew something more than three hundred dollars a month. It all went into the poker game, for even if Vic held a full house someone invariably had four of a kind.

At the end of March, when the Allies leaped across the Rhine and struck into Germany in the blow that finished the war, the Liége paper was left far behind the combat area to which its circulation went. The edition was closed down and the staff scattered among other editions at Frankfurt and Altdorf, in Germany, and those still publishing in France. That was a godsend for Meluskey. The captain hadn't had a nickel of his own pay for three months and on the day of last publication was borrowing ten-franc notes from the sergeants and corporals so that he could buy coffee and doughnuts at the Red Cross club to make up for the luncheons he missed because he was busy losing his money playing poker.

Most of the censors who came to the various *Stars and Stripes* offices accepted, as did the staffers, the doctrine that within the city room of *The Stars and Stripes* the man running the Desk was boss. He wasn't ordering the censor to do this or that, but he was the best man in the room or he wouldn't have been on the Desk.

There was one censor, who had friends and relatives in France and who liked to spend as much time as he reasonably could at their château, who possibly went a little far in accepting the authority of the sergeant running the particular edition to which he was attached. That edition was in a rear echelon area and its reporters covered the activities of organizations in which there was little or no military security involved; the censor didn't have much to do.

One afternoon at four, then, the lieutenant-censor telephoned to or came to the office and said to the sergeant running the Desk:

"Er . . . is there any work for me to do?"

Usually there wasn't and the sergeant would look up and say "No."

"In that case could I have the evening off, please?"

The sergeant was very fair about it and gave the lieutenant every other evening off that he asked for.

# PUBLIC SERVICE

IN THE FALL of 1942, when the American soldiers in the British Isles were getting ready to invade Nazi-held North Africa, a lank, earnest young private first class named Dewey Livingston decided that the size 14 overshoes he was wearing in lieu of ordinary footgear weren't exactly the thing in which to go storming the beaches of Africa. Dewey was wearing the arctics because neither his supply sergeant nor any of the Quartermaster Corps's minions that Dewey showed his feet to could provide him with a pair of size 13 EEE shoes.

In desperation, Dewey went over to the Red Cross club one evening and wrote a note to *The Stars and Stripes.*

"Dear Editor," Dewey began, inaugurating a kind of reader-publisher relationship that was to be indigenous to *The Stars and Stripes* all the paper's days. "Can somebody please help me get a pair of shoes to fit me? I wear size 13 EEE. As a matter of fact, I will wear 13 anything if I can get it. I am wearing overshoes right now which are too big for me anyway even with two pairs of socks. I have had this same trouble with shoes ever since back in the States and thought maybe *The Stars and Stripes* knew somebody with a pair of 13 EEEs."

Dewey signed the letter and affixed the address of the infantry outfit to which he belonged.

When the letter reached the Desk, it was handed to Charlie White, who turned out a little piece which ran the next day asking somebody in the army please to find Dewey Livingston a pair of shoes.

It would be nice to chronicle that so great was *The Stars and*

*Stripes'* reach and appeal that scores of 13 EEEs came pouring in to shoe Dewey's naked soles, but that isn't the way it was. Either *The Stars and Stripes* didn't reach the right people or the army in the British Isles was fresh out of 13 EEEs. Charlie White tried another story.

"Won't somebody please turn up a pair of 13 EEEs for poor old Dewey Livingston?" asked Charlie. A couple of days later a sergeant from the Quartermaster Corps came in with a pair of shoes of the right size; would we forward them to Dewey Livingston? Charlie White fortified himself at the Lamb and Lark for a jeep ride and started across England with the 13 EEEs. But Dewey Livingston and his outfit had moved. We ran a story notifying Dewey his shoes were waiting. No response.

Meanwhile, half a dozen more supply sergeants with half a dozen pairs of 13 EEEs found their way to the new daily's quarters in Printing House Square. The place began to look like a shoe shop, and into Charlie White's daily piece asking Dewey to come pick up his shoes or tell us where he was there crept a plaintive note of entreaty. Charlie's stories weren't, perhaps, approved journalese, but neither was an editorially conducted search for 13 EEE shoes.

"Please come get your shoes, Dewey," Charlie wrote. "I'm gettin' awful sick of this story."

The rest of the army wasn't sick of it, however. White's stories publicly aired a grievance most men in the army feel: you never get the right size from the Quartermaster Corps more than half the time. To add to Charles's troubles, there began to arrive each day at Printing House Square, sometimes waiting in the office when the staffers came in for work, a small stream of other soldiers who wore 13 EEE shoes, and hadn't been able to find any either. Charles wrote one last ultimatum to Dewey Livingston:

"Dewey, you better come get your shoes or they're gonna be all gone."

We never got an answer from Dewey Livingston, because he and his outfit had sailed for the invasion of Africa, Dewey presumably in his too-large overshoes. But we did hear in daily increasing queries from scores of other big-footed GIs, and from a few small-footed GIs. Soldiers couldn't find 14 BBs, 14 EEEs, 15 EEs. Neither could they find size 4½ A.

Each of their appeals was duly chronicled, and so naturally

and dryly were the appeals translated into gently satirical stories by the Hoosier humor of Charlie White that they became almost regular features on page one.

Charlie fortuitously one evening used the phrase "help wanted." That started a snowball.

Size-42-waist soldiers complained they couldn't get pants to go around their middles unless they accepted legs so long they tripped on them. Size-28-waist soldiers complained that the leg size with their waist made good knickerbockers. A soldier turned up with a No. 6 hat size, and another one said that the quartermaster had issued him two shoes for the left foot and wouldn't exchange one of them. Two other soldiers had similar trouble with gloves. They all wanted help.

All these things Charlie White chronicled, and there was beginning to rest almost day and night in his blue eyes a bright gleam of delight as he and the rest of us contemplated what the German High Command—whose agents certainly were reading every *Stars and Stripes* they could—must be thinking of the "best equipped army in the world" whose soldiers no doubt one day would go into battle wearing two left shoes and khaki knickerbockers.

By this time, Pfc. Dewey Livingston's original request had assumed the proportions of a good-sized help wanted department. But the army had had enough. The Quartermaster Corps and Lieutenant General John C. H. Lee's Services of Supply were being made to look more ridiculous and inefficient than they were. To the Desk came a peremptory order originating, we were informed by the colonel who delivered it, with General Lee: *The Stars and Stripes* would print no more stories calculated to publicize failures in the Services of Supply system of distribution. That was an order.

We were in the thing too deeply, however, simply to say to the growing thousands of readers, "We're sorry, fellows, but the army says we can't help you any more."

By that time we were hearing from soldiers who wanted to swap kodaks for bicycles, binoculars for stamp collections; who wanted to know if we could find their brother Louie who was with some ordnance outfit, who wanted to get a transfer from one outfit to another and who didn't like the company commander, or maybe wanted to get in touch with the Woman's Auxiliary

Air Force girl who was sitting at the second table from the door at Lyons' Corner House last Saturday evening.

There must have been some wry-humored, eccentric kind of special god with nothing to do except watch over *The Stars and Stripes.* The paper somehow seemed to scrape by one crisis after another through the last-minute intervention of a providence beyond any poor power we had and so the "Help Wanted Department" miraculously was born at a time when shoes were beginning to pile three deep around Charlie White's desk and the bespectacled Hoosier was leaning more on the Lamb and Lark and Alf Storey's mild-and-bitter for a solution to the problems in his mail.

Private Lou Rakin, who had been a police court justice in Linden, New Jersey, before he went into the army, and looked just like that sort of guy, showed up at the *Stars and Stripes* business offices one morning as an administrative clerk. No one knew how the orders assigning him to us were issued, but there he was. He started to work on a pile of Help Wanted correspondence. In a week Private Lou Rakin was running the Help Wanted Department. He was just the kind of man for the job. He wanted to help people.

At his battered little desk in London, the painstaking Rakin began to assume the qualities of a combined Dorothy Dix, Mr. Anthony, the Help Wanted Department of your morning newspaper, Travelers Aid, and an itinerant umbrella mender. Two years later Lou was running a department with half a dozen research assistants, two or three stenographers, and answering as many as a thousand soldier requests for help a week.

"Who is this guy Rakin?" demanded a colonel in a telephone conversation with the Desk one day. "He comes in my office, says do I mind helping him get some fellow transferred from the ordnance to the Air Force as a gunner. You can't do that. But Rakin just left here, and, by God, I'm doin' it!"

"Help Wanted" became possibly the most concrete public service that *The Stars and Stripes* ever performed for the millions of soldiers who looked to it as their voice in dealing with the Army. Lou did everything for them: he got them the right size clothes when the quartermaster didn't have any. Sometimes he used *Stars and Stripes* money to buy whatever it was a soldier wanted, more often he traded with another soldier or some other branch in the army.

He found their WAAF girl friends for them, traded their surplus goods, brought them news from home when their wives had babies. Every time a soldier asked for something unusual, Lou made a point of getting the item into the Help Wanted column to let other soldiers know that here was still another service they could get from *The Stars and Stripes.*

Once in a while the GIs got a chance to help their paper. In the winter of 1944-45, the *Stars and Stripes* editions in Paris and Liége were down to one day's supply of newsprint. The morning's papers carried a modest box at the lower left-hand corner of page one:

> Stars and Stripes has enough newsprint for tomorrow morning's paper. There are twenty-two carloads of newsprint consigned to the S&S somewhere on the Continent. If you know where they are will you call us at Elysees 4149?

Before nightfall the telephone switchboard in the *Stars and Stripes* building clamored with the voices of soldiers who had seen carloads of paper here or there within the previous two weeks. By the following evening we had enough paper to carry us for several days. But the paper's request for help had consequences beyond anything we had foreseen.

For three weeks railroad cars laden with virtually every kind of paper manufactured were funneling into the army-operated Paris switching yards. Some of the paper was consigned to the Office of War Information, or the Propaganda and Psychological Warfare Division of the army, or to French civilian newspapers. It made no difference to the Joes to whom *S&S* had addressed a plea of help wanted. They weren't going to see their paper run short of newsprint.

Only once did *The Stars and Stripes'* concept of public service carry it beyond ability to deliver. In the autumn of 1944, after the American Army had raced across France and had liberated the French perfume business, among other things, Lieutenant Colonel Ensley Llewellyn thought it would be a fine idea if the paper could undertake to do the soldiers' Christmas shopping for them.

He was moved to the contemplated public service by the daily sight of scores of American doughboys, the whiskers, grime and weariness of the front still upon them, standing in queues at the exotic perfume and cosmetics shops for which Paris is famous.

Llewellyn sent to the Desk a "must" item offering the paper's assistance to soldiers who needed help in buying Christmas gifts of perfume or anything else to send back to America. The Desk tried to argue that the paper would do well first to set up a department and a specific modus operandi to handle the requests that certainly would follow. Llewellyn, however, possibly may have come to consider, as a regular staff member, the special if eccentric providence which theretofore had come to the paper's aid so many times. He said it would work out and made the "must" an order.

One announcement and only one of the proposed *Stars and Stripes* "shopping service" was printed in the paper. We said we would find the gift and send it home. All the soldier had to do was send to *The Stars and Stripes* his money and the address to which the gift was to go.

Ralph Noel, a sergeant who probably knew more about army finances than anyone else in the army including chief paymaster, fought manfully to deliver the goods for "shopping service." He had a cousin living in Paris and she helped. At one time there were sixteen paid and volunteer girls and as many soldiers changing marks into francs, buying Schiaparelli "Shocking" and sending it to Dubuque with a card that said "Merry Christmas from Elmer." But we never caught up with the number of requests.

Buried away in some corner of the Paris *Herald* building which so long housed *The Stars and Stripes* in Paris there undoubtedly today are several quietly mad staffers and stenographers still filling soldiers' pre-paid orders for perfume to be sent home as a gift for Christmas, 1944.

We had one other bit of trouble with soldier requests. Early in its career as a weekly, the paper resumed the plan of sponsoring a fund by which American servicemen abroad contributed money to the support of Allied children orphaned by the war: the *Stars and Stripes* of World War I had done the same thing for hundreds of little French girls and boys.

We started out with a plan of permitting any unit—bomber group, infantry company, service battalion—which raised the equivalent of $400 to choose the kind of orphan it wanted to help. The soldiers could specify sex, age, nationality, color of hair, etc., of the orphan to whom they wished to act as a great many Europeans feel Uncle Sam should.

The Stars and Stripes War Orphan Fund helped thousands of youngsters who had lost one or both parents to enemy action to get a start in education, or to get past that critical first year in which slow-moving public assistance would not care adequately for them. The $400 wasn't a great deal, and it wasn't designed to provide all or even a majority of the orphan's care. The American Red Cross, which administered the fund, simply figured on using the $400 to provide a life above bleak and bare subsistence.

Bomber groups which sponsored orphans in England brought their young charges to the airfields for parties and presents far beyond the original subscription of $400. If in the turmoil that fills Europe today there lingers a strain of feeling not thinned by the bickerings of the international talkers who appear after wars, possibly a share of it will be because here and there an unhappy child found out just how generous and kind the average American kid in a war could be.

Some of the motives of the soldiers seeking to sponsor war orphans, however, to get back to the difficulties the paper's public service occasionally engendered, gave the War Orphan Fund staff and the Red Cross administrators a bit of difficulty.

The letter accompanying the sixth contribution to the Orphan Fund, and about one every twenty-five thereafter, said naïvely:

"For our $400 we would like to select a redheaded, good-looking, feminine little French war orphan about twenty years of age."

It didn't take very long for the fund's personnel to insert a clause in the conditions of sponsorship specifying that no orphan would be more than twelve years of age.

In the stories in which combat soldiers learned better ways to fight a war, or in which engineers or ordnance men described better ways of repairing and improvising equipment, *The Stars and Stripes* did a genuine public service. The development of "parachute brakes" for aircraft was one such.

Into the London office one evening came the telephoned story of a Liberator bomber crew which had come back to base from Germany with their plane's brakes and wing flaps destroyed by enemy fire. Faced with a certainty that they would be unable to halt the 30-ton bomber before it reached the end of the runway, the Liberator crew hit upon the idea of tying a parachute to the gun mount at each of the two waist windows.

As the plane with no brakes and no flaps glided in for a landing, and the emergency crash truck and the ambulance clanged expectantly at the far end of the runway, a new safety device for combat aircraft was born.

Just as the bomber's brakeless wheels touched the concrete, the waist gunners simultaneously pulled the two parachute ripcords. From each waist window blossomed the white silk of a parachute. They caught in the blast of the propeller's slipstream and with the effect of giant air anchors slowed the bomber to a halt just short of the waiting crash truck.

*The Stars and Stripes* carried the story in a box on page one. Within a month, at least four other observant bomber crews had used this same device to make safe landings with planes so badly damaged that a crash would have been inevitable before the discovery of "parachute brakes."

Paris, November 11, 1944
*Hancock County Briefs:*

## IRA FISK ELECTED SHERIFF

*"Will you as soon as possible publish the complete election returns by states, with particular reference to the returns from Hancock County, Ind.?" Signed First Lieutenant Melville E. Watson, APO 739.*

This request came by mail to the *Stars and Stripes* news desk on election night. A lot of editors might have screamed, but not on *The Stars and Stripes,* which claims the best Indiana election coverage in France. Here you are, lieutenant, straight from Ben E. Price, our New York political sage:

"HANCOCK COUNTY, INDIANA . . . SHERIFF, IRA FISK, REPUBLICAN; CORONER, CHARLES PASCO, REPUBLICAN; SURVEYOR, CHRIS OSTERMIER, DEMOCRAT."

Bertha Kirkpatrick, Democrat, won something—we think county clerk.

Now that we've shown we can do it, we rest on our laurels. No more, please.

## COMPLAINTS AND MISTAKES

AT ONE TIME *The Stars and Stripes* in Paris alone was getting about 2,500 letters a week. Half of them were complaints and beefs, many of which were directed against *The Stars and Stripes* itself.

Often the beefs against the paper were legitimate. *The Stars and Stripes* made the same number of errors as the average good army organization. Its editors made the same number a good patrol leader made, a tank commander or a corps commander. Graves Registration Units saw the fighting men's leaders' mistakes. They buried them. Mistakes in *The Stars and Stripes,* though, were there in cold black print for everyone to read and reread and file away or clip out. A mistake was never dead.

The greatest single number of complaints was from men in units which had never or only infrequently been mentioned in the paper. They wanted to know why. There was a constant argument among staff members about the comparative importance of play on a local story of great importance to a relative few and a universal story of mild importance to thousands.

The question first came up on Mark Senigo's sports page in the London edition. Were the fights held weekly in the ARC Rainbow Corner more important than a Notre Dame-Ohio State basketball game? Thousands would read of the game played back home with casual interest but the few hundreds who watched the local boxers and those who participated would probably clip out the report of their affair and send it home.

When operations started in earnest, the question answered itself. With several million men reading the paper, no one unit could be given space on a story of interest to that unit alone.

There were, however, many real errors *The Stars and Stripes* made both in general policies and on specific stories.

Maybe the worst mess we ever made of a story was the Third Army's taking of Metz. The strength of the garrison was underestimated by Lieutenant General George S. Patton Jr., and the city did not fall so easily as he first told newspapermen he thought it would.

Jim Grad and Earl Mazo were with the Third Army at the time and they were filing regular news and feature stories on the action leading up to the fall of the fortress city. The 5th and 95th Infantry divisions were hammering away for weeks at the bastion. One night, when the fall of the city seemed imminent, a story came into the Paris office from Jim Grad. It was a color story that told of the fighting leading into Metz. Jim did not have a Metz dateline on for the simple reason that no American soldiers, let alone a correspondent, had been in the city itself. The Desk planned to use the story as it was written.

About eight o'clock a radio flash from some foreign news agency was picked up by the *Stars and Stripes* listening station. On the strength of the flash, which stated that Metz had fallen to American troops, the Desk had Grad's story rewritten. A Metz dateline was added to the story and a new lead was tacked in front of the piece, which said that Metz had been captured.

When the paper got to Third Army troops still fighting a bloody fight for Metz, the following day, more than one infantryman made a mental note to shoot the first *S&S* reporter on sight.

Poor Jim Grad explained to Patton himself, to his staff and to the PRO that he was as surprised as they were at the appearance of the erroneous story under his by-line. The fact that there was a duplicate of his original story in the censor's file there helped officially but not every man in the Third Army could see or hear about the correct version of Jim's story. After that, Grad veered wide around Third Army territory.

The *Stars and Stripes* Metz mess wasn't over though. Several days later the city actually fell to the 95th and the 5th, which had done the toughest fighting of their careers to win the town. Both divisions had entered the city and each guarded its half carefully against infringement by the other U. S. outfit.

The news came through that the two divisions had cleared Metz but somewhere in transmission the phrase 5th Division was dropped and the following day *The Stars and Stripes* had the 95th taking Metz alone. Every man in the 5th Division was ready to pick up his rifle again. They wanted to clean up the 95th and then march on to Paris to wipe out *The Stars and Stripes.* (To avoid the civil war the Desk ran a front-page box next day, giving the 5th its credit.)

Mazo and Grad stayed out of trouble for a while after that with the Third Army until finally Mazo, one of the two officer-reporters on the staff, signed a petition, along with other Third Army correspondents, asking for the removal from office of the colonel acting as PRO. The petition was sent to Eisenhower and when some Third Army checker saw Mazo's name (*Lieutenant* Mazo) he hit the roof. Mutiny, he said. Mazo never went close to Third Army again but he somehow escaped the court-martial charges laid against him.

One of the greatest, if most unimportant, mistakes the paper made happened in London months after the invasion.

Tony Cordaro, a man with more good ideas than he knew what to do with, convinced Pete Lisagor, then editing the London edition, that *The Stars and Stripes* should pick its own man-of-the-year on January 1, 1945. The army paper's own man should be neither Roosevelt, Churchill, Stalin, Eisenhower nor anyone else in the public eye, Tony said with conviction.

"Our man of the year as the GIs' newspaper, should be GI Joe."

So that was it. The *Stars and Stripes* New Year edition carried a three-column front-page picture of a combat-weary soldier with helmet on, unshaven and dirty.

THE STARS AND STRIPES CHOICE FOR MAN-OF-THE-YEAR

The line over the picture read like that; underneath there was a longer caption explaining fully that the picture of the soldier had been picked as typical. It gave the man's full name, rank and home town.

Newspapers in the States thought it was a good idea and quoted the *Stars and Stripes* choice. The alert New York *Times* city editor sent a reporter out to locate the man's family to see what they thought about having their son chosen man-of-the-year by *The Stars and Stripes.*

The reporter talked to the mother of the soldier named in the *Stars and Stripes* picture caption and finally he even got a picture of the soldier, taken several years before when he had been a civilian.

Back in the *Times* offices the two pictures were compared. The difference was remarkable. In one the soldier was a young, carefree-looking boy and in the other, the combat picture, he was a weary man with hard lines in his face and gray streaks showing in his hair from under the helmet.

It was a natural "before-and-after" picture setup. Side by side the New York *Times* ran the two pictures, noting in their caption how the *Stars and Stripes* man-of-the-year had aged ten years in less than a year of combat.

Other newspapers saw the *Times* pictures and copied them. *Time* magazine used the picture and no one who saw the two pictures side by side could help being impressed by the change the war years had brought in the young boy's face.

The pictures got back to England and over to the Continent from back home. And one day, buried in a stack of mail a foot high, a note came into the *Stars and Stripes* office from a combat soldier at the front. He broke the horrible news.

"That was a very fine picture of your man-of-the-year," he said, "but it was not a picture of me as your caption stated."

The awful truth was that *The Stars and Stripes* had given the wrong name to their combat soldier and when the New York *Times* reporter got the picture of the man whose name appeared in the army paper, he got the picture of an altogether different man. Naturally, when the two were compared the editors noticed a great difference.

Tony Cordaro, formerly with the Des Moines *Register,* glibly explained to interrogating authorities that, while he admitted he had made "a little mistake," it didn't seem important. After all, Tony told them, the man was just a symbol to represent all fighting soldiers. It didn't really matter that *The Stars and Stripes* used the wrong name under the soldier's picture, he said.

Mistakes like that were made only once but somehow editors of the various editions never really learned to avoid one thing, which, whether it was actually in error or not, always brought in basketfuls of complaints. We were always giving someone credit for being first somewhere; being the biggest or having the most of something or the least. *The Stars and Stripes* staffers finally decided that no one ever was first anywhere. If we found a man fifteen feet tall in the army and said he was tallest there were bound to be fifty letters in the mail the following day from fellows who claimed to be sixteen feet tall.

We find a soldier named Aach who says the War Department told him his name, alphabetically, leads all the rest; a guy named Aaberg writes us and wants to know what about him.

We use the name of the soldier who climbed off the boat in Ireland in January, 1942, as the first American soldier to set foot in the British Isles after America declared war and a sergeant who came over to serve at the American Embassy in London a few weeks before that wants to know what about him.

On January 26, 1942, when the Eighth Air Force bombers hit Germany for the first time at Wilhelmshaven, a *Stars and Stripes* reporter got the name and home town of every man in the bomber leading the formation that day so that the paper would have the names of the first Americans in the U. S. Air Force to fly over German territory. The B-17 in which Brigadier General Frank Armstrong flew as an observer led the formation, but after *The Stars and Stripes* stated the following day that they had been the first American crew over Germany, the crew of the B-17 which flew on their right wing wrote in and said that actually they were first because of the angle at which the formation flew into Germany.

You couldn't beat it. After a few years with the paper most of its reporters wouldn't believe any "first" claim. If it had been an American soldier who shot Hitler dead, most *Stars and Stripes* reporters would have been leery about saying it was the first time it had been done.

We made lots of mistakes in giving credit to one outfit for a job another had done. One reporter, in the early days ofter the invasion, reported that the Rangers had taken Carentan, a tiny but once strategically important French town. The 101st Airborne Division, a rugged bunch of Americans who worked full time at the job of being a tough outfit, actually lost a good many men in clearing Carentan and for months after the mistake it was not safe for an *S&S* reporter to go near the division.

Joe Fleming did a piece in London on an ack-ack outfit which was reported to have been the first American anti-aircraft battery in the British Isles to bring down a German plane. The following morning a captain called the office in a plaintive voice. He did not dare distribute the papers to his men, he said, because twenty minutes before *The Stars and Stripes* said that the first German plane was destroyed by the other flak battery, his outfit had knocked a Ju 88 out of the air.

Joe did a humorous apology piece on that one but for the most part the paper had to let the mistakes stand. When the Jewish chaplain wrote us that the Catholic ceremony we had reported as the first American church ceremony in Germany was actually preceded by three days by an informal Jewish religious meeting on Friday, there was nothing we could do. A correction was worse than the mistake—if it was one.

Some of the mistakes were more a matter of poor judgment than actual error. At Thanksgiving and Christmastime, the quartermaster public relations office invariably issued some sort of statement on the meal they were going to provide soldiers on the holiday.

"Every GI will have at least a pound of Turkey with ice cream for dessert with nuts and cigars and cigarettes on the side," the handout read one year.

Knowing that food was always big news to soldiers, *The Stars and Stripes* printed the pound of turkey per soldier story. For the following week the office was flooded with letters and cluttered with personal visits from cooks who first swore at us and then pleaded, if we had an ounce of mercy in us, not to do it again.

The cooks who were forced to serve warm corned beef, fresh from the can, were nearly lynched by soldiers who had read the *Stars and Stripes* turkey story. Others who got turkey, and they were in the majority, were almost lynched too when they cut the soldiers short with a very small bit of turkey in an ocean of mashed potatoes. Some, of course, got their full turkey ration but the quartermaster had issued the statement assuming ideal conditions and the figure was probably strictly an arithmetical one which did not take into consideration problems of distribution, losses, etc., which inevitably appear.

Chaplains, next to cooks, were one of the paper's major sources of trouble on those special holidays. The Desk was always fair about news of religious interest because usually the man putting out the paper could view the subject with considerable detachment. In London, on Thanksgiving, the Protestant story generally got the biggest play in the paper simply because the Protestant chaplains arranged to have their services held in Westminster Abbey. The American flag was hoisted over the Abbey, and because this marked the first time in history that any but the flag of St. George had ever hung over the great English shrine, it was news.

The Catholic chaplain could not see it that way, however. The Catholics were having a pretty important Mass said in Westminster Cathedral the Catholic chaplain contended, and he felt their story should be told in the same size type and for the same length as the Protestant story, at least. His argument, not an unreasonable one, was that more soldiers would attend Catholic services than Protestant services that day. The Jewish chaplain had nothing to say on Thanksgiving.

On December 16, 1943, the news was a little slow and the London edition went overboard on a story Arthur White brought in about plans for installing regular ice-cream soda fountains at American bases all over England. The story was true when printed and the fountains were already bought by army post exchange authorities but they hadn't wanted that much publicity. London newspapers picked up the story and before long all England knew that the American Army in the British Isles was going to have ice-cream sodas for itself. There was so much unfavorable comment from within the army itself about "pampering the soldiers," and so much criticism from the British who were already outeaten about four to one by the Americans who brought their own food with them, that the plan was abandoned and the soda fountains never were installed.

Probably one of the most valid criticisms which could be leveled against the paper was its ever overoptimistic slant on the news—like the soda fountains and the pound of turkey. We were never quite skeptical enough.

We were always taking reports from the States that a new model B-17, which was capable of carrying ten tons of bombs, was being produced, when men on the staff who knew airplanes knew very well that no B-17 would ever cart ten tons of bombs to Germany and fly back the same day. With great optimism we reported new American weapons which were going to make the invasion easier. Somehow most of those weapons seem to have been left in *Stars and Stripes* files. They never showed up on the war front.

We were criticized because the paper always had the war coming to an end. The answer to that was, of course, that it always *was* coming to an end. That was the answer to many of the criticisms that we presented nothing but optimistic news. For almost two years there was little but good news about the progress of the war on all fronts. On the few occasions when the war did not go so well, when things looked black, the paper usually presented the facts to the extent censorship allowed.

With the air force, the bombing of Germany in daylight looked like an impossible task after the beating the Eighth Air Force took over Schweinfurt on October 14, 1943, when it lost sixty planes. Just after the invasion, during the four-day storm which made beach landings almost impossible, it looked as though the beachhead might have to be abandoned. In December, after the Ardennes breakthrough by the Germans, it appeared as though their armor might cut off our First Army supply link into Liége and run riot through France behind our lines.

In all those cases *The Stars and Stripes* presented the black news as it was, when censorship permitted.

Before the invasion, guessing the date was a great game. In December, 1942, just before Christmas, a reporter went around to see the chief chaplain in the ETO. The chaplain, a full colonel, said that the invasion would come off very shortly, that the war would be won soon afterward, and that all American soldiers in England would be home by the following Christmas. The high command had obviously not let their chaplains in on anything.

A year later at Christmastime we were still getting letters: "You said last Christmas that by now we would be home," etc.

We always ran into that trouble, as every newspaper does. If the letter was answered, and letters usually were answered by a staff of letter answerers, it was explained that the chaplain had said that he thought the war would be over. *The Stars and Stripes* had nothing to say on the matter.

It happened that way no matter whom we quoted. If we used a story saying that a War Department order had just been issued stating that all troops in Europe would go direct to the Pacific, we were damned all over the army the following day.

"The Stars and Stripes says we aren't going home first when this war is over."

"The Stars and Stripes says . . ."

The editorial department of *The Stars and Stripes,* or more properly the Desk and the other people who handled the news, seldom made any statement on their own authority. One of the biggest mistakes, probably the biggest, that *The Stars and Stripes* ever made, however, appeared in the editorial content of the paper. That was the publication of editorials designed to "orient" the soldiers' thinking.

That series of editorials was, the staffers felt, the one completely unethical and immoral thing *The Stars and Stripes* ever did.

The editorials were bitterly opposed by the Desk and the staff since they were thought to provide the opening wedge by which the army Information and Education Branch might eventually pry its way into the news columns of the soldiers' newspaper, producing a publication thus in many respects similar to the state-controlled press of the enemy.

The inroads the army's official propaganda department began to make on *The Stars and Stripes* started back in the days just prior to the invasion of June 6, 1944.

Armed with a War Department order, which found it convenient to overlook General Marshall's original dictum that *The Stars and Stripes* should be the soldiers' newspaper and as free as possible from army control, Arthur Goodfriend, who had written for some newspapers back home and had prepared several War Department pamphlets designed to teach the soldier what he was fighting for, descended on *The Stars and Stripes* to convert its eight-page weekly magazine section into a publication to be called *Warweek,* conceived as a vehicle for carrying to the combat man the contents of War Department directives which the soldier wouldn't read if they came to him as directives.

The *Stars and Stripes* staff had fought successfully against just that sort of thing from the day the first paper was printed, and in the course of fighting had made the paper so obviously an unoriented creation that the soldiers had come to trust in it pretty much implicitly.

"The orientation people," as the staffers referred to them, took advantage of that reputation and with orders from so high that the sergeants and corporals couldn't buck them, began to teach the soldiers how to think.

The combat man in a bomber or on the firing line feels that there is no particularly good reason why he should be told how to think by someone two or three or five hundred miles from the conditions under which he is doing his thinking.

Although the soldiers resented the "Tips on How to Destroy Your Foe," written by rear echelon orientation men, it wasn't until October and November of 1944, when the fighting became bitter along the western German border, that there was any really audible protest from the front.

During that period, Goodfriend, who had become the "editor in chief" through a series of higher echelon movings, began to write almost daily "picture editorials," which were ordered into the paper over the vehement protests of the editors and reporters who alone really put out *The Stars and Stripes.*

These editorials comprised lectures on what the army wanted the soldier to believe and think about, illustrated by an appropriate and, if possible, interesting photograph. Most notorious of these was a neat little gem entitled, "So you want to go home?" That one came close to demolishing completely *The Stars and Stripes'* reputation as the GI's newspaper.

The editorial exhorted the fighting men to slug on down the road to Berlin with undiminished fervor, hating all that Nazism stood for and stopping not for a single reason before Victory. It censured them for any occasional moments of doubt, bitingly scored any soldier who had the temerity to express a wish to go home.

The editorial referred scathingly to soldiers who might "raise their heads at night from tear-stained pillows . . ."

A *Stars and Stripes* reporter couldn't safely go within two miles of the veteran by noon the next day. Those staffers who were up there slipped off to cover divisions where they were unknown, and palmed themselves off as being from the Associated Press, or maybe *Yank.* Anything but from the paper that had demanded of the fighting men "So you want to go home?"

Every soldier fighting the enemy in the mud, cold and fear and death of the Western Front wanted to go home. Naturally. He knew the job had to be done first, and knew it would be done first, but he was goddamned if he could see anything wrong with wanting to go home.

Quite possibly from a completely detached point of view the sentiments of the editorial were fitting and proper. But *The Stars and Stripes,* as any enlisted man staffer who lived with the Joes could have told Goodfriend, was not published for people with a detached point of view. It is very hard to feel detached when you're going to get killed the next night or the next hour or the next week.

For that editorial there were some major generals commanding divisions who seriously considered barring *The Stars and Stripes* from their areas. At least one of them wrote his old West Point friend, Supreme Commander Dwight Eisenhower, decrying that and other *Stars and Stripes* editorials and asking that something be done.

For that editorial, some of the ordinary staffers for months lived almost without surcease in the midst of the fighting, trying their best to restore by their presence where the fighting was the paper's prestige with the guys who were winning the war, the guys who wanted to go home.

February 3, 1945

## JUST A NEW GUY FROM BROOKLYN

by Bud Hutton

*Stars and Stripes* Staff Writer

WITH THE 90TH INF. DIV.—The new guy from Brooklyn looked across the snowy fields in the moonlight, saw the German tanks coming toward him. The German infantry was with them, black against the snow, and he must have known what would happen if he stayed.

He came up to D Co., in the regiment's first battalion, at Christmas time, and they made him an ammo bearer with the machine guns. He was a private, and he didn't have much to say. If there was a job to be done he'd do it and that was that.

He was 20 years old, about five feet seven, with kind of brown hair and a sort of medium build. He was one of a batch of reinforcements, and it was easier to remember the names of some of the others, so mostly Dog Company called him the new guy from Brooklyn and let it go at that.

The outfit moved north to cut at the south flank of the Nazi bulge, and the new guy did a good job in the rough going east of Bastogne, so Captain John McLean, the Los Angeles skipper of Dog

Company, made him a machine-gunner. The new guy said that'd sure be good and slipped back into the obscurity of the company.

So they came, the night of January 23, to Binafeld, which is a little town the Yanks had to have for the jump-off to the Our River and the crossing into Germany.

They caught the enemy facing the wrong way and chased him out of town about one o'clock in the morning. Then Dog Company hurried in the bright moonlight to get set for the counter-attack which always follows.

There were three houses in a triangle on the far edge of town, and in them T/Sgt. Paul Landolt, of Aberdeen, Idaho, first platoon sergeant in Baker Company, placed his men. He found the new guy from Brooklyn, from Dog Company, already in the house nearest to the Germans.

The new guy had set up his caliber .50 in a window on the second floor, overlooking a road and the fields from which the Nazis probably would come. Landolt didn't know the guy's name, but he'd seen him around. He asked the new guy was he all right, and the kid said yes, and Landolt said did he know the bazooka ammo was gone. The kid said yes again, and then the counterattack began.

Three hundred yards away, out of the black shadows of the woods beyond the fields, came two German tanks, silhouetted clear and sharp in the moonlight against the snow. They began to clank toward the three houses, and behind them came the infantry.

As Lieutenant Colonel Bill Dupuy, the Sioux Falls, South Dakota, commander of the first battalion, or anyone else will tell you, the tanks don't like to come into a thing like that alone; the bazooka will get them. So the infantry comes along and it consolidates the position if the tanks clear it out.

The new guy was a reinforcement and he had been with the outfit only a month, but he knew if they could kill the Nazis' infantry, the tanks probably would stop, because they wouldn't know how it was about the bazooka ammo.

The noise of the tanks was getting loud across the field, and the new guy must have been thinking about it. He could fire a little and have a jam in his gun, or he could run out of ammo, and then the red and orange flash wouldn't be there for the enemy.

The other men in the houses heard the new guy's gun begin to yammer, saw figures out beyond the tanks stumble, fall, less than 100 yards away.

The tanks came on until they were 20 yards from the nearest house, where the machine gun was, and stopped. The new guy's gun kept firing.

The men who are left in Dog Company will tell you what happened later: how some German infantry surrounded the three houses and First Lieutenant Bob Smith called down artillery around the houses; how they fought the Nazis off till daylight came and the American tanks got up to give them support.

Mostly, though, they'll tell you about a new guy from Brooklyn and how he kept firing at the tank turrets until they turned. They'll tell you that by that time there wasn't enough infantry left to cover the tank. They'll tell you they could see the reflection of the machine gun's flare on the sides of the tanks, and they'll tell you that the new guy must have known what would happen if he stayed there and fired.

The first shell from the tanks smashed the house wall next to the new guy and he kept firing. The second shell passed through the red and orange flare at the muzzle of the new guy's gun and exploded, and because the censor won't pass the name of a soldier killed in action until it's certain his folks are notified, the story has to call him the new guy from Brooklyn, which is the way it was to most of Dog Company.

Not long after "So you want to go home?" General Eisenhower sent a call to *The Stars and Stripes* for the editor to confer with him. Max Gilstrap, a captain who acted as administrative officer for the editorial department of the principal paper in Paris, went along to see General Eisenhower with the sergeant who had been recalled to run the Desk for a month or so in an effort to restore some of the paper's standing. The sergeant, who had received the summons from General Eisenhower's office, didn't see any point in inviting Goodfriend to come along.

General Eisenhower said he wanted to express some concern about some of the editorials which had appeared in the preceding month or so. He pointed out that almost never had he tried to influence in any way what went into the soldiers' newspaper. He said flatly he didn't want anyone else doing it. But editorials such as "So you want to go home?" and some others in that vein, he said, had brought a most unfavorable reaction from the fighting men and their commanders.

General Eisenhower said he felt that from time to time *The Stars and Stripes* had a duty to remind its readers of the basic cause for which we were fighting, but that "perhaps it would be better to do so in a straight, factual manner."

The sergeant agreed wholeheartedly with everything the Supreme Commander said. He said the staff felt that way about it too. Finally, he explained as diplomatically as he could that the editorials had appeared as a result of direct orders from various generals and colonels under the Supreme Commander.

The sergeant went back and told the staff about the conference. He told the colonel, too, and the other colonels and a general who filled out the ranks of command above *The Stars and Stripes.*

The colonels and the generals said yes, they knew exactly what the Supreme Commander "really meant" and they interpreted the message the sergeant brought. The sergeant naïvely said he didn't think General Eisenhower's declaration of policy needed any interpreting. The colonels laughed indulgently.

The orientation editorials continued to be published, by order. There wasn't anything the staff could do.

The staffers who brought out the paper could have gone back to General Eisenhower and asked him to put a stop once and for all to the negation of General Marshall's original directive that the paper was to belong to the soldiers. But they didn't. They wanted to, but that was in midwinter of 1944-45 when Dwight Eisenhower was beset on every side by pressure to do this or demands to do that, to stop von Rundstedt's Ardennes offensive. And after that the Supreme Commander had all the worries one man should have in driving home the final blow that brought victory in May. The *Stars and Stripes* staff was not willing to add to the burdens of that one man who could have helped.

Personally the authors of this story and possibly a majority of the *Stars and Stripes* staff were friends of Arthur Goodfriend. Outside the sphere of the army newspaper, Goodfriend was a gutty, friendly individual who never stood on army ceremony or rank. Most of us felt that in his efforts to propagandize the American soldier he was carrying out what he sincerely believed to be a worthy project. He simply didn't understand what we considered the American way of a straighforward, unbiased chronicle of things the way they were.

About the motives of the polished Information and Education brass which glittered up to the top of the noncombatant pyramid of command from Goodfriend to Washington we held another view.

# THIRTY

Paris, May 22, 1945

## A JOE *CAN* DREAM

### This Army Life at Times is a Bit of All Right When Viewed From a Deep and Cozy Bed

By Andy Rooney

Between white sheets in a hotel in Nice a Joe fell asleep and he dreamed:

He was assigned to a division made up of the best from the First, Second, Third, Fourth, Ninth, 82nd Airborne and a few more crack divisions. They just took the old-timers. Terry Allen was division commander.

The infantry division was reinforced with tank battalions selected from the Second, Third and Fourth Armored divisions: they all had new tanks with three feet of armor all around and a quick-traversing high-velocity 105-mm. gun.

Every man in the division kept his M-1 and was given a German Luger and a Schmeisser machine pistol in addition. Each man also got a pair of 16-power Zeiss binoculars and a Leica.

One of the best things about the outfit was that there was a jeep for every four men and the jeeps were armed with handy twin Spandau machine guns taken from the tail of captured J U 88s.

The division artillery was equipped with German 88s, which artillery officers had been careful to see that the War Department had not "improved and modified" and with our own 105s, 155s and 240s. Each platoon was supported by a battery of 4.2-mm. chemical mortars and, of course, had their own cub observation planes.

The division fought only on weekdays and the men were paid in American dollars, not cigar coupons as formerly, every Friday night, whereupon their CIOs would turn them loose on the nearest town on the boys' promise that they would report back in time for the war first thing Monday morning.

Both EM and officers in the division were given a weekly liquor ration and the PX ration had no tropical chocolate bars in it. Each man got a carton of cigarettes each week and if he didn't smoke them himself he could turn them back to an officer whose job it was to take them to the best local market and sell them. The soldier was given all but three per cent of the return on sales. The other three per cent went into the division fund which gave every man $100 when his turn came to go home on a 30-day furlough every six months.

Special arrangements were made with the postmaster in New York to have the division's mail sorted there and it was then put on special planes which flew directly into a field near the division CP, giving the boys four-day mail service even from the West Coast.

Each infantryman who received four or more air-mail letters each month got flying pay and the Air Force fellows were mad as the very dickens about it because no matter how many letters they got they couldn't get the infantryman's $10 combat pay. The dreamer was heard to chuckle in his sleep by a chambermaid who was passing the door with four sheets over her arm, whistling "Off We Go into the Bright Blue Yonder," in French.

When the division got in a tight spot the cooks were issued class B ration; usually, however, they got regular garrison rations, with a chicken in every messkit every Sunday. Some C rations were issued the fellows who wanted them to feed friendly animals they had acquired and K rations were fed to German prisoners who wouldn't talk.

Each jeep was equipped with a blowtorch instead of the regular GI stove and the canteen cups they heated their coffee in were of a new design which did not burn the lip when full of hot coffee.

In the winter the men were issued German sheep-lined jackets instead of the regular or irregular field jackets. Issue shoes were always paratroop boots instead of cold, leaky, buckle-top boots.

Underwear, towels and handkerchiefs were white, not olive drab, when issued, and to keep these dainties clean the quartermaster provided the division with a mobile, foolproof, 48-hour laundry service. The laundry almost never made mistakes except when some careless worker slipped an extra shirt or pair of shorts into a bundle.

Because of the division's experience, it often was given towns to take which were being defended by Italian prisoners whom the Germans had ordered to fight. By a great stroke of luck the cellars in the towns were always as full of good things to drink as was the cellar of the Excelsior Hotel in Cologne.

The division's actions were closely and accurately followed in *The*

*Stars and Stripes* and on the average day most of the men in the division had their names mentioned at least once. The paper always reached them the same day it was published.

The dreamer, who had 110 points toward a discharge, awoke. Next day he was shipped to a repple depple and moved as an essential through the Mediterranean to the CBI, where he lived unhappily ever after.

On the Western Front the guns are quiet. The dust settles on the rubble of Germany. Some of the Joes turned west and went home; some of them to the Pacific; some of them stayed to guard the peace they won. *The Stars and Stripes* is already established in the Pacific for those who are occupying Japan. Some editions of the paper—Paris, Nice, one or two in Germany, and for a time the one in Rome—will stay with the Joes in the ETO as long as they need it.

Here and there across the newspaper empire, which a bunch of soldiers built, a press slows and the last copy of the local *S&S* has been printed. The staffers go away to a new job, or maybe home, and the city room returns to the kind of normalcy it knew before the pinwheels came.

Probably it can't be, but as the noise of the presses dies away you have a wishful sort of feeling within you that maybe the paper won't have disappeared entirely from this place. That maybe, when it's quiet again and the civilian staff of whatever paper normally publishes there is back on the job, someone once in a while will light a newspaper under a rewriteman's chair or hurl a pastepot at an erring reporter; that maybe where the soldier-reporters have been something will stay on which will continue to speak out for the ordinary folk who can't speak out for themselves. You hope there will be someone to stop in now and then at the Lamb and Lark . . .

On the way home one of the old gang paused in London. He went to the Lamb and Lark. As he stepped from Printing House Lane into the cool shadowed pub, and smelled again the dank old-beer-and-cigarette-smoke smell of the place that was home to *S&S* for so long, the staffer heard the phone ringing. Alf started to answer the phone before he saw the staffer.

Alf put the receiver to his ear and out of the corner of his mouth he said, "City Desk." The staffer said that Alf's voice was a little lonely, like a man saying over again a line from a story he'd read a long time ago.